Uneasy Lies
the
Crown

A Novel of

Owain Glyndwr

Also by N. Gemini Sasson:

The Crown in the Heather (The Bruce Trilogy: Book I)

Worth Dying For (The Bruce Trilogy: Book II)

The Honor Due a King (The Bruce Trilogy: Book III)

*Isabeau, A Novel of Queen Isabella
and Sir Roger Mortimer*

*The King Must Die,
A Novel of Edward III*

Uneasy Lies the Crown

A Novel of
Owain Glyndwr

N. GEMINI SASSON

cader idris
press

List of Characters

Owain Glyndwr – Welsh nobleman. Later Prince of Wales.

Gruffydd Fychan – Owain's father. Descendant of the princes of Powys Fadog.

Helen Goch – Owain's mother. Descendant of the princes of Gwynedd and Deheubarth.

Tudur Glyndwr – Owain's younger brother.

Margaret Hanmer – Owain's wife.

Gruffydd Glyndwr – Owain and Margaret's oldest son.

Maredydd Glyndwr – Second oldest son of Owain and Margaret.

Madoc, Dewi, Tomos and Sion Glyndwr – Owain and Margaret's other sons.

Catrin, Alice, Isabel, Janet and Mary Glyndwr – Owain and Margaret's daughters.

Iolo Goch – Bard to Owain.

John Hanmer – Margaret's older brother.

Philip Hanmer – Another of Margaret's brothers.

Rhys Ddu (Rhys the Black) – A former sheriff of Cardiganshire. Owain's general and friend.

Nesta – Rhys Ddu's daughter and Owain's mistress.

Gethin (Rhys Gethin) – An outlaw who becomes one of Owain's generals.

Gwilym and Rhys ap Tudur – Owain's cousins.

Lord Reginald de Grey of Ruthin – A Marcher lord. Owain's neighbor.

Elise – Niece of Lord Grey and Gruffydd's love.

Sir Edmund Mortimer – Uncle to the young Earl of March (heir presumptive to King Richard II). Married Catrin Glyndwr.

King Richard II – Grandson of King Edward III and son of the Black Prince, Edward. King of England until 1400.

John of Gaunt – Duke of Lancaster. Son of King Edward III. Uncle of King Richard II.

Henry of Bolingbroke – Earl of Derby. Son of John of Gaunt. Later King Henry IV.

Prince Harry (Henry of Monmouth) – Son of King Henry IV. Later King Henry V.

Henry Percy – Earl of Northumberland.

Harry Hotspur (Sir Henry Percy the Younger) – Son of the Earl of Northumberland.

Archibald Douglas – Scottish Earl of Douglas.

Some Welsh Pronunciation and Words

When reading Welsh place names on a map, it may at first seem that there is an absence of vowels, but a few rules will vastly ease the challenges that Welsh proper names present at first glance. For instance, 'w' is usually pronounced 'oo' and 'y' is pronounced like a short 'i' or long 'e'. 'Dd' is pronounced like a soft 'th', so the English equivalent of the Welsh name 'Maredydd' would be 'Meredith'. 'Gruffydd' in English is spelled 'Griffith'.

ab or *ap* – son of
cariad – my love, sweetheart
Cymru – Wales
Cymry – the Welsh people
Darogan – Prophecy
Ddu – Black
Fychan – Younger
Glyndwr – of the Glen of the River Dee
Goch – Red
Llyn – Lake
Mab – Son

Author's Note

In the latter part of the thirteenth century, Edward I of the Plantagenet dynasty rose to the throne of England. King Edward I, or Longshanks as he was later known, was determined to secure his borders and bring the whole Isle of Britain under his domain. He subdued the Welsh by hiring the brilliant James of St. George to design and erect formidable castles throughout Wales and he also invaded Scotland innumerable times, finally setting the pliable John Balliol on the throne of that country. While Scotland struggled for its independence, Wales lay in a state of tacit subjugation that was to last for over a century—until Henry of Bolingbroke seized the English throne from Richard II in the year 1399 and circumstances thrust Owain Glyndwr into the forefront of an Anglo-Welsh conflict.

Shakespeare best captured the essence of Owain Glyndwr when he gave him these words in his play, *Henry IV*:

> "*. . . At my birth*
> *The front of heaven was full of fiery shapes,*
> *The goats ran from the mountains, and the herds*
> *Were strangely clamorous to frightened fields.*
> *These signs have marked me extraordinary,*
> *And all the courses of my life do show,*
> *I am not in the role of common men.*"

Iolo Goch:

Humble and good-hearted was my lord Owain. He loved his wife, his children, and his home. Above all, he loved the land unto which he was born, as any true Welshman does. He wept quietly when the English scorched the crops and razed our towns, as if he had been burned and beaten himself. He smelled the smoke of fired thatch miles before anyone else ever saw the plumes lifting skyward. He sensed storms upon the wind a day before they came. When the rains arrived, he would lift his face and thank God for the gift, as those around him cursed, shivered and complained.

Like him, I should have married in my youth and littered the world with children to carry on my good name—although Owain's eleven was almost too many for me to keep straight. Alas, I have no sons, no daughters. Not even a bastard to carry my blood. Only worn quills, empty inkwells and piles of parchment, black with words that speak so little of my own life and so much of his. My hands now, though—they ache when I hold my implements. My fingers do not always do as I will them and the words come out blotched, looking like flies squashed beneath my fist. Even in the daylight my old eyes strain to see what I have written. I must stoop so low to the parchment at times that the ink smears my chin and nose.

When I first came to his household at Sycharth, it was only as a passing guest, a bard traveling from manor to manor. Like too many, I stayed overlong. I was free and content, trading my love of song and words for my keep.

Myself—Iolo Goch, Lord of Lechrydd—I own a parcel of land which is, more or less, a weedy pile of manure on a scattering of rocks. Scant enough to live on, let alone pay English taxes. Because my father could not pay them, he was taken away by the English, beaten in the stocks at Chester, lashed raw and tossed into prison there, where he died of a fever from the infection in his wounds. All I had of his was his harp and the lessons on it that he had taught me.

Now, I have returned to the home of my childhood—a place forgotten by all but me and one or two others—and here it is that I sit upon my wobbly stool, night after night, wondering if I've enough candles to finish what it is I set out to do before my weakening heart gives up the fight.

Let me tell you, then, of my lord, his wife, and their children. I will tell you, as well, how fate taunted and beckoned to my lord and set him on a path he would rather never have known, but for which he was destined.

1

Treffgarne, Wales — 1359

O N THE THRESHOLD OF heaven lies Wales. Rugged and remote, it is a land more suited to hunting and shepherding than planting crops or building cities; a land of sweeping moors and verdant meadows; of forests deep with shadow and bottomless lakes concealed in deeply cut valleys. Along its jagged spine running from north to south, the rocky earth thrusts upward, parting the clouds as they drift by. Rivers that begin as a trickle from melting snows grow until they are broad and sluggish with silt, finally disgorging their burden into the mouth of an angry sea. Across the water, beyond the setting sun, lies Ireland. To the east, beginning at the fertile, undulating Marches, is England, ever present and ever persistent.

In late May of the year 1359, a gathering wind marched down from the Irish Sea and collided with the Welsh shore. Battalions of marram grass held their ground while nesting terns stood guard over their clutches beneath the hammered blades. A line of thunderheads, dark as death, advanced. Daylong, storm clouds had convened over the cold, restless waters—building, growing and waiting for nightfall just as an army amasses before descending upon the enemy.

There had been no sunrise or sunset, just the slow, subtle change of hue from blackness to shades of gray and back again in a sky without sun or moon or stars.

While nature raged, inland the first drops of rain gently splattered on the roof of a manor near the little village of Treffgarne.

Owain ap Gruffydd Fychan was shoved into the world a bloody mess. His purple fists, balled tight in protest, quavered at the chill air. From between his naked gums a mighty wail issued forth and rent the heavens. In answer, the gods rumbled.

Outside the stone-clad house, daggers of rain slashed at the windows. The sky was a splendid show of terror. In the thin-soiled hills beyond Treffgarne, snowy-faced sheep ran and scattered. The hill cattle, with their sturdy frames and shaggy hides, being of a more obstinate constitution, packed themselves brisket to flank in the windbreak of a craggy cirque.

On that lightning-scoured night—a decade past the purging of the Black Death, which knew neither class nor calling, and less than a century after the exigent Edward I had thrown his stone yoke of castles about the necks of the Cymry—a life was delivered to Wales. A beginning amidst the cataclysm. And a glory, as any child, in the making.

The midwife Enid pinned the wriggling babe under an age-spotted forearm. She blotted at his cheeks with a frayed strip of linen and hoisted him up, unclothed, for his new mother to see. His legs kicked at the air with all his might.

"He has strength, 'tis certain," she heralded as he gulped in air. Dried blood tinged the creases in her knuckles. She laid him in his cradle. "You'll not get a wink of sleep till his belly's filled."

With a steady hand, Rhiannon helped her lady to bed and moved the peat brazier closer. Elen, wife of Gruffydd Fychan, who was off fighting in France, had delivered the boy straining and squatting upon the planked floor of her parents' chamber. She had cried out not once, though the pain of birthing had been fierce enough for her to wish herself unconscious. It was only the wooden handle of a spoon, clenched hellishly between her teeth, which rescued her mind from the stony bulging in her loins as the baby had rammed his way out of her.

The old midwife dabbed her wrinkled fingers in a hornmug of water, then caked them with salt from a wooden bowl. After rubbing little Owain's slimy skin with the paste, she wiped her hands clean and dunked a honey-smeared finger into the infant's mouth. He sputtered and finally swallowed. Soon, his pink tongue licked at the roof of his mouth and his lips puckered into an 'o'. She settled the boy onto his mother's bare stomach, still bloated and tender.

Dark blue irises, like sapphires sparkling in the bed of a mountain runlet, gazed in adoration at Elen. His left fist, with fingers barely broad as a spike of sedge grass, opened up and kneaded at her blue-veined breast. All the while, his bright eyes never strayed from his mother's worshipful face as he studied every detail there.

Faintly, Elen smiled. He winked, or so it seemed, and curled his strong digits around her thumb. Elen crooked her neck to place a kiss upon his salty knuckles, and her tousled auburn hair brushed against his skin. Deep in his throat, Owain gurgled in delight.

"There now . . . tall and strong he'll be," Elen beamed, then added with a mother's vain pride, "and charming as a fresh born lion cub. Small and helpless this day. A danger to those who would cross him later."

"Lion indeed." Rhiannon tugged at a heap of blankets to cover her lady. "He's a babe and soon to take chill if you don't cover him."

Children were born every day. But he was no common child, this smiling little Owain ap Gruffydd Fychan. He had noble blood and much of it. His father had inherited two rich lordships through his descent from the princes of Powys Fadog. His mother's house traced its lineage from Llywelyn the Great, Prince of Gwynedd, and Lord Rhys, last Prince of Deheubarth.

So much greatness to be realized. So little matter as he clutched his mother's thumb, anchoring himself in a world that was new and full of wonder for his glittering eyes to behold. An infant yet, he knew nothing of freedom . . . or what it meant to be without it.

2

Glyndyfrdwy, Wales — 1370

A CASCADE OF SUNLIGHT danced like hand-flung jewels upon the River Dee in North Wales. On its twisting banks, two boys eyed each other with grave concentration, wooden swords gripped fiercely in their blistered hands. They might have passed for twins, but for a slight difference in height.

"Tudur, think . . . just once," Owain, barefooted and stripped to the waist, said to his brother. He stepped backward and lowered his weapon as he drew himself up to full height to accentuate the authority that two more years had afforded him. "How do you reckon David beat Goliath? He was not bigger or stronger. He did not batter him to death or dizzy him into unconsciousness. Think now. How did he win?"

"You're no Goliath," Tudur protested between ragged breaths, his fingers flexing on his splintered hilt. "We're close to evenly matched, don't you think? Besides, Owain, how else am I to make myself stronger if I don't fight hard? It's good practice."

"Agh. Have you ears?" Owain tucked his sword into the hemp cord that held up his hose, turned his back and sauntered away, whistling a made-up tune.

Tudur squinted at the target before him, and then lunged toward Owain as his blunt weapon parted the air with a whoosh.

Barely glancing over his shoulder, Owain whipped his sword free and deflected the blow, sending Tudur's sword hurtling end over end. It landed with a dull thud on the far side of the bank, stirring a cluster of violet-crowned teasel into an abrupt dance. The river between gurgled in mockery.

"Will you ever learn?" Owain admonished.

Tudur rubbed the sting from his hand. "That wasn't fair."

"And you rushing at my back was? At least you knew an opportunity when you saw one, I'll grant you." Owain planted a fist on his hip as his brother's lip began to quiver. "Oh, not that. I suppose you'll start to cry now."

Tudur clenched his fists. "I will not!"

"Good." Owain returned his sword to his belt like a seasoned warrior and pushed back a yawn with his fingertips. "Leave me be, then. I've had enough of trying to teach you what you refuse to learn or even think about and my whole head hurts from the effort. I feel like I've been beating a stone against my own forehead. If you would only listen better to Father when he's about."

Beneath the flickering shade of a willow, Owain plopped down on a bed of wild oats. Below, the trickling water of the Dee chimed a lullaby. If not for the stir his brother was causing, he would have fallen asleep as fast as his cheek nestled against the pillow of his forearm. One eye propped open, Owain watched in lazy amusement.

Intent on retrieving his honor, Tudur hopped over the slick stepping stones that bridged the river and plucked up his weapon, entangled in its grassy bed. As he returned along the slippery path, his balance failed him. Arms flailing, mouth agape, he tumbled backward into the swift waters. Moments later, he emerged in an explosion of curses, his sword lost to the taunting current, and struggled up onto the bank. He wrung out his shirt with a grumble and flung it onto a jagged tree stump, then collapsed, cross-legged, beside his gloating brother. He sniffed and bit his lip hard. An easy silence settled between them.

A long time later, the sun warming his skin, Owain pushed himself up on one elbow and gazed across the river. His eyes skipped over an argent glint on the water's rippling surface.

"Tudur—a pike," he whispered, touching his brother on the knee through soggy breeches.

But Tudur took no notice. Instead, he stared down wistfully at a shiny green beetle clinging upside down to a blade of bent grass. He flicked it to the ground and then pummeled it beneath his fist.

"Will Father be home soon?" Tudur asked thickly.

"Today . . . or tomorrow." Lies were not so easily put upon one as hopeful and fragile as Tudur. Yet what Tudur lacked in confidence or conviction, he more than made up for in his devotion to his older brother.

They were seldom apart, Owain and Tudur. Although Tudur hovered in his brother's shadow and always let Owain lead the way, he did not seem to reflect much of his brother's quickness in learning, whether at swords or books. Where Owain was brave and reckless to a fault, Tudur always gave voice to better judgment. Owain may never have admitted it, but Tudur, in some ways, was wise—wise enough to know better when to yield to caution. Together, they invented stories and explored, turning over rocks at the river's edge and climbing to the highest boughs of the forest groves.

Their home for most of the year, through winter dark till sodden spring, was Sycharth. It was only during the height of summer that their mother, Elen Goch, daughter of Thomas, Lord of Treffgarne, preferred to retreat here to the cool glen of the Dee. Glyndyfrdwy—meaning glen of the River Dee—was perched on the pastoral slopes of the valley like a nesting eagle. Somewhat smaller than Sycharth, it was a perfect place from which to launch hunting parties in the nearby fields and forests.

They had last laid eyes on their father, Gruffydd Fychan, a year and a half ago at Sycharth. Father's umber beard then had been patched with new gray at the chin and there was a hitch in his once steady gate from a deep slash to a calf muscle he had received at marshy Auray. What little they had seen of him then was mostly a man too weary to talk, too absorbed with long overdue business to teach or mold his children in any way. What little they knew of him was formed in fleeting snatches—a hastily scribbled letter that all was well, an obligatory kiss on Elen's cheek before leaving once again. All but for that one last winter. Tudur, moon-eyed with awe, and Owain, his forehead tight in concentration, had sat many an evening that rare winter at their father's knee barraging him with questions that only children could invent. They knelt humbly at the feet of their idol. Every word was a nugget of gold. In the company of their father, they were rich beyond belief.

"Du Goose-ling, is he a giant?" Tudur wrinkled his nose and swallowed a yawn.

"Du Guesclin, a giant?" Gruffydd scratched at his beard, chuckling. "Eh, he's no giant. A pugnacious bastard, maybe. A burr in old Edward's arse. A crafty one at that. But no more a giant than you, Tudur."

Owain peered at his father, who was growing more ragged with battle scars every year, frayed about the edges like a piece of parchment carried too long. "Why has Edward failed?" he asked, his lips pressed in a serious line, curious to know more about this King Edward of England, third by that name.

Gruffydd touched Owain's golden brown locks. He shifted forward and grimaced at the hard frame beneath the thinning cushion of his chair. "King Edward is far from done where the throne of France is concerned."

"But what right has he, Father, to another king's crown?"

"It's not about right, my boy. It's about revenues garnered from Bordeaux wine."

Tudur was by then lost from the ring of conversation, his cheek pressed against his father's shin and sleep dragging down his lids.

Owain inclined his head quizzically. "To deepen his purse, then?"

"Ah." Gruffydd nodded, one side of his lips curled up in amusement. "You understand the English already."

Then Elen came to hover at her husband's shoulder, her face shining as she looked on at her two fine sons. Her slim fingers gently kneaded Gruffydd's neck. She hummed a lover's tune and slipped her arms around him.

"Promise me," she begged in his ear, "promise me you're here to stay."

He pulled her around to him and down into his waiting lap. "Yes, *cariad*. I'll tell the king my wife wishes me at home. One less soldier. What would he care, anyway?" He winked at her, sending oaths of delight in his strong gaze. In a lingering moment, their lips came together.

That was how Owain would choose to remember them. When peace and family and love were God's undeniable gift. When all was as it should be. His mother there in his father's arms and he and Tudur at their knees.

But such are children's dreams.

A fortnight later Father was off again, summoned back to duty as Charles V of France swung his operations toward the English in Gascony. Every time Gruffydd Fychan left his wife, she became a puddle of worry. But this last time, as the months dragged on, even as word spread that the king's son Prince Edward was returning, her hope had withered like daffodils that have bloomed before the final frost and must suffer winter's cruel kiss.

Now the two brothers lay groggily beside the river, wondering when they would see their father again so they could hear more of his stories.

"He'll make knight soon," Owain assured Tudur. Another lie, Owain knew it even before the syllables sprang from his lips. Welshmen were seldom granted such accolades.

Tudur's eyes brightened. "Perhaps he has already been knighted on the field by the Black Prince himself."

"The very day he cut through fifty French soldiers."

Abruptly, they both fell silent, aware they were only giving breath to wishes, and turned their faces to the sinking sun, now a hand's width above the horizon.

Tudur stretched out his knobby-kneed legs. "Time to head home."

"If I were invisible I could catch that pike." Owain rolled over and crawled on his belly until he dangled from the lip of the bank. He dipped his hand in the clear, cool water, watching minnows dart from his grasp in broken shards of silver.

"Time to head home," Tudur dully repeated.

Owain shrugged. "Go on. I want to wait here."

"Ach, try to catch him. Invisible or not, you won't catch anything but a scolding." Tudur snatched up his shirt. Before he set foot on the path that wound homeward, past the wild cherry and gooseberry and beneath a cloud of flowering rowan trees, he dared one last glance, and then sulked off alone.

Time forgotten, Owain scrambled onto a slab of rock jutting out over the riverbed and perched there like a proud captain standing at the prow of his ship. There he waited, for nothing in particular, watching the serpentine ribbon of the Dee darken as the silhouette of the Berwyns purpled beyond.

3

Glyndyfrdwy, Wales — 1370

THAT HE HAD NOT the springing feet of a hare, Owain was certain. Already as large as any full-grown man's, they were more like the plodding hooves of an ox: steady and sure at a measured pace, dreadfully clumsy if forced to a trot. Before he made it home, his path lit only by a scattering of stars, he had fallen twice and his knees were sore and bloody. And while racing Tudur earlier that day to the top of a hill, he had caught his sleeve on a bramble bush and now it dangled from his left shoulder by only a few threads. If he could manage to charm Rhiannon, he could have his clothing mended before his mother ever took notice. He grinned at his own resourcefulness.

Above the broad, rolling fields that surrounded the manor of Glyndyfrdwy, a patrol of yew trees loomed on a bulging ancient mound. From one of the higher boughs, a sentry could see nearly all the way to the ruins of Dinas Bran. The small, slate-roofed manor denied the vastness of Gruffydd Fychan's holdings, but in the many outbuildings and animal pens that clustered about it there spoke its riches. A bleating cloud of wool, ewes twitched their ears when Owain sprinted past. Unconcerned, they ambled to the nearby sheep cote and tucked their legs neatly beneath them to bed down for the night.

Owain bounded up the steps to the upper level three at a time. Assaulted by flies, his dinner sat untouched on a soggy trencher of bread at the trestle table's end. No doubt his mother had ordered it left there to serve as a statement: that he should suffer mutton on the verge of turning rancid and a congealed bowl of leek soup in castigation for his tardiness. Weak punishment for a boy who loathed the dark taste of mutton anyway.

He crept toward his father's chair at the head table and carefully inched it back. The stout legs groaned against the floor planks. Owain flinched. His mother had forbidden anyone to sit in his father's place, but every night Owain had slipped down to the hall when all was still and silent. He would climb onto the tattered cushion and sit there with his fingers curled around the arms of the chair, imagining the resonating boom of his father's voice, the chink of his spurs, his arms spread wide in greeting. Owain closed his eyes and pulled his knees up to his chest.

"Your father often falls asleep in that chair," Elen said softly.

Owain's eyes flew open as he tumbled from his post.

His mother floated across the empty expanse of the hall, each step releasing the scent of mint and rosemary sprinkled among the golden rushes. The plait of her auburn hair was frayed and the front of her light green skirt soiled from an honest day's work. That day alone she had probably overseen the beehives, the milling, the brewing of ale, nursed a sick lamb, collected eggs, and embroidered for endless hours while she rattled off the rest of the day's duties to her collection of servants. Lady Elen was like a hummingbird—never at rest, never weary.

She imparted a fluttering kiss in the tangle of her son's hair. "To bed."

"Yes, Mother," Owain said. He had no wish to displease her—

a frown was enough to correct him. His head hanging low, Owain waited for the chiding that was sure to ensue over the deplorable state of his clothing, but it did not come. His mother merely pursed her lips as her fingers grazed over Owain's dangling sleeve.

"Tomorrow I shall have Rhiannon draw you a bath. We will scrub the mud from behind your ears. Now off with you . . . and say your prayers twice," she said, as she prodded him along, "for having missed your studies."

After a few steps, Owain paused, looked back at her through a stray lock of golden hair and nodded dutifully. He scratched behind his ear. When he looked at his fingernails, the dirt was there, black as peat. How could she see it, in the half-dark, with such a cursory inspection? From behind the kitchen door, Rhiannon gossiped with the kitchen maids. The prospect of her scouring his flesh with hot water and a brush caused Owain to cringe. If only Father were here, surely Owain could have begged a day of fishing from him or some other distraction. But as things were, he was relegated to the company of womenfolk—coddled, cajoled and ushered off to bed barely past sunset. He had been sentenced to the solar more times than he cared to recollect, forced to read French verse to them as the womenfolk's fingers raced across the looms. Mother told him it was part of his schooling. What good was it to speak French when you lived in the cloistered repose of the Welsh hills? Without the bustle of sport with other boys and the vivid tales his father provided, living amongst a flock of women was a dreadful, tedious existence for a boy poised on the verge of manhood and pining for gruffer company.

As he reached the door, beyond which was the chamber he shared with Tudur, a faint clattering of hooves from outside reached his ears. It could only be one person! His spirit on wings, before his mother could utter his name, Owain was bounding across the hall and out the front door, his long legs churning like the wheels of a runaway cart.

Halfway down the front steps he skidded to a halt. His heart leapt into his throat as he strained his eyes in the darkness. Half a dozen riders were crossing the wooden bridge over the ditch surrounding their home—the sharp ringing of horseshoes cutting through the night air. Dark cloaks flared behind the riders like eagles' wings straining to soar. But as they entered the courtyard and the first of the company reined in his horse and dismounted, Owain's heart plummeted.

Richard Fitzalan, the Earl of Arundel, in whose name and company Gruffydd Fychan had served in France, paused at the base of the steps. He slapped the dust from his leather gloves, tucked them into his belt and took something from another of his company. With sorrow plain in his old gray eyes, he gazed up at his neighbor's son. In his arms he cradled a long object, swaddled in a plain white cloth.

Elen and half the household poured from the front door in mute stupor.

"My lord earl." Elen moved reluctantly toward him, the fingers of one white-knuckled hand clenching her skirts. She beckoned for a rushlight. "What brings you at this hour?"

Arundel's balding head reflected the wavering light as he bowed. "Lady Elen, your husband was on his way home aboard a ship with Prince Edward when the flux set upon him." He glanced briefly into her limpid eyes and then back down at the shining row of buttons on his gypon.

Reaching out with a trembling hand, Elen touched his forearm. "My Gruffydd?"

Arundel's eyes moistened. Gruffydd Fychan had been both friend and retainer to him. He cleared his throat and raised his angular, clean-shaven chin. "He succumbed to the malady before the ship put in to Dover. I'm sorry."

"You lie! You lie!" Tudur screeched. He flung himself down the steps and hammered his fists against Arundel's chest, the blows muffled by the thick quilting of the earl's clothes.

The earl merely blinked at Tudur's assault. Behind him, his men shared blank looks, unsure of whether to come to the earl's relief, or let a grieving boy have his moment. Then Elen pulled her youngest into the circle of her arms and held him tight against her breast. They clung to each other as she rocked him, her tears cascading over Tudur's tousled mop of light brown curls.

Peeling back the cloth, Arundel extended Gruffydd's sword to Owain.

"This belongs to you now."

Shards of moonlight danced on the blade. The sword's fuller, Owain knew, had run with a river of blood. Owain stood frozen, staring at the macabre gift, the shock of Arundel's tidings still seeping into him. The blood drummed in his ears. He shook his head and stepped back.

"Why? To kill in the name of *your* king?" They were biting words for one so young. He had always known that his father might not return home, but he was not prepared to accept the circumstances surrounding his death. His father was a Welshman, through and through; he should not have had to fight and ultimately die in the service of an English king.

Arundel glowered at him. "Edward is your king as well. You owe the comfort of your very existence to him and in turn you must pay your dues. Don't forget that so readily. It is a heavy burden for now, I know, but in time you will take to it as your father did."

"Never," Owain whispered. His throat tightened. He would have none of it. Hours before he had sported with Tudur by the river, buffeting each other with play swords—but it was only for amusement, a game to pass time. Mere child's play. The weapon that Arundel proffered was not meant for sport. It was a symbol of servitude. His stomach contracted into a knot.

Overhead, the sky was as black as coal dust and so was his heart.

Suddenly, he felt cold, as if it were a January night and not the middle of June.

Arundel sighed and lowered the sword. As if unwilling to battle with an outspoken man-child, he handed the weapon to a young nobleman to his right.

"I know this news is hard to bear, my lady," Arundel began, brushing off Owain's sedition with little more than a harsh stare, "but there is yet another matter I must press upon you. Your husband accrued many debts these past years owing to misfortune. His loyalty to king and country are to his merit and not to be forgotten. I will take your hardship into consideration, arrange agreeable payment . . . upon one condition."

Several cruel winters had nearly decimated their flocks. Elen had tried to compensate in other ways, but if it was not the blight ruining the orchard yields, then insects were to blame for gnawing the crops down to stubble long before harvest. The times had been exceedingly hard, especially with Gruffydd so often gone.

"I am a widow now," Elen said, her voice thick with sorrow. "What else would you take from me?"

"Your oldest son is to become my ward."

It was as if the words were spoken from some faraway place. Owain felt as though he were elsewhere, watching a scene among strangers unfold. His fate had been marked and sealed the moment he was born. His father was dead. And he was to be taken from his home and family when he was needed most.

Boyhood's Eden faded away like sunlight banished by a storm cloud. The steps on which Owain stood seemed to crumble beneath his feet. He sank down on his haunches, averting his eyes from Arundel's commanding gaze and the sight of his father's sword.

4

Sycharth, Wales — 1393

OWAIN RAN A CALLOUSED finger over the flat of the blade: smooth, cold, unyielding. As he reached toward its tip, the sharp edge sliced into his flesh. His indrawn breath whistled through clenched teeth and he snatched his hand back to his chest. A bead of crimson welled on the tip of his forefinger, dark and glistening. With each pulse of his heart, more blood oozed from the fine cut, until it began to drip onto the floor. His wife would give him a tongue-lashing for the mess he had made.

Lifting his father's sword above his head, he rested it gently on its hooks on the wall above the mantel. So many years had passed since that fateful day that the Earl of Arundel delivered his father's sword to him. A lifetime ago, it seemed. The memory of his father's voice had long since faded, but he had far from forgotten his stories: of bloody battles and stormy voyages, long days riding in the saddle, the many nights gathered around the soldiers' campfires. It had been a hard life for Gruffydd Fychan and one Owain had been determined not to repeat, even after his early years training as a page and then a squire in Arundel's household. But it was only a few years after he and Margaret had begun their life together that King Richard had resurrected *servitium debitum,* calling on him to gather his own forces and report to John of Gaunt in York for the king's campaign in Scotland.

Owain turned and strode across the floor of his library at Sycharth, each step prompting a small but distinct ache in his bones. He was only thirty-four, but already he could feel the effects of having been tossed from his horse once too often. A stinging finger reminded him of his cut and he pressed it between his lips to suck away the blood.

"You have no need of your sword anymore, Sir Owain." Margaret stood at the doorway with one fist propped smartly on her hip. In her other arm, she held their two-year old son, Dewi. Ever since the arrival three months ago of their ninth child, Tomos, tottering Dewi had trailed behind his mother's skirts with petulant possessiveness.

"Ah, Marged. How I wish that were so." Owain settled down in his chair and put his feet on the writing table. "Forgive me for reminiscing with an old friend. She served me well at Berwick when —"

"When you held off a charge of Scots singlehandedly with a broken lance. Yes, yes, we all know the story—how King Richard was so dazzled by your reckless bravery that he knighted you on the battlefield that very day." She shoved back a lock of sun-gold hair that had sprung from its pins and set the child at her feet. "Your quill has served you just as well, wouldn't you say?"

"Indeed, I much prefer it. But we must ever arm ourselves against those who refuse to live by the word of the law."

The year that the old Earl of Arundel died, Owain had gone to London to study law at the Inns of Court. There, after finally becoming an apprentice-at-law, Sir David Hanmer, a justice of the king's bench, took young Owain under his tutelage. Soon, Owain became a frequent visitor to the Hanmer household. In truth, it was Sir David's long-lashed daughter, Margaret, who had captured

Owain's attention far more than discourse about legal matters. In her presence, the smooth-tongued esquire was a speechless buffoon. A full six months lapsed before Owain could summon the courage to speak to her and even then it was by accident—he bumped into her at the marketplace. But the more he tried to put things right, the more tongue-tied he became. Margaret put him at ease not by laughing, but by saying, "I am so glad for your clumsiness, then. I thought you might never speak to me." One year later, they were married in the little church in Maelor Saesneg.

Since then, the patter of babes' feet had become a constant through the wooded warmth of Sycharth's halls—a bright, cheerful place with tables full and tankards overflowing and where no guest, high or humble, was ever denied.

Just as their marriage had proven a fertile one, in the orchards beyond the manor, pears and apples exploded from the trees. So many weighed down the branches, gnarled like the fingers of old men, that bushels tumbled to the ground only to be eaten by the shy, roaming fallow deer.

In the bloated hush that followed the evening meal, dulcet ballads were plucked on Iolo Goch's harp in the main hall. The home of Margaret and Owain became known far and wide to bards and Iolo was like their king. In winter, the bards would spread their pallets by the fireside to sleep and in summer bed down in mountains of straw in the barn. Their ancient yarns passed from the lips of one directly into the heart of another, there treasured and revered, to be later resurrected in the halls of Wales' *uchelwyr*, or gentry.

Whenever Owain was feeling amorous, he would tap a single finger on his knee until Iolo looked his way. Then, Iolo would cradle his harp to his breast, claim the center of the hall and all fell silent while the great bard sang of Owain's love for his golden-haired lady. Whispers and winks circulated among the onlookers as Margaret glanced at her husband, a blush spreading from her cheeks to her ivory forehead.

Fighting a grin at the thought, Owain rose from his chair and tousled little Dewi's hair.

Fingers in mouth, Dewi looked up at his father, and then pointed at the sword on the wall. Owain shook his head at his son, but the boy was determined. He pushed himself to his feet, wobbled two bowlegged steps, and collapsed onto his rump. A moment later, the child had forgotten about the glimmering weapon and instead busied himself studying an insect scampering across the floor.

"Can I steal you from the children for a few hours, *cariad?*" Owain said to his wife.

Margaret arched a skeptical eyebrow at him. "For what purpose?"

"What purpose?" He brushed Margaret's cheek with his fingertips. "To look over the orchards, the fields . . . Dobbin says the hay is ready for cutting already, but I disagree."

"The children are not the problem, my lord." Drawing her head back from his exploring touch, Margaret warned her husband away with a stern glare. "Rhiannon is always at hand. It's tonight's supper I need to finish overseeing. Some of the . . . help is new and . . ."

Slipping around behind her, Owain's hands skimmed over the ridge of her hips to encircle her waist. Breathily, he kissed her on top of her head, then her ear, and whispered, "One hour, then?"

She yielded to his tug as he drew her closer. "One hour." Ever so slightly, her head lolled to the side, inviting more of his attention. "But no more. My brothers Philip and John are coming—or have you forgotten? I should think you'd like this evening to go well."

"Who cares about this evening? This afternoon I promise you a paradise."

"All boast, are you? We shall see about that."

AFTER LOCATING RHIANNON AND placing little Dewi in her care, Owain led Margaret by the hand down the front steps, along the foot-worn path past the glutted orchard where the pale green apples were not yet riddled with wormholes, and to the sloping banks of one of the fishponds. Argent fins flicked at the surface, breaking its mirrored sheen and sending ripples to pulse against the reedy shores. Insects buzzed with complaint as Owain and Margaret's passing stirred them from their task. The midnight plumage of a party of swifts cut across the sky as they hawked for a meal.

Suddenly, a screeching shadow dove at them, its banshee cry shattering summer's song. Owain tackled Margaret to save her from harm. In a deep sea of grass, they rolled over and over, drowning in their own laughter. They did not come to rest until Margaret's kirtle dipped into the pond waters. After she plucked the grass from her hair, Margaret crawled further up the bank, a stockade of spike-rushes surrounding her.

"Are we safe now?" Standing, she wrung the water from her hem.

"For the moment." Owain clambered up after her, grabbed her by the waist and pulled her down on top of him. From where they were, overlooking the pond, they could gaze until sunset at the sapphire reflection of the sky and the titanic Berwyns on its rippling surface. Owain's mind was hardly on the view, however, for he was stricken by the beauty of his wife, his love, his soul. He wanted nothing more at that moment than to hold her forever and lose himself in her. "You are safe here with me. In my arms. Safe from all harm. I will build you a castle and slay the dragon that dares look your way."

"Ah, pity. You would lock me up in a castle? I much prefer the roving shepherdess's life to that of a captive lady." She outlined his mustached mouth with her fingertip. "But you said you were going to show me more of the orchards . . . and the fields. Come now. The children will think us lost. Rhiannon will send out an army to find us if they carry on."

"The children and the fields will wait. They will be there when we are done."

"Done with what?"

He caught her hand and pressed her open palm to his lips, dousing it with a kiss. "Making love, Marged. But then, am I ever done loving you? Do you know that every morning, before I open my eyes, I breathe you in and hold it in my lungs? Then I know 'tis not a dream I'm living, although it would seem so. Ah, I cherish each groan you give when the sun marches in through the shutters, every little protest when I steal too much of the blankets —"

"Which you do all too often." She puckered her brow in scolding. "I have right to protest. A woman with child —"

"That was months ago, my sweet. Have I mistreated you since then?"

A yellow strand of hair fell across her face as she rolled from him. Finally, Margaret turned her head and gazed at her husband.

"It has happened again," she said, one hand upon her still slim abdomen.

Owain bolted up. "So soon?"

She rolled her eyes. "You were there. Or have you forgotten?"

His strong arms wrapped her in a protective embrace. "Do you know the servants say that all I have to do to impregnate my fair wife is wet her fingertips with a kiss?"

"I think all you have to do is look at me . . . nay, *think* of me in that way and suddenly I'm heavy with child."

"Could you love me forever?"

She smoothed the waves of his hair and contemplated the thought. "I will love you, Owain, long after forever is done and gone."

Catching her hand in his, he gripped her fingers firmly. "They say there is trouble in Ireland again."

"When is there not?"

"True. But there are rumors King Richard wants to quell the rebels there. I will be called to serve him."

"Must we speak of that now, Owain?"

"I'm sorry. I shouldn't have said anything. Now,"—he lifted himself up from the ground and with his hungering mouth left a trail of kisses from her lowest rib to her shoulder—"I shall remind you why it is I brought you here."

Sweetly, lovingly, longingly, he kissed her neck. Her arms went round him as she pulled him closer, losing herself in the fevered heat of his kisses. He pulled off his shirt and tossed it in the reeds. Margaret reached to touch his tautly muscled stomach. Then, in shameless invitation, she drew her skirts up.

He glanced at her nakedness and though he had seen it infinite times before, her beauty was still a rapturous wonder to him. "Dare I ask how God so blesses me with the miracle of you?"

"'Tis not the time to be talking of God," she said lowly, a dreamy grin on her lips.

"You will say otherwise shortly," he promised and kissed her throat, hard and hungry. Then his mouth closed over hers.

The sun paused at its zenith and shone gloriously down on them—two lovers seeking and devouring each other, becoming one. Their murmurs intermingled and climbed in pitch as Owain moved faster within her. Blood and heart and breath all pounded through his body as he ascended toward the plateau that always lay in the next moment.

Then he felt Margaret shudder beneath him and her breath catch. Every muscle and fiber of his being contracted. Inside his head and all around him the world went white, like a wave crashing around him . . . pulling him under.

Slowly, he felt himself coming down from heaven—soaring like an eagle above the earth, drifting lower, looking down on all creation.

The sound of the wind became his own breathing and the strong beating of wings his heart.

5

Sycharth, Wales — 1394

ONE WEEK BEFORE OWAIN was to accompany King Richard to quarrelsome Ireland, Margaret gave birth to twins: a boy and a girl, Mary and Sion. They had not come with the usual ease that Margaret had previously delivered her children. The boy child had been turned around when her pains began. The labor went on most of the day, at first intense and excruciating. Then later, as Margaret drifted in and out of consciousness, the physician was finally able to turn the child inside her and deliver each one. Margaret was oblivious to their incipient cries. When the babes were washed up, Owain was called in to see them. A nurse cradled them protectively in the crook of each arm. Their small red faces peeked from cocoons of swaddling. They were tiny—born early. Their attachment to life was a hair so fine a single tug might snap it.

Owain leaned against the bedpost, gazing at Margaret, who was swept away in a sea of exhaustion. For a long time he studied her, worshipful of her, thankful and yet gripped with a fear that paralyzed him. Lamplight flickered upon her face, pale and sparkling with perspiration like a fine dusting of crystal. He glanced at the physician, who was packing his instruments and washing his hands as if there were nothing more he could do.

His voice tremulous, Owain probed, "Will she . . . will she be well soon?"

"More likely so than not," the physician said. He was a Jew named Abraham that Owain had brought to Sycharth from London to attend to his large family. He wiped his hands on a towel, and then gathered the bag that contained his mysterious tools. "But there were complications. If she were to deliver another child, she could die. Do you understand?"

The strong cries of his new son and daughter filled his ears with the assurance that they had gained their place in the world and were not letting go.

Owain nodded dully. Then he knelt beside his love and wrapped his large hands around one of hers. He kissed her knuckles, and then pressed them to his whiskered cheek. "Marged, the children need you. I need you." And he buried his face in the sea of down coverings that surrounded her and wept more tears than he had ever in his life shed.

Waterford, Ireland — 1394

THE SIGHT OF A green-faced man retching over a ship's railing is not the image one usually conjures of a king. For Richard, the passage over the Irish Sea was a necessary evil. He was on his way to subdue the latest uprising precipitated by the mutinous chieftain McMurrough. The voyage, however, was treacherous. Fickle gusts of October wind hammered at the sea, pushing the waves mountainously high and tossing the ships like fallen leaves in a rampant river.

Among Richard's personal guard were his Cheshire archers, bearing the king's livery of the white hart, renowned for their prowess with the longbow and as arrogant as they were accurate. The king had also summoned Owain to attend him. For now, Owain had been relegated to the honor of holding onto the king's shoulders as Richard leaned out over the sea, puking up the last gulp of water that he had cleansed his mouth with.

Owain passed him a sodden scrap of cloth as the king pulled back. Richard buried his face in it and moaned grievously. Low, gray clouds trudged across the sky. Owain blinked away the stinging mist and some minutes later, when the king was standing on his own and the hue of his face was less blanched, he ventured a comment. "I see you have your legs under you now. Are you feeling improved, then?"

A scowl crossed Richard's mouth. "I will feel better when I have been at Dublin three days and the earth stops pitching beneath me." He laughed, but almost instantly the humor slipped away. "Who do you trust, Welsh?"

"Your pardon, sire?"

Richard sniffed, then drew a damp kerchief from his sleeve and blew his nose. "I mean—who do you trust with your secrets?"

Uncertain of the intent behind the question, Owain answered safely. "My wife, I suppose. There is nothing I would keep from Margaret. And there is nothing she would ever judge me too harshly for."

The wind whipped harder at them, winter's promise on its breath. Racked with tremors from the cold, Richard shoved his hands under his armpits.

"Damn it! Hurry, boy! Where is my blanket?" Richard railed at his page. "Your negligence will be the cause of my ague."

The king's page, his hair dripping with rain and his lips blue from the permeating chill of sea air, bolted off and returned with a dry, woolen blanket from below deck. Richard held out his arms stiffly and the page draped it in rehearsed fashion, pulling the blanket over the king's head to serve as a hood. Richard swooned as the ship's prow lifted over a swell, then plummeted. He grasped at a rope secured to the mast.

White knuckled, he confided in Owain. "Trust no one, if you can. Those that swear they live to serve you will plot your demise while you sleep."

"Someone seeks to betray you, my lord?" Owain brushed the stream of rain from his forehead.

"Have and will again, I fear." He beckoned Owain close and whispered into his ear, "Bolingbroke." Richard leaned back, his pupils searing the warning into Owain.

"Why do you tell me this?"

"Because I trust you. And I must trust someone. My first wife Anne is gone. Curse the plague that took her. My friends Burley, Pole, Vere—they called them all traitors to the realm. But you, Sir Owen de Glendore,"—he grinned at the endearment—"they would never suspect me of bending the ear of a Welshman. Here." He delved beneath his opulent folds of clothing and produced a coin, then pressed it into Owain's palm.

An old coin with a mottled patina, Owain flipped it between his fingers. "Roman," he remarked with great interest.

"I found it on the beach at Milford Haven before we set sail. Have it." The king scanned about him. "Be cautious, my friend, the man will turn against you as well one day." The ship's captain and sailors were beyond earshot, but Richard appeared not to trust that supposition. Thomas Mowbray, the Earl of Nottingham, was wisely below deck and his uncle Gloucester was on another vessel altogether. Richard huddled against the mast, rain pelting down on him. His teeth chattered and he pulled his blankets as tight as a mummy's wrappings. Suddenly, he gripped Owain by the collar. "The time is nearing for those who have tried to subvert their king to pay for their crimes. Near. So very, *very* near. But the moment . . . it must be exact. They will learn they cannot treat me like a child forever. God, I have waited too long already."

His eyes were fixed wide, like the mouse that freezes beneath the shadow of a hawk, knowing it is marked as prey and is doomed to feel the piercing of talons. How piteous to see a king trembling for fear of his life. But his words were not those of a madman. Richard's uncle, John of Gaunt, had ruled during his minority in a steadfast manner. But in regards to Gaunt's son Henry of Bolingbroke, the Earl of Derby, Richard was not in admiration of his cousin. The mistrust was known to be mutual.

Owain may have resented his obligations to the English crown, but perhaps it was because of Richard's appreciation of him that he felt some degree of loyalty to him. "Know this, my king," he swore, "if there is but one man in this world to stand behind what is God's wish—that you are to sit upon the throne of England—that man is me."

Richard gazed blankly at him for a long time, as if weighing the allusion. His smooth fingers rubbed at the ruby broach at the base of his slim neck.

"Land ho!" came the captain's shout.

"Waterford," Richard heaved in relief, flashing a meek smile. "Have you ever been to Ireland before, Welsh? As beautiful as it is uncivilized, I regret." He stumbled toward the railing. "I shall send some of the others inland to wrestle with the scoundrels. You will accompany me to Dublin. My back needs watching."

"Have we arrived yet?" A boy of nine or ten peered above the ladder to below deck. He craned his head around, wind whipping his auburn hair across his face, and scrambled over the last few steps to stand above deck, hands on hips, impervious to the storm.

"Nearly so, Cousin. And none too soon," Richard answered with obvious relief. Then, he motioned Owain in close again and, indicating the boy with an incline of his head, said, "A clever lad, my young cousin Harry of Monmouth, unlikely son of that ingrate Henry. I do think he seeks to emulate me. There is promise in the boy, despite his father."

"Who are you?" Harry said, approaching them on a sturdy pair of sea legs.

"Owain Glyndwr, my lord," Owain answered with a swift bow.

Harry studied him with intense hazel eyes that shifted in hue with every tilt of his head.

"You are tall, like a giant," Harry stated. Then, he spun about and raced over the rain-slick deck to the prow of the ship, where he stayed, unbothered by rain or wind, until they docked.

RICHARD HAD LITTLE STOMACH for bloodshed and it came as no surprise that he opted to spend the following winter where it was most comfortable—at Dublin Castle, consulting with his advisors and receiving capitulation from the native chieftains. With due squabble, even McMurrough was brought to heel. Richard was chided by Parliament to return. They would no longer pay for the mounting expenses of his latest campaign.

It was May of '95 before Owain returned to Sycharth. He rode upon a new gray steed of fine Irish blood. Margaret waited for him on the road beyond the manor. The glow was back in her cheeks and her eyes were bright with joy to see him. He dropped from his horse and ran to her. In either arm she clutched their youngest ones, their heads tufted with the same silken yellow as their mother. Before Owain could grant his wife a kiss, she put little Sion down. For a moment Sion tottered uncertainly on his plump, bowed legs. Then he took one step, and then another, and fell into his father's strong arms.

Iolo Goch:

The year following King Richard's marriage to seven-year old Isabella, daughter of King Charles of France, three of the Lords Appellant were suddenly arrested— by order of the king himself. The Duke of Gloucester, Richard's own uncle, met his death by suspect circumstances while imprisoned at Calais. Richard Fitzalan, Earl of Arundel, was executed. The Earl of Warwick was spared his life, but doomed to lifelong imprisonment on the Isle of Man. Only Thomas Mowbray, the Earl of Nottingham and a new favorite of the king, and Henry of Bolingbroke, son of John of Gaunt, were spared. To their astonishment, Mowbray and Bolingbroke were vaulted to the dukedoms of Norfolk and Hereford, respectively. They were gifts accepted with great misgiving.

Mowbray made the horrific mistake of confiding in Henry. So great had grown Mowbray's mistrust, that he was noticeably absent when Parliament convened in Shrewsbury on January 27th, 1398.

If there were troubles in Richard's reign, much of it was of his own making.

6

Shrewsbury, England — January, 1398

IN HIS PRIVATE CHAMBERS at Shrewsbury Castle, Richard II, King of England, sat hunched over the chess board, tapping at one of his pawns. He lifted it, twirled it between his thumb and forefinger, and then put it back down. Twice more, he reached for a piece, but drew his hand back.

Across from him, John of Gaunt groaned impatiently. "You're testing my patience, Richard."

"Uncle, Uncle . . ." Richard laced his fingers behind his head and leaned back on his stool. His father had died when he was only nine, after having just returned from the battlefields of France. The following year, his grandfather, the resolute Edward III, also died, leaving the crown to young Richard. Gaunt had stepped into the role of his guardian almost immediately and served him capably in that respect. They may have differed in opinion from time to time, but Richard didn't love or respect his uncle any less for it. "You're rushing me in the hopes I'll make an impetuous move."

"You, Richard, are stalling. You have no idea what to do, because any move you make will be a deadly one."

"I am not stalling. I'm considering my options."

"None of them are good, so just be done with it, will you?"

Richard nudged a pawn forward and snatched his hand back. The door flew open. The fire sputtered and went low momentarily as it battled the draft that marched in on Henry of Bolingbroke's heels. Shivering at the January cold, Richard tugged his fox-trimmed mantle up to his ears.

Toying with a knight, Gaunt glanced at his son. "Close the door."

Henry flung the door shut with vehemence. His concentration unbroken, Gaunt executed his move, then pinched the stem of his green-tinged Bohemian glass and triumphantly doused his throat with wine.

"Ah, damnation. I'll lose yet another." Richard twisted his face. Quick to find distraction, he peered at Henry. "How goes it, Cousin? Where has Mowbray been these past two days? Not like him to avoid Parliament. I pray he has not taken ill."

"It would be to your great advantage if he were," Henry said.

Hands now clasped before him as he rested his elbows on the table, Richard caressed his jewel-encrusted rings. He wasn't sure he wanted to know the reason for Thomas Mowbray's absence. Even though he had vaulted him to the dukedom of Norfolk, he had lately been nagged by an inkling of mistrust of the man. But more than Mowbray's scheming, he feared Henry's ambition. This sudden revelation was just one more instance of his cousin seeking to advance his worth in Richard's eyes.

Gaunt lifted his chin, stretching the folds of skin that marked his many years like the rings of a tree trunk. "You have news for the king?"

"Oh, enough!" Henry grumbled. "It was you, Father, who urged me to do this. And by God, though I detest my mission, it must be done."

Above his glittering knuckles, Richard studied his cousin: the epitome of knighthood. A constant champion on the tournament field and possessing all the piety of an anointed crusader, he was a power worth recognizing. Even the ornate tapestry on the wall behind him depicting St. George slaying the dragon could have been spun in laud of him.

"*What* must be done?" Richard said.

Striding forward, Henry planted his rock-like fists on the table, rattling the chess pieces. "Thomas Mowbray says that you seek to plot against him. That all your pardons were for naught. He also says that I have every reason to plot against you, which I swear by all that is holy is untrue. I will not have him utter such lies about either myself or my king."

Richard lowered his hands, then rose and straightened his robes. "You speak of treason."

"That I do."

"Then you must bring this before Parliament."

"I know." Henry's gruff voice lowered. "I know as well that it was Mowbray himself at whose hands Gloucester died."

Richard tried hard to control his expression. The web of lies he had guarded until now threatened to tear. It had been the official statement that Gloucester had died of natural causes. He would have preferred that version to remain undisputed, for suspicion to simply vanish. "He will challenge you."

"I am well aware of that."

Richard moved a few steps, stopping behind his uncle. He could have pressed himself through the very cracks in the walls and not been far enough from Henry at that moment. "Henry, my dear cousin . . . this is a complicated matter. Perhaps it was no more than a thought spoken aloud and just as quickly dismissed. Or a rumor that —"

"It was no rumor." Henry's face took on a revealing shade of red. His fingernails dug into the tabletop. He was not known for his ability to control his temper. "I was there. I heard him say it."

"All the same, you may wish you had never spoken of this without further proof. He will deny it. His supporters might well retaliate against you."

"And if I had kept it to myself, would I not then have been guilty of treason, as well? That I would not do. I have no wish to destroy your faithful followers, or myself for what it matters . . . but I will not stand idly by while such sedition grows and festers in your realm. Soon enough, it will stink like plague-rotted corpses in your court."

His fingers again nervously probing the dazzling facets of his jewels, Richard nodded, half-convinced and wholly disturbed. "Very well. Your accusations will be heard before Parliament adjourns this session. Gather what evidence you have. Present it. I thank you for your . . . your concern." He reclaimed his seat. A cool minute later, with Henry still looming, the king drummed his fingers on the table. "You may go. Spare me the details for now."

Jaw clenched, Henry stormed from the room.

Unwilling to accept defeat prematurely, Richard slid one of the marble pieces strategically forward.

"I hear the young Earl of March received a hero's welcome this morning," Gaunt imparted. Edmund Mortimer, the Earl of March, was a seven-year boy old whose great-grandfather, Lionel, Duke of Clarence, had been the second oldest son of King Edward III and Queen Philippa. As the direct descendant of the next oldest of King Edward's sons, many believed that little Edmund Mortimer was next in line for the throne. Richard still had no heir and with his new bride, Isabella, being a young girl still, it was not likely he would have one for some years yet. Anything could happen in that span of time and Richard was well aware of it. Although John of Gaunt had long wielded his influence over Richard, he was King Edward's fourth son and not even he would have asserted to hold the stronger claim.

Richard sensed otherwise about his hotheaded cousin Henry of Bolingbroke, however. Henry was ambitious and would have thought nothing of grasping for what was not his if he wanted it. Richard did not trust him.

"Oh yes, the heir presumptive." Richard sneered. Henry's appearance had put him in a foul mood. He flicked his queen across the board, toppling Gaunt's army of pawns. "I have wearied of this. I wish to retire now."

It was an unsettling revelation for the king. Henry pitted against Mowbray could prove to be extremely ugly. For all he knew, his cousin was merely trying to earn favor by alerting him to Mowbray's remarks. A contrived delay was in order. If Richard was to rid himself of the bur that was Henry of Bolingbroke, without alienating his beloved uncle, it would take some delicate planning.

Iolo Goch:

A parliamentary committee decided, most conveniently, that the dispute between Bolingbroke and Mowbray should be determined by trial by combat. The chosen place was Coventry. The date—the 16th of September of that year: 1398.

As the duel was about to begin, Richard intervened. He banished both men: Mowbray for a hundred winters and Henry for ten years. Henry withdrew to the French court, where he was received with great civility.

The next winter, Henry received the ill tidings of his father's death. He expected that Richard would summon him home and bestow upon him the titles and holdings that had been his father's. But to Henry's astonishment, instead of a cousin's welcoming arms and tepid apology, Richard disinherited him—from everything.

Vengefulness is a dangerous quality in a king. More so to Richard himself than to those he sought to punish. Henry swore himself the king's enemy. Richard would pay.

7

Waterford, Ireland — May, 1399

IT WAS THE 31ST of May in 1399 when King Richard's ships pulled into the harbor at Waterford. Art McMurrough had once again reared up in revolt—this time claiming himself as the rightful king of all Ireland. So it was that Richard had departed for that unruly isle, the funds for the expedition duly augmented by the seizure of Henry of Bolingbroke's lands. There was great risk at leaving his kingdom, especially so shortly after the cutting affront to his cousin, who was not without his supporters. But it was with calculated foresight that Richard brought with him Henry's own son: Henry of Monmouth, more affectionately known to his godfather the king as Harry.

The ride inland toward Kilkenny was intoxicating. The persistent mists had summoned from the earth tender blades of grass that flooded the island in a rippling sea of green. When the clouds broke and drifted away, sunlight coaxed forth tight buds so that the trees and hedges lifted up their emerald crowns beneath an endless sky.

Numerous reports confirmed the king's army was on the trail of McMurrough, but always, the rebel was one slippery step ahead. Then they stumbled upon him almost by accident. An Irishman from the nearby village with a grudge against McMurrough decided to take advantage of the king's presence and revealed McMurrough's whereabouts. A small party of scouts on the swiftest horses rode on ahead to find him. Meanwhile, the English pressed on as fast as they could, their pace hampered by the king's wagon train. It was a short hour later that one of the scouts returned to the king's army.

The breathless soldier dropped from his saddle before his horse had even completely stopped. Sweat poured from his jaw line, drenching the front of his shirt. He bowed hastily before the king, who was enthroned upon his gray destrier, then looked up uneasily. "Sire." His eyes plunged. "We lost him. Over the next ridge. By the time we reached the place we had last seen him, there was no trace. Three rivers converged nearby. He could have crossed any one of them to hide his tracks."

With pinched lips, Richard studied the countryside. Beyond the nearest line of hillocks, the rambling edge of a thick forest wandered. The tree trunks stood like the masts of ships, firmly entrenched, their leafy sails buffeted by the hot, insistent wind. He clenched his reins, feeling the earth tip beneath him. A queasiness reminiscent of his channel crossing soured his stomach. He choked back the bitterness. "So hunt him down. However long it takes. Bring him back to me."

"We tried, sire, but . . . the ground has been used for grazing cattle recently. The tracks will be hard to find—if there are any. And there are several more streams to swallow up hoof prints by the score, as well as forest trails leading in a dozen directions. He knows this land too well and we not at all."

"You failed?" Richard resisted the urge to strike the man.

Beside him, Harry, fourteen years of age, spoke out. "Burn the closest village."

Richard's eyes snapped toward him. "What?"

Above a dimpled chin, Harry's angelic mouth curved into a smile. "If you can't shackle the criminal, punish him otherwise."

"M'lord?" Thomas, Duke of Surrey and the king's nephew

through his mother's second marriage, edged his horse closer. "It was a villager who led us to McMurrough. If we burn it . . ."

Richard dabbed at his upper lip with a kerchief. He wasn't comfortable with the idea, but he wasn't about to go back to England without making some sort of statement that rebellion came with consequences. "Perhaps it was all a ruse, Thomas? Carefully planned from the very beginning. They think to mock their king. My young cousin here is a clever lad. Do as he says: burn the village."

An hour later, as Richard rode on to Dublin at the head of his army, the smoke of burning thatch blotted out the sun.

Dublin, Ireland — June, 1399

YOUNG HARRY WAS SITTING cross-legged on his bed in Dublin Castle, bent over a cherished copy of *Troilus and Cressida*, when the king rushed into his private chamber at well past Compline, startling him. They had been ensconced in Dublin for nearly two months now, with no apparent cause keeping them there. Already, Harry had begun to feel himself a prisoner of circumstance, subjected to Richard's increasingly unpredictable moods.

The lamplight drew long shadows on Richard's thinning face. The corners of his mouth were weighed down with a hundred years' worry. He trailed his hand along the rough stone wall. "Oh, poor Harry. Do you know what your father has done?"

Harry closed his book, studying the king. Yes, he knew. Half the world knew by then. Henry of Bolingbroke had set sail from Boulogne and landed at Ravenspur at the Mouth of the Humber earlier that month. He had then headed toward Pontefract in the north and along the way the people had joined him, shouting and cheering. Even the mighty lords of those northern lands—Henry Percy, the Earl of Northumberland, and his son Harry Hotspur—had merged with Henry of Bolingbroke's ranks. They were more than mere rumors, as sources had been highly reliable, and with each report Harry had watched his cousin rant and worry endlessly.

While Harry understood his father's yearning for justice, it grieved him to see the king so helplessly cornered. For several tense, volatile weeks, Richard had paced the floors of Dublin Castle, bestowing precious time on Henry's cause. The loyalties of those that the king had left behind had proven to be as shifting as sand dunes in a gale. Left and right, Richard's closest councilors had submitted to Henry. If Richard remained in Ireland much longer, soon enough he would have no kingdom at all to return to.

Pressing his back against the wall, Richard covered his face for a long minute. Finally, he raked the woven tangle of hair back from his forehead. "He invaded my land. Beautiful, glorious England. And . . . and without trial or cause or mercy he has put to death my faithful subjects. Oh, Harry, I do love you. I am so sorry for you. Your father's doings will cost you your inheritance. I would not have had it so. Dear God, you don't know how this pains me." Tears washed over his cheeks. "My friends, my own kinsmen—they all turn from me. It feels as though my soul is in flames and there is nothing left inside me but ashes." He crumpled to the floor, his head upon his knees, sobbing.

In his nightshirt, Harry slid from his bed. He approached slowly, knelt down and laid a hand on the king's shoulder. He had spent far more years of his youth at the king's side than his own father's. The affection he felt for Richard was genuine, as was his pity of him. "I had prayed the rumors were not true. But please, please . . . I had no part in my father's deeds. None. I am innocent."

Grasping Harry's fingers tightly, Richard raised his watery eyes. "Yes, I know. You had no part in his crimes. I don't accuse you of anything. Still . . ."

Harry wrapped his arms around the king. Richard, unable to

endure the embrace, bolted up. He went to the doorway and hung there, both hands braced against the frame as if there existed some degree of safety in its structure.

"Harry?" He glanced over his sloping shoulder. "If I could have chosen a son . . ." Quickly, he averted his face. "I must return to England. Try to amend matters there. Tomorrow, Thomas will take you to Castle Trim in Meath for your own protection, where you will remain until this is over."

Over? It would not be over until Harry's father had his way. Only one end could come of Richard.

8

Sycharth, Wales — Summer, 1399

MARGARET FANNED HER SUPPLE fingers over the ridge of Owain's knuckles. They sat side by side at the head of the table in Sycharth's hall. Their home was thronged with family and friends. The rafters rang with the echo of laughter. The day was bright with summer's splendor. Owain's family was celebrating the sixteenth birthday of his oldest son Gruffydd and it was much to Gruffydd's chagrin that Iolo had chosen as his verse the woeful romance of Tristan and Iseult. Only yesterday, Gruffydd had confided in Iolo that the object of his every waking moment was a young maiden named Elise, a niece to Owain's petulant neighbor Lord Reginald de Grey of Ruthin.

Owain poured a cup of usquebaugh and pushed it in front of Gruffydd, who regarded it with disdain. Gruffydd had never liked the way it warmed his veins, made his tongue feel thick and filled his head with fog. Besides, to him it tasted no better than vinegar.

"The Irish call it 'water of life'." Owain winked. "It will put a beard on your chin."

Gruffydd brought it to his nose and inhaled, then plunked the cup down on the table. "The devil's own piss. It will burn my insides on the way down."

"Only the first time." Owain cuffed him on the shoulder. "Ah! The mummers have arrived."

Owain and Margaret clapped gleefully as a small parade, led by their second oldest son Maredydd, entered the hall. The children drew out in a line, from tallest to shortest, all ten of Gruffydd's younger brothers and sisters. Sweeping down from their shoulders were brightly colored cloaks borrowed from their parents' wardrobe. Sion and little Mary, now five years of age, were more concerned with gathering up the ends of their trailing encumbrances to keep from tripping than playing their parts. Madoc, one of the middle children, stood beside his twin Isabel with a grin that was spread from ear to ear. Dewi and Tomos traded punches. Janet clutched a mended doll, the stitched features on its face frayed, its dress a patchwork of color. Holding Janet's free hand was her older sister Alice, the very image of her mother. Each of the children, except Catrin, who was second oldest after Gruffydd, had a wooden sword tucked beneath their belts of rope. Circling Catrin's pale brow was a crown of yellow-faced daisies.

Plucking up Catrin's hand, Maredydd strutted forward. The pair stopped in front of Gruffydd and swooped low at the waist toward him.

"I am King Arthur. Let me present my lovely queen, Guinevere. And these," Maredydd proclaimed, spreading his arms, "are the Knights of the Round Table!"

The audience hooted. Mugs banged on the tables and feet stomped louder and louder until the clatter was deafening. Then Maredydd swept aside the plates still in front of his parents and sprang atop the table. He held up his palms to hush the crowd. Behind him, Margaret and Owain exchanged glances of delight at their son's ability to cast such a spell of amusement. Gruffydd, however, was bored of all the regalia and would rather have been alone hunting with his bow—or better yet, somewhere secluded with Elise—than be forced to watch such meaningless child's play.

"But wait, good people!" A deep seriousness weighed down Maredydd's voice. Slowly, his hands drifted downward. "There is blight in my kingdom. One of my knights, my own nephew Mordred, has fallen from grace and seeks to destroy me." He pointed accusingly to the far end of the hall, where Tudur sprang from behind a tapestry.

Tudur flashed a grin at Owain and Margaret and shrugged. In mocking fashion, he flipped back the ends of his long black cloak and strutted into the middle of the hall. Jeers and whistles followed him.

It was in the midst of this earsplitting folly that the doors to the hall swung open and a sagging figure stumbled in. There was little cause for notice at first. More than one guest had already had too much to drink and people had been coming and going all day. Gruffydd's first instinct, however, was to claim a weapon from above the hearth to chase away the bedraggled stranger. The man looked to be no threat, but clearly he was either drunk or deranged. Gruffydd turned a questioning gaze upon his father.

The smile now gone from his face, Owain detached himself from his wife's gentle handclasp and moved around the table. Maredydd dropped from his perch to stand behind his father. Tudur whirled around, and then took several steps back. Almost in unison, the children turned to see who had interrupted their play.

Head bowed, Owain sank to his knee. "My lord."

The hall went silent. Not even a whisper rippled the air. Gruffydd had seen the man perhaps once before and then from a distance. But he knew by his father's reaction who it was.

King Richard's eyes were dull and drooping. He moved in a detached manner. The clothes he wore were plainer than even those of Sycharth's servants, unmended and tinged with the dust of mountain trails. Just beyond the doorway stood a remnant of his fragmented army, far cleaner than him, but looking every bit as weary.

"Your guests are lacking in their manners." Richard stole a tankard from one of the tables and wetted his lips. Then he groped inside a torn sleeve and, discovering his kerchief gone, wiped at the split corners of his mouth with the backs of his fingers.

Owain shot a glance at Tudur, who obediently dropped to one knee. Maredydd grabbed at the arms of Alice and Tomos and pulled them down. The younger children, bewildered, huddled together beneath a table. Her mouth hanging aghast, fair Catrin slowly knelt, her eyes never leaving the king.

"What are you staring at?" Richard stomped toward Catrin. Trembling, she lowered her eyes to the floor. "Have your eyes never beheld a king?"

He looked anything but a king as he staggered around Owain's hall. The shadow on his whiskered cheeks from too many days without a shave and a bundle of limp, knotted hair gave him the appearance of a cat that had been stranded in a rainstorm. Halting behind Owain, Richard bent over and whispered in his ear, "Get rid of them."

"Rid of whom, sire?" Owain whispered back.

"*Them.* All of them."

"M'lord, if you wish to speak in private we could —"

"I wish to speak to you here. Now. I haven't any time. I am pressed for Conwy."

Nodding, Owain rose.

Richard grabbed his sleeve. "That one may stay." He pointed at Gruffydd. "He reminds me of my cousin—young Harry."

Gruffydd hadn't even been aware that the king had noticed him. As curious as he was about what had brought him here, Gruffydd had no desire to be privy to Richard's troubles. Life at Sycharth was, for the most part, uncomplicated. English politics were anything but simple. Certainly, Wales had had its share of troubles in the past, but his father had done his best to remain on good terms with both his neighbors and his English overlords—whatever it took to live in peace. Gruffydd, too, preferred it that way.

Owain turned to Margaret and gave the instructions for the hall to be cleared. It was several minutes later before the last guest exited and the doors were drawn shut. Richard stood in the middle of the hall, his eyes fixed on the distant hills beyond the windows as if contemplating some looming fate.

"They gave up Bristol," Richard said. "Opened the doors, let Henry in to murder my men." Then he turned his face toward Owain. Behind his pupils was an extinguished soul. The flamboyance for which he was known was vanished, his fingers unadorned but for the ring that bore the royal seal. "My kingdom is in chaos. My army, hearing rumors of my supposed death, has scattered to the winds. My people . . . they hail Henry and toss petals before his godly steps. Yet they flee from me, as if I were some ogre afflicted with leprosy. Have I even one loyal man to defend my name? One? Alas, he has turned them all against me—every soldier, every nobleman, every beggar and every child." Again, he looked out over the hills and flinched, as if he thought he had seen Henry himself riding for him. "Oh, this I swear, by God I do swear—if ever I get my hands on that bastard Bolingbroke's neck, he will die in such a manner that they will retell the tale even in Turkey."

Richard was rambling as if Henry had woven some spell over the whole of England, when in truth it was Richard's confiscation of the Lancastrian inheritance that had severed any and all devotion he might have claimed. Even Gruffydd, just turned sixteen and more interested in a certain young English girl than English politics, knew that.

The king then turned to Owain, inviting a response with a pleading, doleful stare.

"Say it," Richard challenged Owain. "Whatever it is, say it. I did not come here so that you could tell me what I want to hear. Tell me what I *need* to hear. Say it or I'll damn you every day until my death."

Owain glanced around the room—at the immense timber rafters, at the host of empty chairs and half-eaten plates of food—then at the king. "You must give back to Henry everything you have taken from him."

Gruffydd cringed at his father's boldness, wishing he could scamper beneath the table like his siblings had and crawl from the hall unnoticed.

Richard laughed hollowly. "Everything?"

"Yes. Everything. Including his father's titles."

His hands on his hips, the king paced the length of the head table. He tittered like a madman. Then he thumped a finger on his temple and pointed at Owain. "I don't think there was ever a man in my court who spoke half as honestly as you, Welsh."

"I have nothing to gain or lose by doing so."

"Ah, but you do. You are the wealthiest Welshman west of the Severn. You have a great deal to lose." Leaning idly against one of the tables, Richard picked at the food around him until he found a morsel of still warm capon to his liking. "I upheld your right to the lands that your neighbor Grey so covets . . . but fortune may not smile so pleasantly on you in the future. You in all your golden splendor, with an army of children, rivers flowing in wine, a sea of grain around you—mark me, one stroke of the blade or swipe of the pen and all is gone. All . . ."—he gazed down at his sullied palms as if he were watching a handful of sand sift between his wriggling fingers, his voice fading to a frail whisper—"all is gone."

"No." Owain stepped closer. "All is not gone, my lord king. Go not to Conwy. Stay here at Sycharth. Many Welsh would come to your calling. I can send word —"

"You are already in grave danger for having befriended me," Richard warned. "If you were to speak on my behalf, they would disparage your name and connect to it all manner of lies. And they are such fantastic experts at concocting lies, you would not believe it. If you were to raise an army in my name, they would level every paltry village hereabouts. To house me, they would burn your home for it. Cleave to your family, Glyndwr. In the end, it is the only thing truly your own." Pilfering a loaf of white bread, he tossed a glance at Gruffydd. Then he trudged toward the door and without so much as a cordial nod of farewell, shoved it open, tripped down the stairs and pulled himself up into his saddle. With a scant few dozen guards and archers, King Richard departed for Conwy.

Gruffydd expelled a sigh of relief, but in the very next breath his shoulders and arms were locked with tension. The king's visit, how-ever unplanned, meant trouble. His father may not have been one to seek out confrontation, but he was not one to let injustices go unanswered, either. Gruffydd feared his father would let himself be drawn into a fight that was never his to begin with.

With obvious trepidation, the guests began to filter back into the hall. Madoc, so generally soft-spoken and observant, sidled up to Gruffydd and tapped him on the shoulder. "Who was that?"

Gruffydd rose from his seat to watch the last of the king's company disappear over a hill. "*That*, Madoc, was Richard, King of England."

IN THE CIRCLE OF Owain's fingers rested a cup of flat ale. The log in the hearth of their chamber glowed weakly at its core. He had been sitting on a small stool there for over an hour, thinking about, won-dering, even dreading what news would come.

Margaret knelt at her husband's feet and put her chin on his knees. She looked up at him with her great brown eyes, the last of the fire glimmering in her pupils. "I would tell you to come to bed, but I know you wouldn't sleep. You'd only keep me awake with your tossing and turning."

"I fear for him, Marged." He swirled his cup, then tossed its contents onto the diminishing fire. "I fear for us."

"So bar the door. Throw away the key," she teased, running her soft hand over his thigh. Then she raised herself up on her knees and circled her arms about his neck. "Everything we need is here. In this house."

"Would that were true, *cariad.*"

"Owain, what I'll not have you doing is dabbling in king's games. What's done is done. King Richard has made his own bed. You don't take from men what is rightly theirs without paying recompense eventually."

Setting his cup aside, he pulled her hands down to his chest and held them tightly. "I still think he could have been a good king. He's a peace-loving man . . . and generous."

Margaret scoffed. "Generous at the expense of others. Leave it be, my love. 'Tis not your quarrel."

"It's more than a quarrel. More than that. Far, far more." He shook his head and gazed again into the fire. "Ah Marged, but you are right. You always are. There's little to be done. Richard must crawl to Henry and beg bloody forgiveness for all his transgressions. He'll be a king in name only. A tethered animal. A baited bear."

"He hasn't the claws to be a bear." Tenderly, she turned his hands over and kissed his palms. "Come to bed, won't you? If you can't sleep, it's no bother—truly. I'm not tired, either."

A faint grin crept over his mouth. Longingly, he reached for her. A shiver rippled through her. He curled his fingers around one of her ears and pressed something cold and hard against her earlobe. Drawing his hand back, he revealed the glint of an old Roman coin, its surface speckled with the patina of many centuries.

"What *is* that?" she asked in amazement.

"My magic trick. But sadly it's the only one I know." He

shrugged with the innocence of a young boy caught playing pranks. "I promised you, remember? That day in the market, when we first met, that as we grew older I would amuse you with my magic tricks?"

"I do. A cart full of squawking chickens rumbled by. I bumped into you. My hair was full of feathers. You plucked them away, one at a time, as you told me all the times until then that you almost spoke to me, but didn't." She pulled him to his feet and led him away from the fading fire. "I remember every day with you. Every day."

Invitingly, she turned and sat on the edge of the canopied featherbed, the temple where each of their eleven children had been made and brought into the world. "Every hour." Lying back as he approached her, she gazed up at him, sharing with him the memory of each laugh, kiss and tear of seventeen years. "Every moment."

9

Near Ruthin Castle, Wales — Summer, 1399

CONCEALED IN DEWY BRACKEN, Gruffydd peered through the gray blending of forest shapes. In the boughs far above, a tawny owl bemoaned an unfound mate. He kept his eyes on the trail until they were so strained and weary he fought to keep them open. It was well past midnight . . . and his truelove was late.

The moonlight that had so charitably lit his path to this secret place was now hiding shyly behind a thickening bank of clouds. A sluggish breeze rustled the undergrowth and brushed gently at his cheeks. Below where he hid in a grove of oaks, a lazy brook murmured its lullaby. He closed his lids for only a moment . . .

A gasp turned to a squeak. Gruffydd poked his head above the bracken to determine its source.

Elise's slippered foot plunged from a stepping-stone into the brook. As she threw her arms out to catch her balance, her skirts fell into the water. By the time Gruffydd rubbed the sleep from his eyes and scurried forth, she was standing at the rivulet's edge, a dark, knee-deep waterline marking her yellow skirt and a scowl as convincing as any snarling dog's on her mouth. Her bosom, quite ample for a maiden of merely fifteen years, heaved with indignation. Gruffydd drank her in and braved a step closer, dying to press his hungry lips against hers.

Before he was within arm's reach, she shushed him with a forefinger to her plump lips. Motioning for him to follow her behind the shroud of oak columns, she snatched up her wet skirt. No need for further convincing, Gruffydd stumbled through the waist-high ferns after her. If he could have caught her, he would have pulled her down right there and nothing but the trembling spray of fronds would have betrayed them.

"Elise, I was starting to think you weren't —"

"Shhh." She leaned against a tree, one hand pressed to her lower rib cage as if to control her breathing. "He knows."

"He? Who? Knows what?"

"About us," she said. "My uncle, Lord Grey, knows about us." Her thick brown hair was gathered loosely at the back of her head. She pushed a handful of straying strands behind her ear. Her lower lip quivered.

"But how? We've been so careful." It was crushing news. Enough to make him feel compelled to run like the devil and never look back. But in the very same heartbeat he wanted to wrap her in his yearning arms and never let go.

"One of his men saw you follow me behind the market stall in Ruthin."

They had stolen a kiss. A brief kiss. A fleeting moment of bliss wedged into the mayhem of market day.

She turned her heart-shaped face away for a single moment, but his gaze was too strong for her to resist. She fell into his arms, shaping her body to his. "We cannot meet like this again."

"No, no, don't say it. Please don't say it. We shall give it time. That is all. A month perhaps. Ah God, even that is too long." He buried his face in her hair, wanting to remember the smell and feel of her, suddenly afraid he might never hold her again.

"My love, my love . . ." Her dark brown eyes filling with tears, she pulled back enough to look up at him. "Even now, I fear he has me watched. It's not safe for us to be together. I want no harm to come to you. I . . . I must go."

Though it was hardly possible, he pressed her closer to him. He felt every seam of her clothing and every curve beneath. Sweet Mother Mary, he loved her so much it ached in his every sinew. "Then if I must be without you for a time, give me but one more kiss. Just one."

Leaning close, he closed his eyes and tasted her breath intermingling with his. Her lips brushed his, softly at first, then hungrily, greedily.

He felt her arms tugging him down. His knees swayed and gave way as he sank to the earth with her, their mouths never parting. They lay down upon a bed of bracken, one aligned with the other. The scent of wood and earth filled his nose. Leaves rustled in the canopy above.

A new fear gripped him—that they would be found out. He began to roll away from her, but she grabbed his arm, turned him back to her.

Her fingers grazed his cheek. "Please, Gruffydd, please . . ."

Oh God, he had thought of her in this way for months now, watched her from a distance, longed for her, awoken drenched in sweat after dreaming of her. "But your uncle —"

"Never needs to know."

He gazed upon her face, wanting to remember her just as she was, yet wanting more. Unable to resist her any longer, he brought his mouth to hers and —

"Elise!" Lord Grey bellowed through the darkness. "Where are you, girl?"

Gruffydd froze, his pulse racing, every fiery vein turning to slush.

"Run," she whispered, and shot to her feet. As he reached for her, she plunged through the bracken.

Elise splashed through the brook and bounded up the far side, her feet slipping on the steep bank. She grabbed at a sapling branch, but it bent under her weight and she tumbled to the ground. He wanted to run after, help her up, or haul her back to him, but then he heard the caustic bellow once more. A moment later, Elise was up again, clambering up the incline and back onto the narrow path.

There, she froze, mouth agape, hands clutched to her breast. Her uncle's bay steed barreled toward her. She jumped out of the way barely in time to avoid being trampled under its hooves. Grey wheeled his horse around and plunged from his saddle to storm at her.

"Where is he? Tell me where he is!" He hooked Elise's small arm and reeled her in. "Tell me where the devil's hiding! By God, I'll gouge out that bastard's eyes for having put a child in your belly. I told you he would make a whore of you and the next day deny having known you. Tell me, damn it! Were you to meet the shameless mongrel here? How long have —"

Child? What is he talking about? We haven't . . .

The realization snatched the breath from Gruffydd's lungs. She had already lain with another. He was not her first or her only love. She had invited him here with the intention of giving herself to him so she could claim him as the father of her child.

Elise's voice rose in pitch and protest, but Gruffydd didn't wait to hear more. He ran, as swift as his legs would carry him. In the distance, he thought he heard Elise scream, but he would not go back to save her, not after she had lied to him so. Limbs and rocks nearly tripped his unsteady feet. Branches lashed out as he flew past. More than once he stumbled, but without a thought he scrambled back up and raced onward.

The wind pursued him, roaring threats in his ears, mocking his innocence. By the time he reached Sycharth, his clothes were torn and muddy and he was minus a shoe.

Dawn came not with the habitual brilliance of a late summer morning, but instead it pounded with thunder and poured a bleak, oppressive rain that lasted for three straight days. The heavens were black in mourning and Gruffydd was the prisoner of a love he could neither confess nor continue to pursue. Elise had betrayed him.

Still, he couldn't stop thinking of her. He would have forgiven her, claimed the child as his own, if only to be with her forever. But it would never be. Lord Grey, he knew, would hunt him down and make a hell of his life. He could hardly bear to think what Grey already might have done to Elise to punish her.

10

Near Penmaenrhos, Wales — August, 1399

A T CONWY, RICHARD WAS urged by the Earl of Northumberland to submit to Henry's claims, but with full promise that he should retain all honor and authority due his kingship. Finally, Richard agreed to meet Henry at Chester and promptly sent Northumberland away. He was certain that if he could buy himself more time, appease Henry for the moment, that eventually he would be able to win back sufficient loyalties to crusade his cause.

But time is one thing there is never enough of—not for a dying man, not for two young, ill-fated lovers, not even for a king.

Richard's appetite fled as well as his will to fight. Mindlessly, he shoved small hunks of coarse bread down his throat, chased by entire bottles of wine. When he slept, it was usually while sitting upright in his chair at the supper table. His nights were spent shuffling along the battlements, the sea air cold and biting upon his bare neck, as he argued aloud with himself.

A week later, Richard and a small party of guards and councilors stole away in the night from Conwy, for he did not trust the word of Henry of Bolingbroke, or his envoy Northumberland. Their aim was London—London, where once Richard the boy king had captured the hearts of the people when the peasants revolted, burned much of the city and slew hundreds before they gathered at Smithfield to throw down their demands. They had strangled the great city itself and chased its leaders trembling and fearful into hiding. All hope of reconciliation had seemed utterly lost then, but young Richard had staunchly defied their leader, Wat Tyler. When the king's men killed Tyler, Richard had boldly ridden alone to the rebel mob and proclaimed: "I am your captain—your king! I am your king!"

Would they remember that day and gather as an army of peasants to march behind him? Or would they instead scatter from him and go back to their homes?

As mute as a funeral procession, Richard and his small party rode along a thinning trail, far from the main roads near a place called Penmaenrhos. He was beaten by a lack of sleep and it showed in the manner in which he slumped in his saddle, swaying with every stride of his horse. The king wore clothes borrowed from a soldier before leaving Conwy. He might have looked like a man of no importance, but for the nervous jerking of his shoulders as his head followed his eyes to investigate every cracked twig or rabbit bounding through the underbrush. He had reason to fear for his very life.

Half the day slipped away before he allowed them to stop long enough to relieve themselves and answer the rumblings of their stomachs. While his men sank to the ground in the shade of a dense grove, Richard stood with the reins of his horse clenched in one hand, scanning the countryside, seeking the humble army of Welshmen and peasants that would come to his aid, but also terrified of the vengeful English one that would pursue him to the furthest reaches of the isle. They had not been out of their saddles long enough to chew their stale bread before the king ordered them onward again.

Not far from Llanddulas as sunset neared, the king's company entered a lushly wooded glen embraced by towering walls of crumbling limestone. Every hoof beat amplified in Richard's ears, hammering in his head with relentless mockery. The deep, leafy shadows harbored goblins in hordes. Demons concealed in the burled limbs of trees jeered at Richard's vain folly. Suddenly, one of the demons raised its hellish bow and aimed down at Richard's fair head from a craggy cliff.

"Hold." Richard raised a quivering hand, his eyes locked upon the arrow that marked his shrinking heart. On the trail before them, heavily armed English soldiers poured forth. Behind, above, around—everywhere. From their midst strode the stout Henry Percy, Earl of Northumberland, a forced smile bracing his plump cheeks. At his shoulder was his robust son of the same name, but more commonly known as Harry Hotspur.

"Percy, what is this?" Richard's eyes darted from one man to the next; their hands were poised threateningly upon sword hilts. Perched on the limestone outcroppings were two dozen archers, arrows nocked.

Northumberland strode up to Richard's prancing mount and hooked his fingers through the halter. "There, there." Gently he pulled down on the horse's muzzle and stroked its velvety cheek. Beneath his bushy, peppered eyebrows, he glanced up at the king, then back into the horse's great, round eyes. "We have come to escort you to Flint, my lord."

"Then you go against your word, Percy." King Richard gathered the reins tighter in his sweating palms, his knees gripping his mount's ribcage. "You promised to have but six in your escort party. I count tenfold that and more. And no escort, but an armed guard. Besides, it was Chester, not Flint, that I agreed to."

"And you, sire, said you would wait for my return, so that I could personally accompany you there. My guess is that you were headed elsewhere—and not to Chester either."

Richard glanced at Hotspur, but he could read nothing in the knight's stoic face.

"This is no peaceful escort," Richard said. "It is an armed guard. I'll go nowhere with you under these sly pretenses. I am the King of England. All that you see and more"—he raised his palm in the direction of the road ahead—"is my kingdom. So clear the road, Percy. Let us pass."

"Your forgiveness, but I cannot let you go back to Conwy or anywhere else. You must come with me to Flint and meet with the Duke of Lancaster."

"I will not. Besides, Henry is no longer the Duke of Lancaster. I stripped him of that inheritance long ago." It was a futile protest, Richard knew. The slight waver of a bow caught his sight. Cold desperation crept under his skin and seeped into the very pith of his being.

"My lord, do not force my hand," Northumberland said. "I am not good at this."

"Good at what, Percy? Turning traitor?" Shattered bits of sunlight, broken by the canopy overhead, danced around him, but Richard felt only the chill of the shade and its completeness.

"Order your men to drop their weapons," Northumberland said flatly.

With forced effort, Richard raised his fine chin and gathered in his breast what little resolve he still had. "Speak not thusly to me, Percy. Think again on what you are about to do. Take but a moment. Weigh it. Remember all I have done for you and your —"

"You are under arrest."

Richard was stunned beyond belief.

"Arrest?" he echoed. It was the only word his lips would shape. He heard its sound, but the meaning fled his comprehension altogether.

Behind him, the cascading thud of surrendered weapons resounded in the glen. The point of Northumberland's sword drifted upward to meet the king's eyes. On the glinting tip of the earl's blade tottered the very course of the Plantagenet dynasty.

"Your sword," Northumberland commanded.

Slowly, Richard drew his sword and surrendered it to the earth. Hotspur, at last committing to action, darted forth to seize it.

"And your dagger."

This time, with marked hesitation, the king closed his fingers over the hilt. He never thought himself capable of cold-blooded murder, but self-defense . . .

"Don't." Northumberland pressed the point of his sword against Richard's throat. "I was told to bring you without harm to your person, but if I have to . . ."

"May this haunt you to your grave." Richard flipped the dagger from his fingers. Its finely tapered point pierced the ground.

Northumberland bent to free the dagger. "As will your deeds, m'lord."

Iolo Goch:

The tragic son of the lauded Black Prince became Henry of Bolingbroke's captive. Young Harry was released from Castle Trim and escorted back to England to be at his father's side. Richard's reign was in ebb not because of a tidal wave of insurrection, but because none had stood against Henry. Richard's troops had merely wandered off, his assumed friends were mute on his behalf, and the people had long since ceased to remember him as the idealistic child-king.

The baggage train that Richard had taken with him to Ireland was confiscated by Sir Thomas Percy and the Duke of Aumarle, one of Richard's own cousins. Pelts of ermine and fox; cloth of damask, samite and velvet brocade; jewelry set in silver and gold and encrusted with pearls and precious stones; and coin enough to feed all of England south of the Trent. The confiscated goods were escorted through Wales on a long strand of wagons and foreign-bred horses. Such a spectacle was impossible to hide.

Days later, a band of our Welsh brethren, sympathizers to King Richard, ambushed the train in a narrow glen. They would not share their names, but after they stripped the English soldiers of their weapons and herded them into a clump, they left Sir Thomas with one final comment: "Tis common knowledge the king did not give these trinkets to you. So we shall return them to their rightful owner and let you go on your way. Tell the vile traitor you serve that Wales is not his for the taking, either."

If only Henry had heeded those words. Instead, he took them as a challenge.

11

Tower of London, England — September, 1399

FOR NEARLY A MONTH, Richard's domain had been reduced to the periphery of his chamber's walls in the Tower of London. His apportionment of natural light was limited to the narrow aperture of a single high window. When Sir William Beauchamp appeared in his doorway late one day, Richard was so bereft of hope that he barely raised his bleary eyes to acknowledge his visitor.

"What is it Beauchamp? Come to gloat?" Richard sniveled. "And who is that with you?"

"This is Adam of Usk, sire." Beauchamp tipped his head toward his companion. "Welshman, Oxford scholar, and a cleric as soon as his appointment is secured."

Beauchamp, late in years and short on words, curled his fingers at a pair of mousy servants. They scurried in with plates of food, placed them before the king and raced past the guards before they could become targets. Richard had already launched a few goblets at them.

The king swept the food aside and laid his head on the table.

"Go away," he mumbled into his forearm, "and take *him* with you. Whatever you've brought him along for."

Beneath his straight brown mop of hair trimmed in the old Norman fashion, Adam nodded at Beauchamp, who with a shrug and a sigh shuffled out. The guards drew the door shut. The keys clinked with solemnity. Quietly, Adam lifted an unlit candle from its sconce and held its wick out over the dwindling hearth fire until it took flame. Then he circled the room, augmenting what light there was on that chilly September evening.

Richard raised his head. He groped for the jug of wine just beyond his reach. His fingers closed around it, pulled it to him. Empty, but not without use. He tested its weight, brought it over his shoulder and just as Adam turned to look at him, Richard grinned dully.

"All gone," he said.

"I shall have them fetch more, my lord." Adam folded his hands before him, but made no move to call for the servants.

"So why did he send you? Unless you have a dagger hidden in the folds of your sleeve, in which case you need not answer. Just do your duty. Collect your coin. And enjoy your journey to purgatory. I fancy we shall meet there."

"Harry inquires of your health."

"Don't lie to me!" Richard shoved back his chair, toppling it onto the floor. He whirled away, so that Bolingbroke's spy could not see his face. "But if, if you speak to Harry, tell him whatever lies his father would have him believe. Tell him . . . tell him I am well and think of him daily." The last part was true.

"My lord,"—Adam's steps came closer, his voice steady and sure—"you are correct in that I come at the Duke of Lancaster's bidding. But I assure you, I have not been sent to extract any confession. Young Harry is in distress. He would have come himself, but . . ."

Slowly, Richard turned. "Then if you have come in his place to return with a picture of me more brightly painted than the blanched ghost you see, tell him the whole tale: that this England his father would fain have as his, this wonderful, fickle land, it is severe and merciless. So many kings and men of greatness it has exiled, destroyed and slain. Its soil is tainted with the blood of upheaval and greed. My God, if anyone ever truly realized that, no one would ever want it." His eyes trailed along the dimming shaft of light from the floor to the world beyond. "I don't. Not any longer."

Adam righted the chair, went and rapped lightly on the door.

"Are you on your way now to tell Henry that I have been broken?"

"No, my lord." When the guard opened the door, Adam asked for more wine and another goblet. Moments later, a servant delivered upon the request. Adam filled the king's cup and poured himself a drink, then claimed the chair opposite Richard's.

"I have all the time you will grant me," Adam said. "If we talk until the candles have all burnt down, they will bring us more . . . and wine as well."

Richard slid onto his seat, slumping with the strain of defeat. "Then hear my story, Adam of Usk, if you indeed have all night. And witness the woeful issue of this spiteful throne. Speak of it to Henry . . . and my dear Harry. They will not want to believe it, but England is a rose whose thorns bear a poison that kills slowly. I have been pricked and so will they."

12

Glyndyfrdwy, Wales — September, 1399

"ANOTHER DAY," OWAIN PROMISED.

His back to his father, Gruffydd scowled. Since before dawn, they had been pursuing a stag, but when the beast finally came into clear view, Gruffydd had fumbled too long to nock his arrow and it had taken off. It was long gone by now and Gruffydd had cursed his slow reflexes, then swung the arrow against the nearest tree trunk, cracking the shaft.

His horse tethered to a pliant sapling, Gruffydd slid down the incline until the toe of his boot found water. Crouching over the stream, he scooped a handful of ice-cold water and doused his neck.

In an attempt to convert the glum nature of his oldest son, Owain had called for a day of hunting near Glyndyfrdwy, but the event had only served to aggravate Gruffydd further. Even as much as he tried to turn his thoughts from Elise, they kept drifting back to that night. He should have kept her from going back to her uncle, should have stolen away with her and married her in secret. Given what he had learned just a few days ago, that plan was still not out of the question. Even more appealing was the thought of plunging a sword into Lord Grey's gut. Someone needed to take care of the bastard.

Tudur dropped from his mount and whirled about, one flattened hand shading his brow as he surveyed the forest around them. "Perhaps we should take to flying falcons instead?"

"Lady Margaret would be proud to show you about her mews," Iolo hinted, as he clung, green-faced, to the cantle of his saddle and carefully brought his right leg over his horse's rump. The bard was a reluctant hunter and a poor horseman, but he came along for the company. Gruffydd might have been glad for that, he liked Iolo, but he had not yet forgiven him for betraying his confidence to his father.

Plopping down on the bank next to his nephew, Tudur pulled his feet free of his boots and immersed them in the stream. He glanced over his shoulder at Owain, a half-grin tipping his mouth. "If you had allowed me the shot I could have brought home the biggest red stag ever to grease your spit."

"Hah, you would have fared no better." Owain grasped the thick branch of an ancient black poplar and pulled himself up into the cradle of the bough. Straddling one of the massive limbs, he propped his back against the burled bark of the trunk.

Tudur tossed his boots into a clump of grass. "I wager Gruffydd here has other things on his mind."

"About time, too," Owain said. "I was beginning to mark him for the priesthood."

Ignoring them, Gruffydd crossed his arms over his leather jerkin, lay back and stared up at the dappled mosaic of leaves and branches.

Iolo hobbled over to join them. He uncorked his flask and emptied it. "Can you blame the lad for dreaming of sweeter things than a rack of antlers?"

Why were they talking about him as if he were not even there?

"Iolo, how in God's name can you bear a summer's day with that felt hat on?" Tudur said.

"And how can you bear to have the sun searing into your brains?" Iolo pulled his hat down over his ears to ward off the horse-flies.

"Oh clever, clever, Iolo. You should have been the king's jester. 'Tis a wonder you don't drown yourself in laughter listening to your own thoughts." Tudur smoothed his hair back from his face and, closing his eyes, sank back on a mattress of leaf litter.

They lounged in drowsy silence, their ears absorbing the trill of gay wrens and the busy scraping of a nuthatch as it dangled in an upside down world. The breeze was warm and indolent yet for early September, barely rustling the serpentine of branches above. It was a fair enough day for hunting, but better still for a swallow of ale and a long nap.

The throaty cry of baying hounds echoed among the maze of trees like the ominous straining of banshees. The hair on the nape of Gruffydd's neck stood on end. He sat up with a jolt, grasping at his bow and lifting an arrow from his bag.

In his uncalloused hands, Iolo clasped a weighty, curved falchion, one heave of which would surely throw his feathery frame off balance.

Owain vaulted from his perch, landing cat-square on his feet. Leading the way, he clambered up the wooded slope. Just as his head topped the rise a pair of hooves sailed over, clipping the ends of his hair.

The stag they had spent all morning vainly pursuing landed on twisting forelegs, and then collapsed in a tumbling heap, head thrashing as it rolled toward the little stream. Eyes as wide and dark as the night sky, the noble stag shook its enormous rack, the largest Gruffydd had ever laid eyes on, and bounded to its feet. He slapped the arrow against his bow, pulled back —

It had claimed but one single leap toward freedom when an arrow, sure and swift, pierced its thundering heart. Gruffydd's fingers stung with the twang of his bowstring. Stunned, he watched the stag stumble as if drunk, dip its head and bellow in agony. From its soft red-brown hide gushed a fountain of blood. Crimson spotted the forest floor. Astounded and mortified, Gruffydd approached the animal. He freed his hunting knife from his belt.

The honor was not to be his. The pack of hounds that had chased the beast there poured over the ridge, yapping and panting, frothing tongues trailing the ground. The first dog that reached the weakened stag sank its powerful jaws into the deer's neck and pulled it down. In seconds, the knot of sanguinary hunters was drowning with delight in a scarlet sea.

"No! No!" Gruffydd flailed his knife before him and ran toward the pack.

Owain tackled him. His body pinned across his son's, he cried, "Leave it! You'll make quarry of yourself." He hoisted the angry Gruffydd to his feet. As he was dragging him away from the blood-bath, a party of horsemen appeared.

Lord Reginald de Grey of Ruthin leered at his discovery. Swarming around him was a full corps of fifteen huntsmen, lesser lords eager to impress. One rushed in and rammed a spear into the deer, although it was a task that need not have been done.

"Aha! My gratitude, good men, for bringing down my prize," Grey proclaimed.

"*Your* prize?" Owain started forward. "These are my lands you're on. And well you know it. You are beyond your bounds. Parliament has upheld my claims on Croesau."

"Richard's parliament." Grey clucked his tongue in admonishment. "'Tis a hard task to wield influence from a dungeon."

Owain's arms were locked stiffly at his side, though they had the strength to heave the dripping, dog-shredded carcass at Grey's head. "Take it. Take the hide and the meat and the bloody set of antlers. But don't come back. This land is not yours."

"I'll come as often as I please. These are *my* lands now, everything you see. The Welsh sympathizer is not long to wear the crown and Bolingbroke owes me a good turn." One hand upon his hip, he flexed the gloved fingers of his other hand and nodded with satisfaction. "This hunting ground will do, littered though it is with Welsh beggars. Incidentally, I took liberty to evict some troublesome peasants of yours in the next valley."

Owain sprang forward. "You have no right!"

"Yes, yes . . . hmmm. We shall see who has rights. Anyway, they were a little, shall we say, obstinate. A torched roof is very convincing. It has a tendency to make people into believers."

Owain glared up at Lord Grey, haughty in his pride. Grey's huntsmen gathered up the stag, its great ebony eyes glazed over in death, and lashed its slender graceful legs to a stout pole so that it dangled limply upside down. Heaving the prize onto their shoulders, they began trudging back through the forest toward Grey's estate. The hounds had already been leashed and led away.

"Oh, and Gruffydd is it?" Grey smirked with wicked glee. "I have removed my niece to Yorkshire. I thought it best to tuck her away in a nunnery, given her condition. Once the child is delivered, she will take her vows to serve Christ. Saved from the likes of you."

Owain shot his son a questioning glance.

Fists balled until his fingers were bloodless, Gruffydd cast his eyes downward, trying with all his will to master the anger boiling up inside him. He thought of Elise, far to the north, alone, soon to give birth to a bastard child that would likely be taken from her. Gruffydd lunged forward, but Owain latched onto his arm and yanked him back.

"Lying bastard!" Gruffydd shouted at Grey.

"Leave be, Gruffydd." Owain tightened his grip on his son's arm, almost twisting it as Gruffydd strained to free himself.

"A temper? Like father, like son." Grey snorted as he reined his horse around. "So easily provoked." He pricked his horse's flanks with his spurs and started up the hill.

Gruffydd tore from his father's hold and plunged after him. His dagger glinted before him in the gilded shafts of September sun. He might have beaten Grey's struggling mount to the top of the rise, but his feet slipped beneath him and he tumbled down the same slippery path the stag had succumbed to. The cool, mocking waters of the stream swallowed him whole.

At the top of the rise, Grey dallied long enough to drive the blow deeper. "Looks as though you need to put a leash on that pup, Glyndwr. Were he not so impulsive he might be dangerous—even with only his milk teeth." His laughter trailed behind him through the green glen like the tinkling bells on a jester's cap.

Slowly, Gruffydd lifted himself up. Water poured from the tip of his nose and the clean point of his still clenched dagger. When Grey was out of sight he pushed the last of the water from his face and met his father's gaze.

"The child's not mine," Gruffydd said.

"I know." Owain came to him and held out his hand. "A better day will be ours, son. That I swear."

13

Tower of London, England — Late September, 1399

I N THE GLOOM OF his Tower cell, Richard II, the last Plantagenet King of England, nudged a heavy quill across unforgiving parchment.

'*Richard Di Rex.*'

A battalion of lawyers peered victoriously over his shoulder. Before the table, a handful of lords, some of whom had once sworn their undying loyalty to him, looked on, their hands clasped behind their backs.

As Richard drew the quill into the last letter, he faltered, letting the ink pool. It was Adam of Usk, the only man who had befriended him during his imprisonment, who took mercy and lifted the damning implement from Richard's trembling hands. An eager lawyer with a prominently hooked nose snatched the abdication from the table, sprinkled sawdust on it and then blew upon the ink to dry it before rolling it securely and passing it to his assistant.

"King no longer," Richard uttered.

"You are free of your woes," Adam said softly above him.

The lawyers swept up the remaining documents on which Richard had ceded every right and power to Henry of Bolingbroke and rushed out the door. The others followed him.

"Freedom? Is that what Henry has granted me?" Richard, staring at an empty palm, nodded weakly at the irony. "The truth has never been so clear to me . . . or the world so dark." His hand stretched toward the pale light trailing down from his window, as if to touch something that only he could see. "Or God so near."

Richard closed his eyes and brought his forehead to clasped hands. Moments later, he felt Adam's comforting touch on his head. He looked up.

Adam gazed at him, pity plain in his eyes. "God is everywhere. In all our hearts."

Grasping at the splintered edge of the table, Richard pushed back his uncushioned chair and stood, swaying slightly. Although his flesh was deeply chilled, he did not shiver. He fixed his eyes on the door through which his fate had fled. A fly that stubbornly denied the coming season settled on the bridge of his slender nose and yet he took no notice. Adam swooshed his hand at it and Richard blinked, then staggered toward his bed—a narrow array of planks littered with molding straw, shoved against the damp stone wall. There were several richly adorned chambers throughout the various towers where prisoners had been housed luxuriously, but Henry had not afforded his cousin even the most meager of comforts. Richard was not a prisoner of state to be ransomed for profit, but a declared traitor to the realm, a violator of the Magna Carta—the very things he had been groomed from birth to champion.

Richard was not halfway across the room before his knees failed him. He crumpled to the floor like a sack of boneless flesh. Adam, who was close on his heels, hoisted him up and helped him to the crude bed.

"M'lord?" Adam addressed, kneeling before Richard, who could barely sit upright. Adam removed his own cloak and placed it in Richard's lap. "Tell me what it is you need, anything, and I will have it brought to you."

"Anything?"

"Yes, name it."

"Even though you are not so powerful, I will tell you." Richard curled his blue fingers around Adam's uncalloused hands. "I want . . . *peace*. My own peace. What Henry deserves, by God's will, Henry will get. And that will be anything but peace."

He let go of Adam's hands and lay down. Laughter rattled his ribs so dryly it sounded more like a cough than the amusement of a failing soul. "Oh, dear Uncle John—checkmate. Check . . . mate. Your son never much cared for chess, no patience for it. Always about jousting and pummeling knights with his sword. How he loved the clang of metal and the cheers of the crowd. The noise. The commotion. A little blood if he was lucky. Not his own, of course. Too raucous for chess, he was. Even when he tried it, he would pace the room and keep an eye out the window. But you were a master at it. You tried to teach him how the game was played. If only he had learned. What a fool he is. Oh heaven, what a blithering fool. And I, twice so."

Adam pulled the cloak over the king's chest to warm his ailing core. "I shall call for fresh bread. That loaf they left you would break your teeth."

As he went to the door, Richard's voice was faint as mist. "Call if you will. They will pretend not to hear." He laughed more feebly than before. "For all that the world cares, I am already gone. Just as well. I would soon enough be. Adam of Usk, will you hear my confession?"

"Your pardon, sire, but I am not a priest, only an ecclesiastical lawyer." Adam tugged at his collar.

"Close enough. Besides, you have ears and you are here. Sit." The throneless king sighed. "Forgive me . . ."

UNEASY LIES THE CROWN

Westminster Abbey, England — October, 1399

HENRY OF BOLINGBROKE, DUKE of Lancaster, messiah of a realm hungering for justice, stood before the altar of Westminster Abbey on the thirteenth day of October in the year 1399. His morning had been spent in purification and confession to bring his worldly soul closer to the Almighty on this inviolable day. He was adorned in regal garb—a stiff high collar, a robe of brocade trimmed in intricate embroidery, and a clasp of gold links draped from shoulder to shoulder. Although average in stature, he was thick of torso and with legs solid enough to make him a challenge to overthrow when armored. He looked the part of the warrior king and under no different pretenses did he attempt to claim what he had come for. He wore his fate as comfortably as a newborn infant wears its bare skin. There was no stripping it from him.

Westminster Abbey had been Edward the Confessor's life work—the mark he left to stand for centuries in resounding proclamation of his devotion. It was said that the Romans were the first to build an altar, to Apollo, on the once bur-encrusted island of Thorney, protectively encircled by the Tyburn on two sides and overlooking the sluggish Thames on another. Begun over four centuries before Henry's coronation day, Westminster Abbey was as close to the true glory of God that man's own hands could fashion. Many workers had lost their lives in the undertaking.

As hundreds looked on in a garish sea of silks and ermine, the Archbishop of Canterbury, chanting in a cryptic string of Latin, girded Henry with a length of strapping and placed in the scabbard Henry's own sword. He then put on Henry's finger the ring that bore his hastily fashioned royal seal. After a multitude of incantations, the Archbishop lifted the crown from a velvet pillow.

On his knees, Henry waited, and it seemed to him an eternity that the crown floated through the air from just a few feet away.

Finally, its cold weight settled upon the dome of his skull. A sense of immortality seeped into him—a certainty of righteousness and absoluteness. As he received the archbishop's blessing, his hand wandered up to touch one of the crown's jewels and he was overwhelmed with the moment. Then the archbishop extended his hand and Henry rose to his feet, shoed in scarlet velvet with golden spurs at his heels.

Harry, who had been so hastily spirited away from the pastoral environs of Ireland to the carnival atmosphere of London, peered beneath auburn locks up at his father. The light streaming in from the leaded windows behind Henry alighted on his son, its vibrant colors surrounding him in a celestial corona. One day the boy would thank him for delivering the crown to him. So far, Harry had been nothing but surly and ungrateful, almost as if he resented Richard having been ousted. Small matter. Youth was stubborn. Life as the heir to England's throne would alter his attitude soon enough and he would forget whatever affection he had fostered toward his faithless cousin.

As the ovation of the crowd reverberated to the hefty vaulted ceiling above, Henry turned to scan among the faces. The rotund Earl of Northumberland, Henry Percy, stood just below to his right, wearing as always a look of lazy contentment.

Breath held, Henry closed his eyes. His crown tipped ever so slightly and he thoughtlessly pushed it back with a single finger. When he opened his eyes again and looked out on the array of subjects before him on bent knee, he knew . . . knew beyond doubt that England was *his*.

Iolo Goch:

In far away Yorkshire, in the Red Tower of Pontefract Castle, Richard Plantagenet drew his last breath. Call it what you will, none but the utterly naïve believed his death to be of natural causes. To quell rumors that Richard still lived, Henry ordered his remains, embalmed in wax and spices, to be paraded through Cheapside, London's market district, for the public to see.

Official claims were that he had starved himself to death; however, it did not go unnoticed even among those who loathed the former king that Richard's body was encased in lead so that only his head was visible. What wounds might be concealed beneath the uncommon coffin only a handful of people knew. And what Henry was not told, Henry could not be accused of knowing.

The little child-queen, Isabella, whom Richard had so doted on, remained in England while Henry suggested to her father, Charles of France, that a union be struck between the widowed Isabella and his son Harry. King Charles flew into a rage over the ludicrousness of it.

Lord Reginald de Grey remained in the company of his false king, content that all was well at home and my lord Owain was a coward. What an arrogant, unfortunate fool he was.

14

Sycharth, Wales — March, 1400

MIDWAY UP THE STAIRS to his chamber at Sycharth, Owain paused, too restless to sleep and yet too tired to think clearly on his own precarious future. Turning back, he moved quietly down the stairs. There were troubles looming. He knew it as certain as he could feel the rain coming with a change in the air.

"Owain?"

From the top of the landing, Margaret managed a groggy smile. Around her shoulders was draped the blanket that they usually shared through cold nights such as these. She came down to greet him, one hand clutching the blanket, one hand on the railing, as though she were afraid of falling. Her arms wound around him, enclosing him in her soft warmth. All Owain could do was lean against her and sigh. He took her by the hand and led her to the hall. The untended sconces on the walls were void of flame, but he had known his way in the dark through this house since his boyhood, when he used to sneak from his bed in the darkest hour of night and come down to sit in his father's chair.

Sycharth was unusually silent: cold and hollow like a tomb awaiting the corpse. Owain settled Margaret in a chair and went about stirring the ashes of the hearth. He snapped a handful of twigs and tossed them onto a barely glowing ember, then knelt down and blew on it. A single, meager spark flashed, giving him hope. Grabbing the iron poker, he rearranged the kindling, until one spark became two, became several. Carefully, he placed a few small logs on the fire and sat back on his haunches.

His eyes wandered up to the gracefully arched ceiling beams, higher and wider-spanning than those of any hall around, and he thought for certain something about them had changed or that the long tables and their benches had been moved or somehow altered. Flanking the hall were two impressive and immense tapestries shipped from Flanders. One was of St. George and the dragon, the other of the Last Supper. Owain stared at them as if he had never before laid eyes on them. Even in the scant light cast by his growing fire, their twisted threads of color emanated with the essence of long-ago life. There would be no such tapestries spun in honor of King Richard. By now any that hinted of him had probably already been burned.

"You're home far too soon. It did not go well at Parliament?" Margaret brought her knees up to her chest, her bare toes peeking from beneath the blanket's edge. The faint light from a cloud-veiled moon shone from a window behind her, outlining her form in a silhouette of silver.

"They denied my protests over Grey's actions. Dismissed me like an impertinent child."

"What else? You can't have been there long enough to sit in on the full session."

"It would have done no good to stay. Are you awake enough to hear it all?" he asked with weighty sobriety.

"Well, I am sitting here half bare beneath a blanket with frozen feet and more awake than I care to be. Shall I fetch you some ale? A cup of wine?"

After a long silence, he shook his head and stood. The heels of his riding boots scraped the floor as he paced, his rowel spurs chinking with each sluggish stride.

It was Margaret who broke the silence. "Is it true . . . about Richard?"

He stopped with his back to her. "It is. I saw his funeral procession. Ah, God have mercy on his soul. Whatever his end, he did not deserve it. And now all of England's nobility spews lauds of Bolingbroke. Is it any wonder it has come to this? It is not a good day to be Welsh, my love. *Not* a good day."

"It will improve. Henry is merely unsteady. He needs to prove himself fierce. He will soften in time."

"A crown seized is an uneasy one, my love. He will not soften; only grow swifter to send men to the block." He groaned under his breath, expelling the weight of his disappointment. "And Parliament—they laughed, Marged, even as I stood there and quoted their own laws to them. They roared at me, 'What do we care for these barefooted Welsh dogs?' Ach, I was not worth spitting on. I would rather be a hill cur, though, than one of those frothing pack hounds. Only Bishop Trefor said anything on my behalf and even that was half-hearted. You should have seen Grey sitting there amidst his miniver-wrapped murder of crows. He was ever so smug, so content, so blessed lofty. It was Grey himself who put the golden spurs on Henry before his coronation. He sits in high favor. My disputation was nothing more than the butter to smother his bread. The mere sight of that man rankles me to my guts. And Bolingbroke—it nauseates me to think of calling him 'king'—tapped his ringed fingers and yawned, waving me off the floor before I was even half done. I tell you I have argued law with the best of them and won, but on that day it was as if they all conspired to some enormous secret to which I knew nothing of. I wasn't certain if I was their entertainment or an unwelcome interruption. I could have told them the roof over their heads was on fire and they would not have bothered to roll their eyes upward."

"Should have shot a flaming arrow into the beams," came a rough voice, "and burned the whole damn lot of them."

Owain turned at the words. At a table tucked in the far corner of the room, a hunched, ogreish shape lifted its head. The stranger dragged a leather tankard across the table planks and tossed the last few drops down the back of his throat. The tankard smacked down and his head followed. He rumbled with laughter, and then abruptly clamped both hands over his ragged head, howling. "Aaaaagh, Mother of Christ, this headache is going to make my skull burst if I don't get a drink to dull it. Quickly!"

Margaret shrugged at Owain. "I'm sorry, my love. I had offered him a bed. Apparently, he didn't make it." She rose, shifting her bare feet on the cold floor. "I'll have someone fetch him more ale . . . and you a cup as well. In the meanwhile, if you can do without my company for awhile, I need to go back to bed and warm my limbs. I'm feeling rather tired of late. Too many nights spent waiting for you." She shuffled to him, stood on her toes as she pulled the blanket tight, and pecked him on the cheek.

Smiling down at her, Owain cupped her chin in his large hand. "Marged," he whispered, "you're as beautiful as you ever were."

"You say that as if you believe it."

"I do."

She pulled back to go, but his hand on her arm stayed her.

Owain tilted his head in the direction of the visitor. "Who is he?"

"Hmm, I don't recall. There are ever so many people loitering around this hall, invited or not. Don't be long." She winked and scampered off.

"Fortunate man, you are." The stranger propped his bearded chin on his upper arm.

"Your pardon?" More curious than cautious, Owain moved

away from the struggling fire toward him.

The man stood with a grimace. Orange light danced like fiery demons in his black forest of curls. A servant scuttled into the hall, cradling a sloshing pitcher and two mugs in her arms.

The swarthy man smiled broadly. "Now she was good. Very good . . . and would say the same of me, if I may boast."

The maid, a vaguely handsome woman, giggled, but when Owain shot her a look of reproach, she abruptly fell silent.

Owain took the filled mugs from her, handed one to the stranger and waved the servant away. She flared her skirts as she disappeared through a doorway.

"So," Owain said, trying to regain the man's attention, "you have *enjoyed* the service as well as the food and drink here?"

"Rhys Ddu of Cardigan," he said, as if Owain should instantly recognize the name, and bowed. "Your servant, m'lord."

His paunch gave evidence that he did not miss many meals and when he walked he thrust his abdomen before him as if unashamed of the fact. He had the characteristic dark looks and compact build of his Celtic ancestors. In physical traits, he was as opposite as any man could be to Owain. It was a glimpse of Hephaestus meeting Apollo.

"We are well staffed, Rhys Ddu, but if you require employment in the morning my wife —"

"Ah, never was there a more gracious lady. Your bard has been trilling ballads to her incessantly. But I think you mistake my offer. You see, I was a sheriff of Cardigan . . . that was until I saw fit to shackle a certain perpetual drunkard and put him on public display. The local English baron, who happened to be his father, was rather displeased with me." He shrugged hugely, his brown eyes twinkling with amusement. "And so I am ousted. But a turn in fortunes sometimes leads us to other paths. Just as well, I had tired of my wife, and she of me, long before this. The talk of the taverns is that Lord Grey has dealt you a nasty affront. I'm here to serve you with my sword.

You'll have need of it."

Owain placed his tankard on the table and planted his fists before him, staring at Rhys. "Hear me, Sheriff. I have no need for armed men around me. He who surrounds himself with hired swords invites the contempt of others."

"Ah, well then, if you so believe, I wish you safety. But he who has no swords at all around him will surely fall by another man's sword. You carry one yourself," he observed, eyeing the prize at Owain's hip that had been his father's weapon on the fields of France. "Begun watching your back lately?"

"Highwaymen are seething in the forests . . . even here in Wales." Walking to the window, Owain pressed his palm against the cold glass.

"Highwaymen . . . and Henry's men." Rhys Ddu finished off his drink.

A blast of frosty air marched through the door as Tudur dragged himself in. Owain had nearly forgotten about his brother, who had offered to tend to the horses so he could trudge off to bed. Tudur threw back the hood of his cloak and immediately joined them, grabbing two stout logs and stuffing them in the hearth, as if dissatisfied with its conservative size.

Owain introduced them with a sweep of his hand. "Tudur, this is Rhys Ddu of Cardigan. He comes to pledge me the loyalty of his sword. He says I shall have need of it."

Rubbing his hands together before the fire, Tudur glanced at Rhys and nodded, then looked back at Owain. "From what I saw, Brother, sympathy with your predicament is gravely lacking. Don't toss his offer aside too soon . . . you may indeed need him." He fumbled at the clasp of his cloak. "Forgive me, but I think I am more exhausted than cold. Till morning, then."

They watched as Tudur ascended the stairs, cloak slung over one drooping shoulder and his chin bobbing against his chest.

"Go on," Rhys urged, nudging Owain with his elbow as if they were already old friends. "Do you think I'd be standing here lost in thought over a weak drink if I had a wife such as yours waiting for me on a cold night like this?"

Owain kneaded at his stiff neck and a smile crept over his mouth. "You're good company, no doubt, but I think the maid and I would have different opinions as to just how good."

The slightest chuckle leaked from Rhys and he cocked his head. His eyes met with Owain's and his thick brow flitted upward. They shared a moment of mirth—an odd hour, a cold night, Rhys's head swimming with ale and Owain road-beaten—but yet they understood each other already. Friendship is sometimes made of unlikely pairs.

MARGARET WAS FAST ASLEEP when Owain entered their chamber. He undressed, pulled back the covers and slid under. For an hour or more he lay on his side, studying the smooth line of her ear, cheek and jaw while a thousand thoughts twisted inside him.

That he could find sleep at all was a matter of sheer and absolute exhaustion. When he opened his eyes again it was approaching noon.

"I was dying to awaken you," Margaret said dreamily, her skin aglow with sunlight. "I rose hours ago issuing orders to the children and servants to not so much as drop a spoon."

He reached out and tucked a stray lock of hair behind her ear. Although the sun shone brightly through their lead-paned window, he felt the cold biting at the tip of his nose. "They could have danced 'Thread the Needle' on our bed and I would have slept on like an infant."

"Are you still sleepy?" She grinned. Her robe gaped open and the white of her breasts rose and fell in rhythm with her breathing.

"Oh, no, I am quite awake, quite alive . . ."—his fingers skirted over her clothing—"and quite hungry."

She slipped her robe off, baring herself and all that she had to offer to her husband. Rolling closer, she kissed him wetly on the neck, her kisses falling like soft rain over his thickly muscled shoulder and down his arm. He tugged away his braes—ready to demand nothing by right of marriage from her, but to receive the gift she was offering him with openness and pleasure. Her womanliness enjoined every muscle, every vein and every nerve of his being, commanding him with an absoluteness no king or foe ever could. Owain was thinking nothing of Henry or Lord Grey . . . only of his Marged— tender and generous and magical. His Aphrodite. His world, his sun, his stars. His and only his and this moment all that mattered.

Owain took no notice of her momentary reluctance and pushed inside her until he found the wave that had built up within him. It was at the very moment that his ecstasy arrived that she ripped herself from him.

He was half in shock, half beyond command of his own body, before he realized she was curled in a tight ball on her side away from him, clutching at her belly and shaking with violent sobs.

"Marged?" He bolted up on his elbow, looking her over. Between her legs, she crammed one hand, trying to dam the blood that was trickling over her fingers and seeping onto the white sheets.

"It hurts, Owain. It hurts," she forced, gritting her teeth. Her face was jammed into the pillow, her fine mouth twisting with a soundless cry as she pulled tighter into herself, her knees almost touching her face.

"Oh God." He pulled the sheets up over her and grabbed the blanket that had fallen to the floor during their lovemaking. With it wrapped about his waist, he shoved the chamber door open. "Someone! Help her! Hurry, hurry. Please! At once." He darted down the corridor, almost smashing into Iolo as he came around the corner. "Oh please, Iolo. Oh God, Margaret needs help. She's bleeding."

Iolo placed a hand on his shoulder, motioning to a wide-eyed boy servant behind him. "Fetch Abraham, posthaste. Waste not a moment. Lady Margaret is very ill." Then he led Owain back to the chamber.

"Shhh." Iolo comforted her, wiping at her tears with a corner of the sheet and arranging the blanket around her that Owain had handed him.

Still bare-chested, Owain hovered close as he pulled on his braes and hose. "I don't understand. All was well and she . . . then . . ." His voice cracked and he bent down at her bedside. He laid a hand on her arm, stroking it, willing her pain to vanish. "Have you been ill, Marged? Having pains?"

"Ill?" Iolo's jaw tightened as he looked away. He turned his back to watch the door. "She wasn't ill, m'lord. She was with child. You weren't aware?"

With child? No, she would not have told me anyway. She always kept it a secret until the child had quickened.

Owain's heart clenched. The blood was now spilling into a bright pool that had spread from her knees to her ribs on the sheets beneath her. With so much lost, the child could not possibly —

He embraced her, but in her tides of agony she could realize nothing of his compassion—or his guilt.

When the physician Abraham came, it took him little time to diagnose her affliction. She had lost the child she was carrying. He told Owain in a blameless manner as she lay sleeping. A strong tea of willow bark and chamomile had eased her cramps and brought on needed slumber.

After the difficult birth of their youngest twins, Owain and Margaret had avoided intimacy for awhile, both aware of the danger that another birth could impose upon her life. But in time, their deep love for one another had stirred old passions. They had both forgotten. They would not again.

15

Mid Wales — July, 1400

I N THE VERY HEART of Wales, two cloaked men rode into a deeply cut valley. As the sun bowed behind an abrupt ridge line, a dark shadow crept with cold certainty across the land. Uneasy, the men halted to gather their bearings. Their horses snorted and flicked their ears at every sound.

"You had best discover it soon, Tom . . ." the one said, his dark eyes flitting from hilltop to hollow, "or it will be both our heads on Ruthin's wall."

Tom, the younger of the two, sneered. "No one finds Gethin's hiding place. It's never the same. He'll find us."

Further south, a huddle of cottages smoked with the lure of cooking fires, light beckoning ghostly from the cracks around their shutters.

"Will we be aware of that fact before or after they knock us senseless from these two stolen horses?" The older man pulled his hood up. His name was Griffith ap David and, just like Owain Glyndwr, he had found himself the object of Lord Grey's disdain. Though not a man of great station or wealth, he had been afforded some responsibilities in recent years, only to have them snatched away at whim by Lord Grey. Now near starving, the dangerous life of a rebel against the king held a very unsavory appeal at his age.

"God's stinking breath," Griffith muttered, "I thought you knew where the hell you were going. Well, I won't tarry here waiting for starvation to take me. We'll follow that trail . . . and if his men are watching us, I pray they recognize you in this failing light."

Griffith ap David spurred his horse and lurched ahead.

"Allow me," Tom growled.

"By all means. You can ride in a circle just as aimlessly as I can."

The trail took them directly away from the groggy hamlet—closer to the crags that crowded skyward. They soon found their path clinging tentatively to the thin shoulder of an escarpment. Rocks dislodged by their horses' hooves clattered down the steep slope.

"We should turn back," Griffith said between his chattering teeth. "This wind will send us to our graves."

He thought he glimpsed a figure ducking behind a rock above them, then convinced himself it was only a shadow. Darkness was descending and there was neither moon nor stars to light their way. His stiff muscles protested going on any more, yet they couldn't stop now. Turning his head, he glanced back toward the village, thinking of the food being cooked over its fires, but they had already lost sight of its buildings with all the twists in the roadway. He would have risked his life to beg for a bowl of stew, despite the great price that he knew must be on his head by now. Surely they would die in these hills anyway, with nothing more to claim than what they had fled with and the two horses stolen from Lord Grey's barn in retaliation for his trickery.

Before he turned back to gauge the willingness of his guide, Griffith heard a thud upon the trail before them. His eyes flew wide as a spear tip pricked his throat. Gruff hands ripped him from his saddle. He landed on his shoulder on the road, jagged stones cutting at his cheek.

A well-aimed boot punched him in the kidney. Dark cloaks swarmed above him. He clutched his head in his hands to protect his face, while they rained blow after blow upon his frozen body. The air was crushed from his lungs. His only thought was the need to breathe.

As he gasped for air, they hoisted him up and slammed his back against a rock.

"Who are you and what business do you have here?" one of the ambushers snarled.

Still fighting for breath, Griffith opened his eyes to mere slits. He swallowed and tasted blood draining down the back of his throat. A sidelong glance told him Tom was in no shape to answer. His friend lay in a crumpled heap on the ground. Griffith counted the number of his attackers—only four, but it might has well have been forty, so swift and ruthless they were.

"We seek . . ." Griffith began, as one of them grabbed his hair to lift his head up, "a man named Rhys Gethin of Cwm Llanerch."

A trickle of blood ran from one of his nostrils. It felt as though there were bars of iron squeezing his chest from every side.

One of the attackers pulled a stone cudgel from beneath his cloak and raised it above his head. "There is none by that name here."

"No." A man from behind shoved him aside. He stepped forward and by the dim light of a starless night all that Griffith ap David could see was the ragged outline of a bearded chin. "Let him state his business first."

Fighting against the stabbing sensation in his ribs, Griffith coughed and for a moment it was all he could do not to give in to unconsciousness, the pain was so intense.

"Your business?" the bearded one questioned, stooping to within just inches from his face.

"I come seeking aid. Lord Grey would have . . . my head. Mine and other Welshmen's, as it pleases his fancy. He promised me many things—a pardon among them. But if not for the keen ears of my friend there"—swallowing more blood, Griffith nodded at Tom, who was now moaning, his fingers clawing at the flakes of rock near his head—"if not for him, I would have gotten Grey's dagger clear through my belly."

The bearded man pulled back his hood and smiled in the darkness. "If it's Gethin the Fierce you seek, look no further. But unless a life hiding in the hills suits you, you are lost coming here. If it's retribution you so desire, that would take a true fight. Are you up to that, man?"

A fight? Not presently. Sensing he was at last no longer marked as a foe, Griffith ap David let his eyelids drop down and blackness take him away.

<u>Sycharth, Wales — August, 1400</u>

OUTSIDE SYCHARTH, A PERSISTENT drizzle soaked the earth. In the room where Owain Glyndwr wrote his letters, kept his records and met with important guests, it was dry and warm, yet quite unsettled.

"Two days?" Owain slapped the summons against his palm. He stomped toward the hearth and thrust the letter over the hungry flames. Then he shook his head, crumpled it into a ball and threw it on the floor. "How am I to raise enough retainers to comply with his demands in two days?"

Iolo and Rhys exchanged a glance, neither daring to answer just yet.

The messenger who had delivered the summons quivered in Owain's shadow. He had been dispatched from Ruthin that very morning, sent with haste even though Lord Grey himself had been in preparation for his own departure to Scotland for over a fortnight.

"Get yourself back to Ruthin as quick as you came," Owain said to the youth, "and tell your master this: he will march to Scotland without this Welshman."

The messenger, now shaking visibly, did not move.

"Leave, I said!" Owain was more apt to keep his ranting private and work through his troubles while staring into the shifting waters of the Dee, but this insult had hurled him to eruption. If Grey had been standing in the room himself, he likely would have felt Owain's strong hands upon his throat.

"But . . . your pardon, my lord." The youth glanced up, swallowed, and quickly lowered his eyes again. "Am I to tell him you will be delayed in your arrival?"

"Delayed? It is he who is delayed in having this message delivered. He will get *nothing* from me in this manner." Owain strode to the window. "Get this boy a fresh horse, Iolo, and send him on his way."

Iolo pulled the messenger to his feet and escorted him hastily out the door.

Rhys picked up the letter and smoothed it out on the table. "He meant to do this, you know?" Squinting, he drew out his knife, then plunged it into the top of the letter and pulled it cleanly downward. He separated the two halves, uncorked the leather costrel which he often kept on his person and dribbled ale over them. Ambling over to the hearth, he cocked his head. "He'll make damn certain he gets every kernel of grain and remnant of chaff you own." Then he cast the letter into the fire.

Owain's mind was roiling with anger, but then he caught sight through the open window of movement beyond the bridge over the moat and his attention drifted there. The mist and late hour made nearly indistinct, gray images of everything. If not for the people by the bridge moving into a huddle, he would have found it hard to distinguish them from the buildings and trees beyond.

Only four guards were posted at the bridge. Before them now were a group of mounted strangers numbering a dozen. They appeared to be seeking entrance. Travelers, perhaps, in need of shelter from the dampness? They did not appear to be imposing. On the morrow, he would make certain to triple the guard.

Owain faced Rhys. "Lord Grey does as he pleases and a pretender wears England's crown. Richard's rule may have had its own troubles, but this tyranny is no better. Bolingbroke has no right to sit upon the throne while the young Earl of March yet lives. What will become of the boy, Rhys? Would anyone cry 'murder' if he too met a sudden death?" He crossed his arms over his chest and shook his head. "God help me, but I will not bow to Grey on this or any matter. If I did, it would never end."

"If you stand against Grey, you stand against all of England."

"Do I? Bolingbroke does not stand for all of England. Certainly, he does not stand for Wales."

On the wall behind his writing table rested his father's sword— the very weapon that had been carried through the bloody fields and smoking villages of France and swung by his father's strong arm with unquestioning repetition on behalf of England's king, Edward III. Carefully, he lifted it from its hooks and studied it. The edge had been sharpened many times following Owain's own madly fought battles in Scotland under Richard's banner and the binding was worn, but there was no hint of rust on the blade. Even in times of peace when Owain was seeing to his own lands and growing family, he had taken great pains to care for it.

"Shall we look to our guests?" Owain slid the sword beneath his belt. He had forgotten what it was like to know it was there at his side.

"But Owain —?"

Owain glanced over his shoulder. He knew the question that was coming: *What will you do about it?*

"Don't ask me," Owain said. "For now, I haven't the answers, my friend."

Then he turned on his heel and, with Rhys only a few feet behind, strode through the vast hall, where a handful of servants were preparing for the evening meal and Owain's family and guests had gathered. He passed his place at the table's head with barely a glance at Margaret. An ever-present porter flung the front door open.

Fine droplets of mist hung suspended in the air. Owain stalked down the front steps and over the short expanse of roadway before the bridge, Rhys doubling his steps to keep up with Owain's long stride. As they moved across the bridge, one of the visitors pushed his way past the guards.

A man with a short, dark beard and a prematurely balding head gazed boldly at them. Then, bowing his head, he flung his cloak over his shoulders and held his hands wide, palms up, to show he held no weapons there.

Owain eyed him with caution, keeping a safe distance. The man had a shrewd look to him, with eyes and ears that Owain was sure missed nothing.

"Sir Dafydd," Owain said, addressing an older knight who had taken on the duty of overseeing his guard, "who are these men?"

"If I may speak, m'lord," the bearded man requested softly, looking up.

"You may not." Owain stared him down. "Dafydd?"

Sir Dafydd leaned on his poleaxe. "If I knew I would say. He says he will only speak to you."

"I haven't the tolerance for this today. It can wait until morning." Owain spun about and proceeded back toward the manor. Feet scuffled behind him. He drew his sword and whirled about in one smooth movement.

The bearded man had plunged to his knees, but the guards were swift behind him and had already hooked him under the armpits to drag him away.

"I am Rhys Gethin of Cwm Llanerch and I come to speak of the crimes of one Lord Grey of Ruthin!"

Owain raised his hand, halting the guards. It was the last name he wanted to hear. "I know well of his crimes. I have been the subject of them."

Tearing himself from his captors, Gethin rushed forward. "Then you know the lawlessness that festers in this land. This man, Griffith ap David"—he pointed to him and Griffith shyly stepped forward—"was promised a pardon and an appointment as bailiff of Chirk. But when he came to meet with Lord Grey at Oswestry to discuss the terms, they seized and murdered one of his men-at-arms. He and this other man, Tom, escaped and came to me in the hills of Powys, seeking sanctuary."

"Is this true?" Owain surveyed Gethin's companions, unsure what to make of them.

Griffith ap David raised his chin. "As I stand before you, m'lord, it is the full truth."

"I have heard of your troubles, Griffith ap David," Owain said. He glanced at Gethin whose features were as unreadable as the stones littering the mountain slopes, then returned his gaze to Griffith. "There are Marcher Lords who claim their herds are much depleted due to you. I am not in the habit of granting favors to outlaws."

Clearing his throat, Rhys spoke from behind him. "Yet you are one yourself now. As am I."

"Wales has no voice in the kingdom," Gethin said, "unless you would become that voice."

Half-turning, Owain took a step back. He did not want to be anyone's messiah. He simply wanted to be left to live in peace with his family. "You ask too much of me."

"I ask nothing that is not possible," Gethin said. "I tell you these insults against your people —"

"*My* people? How do you surmise that I hold claim to lead anyone?"

Gethin lowered his eyes, letting the question hang in the air awhile before replying. "I am not a man who disguises my words. I speak plainly, to the point, and I say this—the Cymry will be ground into dust beneath the heel of the one who calls himself 'King of England'. He will take from us whatever suits his purpose, as will his minions. For fear of their lives and families, not a single Welshman will resist him unless he has someone to rally to. That someone is you, Sir Owain Glyndwr. By blood and by brotherhood—there is no one but you. And although I may be the first here to say it, everyone knows it is so."

It was a truth he did not wish to look upon. From inside the house, the clatter of plates rose as the first course was brought to the tables. Merry voices rolled from the great hall of Sycharth, among them those of his own children. Tiny Mary peeled with laughter.

He looked at the faces of these coarse hill men and he was well aware of the insults they had been dealt. Perhaps even more so. Every strand of common sense he possessed told him to turn them away, to disassociate himself. He had a family to provide for, to keep safe. But Grey would be back to make him answer for his insolence. There was no doubt of that. And no law would bring him to reason. If someone did not defy him, Grey would be back to take more.

Owain gazed up at the darkening sky. Above the drifting mist, a crescent moon swung from a cloud of palest purple. Then the wind swept a bank of thicker clouds over the moon. "I have never turned out a soul in need. Sycharth is home to all."

Holding an arm out, he waited until Gethin and the others accepted the invitation and crossed the bridge.

As they ascended the wide steps to Sycharth's hall, Owain stopped Rhys with a hand on his arm. He whispered, "God grant me guidance, for I have no idea what is right and what is wrong anymore."

"Oh, I think you know." Grinning, Rhys winked at him. "But 'right' is not always easy, is it? Grey knows he's wrong. Flatten the bastard. It's the only way you'll keep what's yours."

16

Near the River Annan, Scotland — September, 1400

I N THE MOORLAND OF Scotland, the English army was encamped in a broad valley overlooking the River Annan, a hard day's march north of Carlisle. A cutting wind raced over the dead sweep of heather and slid its icy fingers beneath blankets and hoods.

"Have you uncovered the Scots, William?" King Henry addressed the scout who stooped before him. He scanned the naked countryside around them. His growing army filled up the vast valley that ran between two rock-cluttered ridgelines. On either side, a swarm of Scots could be clenching their spears even now. The wind carried in its howling a whisper of primal war cries from long ago and Henry tried hard to listen for snatches of nearby soldierly conversation, anything, to drown out the madness of it.

"If there are any Scots, sire," William answered with a grumble, "they have disguised themselves as stones. But I do report, with pleasure, that our numbers will be augmented before sunset by the arrival of men from the Welsh Marches."

"At last. Good, good." A servant offered a steaming bowl to the king. He sipped, and then spat it out, his lips twisting in disgust. The bowl fell to the ground, its hot contents splashing on the thinly leathered shoes of the servant. "Toad piss! Find me something palatable. And have them report to me as soon as they arrive," he said to the scout. Then he moved off in search of his tent. Once inside, he buried himself in a pile of blankets.

As night crept over the world, an attendant came to the king's tent and announced the arrival of Lord Grey. Wrapped in his fur-lined cloak, Henry waited on the portable throne that had been transported with him.

Grey bowed as he entered, then eased closer.

"Your numbers?" Henry uttered, his gloved thumb caressing the carved arm of his chair. He gazed into the glow of the peat brazier at his feet.

Satisfaction danced on Grey's smiling lips. "As many as you asked for, sire, and more. And enough archers to plant a dozen arrows in every Scotsman."

Stretching an arm, Henry took a drumstick of goose meat from his plate on the nearby table and sank his teeth into it. It was cold and dry, but he was beyond complaining at that point. Suffering was part of the Scottish experience. "How did you convince that impudent Welshman to follow you here?"

Grey tugged off his riding gloves and held his fingers toward the brazier. "Glyndwr does not count himself among your loyal subjects, I am sorry to relay, sire. He refused to come or send any men on his behalf."

"Refused? The insolent bastard!" Henry hurled the meat at Grey. "He cannot *refuse* me. He knows every river and road from Dumfries to Stirling. This is unpardonable."

"Deplorable, sire. Perhaps even verging on . . . rebellious. And in times such as these, my lord can ill afford such disobedience. Then again, I suppose it comes as no surprise that a Welshman would defy you, does it?"

"No, no it doesn't." The king leaned forward and pointed at

Grey. "You will correct the matter?"

"With delight, sire."

"See to it, then." He sniffed back the stream pouring from his nose and slumped in his chair, his appetite suddenly vanished. "Take whatever measures are needed."

"As you wish, sire." Bowing, Grey backed away. "I'll make certain he does not defy you again."

Iolo Goch:

The English were not long in Scotland. The skies opened up and spewed out not rain but snow, turning the moors into quagmires that sucked at wagon wheels and horses' hooves. The impressive numbers that Henry had gathered amounted to nothing more than a show of strength, as the Scottish army melted into the countryside, never rising to clash with their frozen foes . . . and more than happy to see them go on their way.

17

Sycharth, Wales — Late September, 1400

ALONG THE ROAD THAT paralleled the Dee, a wagon laden with newly bought goods rumbled. A driver and three anxious passengers rode in it. At the reins was an old man, silent except for his sniffing. With him were three women—one of middle years and two younger. The women exchanged comments about the weather and hopes that the snow would hold off until they were back at Sycharth. Around them, meadows of winter-dead grass were frosted with silver. Ahead of the wagon, two mounted guards rode, their hands light upon their reins, for the horses knew the way.

From time to time, Margaret, who was seated in the wagon with her daughters, Alice and Catrin, glanced at the hills, trying to mark how many miles they had yet to go. The sun had not revealed itself that day, so how many hours had passed since they had left was impossible to tell. Margaret returned her eyes to the road ahead. The broad loin of the horse that pulled the wagon swayed with each stride.

She had been at Wrexham for three days, exploring the shops there and visiting her brother John. As much as she had enjoyed her stay, she was anxious to return home to see the rest of her children.

Yet when Sycharth finally came into view, she was met by a very disturbing sight. Every stick of furniture, every tapestry, every plate and spoon in the place was being piled haphazardly onto carts and the backs of horses. She told the driver to go faster and he snapped the reins.

Before crossing the bridge over the moat, she ordered the driver to halt. As the wagon slowed, she took everything in. Then cautiously, she climbed down from the wagon. Alice and Catrin pulled their cloaks tighter around them to ward off the brittle cold and followed close behind their mother, gawking at the chaotic scene around them.

Dobbin the shepherd ran out into the mess, a cage of squawking hens under each arm. He tossed one of the cages on top of a fully loaded cart and then, discovering no room left for the other, darted toward Margaret's wagon and wedged it in between the sideboard and a bolt of new green velvet. Margaret immediately snatched it out and put it on the ground.

"What are you doing?" Margaret demanded. "That cloth came all the way from Flanders. And what is going on here? Why are all my things being loaded up? Where is Sir Owain?"

Dobbin waived his arms frantically. "They're coming. Any moment now. Grab what you can, m'lady. We must be gone."

"They?" She exchanged a look of perplexity with her two oldest daughters. Dobbin scrambled toward one of the barns, weaving around the horses and carts. Margaret bunched up her skirts in clenched fists and flew over the bridge, up the stairs and into the hall. Servants sprinted past, their arms overloaded with sacks of grain, stacks of bowls, and piles of clothing. None stopped to acknowledge her. They were all in too much of a hurry.

She flung open the door to Owain's study and found it empty of all its maps and books. Then she flew through the house, peering inside every door. Finally, she found Isabel in her room, clutching a doll to her chest.

Startled, Isabel burst into tears at the sight of her mother.

"Oh, *cariad*," Margaret said, crouching before her, "why the tears? Where is your father?"

Isabel, at eleven still more little girl than woman, shrugged her slight shoulders and sobbed harder, wringing her doll's arms until they threatened to fall off.

"Why is everything being taken away?" Margaret said, dabbing at her daughter's wet cheeks with her fingers.

Isabel's lip hung low and she sucked in a breath. "He shouted at me, Mother." Then she erupted into an even greater cascade of tears and flung herself onto her bed.

Usually, it was Margaret who raised her voice at the children and levied the punishments.

In the doorway, Isabel's twin brother Madoc loitered. He braved a few steps closer, shuffled his feet to get his sister's attention and frowned in sympathy. Margaret stroked Isabel's back a moment, but at the sound of Owain's voice in the corridor, she abandoned her distraught daughter and rushed out of the room.

"What is the meaning of this?" Margaret planted her hands on her hips, blocking Owain and Tudur's way.

Ignoring her, Tudur pushed past Margaret, plunged into one of the rooms, and began rummaging for valuables.

Reaching out, Owain drew his wife closer. "Lord Grey sent an offer to meet here—to amend our differences."

Margaret narrowed her eyes, not understanding. "But that is good, is it not? Perhaps he wishes to apologize for —"

"Grey has no designs on patching the rift between us, Marged. It is a ruse."

"Why do you say that? You yourself told me if there was any way you could repair the misdeeds that have been dealt to you, any way at all, regardless of pride, that you would."

Tudur emerged from the room, a cushioned stool and a pile of clothing heaped over his arms. Owain nodded toward the stairs and Tudur, with a look of apology at Margaret, disappeared down them.

"Listen to me . . . and do not question what I am going to tell you to do." He gripped her arms firmly. "Nothing is more important to me than you and the children. I will not gamble any of that for a remote chance that Lord Grey has suddenly replaced his seething ambitions with forgiveness. Our things will be hidden away until it is safe to come back here. Meanwhile, you will join my cousin's family. You can perhaps take Sion and Mary with you. The rest, it would be wiser if they were divided . . . placed elsewhere. Too many of them together will raise suspicions."

"Are you mad? I will not leave my home and scatter my children among the hills." Margaret stomped her foot, but already she could tell that her protests were apt to be as effective as trying to topple a stone wall with a handful of pebbles. "This is our home. If we leave it, what is to keep him from tearing down every last timber?"

"I will take that chance to save you. Now please, please,"—his words held an urgency, as if mindful of the danger that every lingering second added—"gather what —"

"No. This is my home."

"Stop! Listen to me. What I ask of you —"

"Ask or tell?"

Owain shook her, his voice full of anger. "Damn it! Let him burn this house. Let him level every stone for miles. I will not have you all dead or taken captive." All at once, the harsh lines in his face went soft. "Tudur and Rhys came not an hour ago directly from Ruthin. Grey's forces were gathering there. Far more men than he had sworn to limit himself to bringing here. And I doubt he was headed back to Scotland anytime soon. We are all in grave danger. I haven't the means to keep him from taking this place, if that is his intent."

"Then we shall all go to Wrexham," Margaret pleaded. "John

and Phillip will help us. You can plead your case with the king or . . . or some other great lord. Surely there is one who will support you?"

"And put your brothers' lives at risk? Henry cares not one whit for my case. He has already proven that. Grey is his pet who may take whatever scraps he can wrest from us as reward for his loyalty. No, we must save ourselves first. Save the children."

Margaret shook her head. The reality was too bitter to accept, the implications too far-reaching, the future too uncertain. "What then? When will I see you again? Where will you go?"

"I . . . I don't know when. And as for where, perhaps it's best you don't know."

He pressed her hands together between his and then kissed the ends of her fingers.

Margaret stood as motionless and mute as a cairn battered by a terrible storm. Minutes passed before she realized that Owain had walked off and her children and servants were scurrying past her, urging her to hurry.

"Lady Margaret?" Iolo touched her back from behind. "It's time. Sir Owain is outside waiting for you."

Waiting to say farewell. For how long? A few days? Months? Longer?

Iolo took her arm and guided her the length of the corridor and down the stairs, through the hall and out into the fading light of evening. She felt nothing but the dismal sadness of winter clouds pressing down on her.

Isabel stood in the roadway, sobbing, while Alice and Catrin desperately tried to console her. The littlest ones were handed up into the wagons. Their eyes were wide and bright and they chattered incessantly. They thought they were all going on a great adventure together.

Margaret took a breath and searched for Owain. Just as she found him, a rider sped along the road and dropped from his horse before her. It was Sir Dafydd, captain of Owain's guard.

"They are only a few miles away, m'lady," Dafydd warned. "You should be safely out of sight and ahead of them if you take the mountain road."

Behind her, Owain circled his arms about her waist.

"I will send for you as soon as I can," he said, his breath stirring the hairs on her bare neck.

She could not turn around to face him. She didn't know what to say. Those days of Owain leaving to fight for King Richard had long been over. How had she been so naïve to think they would never part again?

Owain helped her up into the wagon beside Maredydd, who sat there with his hands gripping the reins and his shoulders hunched, bearing a weight far beyond his fourteen years.

"You know the road, Maredydd," Owain said. "Dafydd, go with them. You'll find my cousin Lowarch south of Dolgellau near the ruins of Llys Bradwen. Tell him my instructions. He'll find a safe place for each of you."

As Maredydd lifted the reins, Margaret grabbed her son's wrist to stop him.

"Owain," she began, holding back the tears that fought to overcome her, and spoke the words that she herself needed to hear, "remember—every day apart, brings us a day closer to being together again. Do what you must, but do not risk your own life. You swore to always protect me. I will hold you to that."

"I will," he said. "Now go . . . and Godspeed."

"HOW MANY?" OWAIN WHISPERED into the lingering fog. He stood on the furthest hilltop from Sycharth where he could still see his home, or should have been able to, but for the lazy bank of fog that obscured his view. Behind him clustered a gathering of Welshmen, their ear rims red from the winter cold and their hearts blazing with contempt.

Iolo pulled himself up the last of the hill and paused for breath. "Thirty. Unarmed, as sworn." He drooped forward, one hand upon his knee and the other clutching the sack that cradled his harp. He waited a long moment before looking up again at Owain. "But on the road behind them are sixty more. With more than enough weapons to kill each man here thrice over."

Hands sought out their swords. Numbering just over twenty, they were more than ready to charge down the hill and rush back into emptied Sycharth, but the odds against them were too great.

"Have they entered the house yet?" Tudur asked timidly of Iolo.

"When I left they were beating at the door."

Gruffydd, his arms crossed and his face molded into a permanent scowl since earlier that day, spat at the ground. "They'll burn it. Every last timber."

"Burn it," Rhys said, "or empty every cask and *then* come looking for us." To Rhys, the wine and ale were of primary importance.

They gazed silently through the drifting billows of mist, watching for spires of smoke to rise above the naked branches. Finally, Rhys pulled his sword free and waved it boldly before him. "We can work our way around to the other side and wait above the road for them. I haven't made good use of this sweet thing for far too long a time."

Gethin moved in front of him and swung the blade away with a forefinger. "Do you think they would actually be surprised by an ambush after finding us all gone from the manor? Act with haste and you will lose your life, for certain. Grey will not burn Sycharth. For now he only wants Sir Owain. Let that be his only aim."

"How do you know?" Rhys said.

"I make it my business to know. Don't ask how."

Rhys's blade drifted back to his side, but he kept his grip firm. "I do ask. You are the one who convinced Owain to abandon Sycharth, so until I see you spear an English noble, I *will* wonder how it is you know such things."

"Yes, how?" Gruffydd said. Since Elise's swift disappearance, he had become perpetually moody.

"You have been gone these past two days," Tudur added. "To where?"

Gethin ignored Tudur and moved closer to Rhys, dry twigs snapping under his feet. "You have no cause as yet to doubt me. Time and circumstances will prove where my loyalties rest . . . and every man's, as well, be he English, Welsh or Scots. You see, Lord Grey is not a difficult man to understand. His motives are plain. I needn't any spies to tell me." He stood so close to Rhys now that his breath hung in a cloud between them. "Land is wealth and wealth is power . . . and power is *everything*."

Rhys craned his neck forward until their foreheads were almost touching. "I'll give you that, Gethin. But swear your loyalty now, so that none here may doubt them."

Chin held high, Gethin backed away and turned to Owain. "I grant my loyalty fully," he offered, dropping to one knee, his bare head bowed. "I lay my life in your hands, Owain Glyndwr, and I will give my all until I die, so that others may live their lives in peace. Lead us, just as your princely forebears did."

Griffith ap David separated himself from the others and bent his knee to the ground in suit. Tom was quick at his side. One after another went down before Owain on the leaf-littered forest floor, until only his son Gruffydd and brother Tudur remained standing.

"You're all mad and desperate," Owain said.

Even Rhys had sunk to the frozen ground on both knees. "We are that—mad as they come. Tears of blood and breath of fire. We'd run naked into battle if it would bring us victory. We are, after all, Welshmen and you—our prince."

Shaking his head, Owain went to his friend and pulled him to his feet. "I don't want anyone's life wasted in my name. No battles. No bloodshed. None of that. I want you all to go home."

"But where will you go?" Rhys gripped Owain's shoulder. "Sycharth? You'll be keeping company with the rats in the Tower if you go back there now. Glyndyfrdwy? That's the very next place they'll look. Where will you go, Owain?"

Drawing away, Owain peered through the diminishing mists. Grey's men-at-arms were pouring out of the manor house and had begun scouring the outbuildings, overturning carts and stabbing wildly at stacks of hay. Owain had been certain to leave not so much as a single hen perched on the roosts. Even the dove cotes yawned emptily.

It would not be long before Grey would dispatch search parties into the surrounding hills to ferret out Owain and his kin. He turned his back on the men and began walking a path that only he knew, a remembrance of youth, twisting between tangled saplings, its course hidden beneath the decaying leaves.

Owain was halfway down the hillside when the shuffle of feet caused him to pause and look back. Gruffydd, whose eyes had the uncanny keenness of youth, had started forward. His son gripped his uncle Tudur by the shoulder and pointed over the treetops.

"They're coming," Gethin said calmly, standing. "To the horses."

In the silent manner of practiced hunters, they plunged down the far side of the hill to join Owain, their polished swords and daggers glinting silver in the brown tapestry of the woods. A quarter mile from their hilltop post, in a hidden gully, their horses were loosely tethered, waiting for the escape.

Iolo Goch:

Christmas came and went without celebration. How I missed the song, the dance, the food, but most of all the laughter and merriment. Lady Margaret and the children were stashed away with Owain's cousins—some in the mountains south of Cadair Idris, others in Anglesey.

In the upland wilderness of Powys, Owain and his small band roamed from cave to cave. Others came to join them, but Owain turned them all away. Yet in each offer of servitude, Owain noted something that he had never been aware of, not even in himself until the hunger and the cold and the solitude bared it: the courage to fight for what was theirs.

Until a man is without that one basic thing, freedom, he can never truly understand the value of it . . . or why men have bled and died for it.

18

Uplands of Mid Wales — February, 1401

WHILE DAWN WAS YET a flirtatious hint of light on the horizon, Owain sat upon the broad back of a sleeping hill pony. There was a sprinkling of frost on its shaggy hide and its head hung low, oblivious to Owain's frequent shifting. Owain's shoulder-length hair was gathered at the nape of his neck beneath a black hood that concealed his features. In his company were Rhys and Tudur, who stood just uphill of a meandering flock of horned sheep. It was St. Valentine's Day and an unusually warm week had revealed irregular expanses of sallow grass on the western slope where they waited. In the vistas beyond, in the kingdom once known as Powys, the dark blue silhouette of the mountains surrounded them.

Rhys stifled a yawn and, supported by a shepherd's crook, stretched himself taller to peer into the distance. "There." He nodded in the direction of the narrow road that wound down from a slope to the northwest. "Three riders. And one . . . appears to be a woman. Unless my eyes deceive me."

Owain twisted around to watch. As the riders came closer, the sheep lifted their heads and moved a more comfortable distance away, then bent their necks to graze again. The middle rider, wearing a long woolen houppelande, lifted her hood briefly and pushed a few stray locks of hair behind her ears. The first rays of sun caught in her golden strands. Owain's heart told him what his eyes could not yet discern. He had not seen his beloved Marged for months now—a string of empty days that might as well have been an eternity. The last of the riders reined his horse to the left and eased it across the gurgling brook.

Turning off the road, the other two riders approached the shepherd's cottage further up on the hillside, a few hundred feet from Owain and his companions. After dismounting, the woman and one of the men knocked and went inside. The third approached them.

The rider tipped the brim of his hat. A plain wooden cross dangled from a frayed cord about his neck. "A fair and blessed St. Valentine's, good sir."

"'Tis fair enough, pilgrim," Owain said. "But if it's a bed you seek, we have none. There is a village in the next valley. You'll find a parish church with open doors there."

"But is the priest a Welshman?" he said. He was perhaps a few years older than Owain, with a long jaw and deeply cut cheekbones where the flesh of his face had hollowed out.

Lifting his chin, Owain edged his pony close and reached out his hand. "Lowarch, you've changed since last we raced barefoot through the hills."

Rhys gestured to Tudur and they strayed over to their wayward flock, leaving the two men alone.

"Verily, good cousin, and for the better, I pray," Lowarch said. "I was once a head and a half taller than you, though 'tis no longer so. The years have seen you prosperous and blessed. Your brood makes enough noise to raise the thatch clean off my roof. But my Gwladys would not give them up, having none of her own. Sion and Mary, in particular, are an inquisitive pair. Gwladys gives them chores to keep them from trouble, but they find it anyway. I caution you,

Owain, she has spoilt them so much you will not want them back."

"That would never hold true. Not in a hundred lifetimes. This winter has been long and lonely—an event I care not to repeat. Christmas spent in a cold, damp cave does not inspire a man to rejoice on God's miracles." He eyed the cottage door. "Tell me, Lowarch, how has she faired these months?"

Lowarch reached out between their mounts and touched his cousin's wrist in reassurance. "She is strong . . . for the children. But I see her in quiet moments, a rare thing at our household these days . . . I see her taking out your letter and reading it a dozen times over, then watching out the window as if her will could take you both home."

The smoke of a new fire spiraled upward from the cottage roof. "I dared risk only one letter and told her to write me none. If the English had intercepted it —"

Leaning his head of gray streaked hair toward the cottage door, Lowarch said, "I brought her safely to you. It was all I could do, though, to hold her back from arriving here two days earlier."

An impatient skylark glided boldly above, fluting its melody. Owain's eyes followed it—so sure of spring and finding its mate.

He pressed his mount to a clip over the short distance. Before it came to a full halt, he swung from its back and threw open the door. Instead of his Marged, Gethin barred the way. He ripped a loaf of bread in two and offered half to Owain. More eager to see Margaret than he was hungry, Owain shook his head.

"Take what time you will." Elbowing Owain out of his way, Gethin barreled through the doorway and out into the rising day. Then abruptly, he turned around and said, "You'll be glad to know our thorny Lord Grey has been called away on king's business."

The news was little relief to Owain, as he knew any Englishman, or even a desperate Welshman, would give him up for a sack of coin. But as he saw a figure part from the shadows and fill his eyes, all fear, all turmoil evaporated. In moments, Owain and Margaret were molded tightly in each other's arms.

"I missed you terribly," Margaret murmured into the rough wool of his cloak. "Can we go home yet?"

"Not yet, Marged. Not yet."

She tilted her head up to look into his face. "When then?"

"I wish that I could say." After closing the door, he took her cloak, hung it on a hook, and then placed his on top of it. The light within the cottage was scant, but it was enough to tell there was a thick coating of dust everywhere. A trestle table and a single bench were shoved against the near wall next to the single, shuttered window. Opposite the door stood a row of shelves lined with half a dozen clay jars and along the other wall was a narrow bed with a mattress of stuffed straw and a wool blanket. The bed at least looked clean, although it would not have mattered to them whether they met in a king's palace or cowshed. They were together again and knew these moments would be rare.

With his fingertips, Owain traced her hairline, her jaw, her lips. Then he held her face, gazing into her eyes for a long while. For days now, he had rehearsed what he might say, but nothing seemed to convey just what it was he felt for her. Finally, he kissed her fully on the mouth, but not for long. He wrapped his arms around her and held her close.

"You'll write to me again, Owain? Say that you will."

"I will. But not often. There are risks. You understand? And I cannot reveal my whereabouts for now."

"Yes, of course. Send word, then. I need to know that you are all right. And if there is any way I can write to you and tell you how the children —"

He kissed her again, gently on the mouth, then her cheek just in front of her ear. "Tell me about them now. Tell me everything. Lowarch tells me Sion and Mary are a handful."

Instead, Margaret turned her mouth to his. Her fingers wandered from his back, fluttering over his hip and lower abdomen. Waves of desire pulsed through every vein of his being. Their time apart had made the sensation of her touch more intense than he could ever remember, the nearness of her more commanding. She tugged at his hand, still kissing him as she stepped backward, gradually bringing them closer and closer to the bed. Moments later, she was lying back on it, pulling him down with her. Her skirts rustled as he lifted them to slide a hand over her thigh, smooth beneath the crisp linen of her chemise. Something brushed against his ear, like the air stirred by a voice from long ago.

If she were to deliver another child, she could die.

His breath caught. He rolled from her, burying his face against a fold of the blanket, its fibers stiff against his cheek. Wadding the blanket in his fist, he muttered, "We can't, Margaret." He twisted at the waist to gaze at her. It had to be said. "Not now. Not ever."

She touched his shoulder. "Not now maybe, but later I could . . . I could take 'precautions'."

"No. It's not worth the risk."

"It's not fair to you, Owain." Her hand fell away. Sniffing back tears, she looked up at the ceiling. "If you strayed from our vows, I would not —"

"Nonsense, Marged." He seized her jaw in his tender grip and turned her face back to him. "It's a small price to pay for keeping you with me. A small, *small* price. One I would gladly pay for the rest of my life."

Even as he said the words, a knot coiled tighter inside him. It was not a small price at all. Many times already, he had been tempted and he knew that as soon as he lay with another woman, it would happen again and again. If only he could be as strong as Margaret needed him to be. It didn't help that she nearly gave him permission to be unfaithful.

Nestling beneath his arm, she whispered, "Hold me, Owain."

He drew her against his chest, pressing his cheek against the silken crown of her hair.

19

Conwy Castle, Wales — April, 1401

IT WAS GOOD FRIDAY, the 1ˢᵗ of April, and the majority of Conwy Castle's fifteen men-at-arms and sixty archers trudged along the dirt road from the castle to the toll of the parish church bells. It was a tenet of Captain John Massey's that men of honor did not engage in acts of war on such sacred days and thus he felt secure in leaving two of his keenest as a skeleton force to guard the castle of Conwy. It was not a tenet that the wily Tudur brothers—cousins of Owain Glyndwr— adhered to, however.

As the English soldiers shuffled past on the street leading out from the castle toward the church, Gwilym ap Tudur and forty of his cohorts waited silently in the heated confines of the blacksmith's shop just off Castle Street. In the hills beyond the upper gate to the town, Rhys ap Tudur lingered with an even larger body of fighting men.

The River Conwy spilled sluggishly into the estuary below the castle, another of James of St. George's masterpieces. A giant slab of rock jutted into the estuary and upon it sat one of the imposing towers. An immense fortress, Conwy was as near to impenetrable as the site—and James of St. George's genius—would allow. On the harbor side, the looming tower and a barbican flanked the castle entrance, accessible only by boat. On the town side of the castle to gain entrance one had to ascend a steep, narrow stairway, cross a drawbridge and then pass through no less than three gates—all winged by a host of walls and towers which were enhanced by timber hoardings pierced with arrow loops.

"Maelgwn?" Gwilym moved through the shadows and clasped his friend's shoulder, his grip pinching until Maelgwn winced. He drew his hand away. "You're prepared?"

Maelgwn nodded, tucking a short coil of rope in with his clanking sack full of carpenter's tools.

"To your deed, then." Gwilym sank back into the shadows with the others as Maelgwn crept away. One by one, the tools, knives and other weapons that had been lying scattered about were passed to eager hands.

A few minutes later, they heard a stifled cry, followed by Maelgwn's shrill whistle. They darted out into the street and raced up the causeway.

Within the gatehouse, Maelgwn stood triumphantly grinning by the corpses of the two strangled guards, their necks banded in violet from the deep bruise of his rope.

Gwilym paused but a second. "It *is* a good Friday, is it not?" he said to Maelgwn.

"The best," Maelgwn proclaimed, pulling one of the dead soldier's swords free of his belt.

"'Twill get even better, I wager," Gwilym said, radiant with triumph. "Give my brother the signal. I want to see Conwy in flames. Let us test whether the thatch on an Englishman's home burns as well as that of a Welshman's."

Denbigh Castle, Wales — April, 1401

ON A GRASSY KNOLL outside Denbigh Castle, Harry Hotspur stood with his arm outstretched. Even in his statuesque pose he was a striking figure. While his nose was perhaps a bit too broad, his height less than average, and his chin a bit too small to match the width of his cheekbones, he commanded attention with his flurry of activity. No other knight could spur a horse to such speed as he did, nor shout across the clang of battle with such force and clarity. He could make women swoon with the smile dancing in his blue eyes and with those very same eyes instill in his enemy the cold promise of death. He was the Lancelot of his day and he was intent on wringing every flicker of glory from life—and if death came to him sooner for living by such passionate degrees, then he would meet death with honor and pride.

A very able commander and quick to act, as his name would imply, Hotspur was the Chief Justice of North Wales at the time of the capture of Conwy. He held a string of other titles, a ratification of Henry's as yet unshaken faith in him, despite the fact that by both blood and marriage he had rather complicated ties. His father was Henry Percy, Earl of Northumberland and Warden of the Scottish Marches, who became even more powerful with Richard's deposition; his wife was Elizabeth Mortimer, whose brothers were the late Earl of March, Roger, and Sir Edmund Mortimer. Their mother had been Philippa, daughter of Lionel, Duke of Clarence, second son of Edward III. Following tradition, the heirs of Lionel should have been next in line for the throne of England after Richard, but Henry had shaken that tradition soundly by his seizure of the crown. Still, Hotspur's nephew, the young, imprisoned Earl of March, also named Edmund, possessed a very valid claim to kingship.

Relaxing his arm, Hotspur's lips curled into an easy smile. There was a steady, but light breeze on which his peregrine glided, her blue-gray wings bowed to catch the wind and her yellow-rimmed eyes scanning the fields below.

"She will be a great one, m'lord," his squire John Irby observed, one hand cupped above his peppered brow.

"I think I shall name her Artemis, after the goddess of the hunt. What do you think, John? Is that a good name for her? I only hope she will live up to it."

"Oh, yes, I —"

Hotspur shushed him. Stepping close to Irby, he whispered, "She has her eye on something. Do you not see? Perhaps a hare that the plowman has scared up. Ah, what keen sight she has."

The two were so intent on observing the falcon that they barely noticed the two riders who had stopped at the castle gate and were now riding toward them. The peregrine's flight broke as she pulled up sharply and banked back toward them. Hotspur scowled at the riders, one of whom was waving anxiously at them.

"Ah, damn it. The afternoon is wasted. Who has come to so very rudely interrupt my sport?" Artemis alighted on the perch of his gloved arm, eyeing his finger as he proffered a small morsel of meat. He scratched at her snowy chest and blew her a kiss. "I would proclaim your beauty, lovely creature, but that it might stir jealousy in my Elizabeth. We'll try again tomorrow. No doubt there is some grave matter that none but I can remedy. Perhaps all the wine barrels have burst and flooded the cellar?"

Irby chuckled with him. As the riders, John Charlton, Lord of Powys, and Lord Reginald de Grey of Ruthin halted before them, Hotspur's smile vanished.

"You have ruined her first hunt, my lords," Hotspur admonished. For Charlton and Grey to have come all this way, it could not be good news. The afternoon had been nothing short of perfect until now.

"My regrets, Sir Henry," Charlton said, repositioning himself in his saddle to ease his sores, "but you are needed at Conwy."

"I know of the rebels. I take it Massey has been unable to remove them?"

Grey's mouth twitched. "They are firmly rooted. The king requests that you treat with them."

"With rebels? And what have they to offer in return for their undeserved freedom?"

"Conwy Castle," Grey growled. "The king is very displeased by this. If they are not removed it will give momentum to the Welsh uprising."

"A pleasing triumph for your nemesis, yes, Lord Grey? I understand your stake in this. But why does the king call on me for help? Unless he has lately gone blind, the letter I recently wrote him should have made it obvious that I have yet to see any of that money which he has so fervently promised me. Am I to feed my soldiers on promises? My tolerance wears thin on this subject." He had already put forth a sizeable amount of his own funds to ensure the timely payment of the troops under him, but Henry had been slow in repaying that debt.

"Troubles in Gascony and Scotland —"

"Gascony and Scotland? This is Wales and it is no less a threat than Gascony or Scotland. Perhaps even more so. Gascony is over the sea and Scotland has no Owain Glyndwr to stir trouble. Have you heard, Lord Grey, of Glyndwr's latest escapade? He took on the guise of a cooper and with one of his sons at his side drove his wagon into the square of Dolgellau, from which the barrels opened up and poured out not ale, but armed men. They set free three Welshmen who had been imprisoned there and were awaiting trial—one, a man of seventy years no less, for hoarding a store of arrows in his barn, another for carrying a sword bundled in his blankets as he traveled through a forest reputed for its highwaymen and the third, and this one I am told most infuriated Glyndwr, for taking as his wife a woman from Coventry—an Englishwoman."

Charlton climbed down from his lathered mount, his fingers kneading at his lower spine. "They broke the king's laws, Sir Henry. Laws that were set in place for good reason."

"Laws? Glyndwr himself ripped those laws from the door of the hall in Dolgellau and burned them with a hundred wide-eyed witnesses staring on. Some, I am told, even cheered him." Hotspur laughed raucously. Startled, his peregrine spread her wings. He turned his face from her and gave her to Irby, then stomped toward Charlton. "Does Parliament think . . . does the king think . . . ah, do they *think* at all? Do they think that law upon law, meant to stifle and restrict a people, will suddenly throw a blanket of order and goodwill upon us? God's teeth, this will get worse before it gets better. And I wager it will not be the king who has to deal with it at every turn. It will be the man you are ogling slack-jawed at. Agh, he'll see the repercussions in time. Let him learn his own lesson, then. There is no sense in arguing with a lackwit, let alone a whole Parliament full of them."

The last comment clearly shocked Charlton. Grey, however, revealed nothing. Hotspur knew he had perhaps said too much, but the king had pushed him too far already.

While Grey remained on the hilltop, Charlton grabbed at the reins of his horse to follow as Hotspur and Irby began the downhill trek back to the mews to return the bird. Charlton's words tumbled out in a stammer. "But, but Sir Henry, please . . . *please*, I beg. You must come with me to Conwy. If you don't, it will be my head as well as yours."

"Heads roll like stones in this country. The loss of mine or yours will be of little significance."

Charlton scurried faster. "Can you be ready by tomorrow?"

"Tomorrow?" Hotspur scoffed. "Do you think me a magician?"

"The day after?"

Hotspur tossed him a look of annoyance, like Charlton was

some fly whose buzzing must be dealt with. He raised his voice more than loud enough for Grey to hear. "Well enough . . . I am the king's slave after all, am I not? Lest you think otherwise, all men are slaves. Even kings are slaves to the acts of outlaws. Unhappily, I am a slave to both."

What Lord Reginald de Grey thought of him was of no concern to Harry Hotspur. His outspokenness was the cardinal point of his character. It was what rallied his soldiers to him. Without it, he would not have become the valuable pawn that he was.

20

Conwy Castle, Wales — May, 1401

A HUNDRED AND TWENTY men-at-arms and three hundred archers flew to Conwy. At their head galloped Harry Hotspur on a chestnut steed, its mane the same brilliant yellow as his own short-cropped, thick crown of hair, the bold sun of May setting sparks to every strand. To his immense relief, Grey had gone his own way, straight back to the king, no doubt to deliver an account of Hotspur's damning remarks.

Arriving at the gates of the town of Conwy, Hotspur gazed upon the whitewashed, heaven-scraping towers of the castle. Although he was loath to do so, he immediately ordered Massey arrested for his negligence. The impenetrable walls, which had been meant to keep English forces safe within, were now the very thing keeping them out. The fortress had been amply provisioned. It would take a protracted siege to oust the rebels, given his limited means. It could be done, but there was a quicker, surer way to retake Conwy.

Hotspur began negotiations with the rebels. But what the Tudur brothers demanded of him Hotspur knew that he could no sooner deliver than he could the moon. They wanted total absolution: free pardons and a promise that charges would not be brought against them. Hotspur countered. Gwilym rejected. Negotiations dragged on.

While Hotspur began to count the sunsets from his camp just above the beach outside town, Henry sent his son Harry to Conwy. In the meantime, word came to Hotspur that the Welsh were raiding near both Bangor and further south beyond Dolgellau. A report that the Bangor raids were being led by the younger brother, Tudur Glyndwr, led Hotspur to surmise that Owain must be the one causing havoc in the south of Gwynedd. As soon as Prince Harry arrived at Conwy with additional forces, Hotspur took advantage of the reprieve. He sent Lord Charlton after Tudur's party, while he went in pursuit of Owain Glyndwr himself. The chances of finding the rebel were small, but if he did, it would change everything.

Near Cadair Idris, Wales — May, 1401

IT WAS NECESSARY, FROM time to time, to gather provisions to feed a burgeoning army. While the English were befuddled by the problem of what to do about Conwy, Tudur remained with most of the Welsh fighters at their camp overlooking Llyn Peris, from where he could launch raiding parties toward both Bangor and Caernarvon. In the mountains between Dolgellau and Machynlleth, Owain's men rounded up a large herd of cattle. Enough to keep his men fed well into the summer. It had all gone too easily, however. A fact which unnerved Owain, although he would not admit it.

As he unrolled his pack to sleep beneath the stars, he listened to the lowing of the cattle. Their plaintive song rolled through the valley, making him grimace. He would have his men up well before dawn to move them on again. There were a dozen men on watch for the night, but Harlech was less than a day's ride away and Dolgellau only a few miles. He gathered his blanket and went to join Rhys.

Owain picked up an overturned cup from the ground and thrust it at Rhys.

"Your friendship is costly," Rhys said, pouring the last of his drink from his flask into Owain's cup.

"As my kitchen maids would attest is yours." Owain sank to his haunches. He took a swallow of ale. It left a warm trail on its way down his throat. In moments, his worries began to dissolve.

"Agh, your kitchen maids are generous wenches. They take little convincing when met with a pair of pleading eyes." Rhys rubbed at his whiskers. "What do you think will become of Gwilym and the lot?"

Draping his blanket over his shoulders, Owain shrugged. "What will become of any of us, Rhys?" He stared at the stars, his knees clutched to his chest, just as he used to do when he was a boy— hours upon hours spent gazing up at heaven.

Rhys emptied his cup and placed it on the ground. "This has become something more for you than just getting your lands back, hasn't it? You hate them. You hate the English. You had no idea Gwilym would be so foolish as to capture a castle he could not keep and yet you revel that he's thwarted them for so long."

"I don't hate the English, Rhys. I don't hate any man."

"Oh, come now. Not even Lord Grey?"

Sighing, Owain looked at his friend. "If you must pry me for an answer, yes, it is men who can never have enough who I detest. More money, more lands, more titles . . . What is all of that without freedom? They don't know the value of it."

Groaning, Rhys lay down and wrapped himself in his blankets. "So much talk of freedom," he said as he tossed a glance at the cattle. "To me it's about being able to fill my belly. I hate people who keep me from my supper."

Owain wadded up his cloak for a pillow and eased back. "You forgot to mention your drink. You'd hate anyone who kept you from your drink, as well."

He turned to look at Rhys. His friend's chest rumbled with a snore. Somewhere in the herd, a cow bellowed for her calf.

HILL CATTLE WERE NOT easily goaded—and they left behind a very obvious trail. Shortly after dawn the next morning, the Welsh were being surveyed from across the foggy valley by a force slightly larger, better armed and less encumbered than their own.

The shout went up in the Welsh camp. "English!"

The Welsh bolted to arms. Gruffydd and Maredydd watched in terror as a line of English archers plunged down the far hillside. Behind the archers, a cluster of armored knights on horseback appeared. In their middle rode a knight in a plumed helmet.

On a gentle slope that fell away into the gaping valley, the cattle twitched their ears and snorted into the damp morning air as they turned their huge brown eyes toward the opposite ridgeline. Owain was among the first to his horse. He grabbed a spear from someone frozen in indecision and began prodding the cattle with it, yelling and swinging it wildly. In protest, their hooves tapped at the rocky ground. Then one of them turned, thrusting its weight into the rump of another, and the stampede began. The herd rumbled toward the advancing English.

Owain bellowed orders to split the party. "Flee! Flee as fast as you can!"

The English knight raised his arm and a call went up to his archers. They halted, forming a loose line, and sent their arrows into the stampede. Cattle fell in their tracks. They stumbled over one another and tumbled down the hill. Those behind plowed their hooves into the steep hillside. Some turned back. Others scattered laterally.

The Welsh exploded in a dozen directions. For those who dispersed on foot, they were aware they were marked. Through the mayhem of singing arrows and the drumming of hooves they took to the higher paths. They knew these would be a challenge for the English horses, which were long enough on leg to prove speedy across open ground and strong enough to bear an armored rider long distances, but also dangerously awkward on the broken mountainsides. The few stragglers who could not gain higher ground soon fell under swooping English blades.

Owain was well on his way south when he turned to look back. He reined hard. Beside him Rhys and Gruffydd pulled up.

"There is no time!" Rhys shouted. "We can only save ourselves!"

Owain glanced at him through the drifting mist. Then a flicker of color caught his eye and he peered across the valley. The banner that his men always carried with them, the bold red hands of a maiden painted on its field, beckoned to him from a precarious ledge several hundred feet away. Tom had always been its bearer, but there was no sign of him.

"Maredydd," Owain mumbled.

Rhys and Gruffydd looked around and saw the quivering banner. Maredydd had gone back to save it. He was struggling along with it, finally tucking it under his arm, but the end of the pole caught on a stone and he stumbled.

"Go on," Owain said. When Rhys and Gruffydd hesitated, he summoned his voice. "Go!" He dug his spurs into his mount's flanks, racing across the ridge until he came to his son, the drumming of enemy hooves bearing down on them.

Maredydd was possessed with that look, that wide-eyed frozen look of young men who flock to battle with dreams of glory and courageous fighting only to discover it is chaos and fear and vomit pushing at your insides. Owain thrust out his hand. An errant arrow landed at Maredydd's feet. He scrambled onto the back of his father's saddle, dropping the banner on the ground.

A bank of fog had rolled around them. Although it gave them some degree of cover, it had also separated Owain and Maredydd from the others. There wasn't time to calculate the best route. Owain heard the hoofbeats, loud, steady, and certainly not those of cattle. He hesitated, closing his eyes to pinpoint the sound and as soon as he was sure of its source, he guided his mount away. With his son gripping him tightly, he forged on into the whiteness.

The mists had grown heavier since dawn. Even the sun could not break through. There was no wind to usher it away. It was a godsend.

21

Cadair Idris, Wales — May, 1401

HEARING THE RASP OF his horse's breathing, Owain at last ceased to urge the animal on. He swung down and helped his son off. Several times, the horse had pitched sideways and Owain had felt Maredydd nearly falling and pulling him with him. But the horse, with its great heart, had carried them this far. The slight limp that came on when it stepped in a shallow hole was now verging on lameness. Now, as he looked on at the animal, he knew they had to abandon it.

Maredydd ducked beneath an outcropping. There was no cover for miles, no cave, no cottage, no thicket of trees, only the little hollow that Owain had guided them to. The hills around them were jagged, broken and steep sided. They could rest safely here for awhile.

"Where are we?" Maredydd's eyes darted from rock to rock.

"Would that I could tell you." Owain slapped at the horse's rump, but it just stood there, wavering, its head hanging so low its lip touched the ground. The sun had broken through and the rising heat was beginning to take its toll. Owain wiped at his forehead and squinted, his face to the south. "That mountain is Cadair Idris. Iolo tells me if you sleep all night on the stone that was the giant's chair, you will awaken either reciting brilliant verse or spewing madman's nonsense." Drawing his long sword from its scabbard, Owain stared hard at the horse and then with two hands on the hilt, drew it back.

"What are you doing?" Maredydd scooted forward, grabbing his father's ankle. "No!"

Owain shot him a look of reproach. His leg flinched as if to kick. He had always been so gentle in speaking to his children, that it shocked even him when his words shot out tight and menacing. "Quiet yourself! Do you wish us dead? I merely want to send him away. He is of no use to us now. We can run faster than he can carry us. We'll have to find our way back to the camp without a horse. Otherwise we are butts for English arrows."

With that, Owain slapped the flat of his blade against the horse's hindquarters with such force that its head shot up. He feared for a moment that it might just fall over from exhaustion—give up rather than go on. But it took a couple steps backward, eyeing him with confusion, and realizing its load was gone it trotted off in a hitched gait, weaving amongst the scattered rocks. He watched it go and finally sank to the ground beside Maredydd. It was some time before he noticed that his son was trembling.

Owain touched him on the leg. "It is never what you think it will be."

Maredydd held a hand out, gazing at his palm. It quivered with each breath. "Tom was . . ."—he squeezed his hand into a fist and tucked it against his chest—"carrying the banner when they came. I was not five feet from him and an . . . an arrow struck him through the eye." He looked at his father dolefully, as if he could read answers there in the depths of Owain's pupils. "He didn't die right then. He was just . . . lying there, the arrow sticking out of his eye . . . clear through his head. He called out and I went to him. I wanted to save the banner. I don't know why. But I wanted to do it for him. I told him I would carry it. I told him I would."

Owain knew that if the cattle had not trampled Tom, the English would have finished him off. He touched his son's shoulder reassuringly. The grass waved across the land with the rising wind, the fog now reduced to scattered patches. "A banner is of no importance. You . . . are."

They sat in their little shelter of shadows for a long, long time, waves of exhaustion beating at them both. There were things Owain wanted to say, questions Maredydd might have asked if he could have found his tongue, but they just sat in silence, close to each other— Owain's hand now on his son's thigh and Maredydd leaning against his father's arm. Gusts of wind were making it harder to hear now, but all was seemingly undisturbed. Even though the fleeting clash and resulting flight were still fresh on his senses, Owain's eyes began to drift shut. Exhaustion crashed through his limbs. Yawning, he stretched his long legs and —

A rock, a very small rock, dropped from the overhang above. It clattered over a half-buried stone and fell silent into a clump of grass. Slowly, Owain reached for the hilt of his sword. He had barely touched it when an armored knight and half a dozen archers with their arrows nocked appeared before them. Maredydd shrank against the stone wall at his back.

A set of gleaming teeth amidst a flushed face was all that Owain could see as the knight flipped his visor up. The plume atop his helmet fluttered in the rising breeze. "Aaaahhhh . . . what have we found? Come out, come out. Have a drink, good fellows. You look parched."

The knight motioned to one his soldiers who quickly unslung his flask and thrust it toward them. Hesitantly, Owain and Maredydd crawled out and stood. Maredydd stared at the flask, his fingers uncurling, lifting.

Owain read his thoughts. "No."

The knight raised his pale eyebrows in amusement. "Yes, you

looked Welsh and that proves it." The knight took the flask himself and guzzled. When he had sated his own thirst, he dragged a sleeve across his mouth. "There. Harmless. Now please, won't you introduce yourselves?"

His request was met with resolute silence. The knight, a rich and important one, judging by his fine new German armor, was taking the encounter with a sense of wry humor. "Very well, I'll go first. Sir Henry Percy, also known as Harry Hotspur—long story to that, we shall save it for later. Now you. Your names?"

Owain stared at him, taking him in. He had heard much of this man, even seen a bit of him in action in Scotland when he was not much more than Maredydd's age. The man may have danced around with his wit, but he meant business.

Hotspur raised his palm up and the archers pulled their bowstrings tight. It was answer the question or die on the spot.

"Owain Glyndwr."

Hotspur tilted his head. A spark of delight shone in his eyes. "Give up your weapons. At once." As soon as Owain and Maredydd had done so, he gave another order. "Now you," he said, indicating Maredydd, "turn to your right. Go with them."

Two soldiers placed their arrows back in their bags and slung their bows over their backs. They hooked Owain's son by both arms and led him some hundred feet away. There, they settled him to the ground without force and drew their short swords. Maredydd did not flinch or turn his head or move in any way. It was as if he already accepted that his fate had come to him—too soon, too sudden perhaps, but altogether undeniable.

"Your son will make a good soldier," Hotspur said. "I saw him take up the banner."

"How did you know?" Owain asked with astonishment.

"I have a son, although he's only an infant. Still, I know. That's not the look a man gives a common soldier. Not even a friend. You fear for his life and you'd rather die yourself than see his life end now."

"Then take me. Let him go," Owain pled. The tenor in his voice was steady, although it took every bit of his courage to keep it so.

Hotspur chuckled. "A noble offer, Sir Owain, but methinks it would serve me better to take him and leave you behind. I'm certain you could fetch a healthy sum to pay his ransom. Perhaps you could even call off your little rebellion to save his skin?"

He was shrewd. Grey would have killed them both on sight, if only to please the king. But this Hotspur—perhaps he was not as rash as his name implied.

"Agh, I will bake beneath this armor." Hotspur removed his helmet. "It is damnable hot in these mountains in the day and freezing at night." His helmet tucked beneath his arm, he walked a small circle around Owain. "I mean you and your son no harm. I want no prisoners, no ransom, no heads for trophies."

Puzzled, Owain glanced at Maredydd, then back at Hotspur. "Then what do you want?"

He shrugged. "The truth. Only the truth."

"Truth?"

"Sir Owain, this is no quarrel about land. You seek to see the rightful ruler of England on the throne."

"Richard is dead."

"So they say." Hotspur plucked at the feathers of his plume. He appeared amused at something. "They also say he's gone mad and lives at the court of King Robert of Scotland. Rumors, no more. But . . . the Earl of March lives."

"He is a boy."

"So was Richard when he came to the throne. The Earl of March is my nephew by marriage. Some would say that he should be the king. Do you agree?"

So that was the crux? Hotspur was not entirely fond of Henry, that much was obvious. But more than that, he was seeking an alliance. It was a dangerous ploy. If Owain answered to the affirmative, Hotspur could use that against him as grounds for treason. Owain would be drawn and quartered mercilessly. If Owain cried out against Hotspur none would believe him. On the other hand, if Henry were deposed and little Edmund Mortimer set on the throne, Hotspur would be a natural choice for a regent or at the least a councilor.

"I would say," Owain replied carefully, "that some are right."

Hotspur smiled. "A safe answer. But understood, Sir Owain. So you see, you and I have a common interest. Should you ever like to make more of it, let me know." He pulled on his helmet, then reclaimed Owain's sword and dagger from the soldier who had been holding them. He tossed them at Owain's feet. "So that we both have the same story—you and I had blows, you knocked my sword away, but upon hearing someone approach you fled on foot. I did not ask your name, nor did I see anyone with you. And don't fear, my soldiers are loyal men. They will have nothing to report. By the time they got here, you were gone."

He signaled to the two guarding Maredydd to leave him and return back up the hill to where they had left the horses. Before going, he nodded to himself, as if to agree with a thought that he had held back. "One last thing—I must finish my business in Conwy. Then, I have matters on the Scottish border that demand my attention. They're clamoring for a truce, whatever that's worth. A piece of advice before I go: select your targets with prudence, m'lord. I hear the garrisons in the south of Wales are less vigilant than those to the north."

Neither Owain nor Maredydd moved from their places until Hotspur was well out of sight. When they stumbled into the Welsh camp at Llyn Peris several days later, Maredydd collapsed as if his feet could not carry him one more step. Owain was helped to his tent by Rhys. They brought him water and food. He emptied his cup and lay down. A young woman with long brown hair, an occasional lover of Rhys's, came to him with a vial of warm oil and massaged it into his shoulders and feet. While Iolo's fingers plucked at his harp, Owain closed his eyes and let sleep overtake him. There was much to think about and he would need a clear head to sort it all out.

He did not know how long it would take him to travel the road he had set his feet on. He did not know what the end would be or what would be the price demanded of him. He did not know when again he would hold his sweet Marged in his arms. But perhaps in order for him to continue on this path, it was better for them to be apart for now. Still, convincing himself of that did not make it any easier.

Llys Bradwen, south of Dolgellau, Wales — May, 1401

TWO DAYS RIDE DUE south of Llyn Peris, Margaret stood on the banks of Afon Arthog, water up to her ankles, the hem of her skirt well soaked.

"Ready. Go!" shouted Sion. His feet slapped water onto Margaret's face as he and his twin sister Mary sprinted past. Sand flew out behind their spinning legs.

Margaret felt the first smile in many months on her lips. Overhead, the sun shone brilliant. A warm breeze swept over the green hills and twisted loose strands of her hair.

"Sion, Mary, time to go back," she said.

They swept the sand from their clothes, clasped hands and scrambled up the sheep path. Rejuvenated by their outing, Margaret joined the children at the top of the path where they had stopped to each gather a bouquet of wildflowers. Mary gave hers to her mother and took off after her brother again. As the slate-roofed manor came into view, Margaret paused. A cart heaped with market goods stood outside the house. Her bouquet fell to the ground. Grabbing up her hem, she ran barefooted toward it.

Sir Dafydd, whom Owain had sent with her when they were ushered from Sycharth, had just returned with Lowarch from the market at Dolgellau. He grinned when he saw Lady Margaret breathless before him and whisked the dust out of his bristly, graying hair. Lowarch dipped his head in greeting, grabbed a sack of grain and went inside.

"A splendid day, m'lady," Dafydd remarked. Grunting under the strain, he hoisted a cask of ale out of the cart and up onto his shoulder.

"Dafydd," Margaret said, "is there anything for me in particular?" That sounded like something the children would say, but there was always hope.

Sion climbed the spokes of the cart wheel like a ladder to peer inside the cart. Lowarch lifted a string of fish from the top and handed it to him. "Away with you."

A thumb and finger pinching his nose, Sion took it, leapt off and raced inside, the string held at arm's length.

"There's a jar of nutmeg for you," Dafydd said to Margaret. "Up near the front."

A familiar emptiness settled in Margaret's stomach, just as it did every week when Dafydd returned from market. A thousand such frivolous favors would not have lifted her spirits. Out of kind acceptance, she rummaged through the sacks of grain near the front of the cart. The only jars she found were one of honey and another of oil. She dug her fingers deeper. Something stiff crinkled at her fingertips. Was it possible? A letter from Owain! She tugged it loose and clutched it to her breast, cherishing the moment and at the same time whispering prayers that the news it contained was good.

Dafydd lingered at the open door to the house.

Although there was no signature, she knew the handwriting by its sharp slant to the right and broad loops. The letter was deeply creased, the ink smeared, and there was a small tear in one corner.

"May God, who knows full well the hell we have endured while we have been apart one from another, reward us with heaven when we meet again."

She read it three more times, turned it over to inspect the back and rushed toward Dafydd. "But where did it come from? Is there nothing else?"

Dafydd shifted the cask. He looked over his shoulder and smiled at Gwladys, Lowarch's wife, who emerged through the doorway to take inventory of the goods stuffed in the cart. Gwladys claimed the jars of honey and oil, heaping words of thanks upon Dafydd. As she shuffled back inside, Dafydd placed the cask on the ground.

"I heard . . . some news, but only a little," he confessed softly. "Gwilym has taken Conwy. But they've sent Hotspur to take it back and . . ."

"And Owain?" Margaret asked, her fingers pinching the creases of the letter.

A broad smile parted Dafydd's thin lips. "Stole their cattle. Chased by Hotspur. Lived to tell about it. Four, maybe five days ago, near Cadair Idris."

Margaret gazed off into the distance. To the east on the horizon, the foothills of Cadair Idris pushed upward. A few days ago, Owain had been only miles away. So close. By now, though, he could be anywhere. "Then we shall have to find him, however long it takes, however far away."

Iolo Goch:

For well over a century, since the murder of Prince Llywelyn the Last on the banks of the Irfon near Builth, the Welsh had bowed down before their English lords. There was peace to be had, as long as we obeyed. But now there was a new king—the Pretender, some called him—a king who sought to destroy that peace.

Laws were set down by Parliament that forbade things we had until then taken for granted. We could not hold office or bear arms within any city. We could no longer serve among the garrisons of the numerous castles in Wales. Welshmen could not bring suit against any Englishman, no matter the offense. We were forbidden from sending our sons to the universities or apprenticing them to a trade in any town. Any Englishman who married into a Welsh family was subject to the same restrictions as the Welsh. Aimed specifically at my lord Owain, the marriage of a Welshman to an Englishwoman was an act subject to severe penalty. Bards were not allowed to travel or perform in groups, in essence cutting them off from their livelihood. Even the practice of assembling to help neighbors during harvest was outlawed.

Still, there was talk. Talk passed from lips of the old farmer who came to town to sell his sheep. The butcher and the cloth merchant talked to any who did business with them and those people in turn went back out into the countryside of Wales and told what they had heard. They talked of Owain Glyndwr's bravery, his long, noble lineage, and his gigantic height. They talked of the Tudurs' trickery and how they had stolen Conwy out from beneath the very noses of the English garrison. They talked of freedom and how Wales was once a place that knew of *such a thing—before the first Edward of England put an end to it.*

In the day of our great-great grandfathers there had been song and ale and food enough to tip the tables. The flowers had bloomed more brightly then. The sun had shone more boldly.

The hills of Wales filled with men, young and old, starving to taste a dream. They flocked to Owain. They called him their 'prince'.

Some even called him Owain, Prince of Wales. Others gave breath to the name 'Arthur'.

22

Conwy Castle, Wales — June, 1401

F OR THREE MONTHS THE Tudurs and their outlaws had been
holed up in Conwy. Three months without an agreeable settle-
ment. Three months during which Hotspur paced and fumed and
shook his fist at the walls while his pupil Prince Harry stood by, asking incessant questions.

In that time, King Henry's tone had changed from one of
patient determination to insult and blame. The letters that Prince
Harry received were very clear on that point, labeling Hotspur's tepid
negotiations as 'an evil precedent'. The letters that Hotspur himself
received went so far as to insinuate that he had grown sloppy and
ineffectual in his jurisdiction. It was an affront that infuriated Hotspur far more than the lack of funds he was meant to operate on. It
was an attack on his character and that is something he did not take
lightly. He vowed to finish what he had started and be on his way.

Three months was a very long time to have your enemy staring
up at you with murderous intent. The isolation had worn the Welsh
captors to a fray. The giddy victory they had enjoyed at their accom-
plishment clashed with the reality that the English were prepared
to starve them out. Despair had a way of bending even the most iron

of wills.

On St. John the Baptist's Day, the 24th of June, the Welsh bound and offered up nine of their own in return for their freedom. Hotspur intended to imprison them for a time, but Prince Harry overruled him and ordered that they should suffer a traitor's fate. Despite Hotspur's vehement protests, the nine men were hanged, disemboweled, beheaded, drawn and quartered.

As the rest of the Welsh filed out of Conwy past the fly-covered heads of their comrades, which were sitting atop the town walls, and went off to their bittersweet freedom, Hotspur's throat burned with bile. He had agreed with Gwilym ap Tudur to take nine prisoners— prisoners, not sacrifices. This despicable means was not how he had meant to close the matter. If Harry had wanted to show himself fierce, it would have sufficed to behead them with all swiftness. Such barbarity was beyond Hotspur's code. He held nothing back when he admonished Harry for the act.

"This is a disgrace to your honor! What man will treat with you now, but one with no memory at all?"

Brooding in a cloud of disgrace, Hotspur left for Northumberland. He had much to say to his father when he arrived at Warkworth and the earl was swayed by every colorful word. His son had been humiliated. It was not wise for any man, not even a king, to insult a Percy.

Hyddgen, Wales — June, 1401

AFTER HIS ENCOUNTER NEAR Cadair Idris with Hotspur, Owain ordered camp moved from Llyn Peris. His followers often called themselves the 'Children of Owain' and their numbers were now in the hundreds. They traveled south, in the shadow of the spine of the Cambrian Mountains and finally made their base, a veritable city, on the western slope of a peak called Plynlimon.

Several days later, Owain's army shifted their camp to a deep glen slightly north of Plynlimon at Hyddgen. The grazing was good there and the breezes cooling. A small river twisted through the glen and the cattle meant to sustain them were gathered on its banks, lying peacefully amongst the fluttering grass and short rushes.

On a peak overlooking the valley was a cairn that had marked the way for many a shepherd.

Gruffydd, who had gone there to steal time alone, scrambled to the top of the rocky cairn and swung his legs over the side. Downy sheep, stolen from the Flemings nearby, wandered the hillsides, content in their paradise. He unfolded the last letter sent from his dear, long-lost Elise and read it for the five hundredth time. Minutes later, he paused to rest his eyes and looked off into the next valley. The sun was blindingly bright and he blinked to regain his vision. As the world sharpened, his pulse began to race wildly. The sheep lifted their heads, then took to flight.

"Holy Mother of Christ!" he muttered, for he saw a great army approaching. As he lowered himself, the letter slipped from his fingers. He dropped to the ground and reached for it, but a gust of wind blew it several feet away. Desperate, he dove for it, but the wind took it again. By now, he could hear them coming. Against caution, he scampered after the letter once more, grabbed it by the corner just as another gust buffeted him and ran for his life back to camp.

It was Gethin who snatched him in mid-stride and put a lock on Gruffydd's shoulders, waiting for the boy to catch his breath. "What is it?"

Owain and several others worked their way through the little city of tents and came to stand behind Gethin.

His heart hammering at his ribs, Gruffydd looked toward his father. "An army!" He pointed toward the ridge line. A line of spearheads flashed against the light of a setting sun.

Moments later, a wave of Flemings broke over the mountain. In recent years, a great number of Flemings had immigrated to these parts to deal in the wool trade and they were indebted to the English crown. Thus, the unrest caused by the Welsh uprising had not been to their liking. Threats had been issued, warning the Welsh army to disperse. Owain had thought it merely idle prattle. Obviously, it had not been. Three times the size of the Welsh army, they flooded down into the valley, a river of swords and spears and poleaxes, rushing unstoppably onward. The Welsh camp erupted in pandemonium.

Owain bounded onto a boulder and thrust his sword in the air. "To arms, brave men! Keep your brothers at your back! Break their lines!"

They grabbed up their weapons. Those that kept their blades always at their sides reached the edge of camp just as the initial impact of Flemings struck. A great clang shook the sky. The screams of dying Welshmen rang out. In every direction, Flemish soldiers beat at the ragged lines of the Welsh, tearing them apart like wet pieces of parchment. The spontaneous defense of the Welsh crumpled under the weighty onslaught. One after another, Welsh warriors fell to the ground in bloody pools.

Gethin and Rhys, side by side, levied their swords against the endless wave of attack with such ferocity that those Flemings they encountered in the lopsided fray yielded. Bit by bit, the two seasoned warriors gained ground and those next to them saw their great courage and took strength in it.

For a brief while, Gruffydd stood clenching his sword, unsure of what to do. He had lost sight of his brother Maredydd. Pushing his way through the confusion, he at last spotted him, engaged with a Fleming twice his age and far more experienced. With a roar, Gruffydd rushed forward. He did not stop until his sword point pierced the Fleming's belly clear to his spine. Gruffydd yanked his weapon free and the Fleming fell face forward between them.

ON HIS HORSE NOW, Owain swept through the melee—a god-like figure with his golden mane flowing behind him and his sword taking down a man with every swing. As he urged his soldiers on by name, the Welsh began to fight with a strength larger than the mountains.

The Flemings had numbers, but they did not have the heart of the Welsh. Their attack was not a well-planned one and soon their lines ebbed. Bodies of Flemings began to pile on top of Welsh ones.

A small pocket of Flemings broke and ran. Soon it was a stream. Then a river.

A short hour after the assault had begun, two hundred Welshmen lay lifeless in a meadow of carmine. Over four hundred and fifty Flemings had given up their lives. Owain walked among the ravaged bodies, searching the faces. Between his thumb and forefinger he rubbed at a coin—the Roman coin Richard had given him. As he bent over and laid hands on a body that was face down—hair the same color and length as his Gruffydd's—the coin fell onto the trampled, blood-stained grass. He grappled at the young man's bloody shirt and, breath held, turned him over. His heart leapt wildly to discover it was not his son.

Iolo Goch:

The tale of Owain's victory at Hyddgen spread far and wide. Welshmen, old and young, uchelwyr and peasants, came to join in the cause. A new age had come to Wales. A golden age, for we had a golden prince. That summer, the hills echoed with the song of bards and an army arose, the likes of which had not been known in the land for centuries.

From the highest summit of the five peaks of Plynlimon, the enemy could be spotted miles away. To the northeast ran the first rivulet that would become the broad waters of the mighty Severn; on the southeast slopes, where a crease formed between two of the peaks, the headwaters of the Wye rushed cold and clear.

The exultant wave of the victory at Hyddgen hurtled them through New Radnor, Montgomery and Welshpool. Heralding their leader, a new banner waved boldly: the golden dragon of Wales. Gone were the days of hiding away in mountain caves and stealing cattle. King Henry IV of England, sitting content in London, would soon learn of their triumphs.

23

Plynlimon, Wales — June, 1401

A GREAT CHEER ROSE up in the camp as Owain galloped into its midst. The returning soldiers passed out the casks of wine they had brought back from their raid into Radnorshire. They whooped with glee as they did so, tossing their loot into greedy hands and unloading sacks of grain and fresh vegetables.

As Owain dismounted, Iolo rushed up to greet him. The bard's once pale complexion was now bronzed by the sun's rays. In the nearly twenty years that Owain had known Iolo, he had never seen his friend's hands so soiled, his hair so unkempt or his small frame so thin that his clothes hung lank and ill-fitting upon his frame. This life of roving outdoors had not been to Iolo's liking, but the tales of their endeavors had filled his genius to overflowing.

"Ah! There will be song tonight," Iolo trilled, his delicately framed mouth spreading into a huge smile. "I've just finished a new ode in your honor, my lord. I think you'll be pleased. I know Lady Margaret will be delighted to hear it. But first, if you could grant your approval, it would mean much to me."

Owain tied his horse's reins to a tent stake. He glanced down at his surcoat and seeing the blood there he unbelted it and lifted it over his head. "Tomorrow, perhaps."

Iolo's smile drooped. "You are exhausted, certainly. A little rest should restore you."

Loud cries of "One, two, heave!" went up as wood was gathered and catapulted into a huge bonfire. The clamor of celebration grew.

Owain started toward the flap of his tent and then paused, looking back at Iolo. "Could you . . . could you bring some wine? Otherwise, I shall not sleep."

"Of course."

A short minute later, Iolo had returned. In his right hand, he held two jeweled goblets by the stem and in the crook of his left arm he clutched a small cask to his chest. "Judging by these goblets, you've had good success."

Owain's page worked with silent speed, fingers flying over the laces of his plate armor. When Owain was finally free of his chainmail, he took a sip of wine from his goblet. Then he set it down on a small table where the page had placed a basin of clean water for him. Repeatedly, Owain cupped the water in his hands and splashed it on his face to rinse the soot away. "Lord Charlton finally stopped us at Welshpool. But this time we left our mark."

"Welshpool? The king will hear of that."

Owain pulled on the clean shirt the page laid out for him and settled himself on a cushioned stool across from Iolo. With a flip of his hand the page scurried out. "He will hear of New Radnor, as well."

"New Radnor? What went on there?" By now Iolo was seated and leaning forward, waiting for the first strand of a story to unfold.

"We captured the entire garrison." He drained his goblet in one swallow.

"You have prisoners, then?"

"No." Owain winced. "They are headless. All sixty."

For a long minute it was painfully quiet inside the tent. Beyond the canvas walls, the drunken song of victory filled the valley.

Iolo studied his benefactor long and hard before asking, "Why so?"

"Conwy," Owain uttered.

But it was only one of many reasons. Owain meant to send a message to other English constables in Wales. Now that it was done it left him feeling anything but vindicated for the usurpation of the English throne from King Richard, the seizure of his lands, and the murder of nine Welshmen at Conwy. He stared at his distorted image reflected on the side of his goblet.

Rhys Ddu popped his head of wild black hair into the tent. "Ah, celebrating alone, I see."

"Owain, I . . . if you don't mind . . . I would like to join the others." Iolo rose. "Every harp in the camp will be possessed with song. Verse flows like a fountain when coaxed forth by good wine."

Dully, Owain nodded as Iolo left.

Rhys stepped inside. "I have just the thing to revive wearied bones. I shall send my girl along—ah, what is her name?" He scratched his head. "No matter. You'll sleep well afterward. Like a babe at his mother's breast."

When she came, Owain recognized her but vaguely from the time he had returned from Cadair Idris with Maredydd. On that night, she had kneaded at his stiff shoulders and although she had obviously been meant to be available for his needs, he had resisted. He lay stomach down on his bed as he had before. She trickled her little vial of oil onto her supple fingers and fanned them over his back. He closed his eyes and tried to forget the heinous scene at New Radnor in the castle yard. But the scents and sounds came back to him, even above the sweet-smelling oil and the warbling of his men: the iron tang of blood filled his nose, the whack of an axe blade falling, and the dense thud of a head striking the ground. He had witnessed only the first few, but the sight of sixty heads crowning the walls of the castle as he rode away were forever seared upon his mind.

How desperately he wanted to forget. Needed something, some-one to help him forget.

It's not fair to you, Owain, Margaret had said. *If you strayed from our vows, I would not —*

The girl's delicate hands worked their way up to his shoulders. He turned himself over, curved his fingers behind her slim, young neck and pulled her down to devour her with hard, needy kisses. Even as he made love to her, this firm-bosomed girl from the hills whose name he didn't know or care to ask, the echo of dying men's screams rang in his ears.

OWAIN STRETCHED AND YAWNED, his eyes still closed. Sweating from the late morning warmth, he bunched the sheets across his tor-so. Muffled voices reached his ears and he rolled over on his side. The nausea of too much wine ground at his insides.

"I had not expected so pleasing a sight, m'lord," chimed a sweet voice.

His eyes flew open. "Margaret?"

He shot up so suddenly that the sheet fell away, leaving him naked. His heart thumped wildly. The girl was gone—thank God.

"It was . . . it was hot . . . last n-n-night," he stuttered.

Margaret glanced at the two empty goblets on the table and then at her husband's clothing strewn about. "I saw Rhys when I arrived. Like everyone else here, it appears, he was in no state to be easily roused. I noticed your horse outside and took the chance that I would find you here. And I have."

She bent to pick up Owain's braes and handed them to him. Her wide cuffed sleeve fell away from her slender wrist. After all these years, eleven children, and a wealth of hardships since Henry had come to the throne, she was still exquisitely elegant and the thought of her lying dead on a mountain road somewhere sparked his protectiveness.

"Marged . . . I told you to stay." Standing, he pulled his braes on.

"You don't want me here?"

"That's not what I meant." As she turned toward the tent flap, he caught her wrist. "You were safer where you were. The English have been scouring the land looking for us. If they had come across you . . ."

She arched an indignant eyebrow at him. "Meanwhile, you appear to have made yourself very evident. If they wanted to find you, they would have had no trouble. Anyway, I had grown weary of hiding. I wanted . . . *needed* to see you. It's been months, Owain. When I heard of your recent successes, I thought the time was never better. I couldn't stay where I was a day longer. At first, I thought I missed our home, but then I realized it was you I longed to be with. A kind old man named Llywelyn ap Gruffydd escorted us here— without his help we would have been wandering in the mountains for days. I brought the children with me. Sion has been asking for weeks when we would see you again. All I could tell him was 'Soon, soon.'"

Owain fumbled with the cord on his leggings. As he turned to snatch his shirt from the floor, he bumped the table and the goblets toppled.

"Owain?" She touched his forearm. "My love, what troubles you?"

His eyes did not leave the pile of clothes at his feet.

She wrapped her hands around his neck and pressed her cheek to his bare chest.

"I didn't expect you, that's all," he finally said, encircling her waist.

"Should I leave, then?" she asked laughingly.

He had forgotten what comfort there was in her arms, even

though the physical nearness of her was bittersweet. "Stay awhile, Marged, won't you?"

Her arms slid down to his back, holding him tight. "Awhile, yes. We'll make the best of it." Her voice, already low and plaintive, softened even more until it was no more than a breathy whisper. "Who knows how long our days together will last?"

For a time there was peace at Plynlimon. Bards' songs filled the long days and starry nights. There was wine and food aplenty. Owain's children plucked wildflowers from the meadows and wove them into crowns. Gruffydd and Maredydd were young men now, proud soldiers boasting of their battles. Catrin, golden-haired Catrin, caught the eye of many a soldier, but simply went on with her sewing as they came to her with garment after garment for mending.

Owain wanted to draw strength from Margaret's presence, to confide in her as once he had, but the nightlong conversations of long ago were no more. Margaret talked briefly of the children's lessons and the goods Lowarch brought home from the market at Dolgellau each week. Owain, in turn, spoke of his plans to thwart Henry and drive the English from Wales, but Margaret had little to say in response, at first merely nodding and then later making it known she didn't want to hear about the war. But what else could he share with her? It was his life, the means to an end, the path to their future. Each day, the awkward pauses lengthened until finally, as they lay side by side at night, he turned from her, the silence as hurtful and baffling to him as it must have been to her.

Every day, he strode about camp and cheered his archers as they shot at their butts made out of haystacks. Afraid of growing soft with idleness, he frequently traded sword blows with young soldiers. He was all in the moment then, completely and ardently. In a way, Owain was merely passing time, for there were plans to be laid far more grandiose than the next battle.

When rumors stirred that King Henry had blackmailed enough funds out of his lords to raise an army, Margaret left Plynlimon to return the children to safety—and in that, Owain found some relief. Soon, his attention returned to the brown haired maiden who had shared his bed. Many times, Owain wondered if Margaret had noticed the longing glances that the young woman had bestowed upon him.

Still, though, he did not know the girl's name and when she came to him again, he did not ask, although it was Margaret's face he envisioned in the darkness as she unclothed herself and Margaret's name he said as he spent himself inside her.

24

Glyndyfrdwy, Wales — September, 1401

BENEATH THE SPRAWLING ROOTS of the fir trees that stood sentry on the mound above the house at Glyndyfrdwy, the bones of long-ago warriors rattled. On the earth above them, a secret gathering had commenced. Men huddled in a loose semicircle, nodding their heads and scratching at their whiskered chins as their eyes swept from west to east and back again along the river's course. Looping through the deep ravine below, the Dee murmured its conspiracy. The leaves upon a great oak that clung fiercely to its banks were mottled with the first brown of the harvest season.

Among those gathered were the Dean of St. Asaph and his two nephews Ieuan and Gruffydd from Powys. Their outspoken neighbor, Madog ap Ieuan, upon catching wind of the meeting, had left his scythe in the barn where it lay and raced northward with nothing more than the handful of coins he had received from the recent sale of his bull. His friend John Astwick, while chancing upon him in the darkness of a roadside tavern as he stopped in for a swallow of ale, offered to join him in any fray that involved the disturbing of the English. Robert Puleston, the often-drunk husband of Owain's older half-sister, who herself was the product of a youthful tryst of Gruffydd Fychan's, was on this rare occasion quite sober and coherent.

Sympathetic to their distant Welsh heritage, two of Margaret's brothers, Philip and Griffith Hanmer, were in attendance, although John, the oldest, would have no connection to this insurrectionist lot. He had, with fiery vehemence, warned them against any such affiliation. But Owain's charisma was far more appealing to them than John's patronizing. Since the death of Sir David Hanmer a year past, they had flocked to Owain like lambs to the shepherd. But of those there, only Owain carried a weapon. The English had forbidden any Welshman from bearing arms outright. To do so was to invite instant death upon discovery.

"Grey will come again," Tudur said, entering the ragged circle's center. The fingers of his left hand worried at the hem of his tunic. "It's only a question of time."

"Then we will prepare ourselves," Philip said. Griffith, at his side, nodded his agreement.

In two long strides, Tudur was before him. He locked his hands on Philip's angular shoulders. "Prepare for what? I tell you, we are marked, every one of us. Lord Grey will bring a hundred men and if that will not rid him of us, then two hundred, or three hundred. And mercy, we all know, is not a virtue he possesses. He will raze our homes and then he will hunt us down. How does one prepare for that?"

"We prepare ourselves," Gruffydd, shining with youth's boldness, spoke, "to fight."

Turning to him, Tudur threw his hands wide. "And how many soldiers do we number, Gruffydd? You are barely old enough to grow a beard. What of you, Robert? Could you fight if you had to? Your head is ever drowning in a barrel of ale. Hywel? You were born to the Church. Your hands will never seek a sword."

"Perhaps." Hywel shrugged. "But even soldiers need their

blessings."

Once again, they all nodded in agreement. Only Owain stood silent. The September breeze pulled at his long hair as he studied the men around him. They were a flock without a shepherd, a clan without a chieftain.

Never one to keep his thoughts to himself, Madog, who kept his head clean-shaven and went about bare legged even in the dead of winter, raised his voice above the muttering. "I will fight him! I will fight for Owain and I will fight for Wales!"

Cries of *'For Wales!'* and *'For Owain!'* rang out. Raising imaginary weapons, they shook their fists at the heavens.

"How? How?!" Owain shouted.

They all looked at him questioningly, except for the doubtful Tudur, who rolled his eyes, as if relieved that someone there possessed a shred of sanity.

With Tudur still in the middle of the circle, Owain ringed him, his steps slow and purposeful. "*How* will you fight him? With hoes? With hammers? With pot-hooks? Will you lie waiting day after day, night after night, waiting for *him* to come to you? Wondering whose house he will burn first? Whose wife he will rip from her bed to rape while you drown in a pool of your own blood? Do you all think that merely rising in anger, fighting madly against all the wrongs that have been dealt to you and your kin will give you the means to stop him? Do you? I tell you, your anger serves nothing." He paused before his son. Only the rustle of leaves answered. Nose to nose with Gruffydd, he screamed, "Do you know *how* you will fight him?!"

Gruffydd recoiled against the forceful wind of his father's words. He closed his eyes for a moment, as though summoning courage from somewhere deep inside. "Tell us," he whispered, opening his eyes, straightening himself. Then louder, "Tell us and we will do as you say."

Owain clutched Gruffydd in his arms and then stepped back. "It will be a long fight . . . and a hard one. You cannot even begin to imagine the agony of it. Such causes have great allure to men whose souls are starving, and dreams are the food of the soul. But you must weigh the price of something you can only imagine with the sound of bones crushing around you and the smell of blood. You must decide if the sacrifice is worth the lives of your brothers and sons. You must know, in the deepest chasms of your heart, that your life is all that you have to give and give it you will. You must believe that someday . . . someday, your children's children will live freely because of you."

He gazed at each man in turn. "I cannot promise any of you glory, or justice, or vengeance, or even freedom. I can only lead you to a chance at these."

Parting from the others, Philip reached a hand toward Owain. "Then lead us, Owain."

Owain clasped Philip's hand briefly. "Your trust in me is blind, dear brother, for I do not myself yet know where it is I'm going, but if you follow me . . . I will show you when, and how, to strike the first blow." With a roar, he pulled his sword from his belt and plunged it into the earth, both hands wrapped over the pommel. "Fight *with* me. Fight for Wales!"

Gruffydd placed his hand over his father's knuckles and soon hand after hand was laid on top. Even Tudur's—although Owain knew his brother would forever doubt not his courage or conviction, but that either of them should live to tell about this at all.

25

York, England — September, 1401

SIR DAFYDD WAS EN route to Scotland to deliver letters from Owain, with orders to give them up to none but the hands of King Robert himself. Other letters had been sent with all haste and secrecy to Ireland. They were offers of alliance. Owain was now looking beyond Wales to further his cause.

When he made it all the way to York, Sir Dafydd was certain he would achieve what he had been sent to do. He made it through the town gates just before they were shut for the night and rode through the muddy streets until he found an inn that was not already full. Before bedding down, he went to a tavern called The Red Bull. He ordered an ale, paid for it with coin that had been taken from New Radnor and found himself a dark corner. Perhaps it was because he had come so far with so little trouble that he felt uneasy, but he couldn't help but notice two cloaked men near the door passing glances between each other after he caught their eyes. Dafydd nursed his drink well into the evening. When the two men finally left and the tavern keeper ushered him out, he skulked along the alleyway toward the inn.

As the alley opened up to the main street, shadows blocked his path. The two men from the tavern had been waiting—like wolves stalking the straying lamb. Desperate, he threw his bag of coin at their feet and spun about in retreat. A fast set of hands snagged his mantle and he crashed to the ground. In the darkness, he saw only an upraised arm above him. Then, he saw no more.

It was not long before the letters to King Robert of Scotland found their way into Henry's palm. He read, with angry curiosity, the words that Owain's own hand had penned there:

> *"Humbly, I beseech you, my lord, upon my knees, that if it please you to send me a number of your men-at-arms, with the help of God, I may withstand your enemy and mine, a pretender, the one who falsely calls himself Henry, King of England . . ."*

Plynlimon, Wales — September, 1401

"IT CANNOT BE," OWAIN'S brother-in-law John Hanmer said. "His treasury hasn't the funds. Parliament forced him to cancel." Although John had been reluctant to openly side with Owain at first, he had been pressured by Henry to reveal Owain's whereabouts, which he refused to do. Eventually, it became clear he would either have to betray Owain or be declared a traitor himself. Blood had won the battle and when he arrived at camp a few days ago Owain had welcomed him with open arms.

"Yes, they *did.*" Gethin wrung his leather riding gloves. Putting a foot up on one of the logs that ringed the fire pit, he rested an elbow on his knee. Another month had passed at Plynlimon and by now the men, Gethin included, were growing restless. "But there are plenty of others who have the money and it would appear that they are with him on this matter."

"Their numbers?" Owain was standing closest to the fire.

Around him were gathered his most trusted advisors and his two oldest sons. The first chill of the season had settled over the mountains. Dark, wet clouds, promising rain, blotted out the stars.

"Forty or fifty thousand English troops already at Worcester," Gethin reported, "and that many more called to assemble there."

Maredydd, his hands tucked tightly into his armpits, was the first to express his shock. "Why so many?"

"He means war, son," Owain said flatly. "We have at last been deemed worthy of his full attention." Doubt began to gnaw at the pit of his stomach. He had expected Henry to return at some point, but not so soon or in such force. "I can only assume my message to King Robert was intercepted. Someone followed Sir Dafydd, took the letter from him and went straight to Henry. He means to crush us before Scotland can be stirred to action."

"Owain?" Tudur scanned the orange-lit faces around him and then looked at his brother with concern. "How are we to hold up against so large a force? How? It's impossible."

"You assume numbers are an advantage." Rhys Ddu's eyes beamed through the darkness. "They are many—and slow. They come with not only fletchers and bowyers, but priests and physicians, carpenters, gunners, cooks, and musicians. Perhaps we should call on Henry's minstrels to do battle with our bards."

"He would lose sorely then," Iolo proclaimed from the other side of the fire.

Owain sat down on the log next to where Gethin stood. Lost for an answer, he rubbed at the back of his neck, but nothing came to him. Without help, they could not stand against such a force. The heat of the flames licked at his face. He leaned back, sweat pooling on his breastbone. Then it came to him.

"Perhaps we should take a lesson from our Scottish kinsmen, my friends," Owain said. "The English fight by formal rules. They are numerous, well drilled and organized. But time after time they have ventured into Scotland only to be defeated by the land itself. Let them come looking for us, here, in Wales. They will spend their lives figuring out which mountain to look behind."

Gruffydd's upper lip curled in disgust. "So back to the caves?"

"My prince?" Gethin stepped boldly in front of Owain. "What if, rather than a spy, we sent someone to The Pretender who promised to lead him to us?"

"I don't quite follow you," Owain said.

Gethin smoothed his neatly trimmed beard. "Someone to guide him through the mountains. You spoke of the Scottish wilderness. Surely, the longer the English march through these mountains, the more they will be convinced this is an unforgiving, hostile land."

"And they would never find us?" Owain said.

"You're asking someone to forfeit their lives," said Rhys.

"We all potentially do that every time we ride from here, do we not?" Gethin replied.

Owain paced a few steps, weighing his options. "Do you know of a man who would do this, Gethin?"

Gethin nodded. "I know just the man. He was the one who brought your wife and children here."

Margaret had spoken kindly of Llywelyn ap Gruffydd. He had a son or two, even a grandson, serving under Owain. There were many men who would have volunteered for the chance to set Henry awry. But he trusted Gethin's choice in this. "Find him. Have him sent to me."

"Father!" Gruffydd grabbed his father's elbow. "You owe him your goodwill, not a death sentence."

"I hold no man in bondage here. He may decline, if he so chooses. And any who values his life above the freedom of Wales may leave us and go straight to the King of England and tell all."

Within the hour, Llywelyn was brought to Owain's tent. Before he could even ask it of the old man, Llywelyn threw himself at

Owain's feet and wept for joy at the opportunity to thwart the English king. He was too old, he explained, to last more than a few minutes in pitched battle, but this . . . this he could do for his prince and his people.

26

Llandovery, Wales — Late September, 1401

IN WORCESTER, LEOMINSTER, AND Chester, King Henry amassed his army. When they at last departed from Shrewsbury with Prince Harry commanding his own column from Hereford, they numbered a hundred thousand strong. Knights and gunners, clerks and chaplains, cooks and spearmen—the very sight of such an army inspired awe and fear. To the onlookers who peered at them from cottage doors, only slightly ajar, they must have looked like terror itself: overwhelming, absolute.

By the time they reached the gates of Llandovery, a gentle, warm mist had developed into a chilly downpour. Henry was in his tent that evening outside the town with a collection of his commanders. By the light of an oil lamp they muttered above a mess of maps. Their bickering drowned out the steady drumming of the rain.

Lord Charlton pointed at a blank spot on one of the smaller maps. "Perhaps there."

Fifteen-year old Prince Harry wrinkled his chiseled nose. "There is nothing there."

"Precisely," Charlton replied. "A perfect place to hide."

"Hide? They are probably right beneath our very noses." Sir

Gilbert Talbot crossed his arms. "I tell you, compared to us they are invisible."

"They are not so invisible when they leave behind their smoking ruins," Henry said.

A cold sheet of rain blasted into the tent as Sir John Greyndour entered. Charlton cursed and threw himself across the table to keep the maps from being soaked.

"Sire," Greyndour announced, his thinning yellow hair plastered to his wet forehead, "we have been approached by a man calling himself Llywelyn ap Gruffydd of Caeo in Carmarthenshire. He says he can lead us to the caves where the rebels are hiding."

Henry, who had been stooped over the maps for hours, straightened with interest. "And how does he know this?"

A confident smile lit Greyndour's face. "He has just come from there, m'lord."

TO SOME DEGREE, THE king's army was prepared for its task. Scotland had taught them about the remoteness of the mountain wilderness and the need to sustain themselves when the land could not. Yet it was that very practice of preparedness that bogged them down. Carts of cheese, mutton, pork and peas rumbled along in formation. Others were packed with the paraphernalia of war: longbows and bundles of arrows, cooking pots, horseshoes, and tents . . . even trumpets and fiddles. Henry was intent that not only would his troops be well armed, but that they would grow neither hungry nor bored.

What the English could not prepare for was the weather. The moment they stepped foot inside the Welsh border, it began to rain. In the marshes and flooded valleys, their encumbered carts became mired. Where there was not mud up to a man's knees, there were boulders around which the carts had to be maneuvered by hand.

With such a vast host, they could not venture far without their supplies. So they crept and crawled their way along, heads hung low and legs wearied to the marrow.

Llywelyn led them skillfully through the hills, sometimes choosing a narrower path which would later join up with a wider one where the footing was better. Although their course was a meandering one, Henry expressed no overt doubts about Llywelyn's knowledge. The old man had described the Welsh camp in such detail and even spoken of the rebel Glyndwr himself with such contempt that there was never any doubt in his mind that if anyone could lead them to the Welsh it was Llywelyn ap Gruffydd.

On the fifth day of their waterlogged expedition, they were strung out along the valley of the Wye under ominous black clouds. A tight line of horsemen were breaking the force of the headwaters just upstream. The king flipped his visor up, watching. He and his guard were still on the western slope, waiting impatiently until they were assured it was safe to cross, when booms of thunder rattled the earth. Beneath his helmet padding, the hair on Henry's scalp stood on end. A second later a stroke of lightning ripped from above and crashed close by. His horse startled. As the steed fought to bolt, swinging its hindquarters toward the lip of the precipice, Henry swallowed back his heart. Then it reared. There was nothing to do but hang on for dear life.

A page dove from his hackney and scrambled to catch the reins of the king's horse, but a hoof smashed him in the chest, hurtling him backward. Henry felt his weight pitching again. Rain slashed at his face, blinding him.

Swiftly, four of his men surrounded the horse and eased it down. The moment it had calmed enough, Henry dropped from his saddle.

"The boy?" he asked breathlessly.

Greyndour peered over the edge. Mindless of his own safety, Henry joined him. Frightened, round eyes stared up at them. The page had landed on a thin, rock-strewn ledge ten feet below.

"He'll live," Greyndour said. "A bit bruised, perhaps, but wiser."

Henry shuffled back and stared into the rain beneath his open visor. It slapped at his face in mockery. His eyelids drew down to slits. "Send me Llywelyn ap Gruffydd. By the Virgin Mary, I swear we were here not two days ago."

A few minutes later, Greyndour appeared with Llywelyn at his elbow.

Rivulets of water streamed over Henry's armor. Small rings of rust encircled the rivets on his gauntlets. He licked the raindrops from his mustache. "I would think the earth could hold no more water. Soon enough it will all be one vast sea. Think you not the same, Llywelyn?"

Rain falling on his bare, silver-fringed head, Llywelyn grinned.

"You know this area well," the king went on. "How long, given our impediments, before we reach this cave where Glyndwr and his men are concealed?"

Llywelyn's grin slipped away. "My lord, I have two fine sons. They both serve the true Prince of Wales, Owain Glyndwr, and, by my life, I will not betray him to you or any other man."

Henry gave a short laugh, shaking his head. When he began to speak, though, the laughter shattered and his voice strained in fury. "Then your life is forfeit. It is my son Harry who is Prince of Wales—not your restive chieftain who strikes at families in their homes while they lie sleeping. A curse on you and your kind. Dogs— all of you!" He slammed his palm into Llywelyn's sternum. The old man would have fallen over the edge had the guards not caught him. They nudged him forward and Henry stomped closer again, his face inches from Llywelyn's. "By my head, your head shall fall from your crooked shoulders and roll through the square at Llandovery! Let all your friends and kinsmen there gaze upon you and see what becomes of a liar and a traitor to the king."

While Llywelyn's hands were being tied behind him, he raised his angled chin proudly. "A liar I am and so confess. But I have not betrayed the king. After your father, you sir are Henry of Bolingbroke, the Duke of Lancaster."

"I *am* the king!" Henry screamed at him. Then he spun about and shoved his foot into his stirrup and vaulted onto his saddle. "Take him back to Llandovery immediately. He will meet his fate there. Or I will strangle him myself."

North Wales — October, 1401

"AND WHAT BECAME OF Llywelyn?" Owain cupped a bowl of bean potage between his hands. An hour ago, the bowl had warmed his hands, but he had not been hungry then. He was even less so now.

Squatting in the darkness of the tent, Gethin delivered the news stoically. A camp cur slunk along the ground to him, licking his hands in submission, but he pushed the dog's nose away. "He was escorted back to Llandovery. There, King Henry watched while the old man's fate was delivered by the hooded executioner."

Owain hung his head. A brutal end. Even Llywelyn had known it would come to that. But the sacrifice had bought them precious time, enough to escape the English, fly north and plunder there. Meanwhile, young Harry and his column had continued to struggle through the mountains in search of the Welsh rebels. But it had been the rebels who found them. As Harry's lines became strung out, almost losing contact with one another, a band of Welshmen led by Gethin descended upon the English in a mountain pass and cut off some of the wagons and extra horses, then rode away with them. In the ambush, a flight of arrows had been let loose. Lord Charlton, riding beside Prince Harry, caught an arrow through the neck and died in his saddle.

"Besides the ambush and Charlton's death," Owain said, "what other news from the south do you have?"

"They said Henry went mad with rage. He ordered Strata Florida Abbey to be leveled when he found some of the remains there of the baggage train Richard had taken to Ireland. The monks were herded into captivity. A few who resisted were murdered to serve as an example. Children from nearby homes were snatched up to serve in English households. Relics were smashed and looted and what could be burned was burned. While the English knights' horses were tethered to the high altar, they drowned themselves in communion wine. Fourteen days after entering flooded Wales, King Henry left with his defenseless prisoners in tow. They say the cries of innocent children still echo in the hills."

Owain scraped the last of the cold potage from the bowl with his fingers and flung it to the ground for the dog to eat. "We'll send another message to King Robert of Scotland. Meanwhile, I know someone else in the north who may be inclined to assist us against Bolingbroke."

Warkworth, England — October, 1401

HARRY HOTSPUR HAD SEEN it coming. His fingers pinched the edge of the table, girding himself for defeat. How many times in one day could this happen?

His wife, Elizabeth Mortimer, slid her queen in front of his king. "Checkmate!"

"Again?" He clamped a hand over his heart. "I am slain once more."

"You are impatient . . . and too easily distracted."

"By your beauty, but who would not be?"

Ignoring his flattery, she began collecting the chess pieces and arranging them in their carved walnut box. Wind hissed between the shutters of their chamber window. Elizabeth shivered visibly. "I dislike Warkworth, you know that. I swear there is no place draftier. Does the wind ever cease to assault this rock? I shall freeze to death before winter's end."

Hotspur leaned across the table, toppling the remaining pieces, and pressed his lips hungrily to Elizabeth's.

Laughing, she broke the kiss. "Trying to warm me, are you?"

"Oh, I can do much better than that, my love. Between the two of us, we could set the bed afire. Care to retire early?"

She answered with a shameless smile and Hotspur kissed her again, longer, more deeply.

The door swung open, blasting them both with frigid air. The Earl of Northumberland stomped into the room with a wolfish growl rumbling in his throat.

With his forehead still touching Elizabeth's, Hotspur turned his gaze to his father. "Would you at least have the courtesy to shut the door? Otherwise, my lovely wife will turn into an icicle that will shatter at my touch."

Northumberland inclined his grizzly mane toward the open door. "Elizabeth, forgive the interruption, but I must speak with my son. Political matters. I do not wish to bore you, my dear."

Rising, she whispered into her husband's ear, "Don't let him keep you long—or you'll find me asleep in a cocoon of goose down." On her way to the door, she touched her father-in-law on the shoulder in farewell, and then blew her husband a kiss. He caught it in his hand. Softly, she closed the door behind her.

Switching to his wife's seat, Hotspur collected a bishop that had fallen to the floor and twirled the marble piece between his thumb and forefinger. "Do you know she has beaten me three times today alone? The truth of it is, I *let* her win—and often. If she is happy,"—he arched a brow in suggestion—"the better my chances of benefitting from her happiness. Small price to pay for delayed reward, wouldn't you say? Now tell me, has King Robert changed his mind again?"

"Not Scotland this time."

"Who then?"

"Wales."

Hotspur stood, his attention now fully derailed from his wife's tantalizing invitation. "Glyndwr?"

Northumberland nodded.

"Well, what does he want with us?"

"Only to carry a request to the king. He'll end his rebellion if Henry will give his lands back and spare his life."

Hotspur scoffed. The wily Welshman was bold, if nothing else. "And do you think Henry will agree?"

"Henry? It's hard to say. If he were wise, yes. It would save him grief in the end to accept, not to mention preserve his treasury. But there are others who would stand to lose too much if he compromised with the Welsh now. The king's half-brother John Beaufort would surely not relish abandoning his new gifts. And Lord Grey . . . the man would sooner cut off his own head than see Glyndwr returned to his estates."

"So you'll deliver the message, Henry will refuse the offer and then . . . ?" Hotspur picked up a knight and placed it in the box, then broke into a smile. "What has any of this to do with us?"

"Us? It's your wife's nephew who bears as much claim to the crown as Henry. With Richard dead now, Glyndwr's not the only one who would rather see little Edmund Mortimer on the throne of England. He wants our support—and not just in word, but in deed."

"Meaning . . . ?"

"I think that is yet to be determined. Right now Glyndwr is playing both sides, but he knows Henry will refuse him. As for me, I'll stand by cautiously for now. And you—tread carefully, son. Ousting a king is risky business. I'd not recommend it."

"Henry did it."

"And look what that earned him: enemies."

27

Ruthin Castle, Wales — January, 1402

THE NIGHT SKY GLOWED deepest violet, clouds veiling an endless universe where clustered a million unseen stars. Before the dawning of the 31st of January, 1402, a dense fog crept from rimed tree to tree, clinging heavily to the glistening snowy meadows in between and crouching broad in the hushed vales. In Coed-Marchon, the twisted woods beyond Ruthin Castle, two hundred and fifty Welsh fighters hid.

Huddled between the mammoth roots of a centurial oak, Owain began his prayer. His lips, cracked from the dry air, moved in hurried whispers.

"*Pater noster, qui es in caelis, sanctificetur . . .*"

Time was short. He turned his face to the reddening sky, where the orange flames emanating from the village of Ruthin reached upward.

"This time, Almighty Father, I beg your forgiveness. I am omitting the blessing of mine enemy."

Pressed against the jagged bark next to him, Rhys Ddu kissed the smooth blade of his sword. "Allow me then: Almighty, bless our enemy with rashness, fuming anger and the gullibility that he might fall into our trap." He winked at Owain, then tucked his weapon beneath his stiff cloak. "And, oh yes . . . bless the bastard with a proper fear of Gethin's sword. Amen."

"Amen."

They fell silent, their breaths billowing in small frosted clouds and mingling with the mist. Dawn came in silver light sparked with ocher demons that danced upon the roofs of Ruthin. The screams began. Soon, Owain heard his small band of raiders riding from the village gates; their war cries cleaved the smoky banks of fog.

The castle garrison overlooking the candent town bolted in alarm. Groaning in protest, the gridded portcullis was lifted. Grey's company rushed forth, lured onward by the triumphant cries of the Welsh. In their midst rode Lord Grey himself, eager for revenge.

Ahead of the English, Gethin led his raiding party. Their rush torches blazed like taunting beacons as they sped toward the woods. They rode well spaced, each horseman following as far behind as the mist would allow.

When they reached an open hollow, Gethin's men dropped to the ground, shoved their torches into the packed snow and remounted. There, just beyond the field of torches in a crowded copse, rose the tops of Welsh helmets and spear tips glinting palely in the mirrored light of snow.

In the frosty air, Gethin sat upon his creaking saddle. Only the snorting of their horses and the scattered jingling of bits broke the silence. They waited, loosely clustered, until the snow-muffled clatter of hooves reached their ears. Then in practiced order, the twenty Welshmen followed Gethin. Swinging south of the thicket, the line of raiders dipped into a frozen swale, then climbed over a hill and plunged into the woods.

As the fog thinned and the first weak rays of sun pushed through, the last of Gethin's party lingered at the forest's edge. The lone rider paused just long enough to peel back the hood of his cloak and reveal himself. His sweeping golden hair glistened damply in the growing daylight.

GREY'S CONTINGENT CRESTED A rise overlooking the valley. Surely, he thought, that was Glyndwr himself, gloating over his destruction. White rage swelled inside him. He raised a hand and they halted. Then the figure turned and disappeared into the tangled woods.

On the western lip of the valley was a rough thicket where a dozen-and-a-half torch fires sputtered. Hastily, he surveyed the scene. A flash of metal caught his eye—a weapon concealed behind a bush there. Dark forms were hunched low in hiding, their tarnished helmets betraying them. Hard to discern in the diffused light of pre-dawn, but there was no doubt they were Welshmen waiting to ambush. Grey pointed to the south and he and his forty men quickly swung far from the copse and into the woods where the last of Gethin's people had disappeared.

TUDUR, WHO HAD PRETENDED to be his brother and was the last of Gethin's party to return, dropped from his mount when he reached the oak-crowded hill where the Welsh lay in concealment. He slapped his horse on the rump. Gethin, still mounted, tossed him a helmet to cover his bare head, and then plunged on his horse back into the thicket, along with several other men.

Catching eyes in the half-dark with Owain, Tudur nodded once then fused himself to a tree next to Gruffydd. They did not have to wait long for their ruse to be discovered.

As Grey and his men came crashing through the woods, the trees came to life. Naked branches transformed into spears and axe hafts. A sea of Welsh blades flashed and engulfed the English on three sides.

In frantic chaos, some of Grey's party spun about, seeking retreat to the rear, their horses crashing into one another. But even as they put spurs to flanks and turned back toward Ruthin, Gethin and his marauders surged from behind and blocked their way.

"Fight, men! Cut through!" Grey screamed.

The first Englishman was skewered at the tip of a spear.

Tighter and tighter, the English huddle drew as their men were picked off one by one, dropping in pools of bloody snow upon the frozen ground. Grey slashed out, his weapon swinging wildly, striking no one. The lopsided fray was as fleeting as it was fierce. The end came when the butt end of a pike smacked into Grey's neck and toppled him from his horse.

He lay face up on the cold earth, eyes wide in shock. His sword lay just beyond his grasp. With a jerk of his arm, he freed his dagger, but as he did so a circle of twenty spears hovered above him.

Owain kept his voice level as he stepped between two of the spearmen. "I believe this is when you beg for mercy, my goodly lord."

His knuckles whitening as he gripped the dagger, Grey swallowed hard. "You heathens bear no mercy toward any."

Only a handful of Grey's soldiers had been spared, enough to carry back the shameful tale of their defeat. The rest had been cut down fleeing or fighting.

"No mercy?" Owain unsheathed his sword. "What a grand idea. I will remember that."

But it was Gruffydd who pressed the flat of his blade, gleaming with blood, firmly across Grey's naked throat. His arm quivered with a barely contained rage.

"You may have kept Elise from me," Gruffydd said, drawing a piece of well-worn parchment from beneath his tunic just enough to reveal its constant proximity to his heart, "but I know the truth."

Jaw taut, Grey drawled, "Truth? You are late in your tidings, pup. My niece left the abbey long ago after bearing your bastard. It was a blessing the whelp was born dead. The Church would not have her, whore that she was, so I convinced a Flemish merchant to take her as his wife . . . She carries his child now." He licked away the trickle of blood at the corner of his mouth. "It is cruel to envision, is it not, her lying there trembling in pleasure beneath the loins of some other man?"

"I never lay with her. I have more honor than that. The child was *yours*." Gruffydd's boot smashed down on Grey's bare wrist. With a shriek, the lord's dagger fell from his fingers. "Rape and incest. Murder and thievery. Is there a crime left you have not committed?"

Then Gruffydd extended his other hand toward Tudur, who gave him a smoking rush light. Slowly, he lowered the flame until Grey's naked cheek reddened from the heat. "I will introduce you to hell long before your actual death." Grinning smugly, he stepped away.

In seconds, Welsh soldiers had shoved Grey's bruised face into the snow and were binding his hands behind his back. Then gruffly, they yanked off his battered helmet and hoisted him up to stand before Owain.

Swinging his sword back and forth at his side, Owain approached Grey. "Much as I want to make a sacrifice of you, heathen that I am, and see you bleed to death here and now for all the wrongs you have caused, I won't grant you such mercy. That would be too kind."

Eyes red from smoke, Grey glared at him. He took two faltering steps, the rope that bound his hands cutting deeply into his wrists. Fast behind him, Rhys kicked at the back of his legs. Grey stumbled forward, landing on his knees an arm's reach from Owain.

Lord Grey knelt before his archenemy on a carpet of blood-splattered snow, the bodies of his garrison strewn about him like squashed flies. Beads of melted snow dripped from the end of his nose. He spat at Owain's boots. "Raise your God damn, bloody sword and take my head. Do it! Get on with it, you fucking bastard! You've killed so many, what is one more? Put my head in a basket and deliver it to London. I care not. You will get yours . . . one day."

"I will get . . ."—Owain lifted his weapon up, then back—"what was mine to begin with." He thrust the long blade forward. Iron sliced the air.

Grey's eyes shut instinctively. Cold metal kissed his neck. When he looked again, Owain held the sword level, a teasing inch from his jugular.

"So easy," Owain said, his lips tight. "It would be so *very* easy to kill you. But it would bring me a great deal more satisfaction to see you suffer and live with what you have done . . . and the knowledge that I have beaten you. I hope you live long."

In slow cruelty, Owain withdrew the blade and then motioned to one of his men. Grey's horse was brought up and they shoved him onto the saddle as roughly as a miller handles a sack of flour. Gethin slung a noose around Grey's neck and pulled the knot tight until he gagged.

Grey glared at Gethin. "Going to hang me from my own walls, then? Fitting justice from the hands of a criminal."

The invitation was a temptation to Owain, but he muffled his amusement in trade for a more suiting punishment. "A sweet sight it would be. But that's not your noose."

"It is a leash, Lord Grey," Gruffydd announced, smiling great and broad. "We wish to keep you close at hand. There's value on your head, ugly as it is."

"Gruffydd," Owain wagged his sword, "I grant you a prisoner."

By the look on his face, nothing could have satisfied Gruffydd more.

The six remaining English soldiers were stripped of their weapons, armor and shirts and tied together to the trunk of a large tree.

It was midmorning before Owain and his men rode out from the woods of Coed-Marchon. Grey, who had left without a cloak that morning, shivered convulsively. As they passed the thicket which the English had so prudently avoided, Tudur went and plucked up the last fizzling rushlight. He set fire to the helmeted figures, which were nothing more than cloaks and tunics stuffed with dry straw and set on poles.

THE BUILDING CONTAINING THE ruthless Marcher Lord was a single room building, wide enough for two men to lie abreast and one and a half times the length of a man, but not nearly tall enough to stand in. Once, it had served as a sheep cote; now it was a prison. The floor was a mixture of dirt and manure, his bed a pile of moldy straw. It was comprised of aged oak beams and a loosely planked roof that acted as a sieve whenever it rained. Between some of the beams of the walls was enough space to slide a man's arm halfway to his elbow. It was through these slats that his meals came and dirty dishes went. The wind funneled and whipped through the cracks like knives flung at his skull. He tried to burrow his way out with his fingernails, but his captors had already thought that possibility through and hammered iron rods deep into the surrounding ground. When they threw Grey in this ignominious cell, they nailed the door shut. He was forced to bury his own feces and endure the stench of his own urine.

As if living in his own effluvium was not enough, his Welsh tormentors would dance and sing outside his tinderbox prison, juggling torches and sprinkling the walls with boiling pitch nightly. Glyndwr's oldest son Gruffydd seemed to take the greatest delight in it, circling with the satisfaction of a hawk above a wounded hare. Occasionally, Gruffydd would cease his pacing, glare with judgmental eyeballs at Grey, and chant, "Rapist, murderer, thief, traitor, rapist, murderer . . ."

Sleep became Grey's only desire. He teetered on the brink of madness, fantasies of revenge filling his waking moments and nightmares of fiery death consuming his dreams.

Iolo Goch:

Before spring's end, Lord Reginald de Grey of Ruthin was escorted by Gruffydd ap Owain under the dark of night to Dolbadarn Castle. The view from his single, barred window was unchanging: wild, rough mountains that pierced the sky's lid, their image mirrored in the sullen black waters of Llyn Peris.

Each evening as the sun retreated, a blazing star trailed its fiery tail across the Stygian darkness. To Lord Grey, it was an omen of ill portent. To the bards who sang of Owain Glyndwr, it was the resurrection of Myrddin Emrys's prophecies—that Arthur had come again.

In order to raise the astronomical sixteen thousand pounds in gold that were demanded by Glyndwr for ransom, Grey's manor in Kent was sold off. The drain on Grey's finances would leave him forever penniless.

28

Harlech Castle, Wales — May, 1402

ETWEEN THE DEEP BLUE waters of Tremadoc Bay and mountains couched in lavender mist, Harlech Castle thrust majestically skyward, washed in the yellow-pink of morning's first light. Owain stood at the head of his army on the ragged shoreline. He coveted every stone.

"How many?" he asked, as his kinsman Gwilym ap Tudur rode up beside him.

Dropping to the ground, Gwilym dashed a coating of sand from the front of his tunic. "Roughly a hundred men-at-arms, give or take a dozen . . . and over four hundred of those nasty Cheshire archers."

"Five hundred? Are you certain?" Owain asked skeptically.

Gwilym's thin lips twisted in a sneer. "I am. Seems they were expecting us."

A warm breeze tossed Owain's hair across his eyes. He turned and peered at his men through a veil of graying strands. "What now?"

"Into the mountains," Gethin answered.

"Mountains? For what?" Tudur's weariness was evident in the slump of his shoulders. "To hide again?"

Gethin shook his head. "No. To Maelienydd: Mortimer lands. There's much bounty yet to be had between the Severn and the Lugg."

"Maelienydd? Maelienydd . . ." Owain shaded his eyes with a hand and gazed at Harlech's titanic walls. "They wouldn't expect us to provoke a Mortimer, would they?"

Rhys Ddu spat. "Ach, only thing Henry expects of you, Owain, is sheer madness."

"Madness, genius, are they not the same?"

Rhys nodded toward the mountains. "Come on then. Maelienydd awaits."

The Welsh army withdrew eastward—back into the wilderness from which they had crawled. Harlech's garrison hadn't even been afforded the satisfaction of sending a caveat of arrows. The castle was safe in English hands. For now.

Pilleth, Wales — June 22nd, 1402

WHEN NEWS OF THE burning of Bleddfa Church in Maelienydd by Welsh raiders reached Ludlow Castle, Sir Edmund Mortimer did not hesitate. Although he was the uncle of the young Earl of March, he had sworn his loyalty to King Henry and leapt at this opportunity to prove himself, for he did not wish to give the king any cause to suspect that he wished his kinsman on the throne instead. Thus far, his sister Elizabeth's husband, Harry Hotspur, had proven steadfast as well, although Hotspur had quarreled with the king repeatedly over the delay of payments due to him.

Lured at first toward Knighton by the latest attack, Mortimer found nothing but smoking ashes. He then led his army southward into the throat of the Lugg Valley, threading along the trails that were once Roman roads. A steady week of rain had left the valleys flooded and so Mortimer kept his army clinging to the slick hillsides. Through crowds of oak leaning into the mired valleys, the English trudged, their eyes alternating between the treacherous path and the rumbling sky.

Slowed by a growing mountain of plunder, it appeared the Welsh were being chased down like fading hares. On the 21st of June, the English bedded down at Whitton. Mortimer's scouts had reported that the Welsh were camped on the emerald skirt of Bryn Glas, a hill less than a mile away from the village of Pilleth. The presence of the dragon standard had been confirmed.

At last. He would bring to battle and destroy the rebel Glyndwr.

LATE INTO THE NIGHT, Owain knelt in fevered prayer before the effigy of the Virgin Mary in Pilleth Church. Sleep, when it finally came, was broken and fraught with worry. When St. Alban's Day dawned, the air was already steaming. He rose, donned his armor, and prayed again before mounting his war horse. Owain's helmet, polished but with many dents, rested on his saddle before him. Sweat trickled over his temples.

Rhys Ddu pulled up beside him on his horse. "Fifteen hundred. And they look very sober about the whole matter."

"Gethin?" Owain began. "As always, should I fall, you will take command."

Gethin nodded only once. His countenance was as rigid as his brass-edged breastplate.

As they watched the English columns advance, tall standards bobbing in rhythm and lance tips pointing heavenward, Owain pulled on his helmet. A page scuttled forth and handed up his dragon-adorned shield and newly whetted great sword. "Did you mark the point, Rhys?"

"I did. We'll be within almost bowshot when they come abreast of that row of hawthorns," Rhys noted, pointing.

"Good. When they get there, but not before, we turn back and go up Bryn Glas."

"And give them our backs as targets?" Tudur said.

"If our timing is right, we'll be just beyond their reach. Archers must stand still to shoot."

"What if Mortimer doesn't follow us?"

"Oh, he will. He will. 'Tis a sure thing in his eyes. They outnumber us two to one. Mortimer needs to prove his loyalty and we're going to let him try."

Tudur scoffed. "Jesus, Mary and Joseph. We should've burnt the damn church and left."

Owain gave him a sideways glance, and then turned his sights back on the nearing English. "Did you find the monk you were looking for at Mynachdy last night, Gethin?"

Gethin weighed his favorite axe in both hands. "I did." His eyes narrowed as he looked east into the low morning sun. "Be mindful of the first flight."

"Positions," Owain commanded. He glanced toward the lines, searching. The smell of mud and sweat rising from his soldiers mingled into one heavy stench. His sons, Gruffydd and Maredydd, were there . . . somewhere. But each face looked like the one next to it— gazing on at the enemy in macabre state as the throb of battle drums shook the earth beneath their feet.

Pushing forward, Mortimer's archers, mostly men from the Welsh brink of Maelienydd itself, packed into their menacing wedge shapes. Clutching the shafts, the bowmen pushed their points into the soggy ground before them, so that they might easily snatch them up for ensuing volleys.

"Retreat!" came Owain's order. The word echoed down the lines as the Welsh turned like a tidal wave breaking against the shore. Hooves and feet pounded toward the hill. Urging his horse along behind the lines, Owain shouted at them to move faster, faster, faster. By all appearances, the maneuver was an inch short of bedlam and a mile short of genius.

The first pluck of arrows nestled against their bow staves. Waxed strings stretched taut.

"Pull!" Death's chorus sang out.

Owain glanced toward the hissing hail. The sky was black and moving.

The first arrow pierced the skull of a Welsh soldier. His body flew forward with the force; then his face slammed onto the trampled ground. No one paused to check if he was still alive, or even to claim his body. They were all running for their lives.

Owain's horse stumbled and then regained himself. They were almost clear of arrow range. Almost.

It was in that moment when Owain thought safety was at hand—the flight of arrows having largely fallen short—that he felt the white heat of a broadhead pierce through his mail and into his flesh. Just below his right calf, a tendon snapped, sending a knife of pain through his entire body. His horse reared as the arrow punctured the animal's ribcage. Owain gripped the reins and pulled them in to his chest, hanging on. The ground whirled. Bodies lay scattered around him in a moaning, writhing sea.

"Owain!" Tudur called as he rode up and grabbed the reins from his brother. "Take my horse!" He abandoned his shield and dismounted as a roar arose from the English ranks.

Swooning, Owain looked down. "I can't." His breath was shallow and ragged as he fought the white blazing fire that consumed him. His horse staggered. His weapon fell from his grasp. His fingers fumbled at the straps of his shield, but he couldn't loosen it. "You'll have to . . . break off the shaft."

Tudur snapped the shaft as close to Owain's leg as he could. Then in one brusque jerk Owain wrenched his leg free. Blood gushed down his leg and streamed onto the ground. Pulling his horse close, Tudur yanked the shield from Owain's arm and helped him onto his saddle. Then, he gathered the trailing reins and sprinted on foot toward Bryn Glas.

Another rain of arrows pursued them as Tudur guided his horse with haste over the litter of bodies. It was a long, arduous run. His breath heaved and his pace began to slow. When at last he reached the Welsh lines, he collapsed.

Faceless soldiers surrounded Owain. Relieved, he kicked his good leg free of the stirrup and tried to swing it over the saddle, but instead his body pitched backward. Arms enclosed him, safely lowering him to the ground.

Strangely, he no longer felt pain. Nor could he discern the words being spoken to him. Or see . . .

CONVINCED THE WELSH WERE in retreat, Mortimer ordered the advance. Mounted knights pressed through the line of archers and the charge began. Fury-bent, the English knights were focused on nothing but the breathless Welsh soldiers cleaving to the slick, grassy slope. So intent they were as they thundered across the plain that they did not sense the torrent of arrows closing in on their backs.

Edmund Mortimer gazed on in horror from behind his lines. His jaw hung frozen. English knights and horses dropped like flies on the open field.

Beside him, Sir Walter Devereux mumbled in disgust, "Your trusted Welsh archers . . ."

The very same archers, who only moments ago had sent their arrows into the Welsh lines, had turned without warning on their English masters.

"Judas." Mortimer groaned as his stomach turned in on itself. He flipped his visor down and headed into the ill-fated fray.

THE GLOW FROM THE oil lamp was harsh upon Gethin's dark features, cleaving grave shadows above his cheekbones and pushing back even further eyes that were already deeply set. He stood in judgment before his commander.

When Owain had finally regained consciousness, he found himself at Mynachdy, his lower leg heavily bandaged and his head light from loss of blood. Iolo described the battle and its aftermath in great detail to him. The defection of the Welsh archers over to the rebels had inscribed Mortimer's lot that day. Near to a thousand Herefordshire men had fallen. Welsh losses, thankfully, were only a fraction and most of those had been in the first flight of arrows. Owain's general, Rhys Gethin of Cwm Llanerch had commanded the fight brilliantly, but afterwards he consented that a rabble of hill women be allowed to pick over the dead and ransom their bodies. And when those women undressed the English corpses and with their knives cut off unmentionable parts, Gethin had walked among them without a word of reproach.

"Sir Edmund Mortimer was taken prisoner," Gethin said.

"So I heard." While pleased with that fact, Owain could not have been more disturbed by Gethin's actions that day. He had trusted the man. Gethin had dishonored the dead. It was unforgivable.

"He'll fetch a healthy ransom," Gethin added.

"If I ask for one."

Gethin eyed him questioningly.

With his wounded leg propped up on the table, Owain straightened in his chair. The shift brought a wince and he slouched back into the comfort of its cushions. His eyes went shut for a moment, and then opened with their accusation. "Enough of Mortimer for now. What you have done . . . it is not war. It is a mortal sin."

The condemnation wafted over Gethin. Clearly, he would not

allow himself to be so casually damned, even by Owain.

Tenderly, Owain rubbed at the dressing around his arrow wound. "I will not speak of it again. Nor shall you. God will judge you for it one day. For now, I've need of you. But don't *ever* let it happen again. If you do, your fate will be the same. I'll see to it."

Gethin's mouth opened, but Owain stayed him with a hand and pointed to the heavy tent flap. "Leave," Owain said lowly, his voice choked with shame. "I find it hard to look at you, knowing."

In the blackness of Gethin's eyes there smoldered something of long ago. He stared at Owain and turned to take his leave, but before he reached the exit, he spun around.

"When I was —"

"I said leave!"

"No, no. I won't scuttle off at the parting of your chastising lips. You *will* hear me out or you will do without me." His words fell with the weight of boulders from a sea cliff. "When I was eighteen, I was newly married and my wife . . . she was carrying our first child. The English forced their way into our home and . . . and they raped her." A single shudder gripped him and he went on, remarkably stoic.

"When she struck one of them, he cut off her hand. She screamed and screamed until he bashed her skull in. And while they did this to her, they had me tied to a post. I watched her die and there was nothing . . . *nothing* I could do . . . until today." Without waiting for Owain's response, he left.

The quiet of midnight suffocating him, Owain clasped his hands in prayer. He stared into the lamplight above his knuckles and whispered, "Almighty Father, I do not want this burden. Why then have you given it to me?"

29

Sycharth, Wales — July, 1402

"GET UP."

Sir Edmund Mortimer rubbed the sleep from his eyes as they gained focus. At the foot of his bed stood the one he recognized as Rhys Gethin. Visions of his possessed nature on the field at Pilleth swept over Edmund and he recoiled toward the wall, waiting for the swift mortal stroke of a blade. Behind Gethin stood four guards, one of them holding a lantern that cast a dim glow throughout Edmund's room of confinement at Sycharth.

"Get up," Gethin repeated with a sneer of contempt.

Edmund had no desire to cross him. He doubted there was any soul at all to the dark heathen.

Never taking his eyes from the man, Edmund put his feet on the floor and asked, "What hour is it?" It had been the first night in weeks he had slept deeply—only to be awakened by this walking nightmare.

"No matter. Get dressed." Gethin nodded and one of the guards threw a pile of clothing at Edmund's feet. "And make haste. You're wasting time."

They were new clothes, the stitching still taut. Edmund felt the suppleness of satin beneath his fingers as he bent to gather them. If he were to die today, why such finery? Why not a tunic of hemp?

While Gethin and his accompaniment watched impatiently, Edmund doffed his threadbare nightshirt and pulled on a pair of scarlet leggings. Once secured, he then picked up the shirt and squeezed his hands through the tight cuffs. The elbows of the sleeves hung in drooping billows. Out of an almost forgotten habit, he straightened the tunic and then belted it. They were trappings fit for a man of his station and somehow they lent him a sense of being refreshed. The shoes that Gethin thrust at him were fur-lined. Slipping his feet inside, Edmund paused.

"Will you impart the purpose of this rude awakening? If my time is short, I wish to prepare myself to meet Our Father."

"You'll find out soon enough. Come."

As Gethin turned his back and the guards ringed Edmund in a tight circle, he mused on the new set of clothing and wondered if it were at all possible that Henry had finally delivered the ransom. He ran his fingers, still stiff from sleep, through his uncut hair, raking the tangles away as they led him through a narrow corridor, down the stairs and through the great hall to the door of another chamber. The walls were lined with copper lanterns housing candles of beeswax, their wicks neatly trimmed. The lead guard knocked at the door and it swung inward.

Edmund shuffled in, blinking at the brightness. A fire had been newly lit, the tinder still sparking, the logs blazing in full. At the far side of the room, behind a writing table sat a golden-haired man, his temples frosted with silver. An inkwell and plumed quill were neatly arranged in the corner of the table and a single roll of parchment lay in its middle. He did not need an introduction.

Owain rose to his feet and without hesitation stepped around the table. As he did so, Edmund was astonished at his height.

"Sir Edmund." Owain smiled with vigor, even though it was late into the night. With a flip of his hand, a servant flew forth with a great tankard of spiced mead. "I never welcome a guest without a hale drink."

"Guest, m'lord?" The term sat strangely on Edmund's lips. He held the tankard loosely in his hands, staring into its depths. "I am indeed grateful that you have spared me, but I wish to return home."

"I would imagine you do." Owain drank from his own tankard. He absently wiped at the corners of his mouth, gazing at Edmund almost with a look of regret. "Bolingbroke has come to Wales . . . and left again as quick. He finds the weather disagreeable." A spark of amusement danced in Owain's eyes. He seated himself again and took another, deeper swallow of mead. Tapping the broken seal of the roll before him, he asked Edmund, "Why do you serve Henry of Bolingbroke?"

"He is the King of England."

"Hmm, yes. So says Parliament." Owain indicated two chairs on either side of the hearth. "But what of your nephew, the young Earl of March?"

Edmund had no ready answer. Feeling the need for warmth, he claimed the chair closest to the fire, but opposite the door, so he could be aware of Gethin's movements. His own room was perpetually drafty and cold. There was no hearth in it and the peat brazier they had given him was hardly enough to warm it entirely.

"Gethin," Owain said, "Wait outside, please. There is no reason for a guard here."

As Gethin exited with his guardsmen, Owain moved toward the chair opposite Edmund. Each halting step brought an obvious grimace to Owain's face. Edmund had seen the arrow pierce his calf, seen his brother Tudur race across the battlefield to lead his horse to safety and then watched Owain fall from the saddle. He marveled that the Welshman was here before him at all, let alone up on his feet already.

"Now tell me outright," Owain began as he carefully lowered himself into the chair and leaned forward, "tell me how it is that you serve Henry of Bolingbroke."

Why the interrogation? There was nothing to discuss. Henry had returned to England, forced Richard from the throne and taken the crown. That was that. Was it really so complicated?

Edmund cupped the tankard between his palms and gazed into its amber depths. "My ransom? Has it been delivered?"

The fire popped and sizzled. Owain pulled at his beard. "No."

"When will he send it?"

Owain stood then and took the letter from the table.

Hesitating, Sir Edmund received it from Owain's outstretched hand. He skimmed its contents. Disbelief, then shock, surged through him. He re-read it, this time more slowly to be certain he had not misinterpreted it. "This cannot be. It's a forgery."

"That is the king's seal, is it not? And the handwriting . . . Sir Edmund, you know Henry's penmanship well. It is no forgery, I assure you. He accuses you of collusion at Pilleth."

Edmund dropped the letter into his lap as his eyes met Owain's. "Why would I—why would any man . . .?" He covered his face with his hands to try to hold back the anger now roiling inside him. "How could he even suggest this? I have been nothing but loyal. The archers betrayed me. It was none of my doing. None!"

"It was convenient for Henry to blame you, that is all."

His hands fell away. "But what of Lord Grey? You took him prisoner and Henry made certain his ransom was met. And he was no kinsman of the king."

"Grey was not in line for the throne, either," Owain said. In three strides he was back behind his writing table.

"Do you think . . . do you think he would harm my nephews?"

"If he did, that would put you closer to the throne, would it not? Perhaps he's betting that I'll end your life out of retaliation for him not delivering on the ransom I requested for you—and it was a modest amount, I might add. He could have found the money, if he had wanted to."

Edmund approached him, the letter clenched in his hands. "So what does this mean? What will become of me?"

"That will be up to you," Owain said. "At this stage it would be rather useless to kill you, wouldn't it? Although judging by your cousin's attitude it would likely please him if I did so. Take the letter. Think on it. Then perhaps you should tell me what I ought to do with you."

"You haven't planned for my execution, then?"

"You have no value to me dead, Sir Edmund. I assure you."

Edmund scoffed. "I fail to see how I have any value to you alive then, either."

"Oh, but you do, you do. Think on it. Call for me when you have an answer."

"You'll let me go?"

"Ah, no, no. You misunderstand me. I'm saying you should take time to think about it. Should you come up with a favorable solution, you may yet gain your freedom."

With that, Owain called for the guards. Edmund was more confused and uncertain than he had been an hour ago. As he was escorted toward the door, he glanced back at Owain. His chin was propped on folded hands, his gaze on nothing in particular. Having finally met the man, Edmund wasn't sure what to make of him. Certainly, he was not the ruthless savage tales had portrayed him as. On the contrary, he was almost soft-spoken, deliberate in his speech.

In his room, while the last few hours of night trudged on, Edmund thought long and hard on his unlikely predicament. He had been tossed away by his cousin the king, at whose command his nephews' fate also rested. Little Edmund and his younger brother Roger were kept under close guard at Windsor Castle. Two young boys who knew very little of the pivotal role they played. He had sworn to his brother Roger, the late Earl of March, sworn on his life that he would protect the boys. It was a stroke of misfortune Roger had been killed in Kells. How very different this whole thing would have played out if his brother had lived to fight for the inheritance that Richard had named him to. How different it all might have been if Richard had ruled more wisely.

How different it all might have been . . .

Henry had accused him of taking sides with the rebels. Glyndwr was right. His capture, this fabrication of treason, was all a convenient way for Henry to rid himself of little Edmund's only remaining protector. Did Henry indeed wish him dead at Glyndwr's hands? Yet Owain Glyndwr seemed unlikely to send him to his death. So what then was it that Glyndwr wanted from him?

As the first silvery glow of dawn pried through the cracks around his window, Edmund took out the letter and read it once more. Then, he gave its words up to the flame of his candle.

MARGARET WAS FIXATED ON a piece of needlework when Owain limped into the room late the next morning. Startled by the opening of the door, she pricked her finger and gasped. "Owain! I didn't hear you arrive."

"I have been home some time now." Each word was thick and clumsy on his tongue. He was beyond exhausted. The journey had drained him. It had taken nearly two weeks for Owain to recover from his arrow wound well enough to travel from Pilleth to Sycharth.

"Oh, how long?" Margaret placed her work in her lap.

Trying to rid himself of a clawing ache, Owain rubbed at his forehead. "We rode in late last night. I didn't want to awaken you."

She did not ask where he had been or how long he would stay. She did not even rise from her bench, although it had been weeks since they had seen each other. Her fingers busied themselves with the needlework, flying deftly among the colored threads. When Owain's foot scraped the floor heavily, she finally started toward him. "Your leg —"

He waved her away. "Improving quickly. Although it begins to throb still if I stand too long."

In actuality, there wasn't a waking moment when it didn't pain him and the scar was hideous, but no need to concern her. The less she knew of such things the better. He pulled off his boots and began to undress. "Marged?"

"Yes?" She came to him then and sat down on the bed an arm's length from him, her body rigid, as though they were mere acquaintances and not a husband and wife of nearly twenty years.

"Mortimer? Has he fared well in his stay here? I trust he has given you no trouble?"

"No, none. But Catrin, I am concerned, my love. I know she is of an age, but she seems overly intrigued by him. He is considerably older . . ."

"Ten years, perhaps. 'Tis not unnatural." He slipped under the covers and turned away from her. "And the children have been well, I trust?"

"Yes," she said softly, "very."

Owain heard the disappointment in her voice. He wanted to ask more, wanted to tell her about events, carefully abridged for feminine ears, but the effort was more than he could bear. *What does one say when there is nothing shared? Would she understand anything of politics and strategies?* He had come here mainly to break the news to Mortimer about Henry's bold-faced accusations. He and Marged would need time to get to know each other again . . .

If only he could promise her that he could stay for awhile. But there was so much to be done. So great a price to pay for freedom.

Iolo Goch:

Far to the north, Scots poured across England's border and raided into the Scottish Marches. The Earl of Northumberland was consumed with defending his holdings. Meanwhile, coastal towns along the English Channel were harried by French fleets. With Henry conveniently distracted, the Welsh, who were still riding on the crest of victory at Pilleth, stormed through Gwent and Glamorgan in southernmost Wales to take Caerleon, Usk, Caerphilly, Abergavenny and a string of other undermanned castles.

Castle by castle, my lord Owain was driving the English out of Wales. He was indeed Y Mab Darogan: the Son of Prophecy.

30

North Wales — September, 1402

THE WELSH WHO HAD once relied on the English for commerce and protection, now flocked to the golden dragon banner of Owain Glyndwr—and that infuriated Henry. Their defection was an insult he could no longer ignore. Once again, preparations were made to march. By now, he so hated Wales and its people that he would just as soon cut them loose as reel them in.

Plagued by reoccurring bouts of subtle illness, Henry was in a reluctant state of commitment. At first, he thought he merely suffered bruises that were slow to heal, but time betrayed that the strange discolorations of his skin were something more. His fingertips were numb extensions and if he did not watch what he was doing, he sometimes found it hard to perform even simple tasks, such as dressing himself or cutting his own meat. More and more he called on a page to do these things for him. It humiliated him to do so and stripped him of his pride, but he would not have others see him perform menial tasks like a clumsy buffoon. Even a sword felt so much heavier to hold than he remembered.

A king must not show any sign of his failing strength. A king *must* be strong, mighty, indomitable. But how his bones ached. Where was the suppleness of youth? Was this what it was to grow old and infirm? Sometimes it was hard to rise from bed. It was particularly true when the weather turned cool or rain fell. And Wales . . . cursed Wales was rife with rain. But he could not allow the rebels to mock and taunt him. He would keep his crown. And he would keep Wales.

When September came, Prince Harry was dispatched with a sizeable force into North Wales, while the Earls of Warwick, Stafford and Arundel were sent to South Wales. Henry left from Shrewsbury to delve into the mountainous heart of that rugged country. The weather was the most horrific that any under Henry's command had ever seen. It did more than rain. It was the modern version of Noah's flood. They lost as many men and horses to drowning as they did to sickness. Henry himself was consumed by a fever even as he witnessed a dozen of his archers being swept away by the raging Severn during a crossing. The cold rain that had drenched them earlier was turning into icy daggers of sleet that slashed at their frozen faces.

Only once did they find any sign of the rebels. Scouts had discovered the tracks of horses that led deep into the remotest moors. It was not until much later that day that they discovered the ruse: the Welsh had put their horses' shoes on backward, leading the English in the opposite direction. Yet another day lost in this shit-hole of God's creation. Why did the Lord test him so?

The following day, the wind shifted direction and the air warmed, but the rain came again, this time driving hard, so mercilessly hard it was blinding. When the English reached a ridge atop a gentle incline where the ground appeared driest, the king ordered camp to be set up. The order was carried out with disinclination. None of them wanted to stay in Wales any longer than they had to and what was the sense of setting up camp if they could not build fires? But Henry could not move on any further. He would not tell anyone, indeed he would sooner die in his boots than admit it, but he was very ill. If he did not find a bed soon, he would fall from his saddle and die of a broken neck.

The ground into which his tent poles were sunk was sodden. His blankets were damp. Having abandoned the prospect of sleep, his soldiers huddled in tight packs, their knees clutched to their chests and their heads buried beneath their arms. As night crept on, the wind gathered force. And the rain kept coming.

"He is a wizard! Glyndwr is a wizard and he'll kill us all!" someone cried.

"He conjures up the clouds!"

"And summons the lightning!"

Henry, in his tent, heard their claims . . . and he half believed them. But he was too tired, too beaten by fatigue to rise and shout at them to cease their prattling. Although he was desperate for sleep, he could not find it either. The roaring wind was the voice of the devil to him: *Glyndwr will beat you*, it wailed. *He will beat you without ever coming before you.*

He tried to turn over onto his side, but between his encasing armor and his infirmity it was too much effort. Fearing the Welsh might attack at any time, he had taken to sleeping fully protected, with his armor intact and his shield and sword always at this side. Another roaring gust hammered at his tent. The flap ripped open and a tempest rushed in. He shut his eyes against the rain that drove into his quarters. Then he heard the sucking of mud. The center pole of his tent strained against the force, leaning dangerously his way. He barely had time to open his eyes before the massive pole came crashing down on his chest and the tent collapsed around him in a dripping shroud.

The sound of boots slapping through mud could barely be heard above the pounding rain and roaring wind.

"My lord? My lord" Sir John Greyndour shouted, over and over. But Henry could not answer—the blow to his chest had knocked the air from his lungs.

"Heaven save us. The king is dead," murmured an old voice. Henry could not make out whose it was above his wheezing gasps for air.

"The stakes. Free the stakes," ordered Greyndour.

They jerked at the stakes, but the rain must have made them difficult to grasp. Then someone whacked at the ropes with a sword. Soon they were peeling back the soaked cloth of the tent. Henry lay mumbling, helplessly pinned beneath the weight of the post.

"Dead? Dead?" he groused. "Imbeciles. I am not *dead*."

When they had finally freed him, they helped him to his unsteady feet. Henry's armor had saved him from being crushed to death.

"By St. George, I will not be so easily or haphazardly killed!" He stomped through the pelting rain to reaffirm that his feet were still beneath him. His hands shot up into the air, defying the lightning to strike him. "Damn you, Glyndwr! Damn you to eternal hell!"

He pressed his fingers to his frozen cheeks and laughed crazily. Rain filled his mouth, confirming that he was indeed alive. Around him, his soldiers gawped at him.

"Why," he said, suddenly sober, as he grabbed the nearest man by the shoulders of his sodden cloak and shook him, "this *is* hell. And I will gladly leave it to him!"

Henry abandoned Wales as fast as could be managed. The weather, in cruel irony, tortured them even more during their exodus. A rare September snow, wet and stinging, followed them with every stumbling step.

It mattered not to Henry if he ever returned to that godforsaken land. Let his son Harry have his way there.

SNUG IN HIS WOOL cloak, Owain watched from a distance as the army of Henry of Bolingbroke crawled on its muddy belly along the

Severn valley back toward Shrewsbury.

"Do you think he will ever learn?" Rhys Ddu said, peeking above the boulder that concealed them from English scouts.

Gruffydd snorted. "He's too proud."

Owain patted his son's shoulder with a gloved hand and nodded. "Three times he has gone home, beaten by rain and having lost his boots. Three times we have won. He cannot play our game. With every try he grows weaker . . . and madder." He sank to his haunches, satisfaction swelling his chest.

"Go home, Henry," Owain said. "Go home to bloody England."

31

Northumberland, England — September, 1402

Hotspur had it on good advice that the Earl of Douglas was an impatient man. When his troops checked the retreat of a Scottish army of ten thousand, rich with pilfered cattle, near the River Till, he rehearsed his options in his mind. It did not take him long to decide what to do next.

With his own army stationed securely on Harehope Hill, the sun flaring behind them and the wind pushing at their backs, Hotspur sent his five hundred mounted archers down into the valley. They left their horses out of range of the Scottish archers' shorter bows and advanced on foot. When they had gone far enough, they rammed their long, pointed stakes into the earth to serve as defenses against the charge of Scots cavalry that was sure to ensue. At their feet, they arrayed their arrows, with swords and mallets close by for the inevitable hand-to-hand combat. Opposite them, on Homildon Hill, the Scottish schiltrons stood defiantly.

Hotspur signaled and the command was relayed to the archers: "Engage the enemy!"

Arrows arced through the sky and found their targets. Scots tumbled dead down the hill. With certain death singing its requiem overhead, the Scottish archers broke and ran back through their own lines. Douglas ordered his men to advance. It was a completely suicidal move and the very thing that Hotspur had counted on.

Although fewer in numbers, the English—blessed with their longbows and a more calculating commander—won the day decisively. Late into the evening they were still pursuing Scots through the countryside. The Earl of Douglas, one eye injured thanks to an English arrow, was taken prisoner.

HOTSPUR WAS HEADED BACK to Dunstanburgh, his prize captive in tow, when he spied a small party out ahead on the road. The Percy banner that heralded his father's presence snapped in the stiff northern wind.

Waving his sword above him, Hotspur rode out to greet his father and gave the Percy battle cry. "Esperaunce!" Within a couple of minutes he had delivered the entire account of the battle.

Northumberland leaned back in his saddle. "What chance! Douglas will command a high price." He spat at the ground. "But Henry will want him. He has debts to pay."

"Hah! I think not. Have you forgotten, Father, that he still owes me? Out of my own purse, I paid to defend his castles in Wales and have yet to see a shilling. Douglas is mine."

"You would be violating articles . . . *blatantly* violating articles if you do that. And rest assured the king will hold it over you. I know you bear him a grudge, but —"

"A grudge? 'Tis a bit more than that." He motioned his father beyond earshot of the other knights and they began down the road toward home riding abreast of one another. "I have spoken to Douglas. He says, nay swears, it would be easy enough to sway King Robert to take up arms against Henry. And not just these senseless skirmishes, but full force."

"Harry, Harry," Northumberland said, shaking his head, "the Scots are always eager to brawl with English kings. Take it with a grain of salt. It will just as easily blow over when their people weary of being trampled by English troops."

Hotspur clenched his reins. "We have spoken of this before. Think on it, Father. Think. Henry uses us like mindless puppets. And he does so begrudgingly, with very little thanks and even less favor. Each time it costs us and he is the one whose crown is protected—at our expense, I remind you. My wife's nephew is the rightful heir to the throne. Richard himself named Elizabeth's brother, Roger, as his successor. By Richard's own tongue and by every law under the sun it ought to be the young Edmund to sit on the throne. It is wrong, *wrong* for Henry to take it. You know it as well as any. With Scotland behind us,"—he raised his face to heaven—"and Wales . . . what chance would Henry have?"

Northumberland gave his son a sidelong glance and shrugged, but said nothing.

THREE WEEKS LATER, STILL drying out from his miserably failed Welsh campaign, King Henry sat wrapped in furs in front of a sputtering fire in Westminster Palace. There, he received the news of Hotspur's victory. It should have pleased him, but it only served to infuriate him further. Hotspur was refusing to hand over the Earl of Douglas. In doing so, he had violated a slew of articles in the Ordinances of War. A subject could not refuse his king any captive. He would dare not, unless . . .

Hotspur's defiance reeked of collusion. But with whom?

32

Sycharth, Wales — October, 1402

ALTHOUGH CONFINED UNDER HEAVY guard at Sycharth now, Sir Edmund Mortimer could not deny that he had been treated like a prince. The chamber where he had spent these past months was a comfortably furnished second-story room, the window of which overlooked the withering stubble of the herb garden and an orchard pregnant with apples. The wounds he had received at Pilleth had been superficial and healed quickly. A few deep bruises had made him sore for a short while, but all in all he had been far from bedridden. It was a quiet, contemplative existence that left him feeling more restless than anything.

As a burning summer gave way to the sharp chill of October, he yearned to walk freely—without a small army of Welsh soldiers eyeing his every move. Even as he gazed out his window, three guards stared up at him in warning and yet more paced their watch at every turn of the manor grounds. No, he was no prince after all.

Edmund barely heard the soft rapping of knuckles at his door. "Enter," he bade.

The outside bar slid heavily across its anchor and the door opened only slightly. It was several seconds before the fair features of the young Lady Catrin's face presented itself.

Swallowing, Edmund clasped his hands firmly behind his back. During the few occasions that Owain had granted Edmund the favor of sharing supper in the great hall, he had introduced him to several of his children, but one in particular caught Edmund's attention. Still, it had been an awkward affair for Edmund to sup in the presence of his captors, although both Owain and his lovely wife had charmed him beyond belief with their generosity. He had never received such kindness from King Henry.

When not chasing after English troops, Owain came to Edmund's chambers often, merely to talk with him. It had surprised Edmund how learned a man he was. The Welsh prince's eyes lit brightly as he talked of Charlemagne and Alexander the Great with obvious admiration and Julius Caesar with a twinge of pity. He had even taught Edmund a thing or two about the dark maelstrom of Welsh history—always pointing to its power struggles among kinsmen as its downfall. It was through these musings that Edmund began to understand more of the man than just the shrewd general he had seen from the other side of the battle line. Edmund was well aware that Owain was playing to his sense of loyalty and the frequent visits of this long-lashed, golden haired daughter were a ploy of genius to weaken him.

"I have brought you some books," she said softly, as she set a tall stack on the round table where he took most of his meals alone.

Turning his unfocused gaze to the world beyond his window, he said, "I don't think I have ever seen so many books in one household before, except for King Richard's."

"My father says you can never have enough." She selected a book and, clutching it to her chest, moved in front of him. When he finally turned to look at her, she was blushing.

He offered his palm and it was a long moment before she extended the book to him. He walked in a small circle, flipping through the pages. He settled himself in a chair at the table, pressing the stiff parchment open and propping his chin with the other hand. After a minute, he gazed up at Catrin, who stood wordlessly behind the opposite chair as if waiting for an invitation to speak. He had tried to ignore her, but it was impossible to forget she was there. Even when she wasn't in his presence, he had found himself thinking of her lately.

Her lips parted and she lowered her eyes. "Would my lord care to walk with me in the gardens?"

He closed the book, staring at her incredulously. "Your pardon?"

"I know it is past its splendor, but —"

"Have you forgotten I am your prisoner?"

"You are not *my* prisoner, Sir Edmund. So do not rebuke my generosity with mistrust." She raised her head boldly. "The clothes— they hang well on you."

"They do. Very well."

She grinned brightly. "I made them. With a tiny bit of help from my seamstress, Emma, I confess, but I had only your old clothes to go by. They were too far shredded and bloodied to be of much help, but I guessed them to be about the same size as what my oldest two brothers wear. It was a lucky guess."

Edmund stood. How brave she was in her innocence, he mused. He could have been a lascivious ogre, for all she knew. "Why . . ." He looked down abruptly, uncertain how to pose the question so as not to insult her again. "Why have you come here? Surely, you have better things to attend to than a guest who —"

"Wishes himself elsewhere?"

Edmund meant only to glance at her, but when he met her eyes he could not look away, so entranced he was. What was it about her that so intrigued him? Indeed, she was beautiful, but —

"Look," she said, rushing to the window. "The apples are ripe.

And the sun may not be so bright again until spring. This room must be a dreary place when it is your whole world."

Suddenly, he realized that his stay at Sycharth was not as gloomy as he had painted it. She was refreshing, this young, excitable creature—almost childlike in her joyfulness and innocence. A thought entered his mind. Some good could come of this predicament of his after all.

Catrin tilted her head. "Is that smile a 'yes'?"

"It is," he replied. Shoulder to shoulder, they walked to the garden together. There were watchful eyes everywhere, but as Catrin bent over to pinch off a rose hip, Edmund forgot all about them. He saw nothing but her—so youthful, so vital, so in awe of the world's beauty. He could not help but feel a little imbued by her spirit.

It did not take Edmund Mortimer long to give Owain Glyndwr an answer about what to do with him. He was more than pleasantly surprised when Glyndwr agreed to his proposal.

Not long afterward, Edmund wrote a letter to Sir John Greyndour asserting his nephew's right to wear the crown and elaborating on his consent to join in cause with the Welsh. Also, along with the letter was the news to be delivered to King Henry that he, Sir Edmund Mortimer, had married Catrin, daughter of Owain Glyndwr.

33

Sycharth, Wales — March, 1403

THE WELSHMAN HAD BOASTED once too often and too loudly.

The first buds of spring were on the trees when Prince Harry came upon deserted Sycharth with his army. He grabbed a torch from his friend and mentor, Sir John Oldcastle, and raced his horse madly through the maze of outbuildings, touching the hungry flame to dry thatch. When no signs of inhabitants were found, he tossed the torch to one of his soldiers.

"Burn the house," Harry ordered. "Burn it all."

"Your uncle, Beaufort, will not take kindly to this," Oldcastle warned him. After outlawing Glyndwr, the king had granted his lands to his half-brother John Beaufort, the Earl of Somerset. Mindful not to destroy Beaufort's property, Henry had thus far left it intact—a mistake Harry would not repeat.

"Beaufort has reaped nothing from these holdings and will not unless we destroy this manor and give Glyndwr nothing to come back to. If Beaufort thinks otherwise, he's merely pissing himself."

Oldcastle nodded to the soldier holding the torch.

With mounting satisfaction, Harry watched the beacon of flame rise into the brightening dawn sky, the tail of its smoke twisting eastward. "The only thing more satisfying than burning the Welsh bastard's home, John, would be knowing he's inside. He's a clever rascal. Always a step ahead. The braggart will reckon with me now and he'll not find it so easy a task. He'll come to his knees, by God's eyes, he will. I will see to it, even if it takes me the next ten years. And centuries from now all that will be remembered of Sir Owain Glyndwr is the ruin he brought upon his own land."

Harry had known since his tortured days at Oxford that the scholar's life was not for him. He was a soldier and by a soldier's ways he would win what was his. For now it was under the premise that he was guarding his father's realm, or so others would see it, but he was thinking ahead of the years to come. His father was plagued by some mysterious illness. He would not, could not last much longer.

Carmarthenshire, Wales — Spring, 1403

IN THE BROAD TYWI Valley, which meandered lazily through a jumble of low emerald hills in Carmarthenshire, the army of Wales spread like a vast city sprung up overnight. They had grown bold in their movements at times, less inclined to seek cover, quicker to strike and resolute when they did so. But there was a delicate balance to be struck between decisiveness and patience, for Owain knew that Harry's soldiers had not been paid in some time. Their food would be rationed; discontent would burgeon. If he drew things out long enough, that could all work to his advantage.

Steadily, Owain was gaining an advantage. His men were well fed and well provisioned. They were in bold spirits. His newly vowed supporters had proven faithful. Some noteworthy warriors had joined his flock—men of station, influence, wealth and wisdom. The Welsh were no longer a band of roving brigands. They were an army, fully armed and numbering in the tens of thousands.

Sunset was in its blazing glory when the night's song began. Walking amongst his men, Owain was drawn on by the silken strands of a female voice, one that he had not heard before, he was certain, for he would never have forgotten it. He wandered past the tents and threaded between the woolen blankets spread around small cooking fires. His soldiers smiled and bowed in salutation. Owain put on no lofty airs. He had been the same in the early days with his family at Sycharth, when people would travel from across the land to share in the merrymaking of his hall. But somehow that all faded from his thoughts when he came to the clearing from where the golden song emanated.

Her hair tumbled to the small of her back in rebellious, satiny ringlets of jet black. She was dark of complexion and small, betraying her ancient Celtic blood. Her fine hands floated from her side as she sang and gave her the likeness of a songbird stretching its wings as it trilled. Perched on a felled tree stump, her bare feet peeked from beneath a plain dress of green, tattered at the hem.

Owain was mesmerized by her sorrowful ballad—a song of lovers too often and too long parted. Iolo plucked his harp softly, his notes encircling her heavenly voice. Owain did not feel the first tug at his sleeve.

"You like her?"

Owain turned to see Rhys's cheeks lifted by a smile as huge as his lips could manage. He nodded. "The sight of her makes me drunker than any wine."

The corners of Rhys's mouth sank. "Her singing . . . you like her singing?"

"Her singing, most definitely." He leaned against the trunk of a solitary willow, its yellow catkins hanging low. "But I am certain there is more of her worth liking than that." It made him feel young again, this gush of lustiness. She was so delicate of form, yet so incredibly powerful in the conveyance of her song. What an exotic beauty. Helen of Troy could not have rivaled her. "Who is she?" he whispered.

"My daughter Nesta," Rhys said.

Owain blinked. "*Your* daughter? She cannot be. She's too beautiful."

Fists clenched, Rhys looked away. "Have I ever struck you before, Owain?"

"You have. On several occasions."

"Have I ever struck you when we were sober?"

"Not that I recall."

"You're damn close to feeling my fist breaking your nose."

Owain grabbed his belly as he shook with laughter. "Oh, try. You couldn't reach that high."

Rhys's fist reeled around and struck Owain on the underside of his chin. Owain stumbled backward. When he finally caught his balance he stared wide-eyed at his friend. He swallowed back the blood that trickled from his tongue. "You missed."

"Keep your eyes from her. I know you," Rhys spun away, mumbling. "All you have to do is look a woman's way and the next morning she's feeding you cherries from her fingertips."

In his youth, Owain had been too tongue-tied around girls to do more than draw their glances, but of late there had been no shortage of flirtatious maidens darting around him. He would not say so, but he found the attention invigorating and flattering, almost intoxicating. He wrapped an arm over his friend's shoulder. "You're talking about yourself again. Who is it that boasts about kitchen maids and shepherdesses from town to town? And wasn't it you who sent that dark-haired girl to me at Plynlimon and —"

"You mean Madrun?"

"I don't know. Does it matter?"

"Not to you, I suppose."

"Whatever happened to her? I couldn't find her after awhile."

"She went home, Owain, to marry some local boy, a farmer. She tired of you calling her by your wife's name, she told me."

The two men fell silent as Nesta's song filled the air. By now, a lute-player had joined her and Iolo and she was singing a merry tune. Around her, a few girls had begun to twirl in a dance and the men clapped and whooped.

Rhys sighed and gazed at the darkening hills. "She is beautiful, isn't she?"

"She is. Be proud, my friend, be proud. What a joy to behold. She is proof there is yet heaven in the world."

Nesta's lovely strains did not waver as Gruffydd, who had been standing among her admirers, reached out and tucked a single daisy behind her ear. Gruffydd bowed before her and plucked up her dainty hand to place a kiss upon her knuckles. Nesta's eyes swept over the crowd and as they met with Owain's her voice lifted up and her smile broadened.

"It would seem your son thinks so, as well," Rhys said, not noticing his daughter's exchange with Owain. "I should introduce her to your boys. Gruffydd, he needs to cease pining for that daughter of Grey's—she's long gone. And Maredydd, ah, he's a bright lad. Keeps his wits about him when everything around him is in mayhem. He'll outshine you one day soon, he will."

"Outshine me soon? Are you saying I'm getting too old?"

"Nothing of the sort. We're both fresh as spring lambs." Rhys leaned toward Owain. "Then again, you're soon to be a grandfather now, are you not? I hear Catrin is with child. She must have conceived on her wedding night—or before."

Owain gave him a sharp look. "They wasted no time, I grant you. It's breaking Edmund's heart not to be with her. Most men would wish for a son, but he wants a daughter with a head full of golden curls, just like Catrin's." He remembered thinking the same before Margaret gave birth to Catrin. It had been weeks since he had written his wife or heard from her in return. How quickly the twenty years had passed since he had opened his shutters to find her on the London street below. How magical it had been to gaze upon her from across a room and feel the rhythm of her heart echoing inside his own chest. But now . . . now they were worlds apart. Looking into Marged's eyes was like dropping a stone into a bottomless well. He could not even hold her close without the wrenching pangs of guilt reminding him that he had almost caused her to die.

Holding out a flask, Rhys elbowed him. "A bit of fire down your throat to celebrate, old man?"

"I would rather compliment your daughter . . . if you trust me, that is?"

Rhys groaned, and then chugged from the flask. "Ah, come on then. Devil take you, anyway."

They were edging through the crowd of Nesta's admirers when Edmund came flying forward. Breathless, he pushed a slightly crumpled letter into Owain's hands.

"What is this?" Owain asked. But the look on Edmund's face betrayed the ill news. Owain cast his eyes down and as he absorbed the words there his hands began to shake.

Rhys peered past his arm. "Curse him."

Gruffydd, who had noticed his brother-in-law's frantic race through the camp, approached his father with trepidation. Maredydd was close behind him.

"What is it?" Gruffydd said. "Is mother well? Sion and little Mary? Catrin?"

"They are all fine. But our home . . ." Owain said, his voice quavering, "is no longer. Sycharth and Glyndyfrdwy both are but piles of ashes left to the ravishes of the wind. Prince Harry has descended like a winter gale upon Wales."

Carefully, Owain rolled the letter up and tucked it into his belt. "Fetch Gethin at once. Rhys, I want an accurate count of our numbers. We will reinforce our siege parties at Harlech and Aberyst-wyth. Send word to Tudur, posthaste. He will be greatly relieved. Tomorrow at daybreak, we head for Llandovery. I will send another force on to Llandeilo. Gruffydd, you will accompany Rhys there. Maredydd, Edmund, you will follow me. If Henry and his son Harry want all out war, they shall have it."

Edmund's eyes sank with the blow. The child was due any day now; he would not learn of the birth until long after the fact.

AFTER A HASTY MEETING with his commanders, Owain wandered from his tent into the starlight and sat down on the riverbank. Silver moonbeams glistened at the water's surface and the gentle murmur of its gurgling brought him back to his childhood days. He did not hear the rustle of bare feet in the grass until she was before him.

Nesta's smile broke through the darkness. "So, you are him— Owain Glyndwr? The glorious warrior? You are tall, I can see that even though you're sitting, but I had imagined some giant with a lightning rod as his spear." She sank to the ground and deftly arranged her skirts in a swirl around her.

"Such glory is spun from bards' songs," he said. "'Tis a myth, nothing more."

"But you are no myth. It was not so long ago that the bards sang of Cadwaladr who drove out the Saxons. He was a real man, like you—a conquering hero fed by great vision. Now the name of Owain Glyndwr is upon their lips. They call you their Lord, their Prince of Wales . . . *Y Mab Darogan*, Son of Prophecy. I hear it everywhere. They are calling upon you to take the crown and lead them."

He shook his head. "A lofty calling . . . but you see, crowns never came to princes of Wales without great bloodshed. I am not that heartless or ambitious to seek it. It's a life I would sooner not lead."

She drew her knees up and hugged them against the cool air. "So you would rather live as you did before? A servant to Marcher lords? A slave to the wagging finger of a king?"

"Neither of those. I simply want the English gone from Wales, but I don't long for any diadem, especially not one as transient as the mist in the valleys. If I could declare peace through courts and laws, by the saints, I would do it. Reality, however, is like the face of a leper: we all know the truth, but we hesitate to look at it because of its ugliness. What I have to do is not what I would want to do. Peace and freedom are the products of war. And I fear their price will fall on my head, crown or not."

"A heavy price indeed, but there is yet joy and beauty in the world—and hope, is there not?"

He tried to hide his smile from her. He had said much the same to Rhys in regard to her. How quickly she had wiped away his cares by reminding him.

She turned her face toward the firmament so that starlight glittered upon her brow like a circlet of diamonds. "Yes, maybe it's hope they most want and need—and who will give them that if you do not?"

"But why me?"

"Who else? Does it matter if the prophecies are true or not? If the people believe them, if they believe you are *Y Mab Darogan*, then let them. Maybe they are right."

He nearly asked her if she believed it. Certainly, he did not. No, he was nothing more than a country landowner of a long and distantly noble lineage who had been robbed of his lands. And even though he acknowledged her point—that the Welsh cause was worthless without a leader and he had fallen into that role, whether by design or accident—it did not sit comfortably on his shoulders. But if he listened to her long enough, he might find ways to use it to his advantage to ensure the freedom of Wales.

No, he must not allow her adulation to inflate his own self-image. Still, she was alluring. "You're as clever as you are beautiful."

"And you, my lord, are drunk."

He hadn't had a drop from Rhys's flask, nor any drink that whole day. But yes, he *felt* drunk, sitting there next to her. Perhaps he should walk it off, clear his head a bit? "I have it in mind for a stroll along the river. Will you come with me?"

He stood, towering above her, and reached down. She fitted her tiny hand inside his strong grasp in answer.

As they strolled beside the river, Nesta moved closer so that his knuckles brushed her arm.

"I wonder," she mused, "what will happen after you rid this land of its English demons?"

He shrugged. "What do you mean?"

"How many years ahead have you thought, my lord? A general can lead an army to victory, but a country is made of more than just soldiers. I, for one, carry no bow or sword. What will you do when the English have gone?"

"Go home . . . and live in peace."

"But they will come back eventually, don't you think?"

Owain stopped, turning to face the river as he weighed her question.

Nesta twirled around and planted herself before him, the riverbank dropping away steeply just inches behind her. She tilted her head to pose an even more difficult question. "How will you keep them away? Beg for their kindness?"

"I will do"—he stepped closer to her—"what I have already done . . . for as long as I need to do it."

"Hmm, then you will not have your peace after all." Nesta tapped a finger in the middle of his chest. "Something tells me there is more to you than being a soldier."

Owain pushed away a curling strand of hair that had blown

across her cheek. Leaning closer, his lips parted, seeking a kiss, but she shoved her finger hard against his chest, pushing him back.

"If you want your peace to last, take the crown. Build a nation stronger than its army—strong from within. *You* could be that strength."

She took her kiss then, as if she would be the one to determine where and when. She parted from him silently, her hand trailing down over his chest, a lingering look between them.

As Owain lay awake in his tent that night, a tiny seed took root in his mind. If he accepted the crown, as some had called on him to do, he could bring an end to untold centuries of wars and raids. He could bring lasting peace and knowledge through places of worship and learning, by maintaining a trained army, by making laws to protect the people's rights, by forming alliances that would open Wales to trade and prosperity. For hours he stared at the walls of his tent, a gentle breeze fluttering against it, as he thought on a whole new world. It seemed he had barely closed his eyes before Rhys was shaking him from slumber.

While the rising sun was but a sliver of gold above the eastern hills, before Owain set off with his men, Nesta appeared at the edge of camp. She did not approach him while his squire slipped his surcoat over his armor and handed him his helmet. She said nothing while he climbed up on his mount. She just stood there watching, her fingers twined together before her.

When he took up his sword that day, it was no longer merely to chase English soldiers from Wales. A larger purpose, a grander scheme now lay ahead.

Iolo Goch:

Over eight thousand spearmen strong, we took not only Llandovery and Llandeilo, but also Newcastle Emlyn and Carmarthen. In the early weeks of summer, an envoy was dispatched to the Percys with news of Owain's conquests and an invitation which was sure to shake the very roots of English nobility. Soon afterward, Owain received a reply: Hotspur and his father agreed that the time to strike against the king was now. The Percys had already sent word to Henry that his aid was required to put down the Scots—bait meant to draw the king away from Wales.

Evidently, Henry still trusted the Percys, for he brushed aside the urgently scribbled appeals from the panic-stricken English gentry on the Welsh border. What the king was unaware of as he began the ride north to join the Percys against Scotland, was that they were now fully in league with Owain and the Earl of Douglas and were themselves on their way southward.

34

Carmarthen, Wales — Summer, 1403

OWAIN'S TEMPORARY RESIDENCE WAS a spacious half-timbered house less than a mile from Carmarthen. He had spared it from the torch in a moment of forethought, because it reminded him vaguely of Sycharth with its sheep pens and barns clustered about. For weeks he had longed for a bed contained within a room of solid walls, for there was too little privacy to be found in a tent surrounded by other tents. And the need for privacy was an increasing concern.

It had happened so . . . naturally, so unforced. Like bending to drink from a stream when his throat was parched. One night, he had been lying in his tent, unable to sleep, his senses a heightened whirl of awareness. The air was hot and breezeless. Sweat trickled over his temple, pooled on his breastbone, and dampened his clothes. Sitting up, he had ripped his tunic off and tossed it to the ground. It did not help. There were no books to read, no hall to wander into to demand a tankard of ale. Then, from somewhere in the camp, the sound of lowered voices had drifted to him. Perhaps he could talk with his men, encourage them? Too hot to don his shirt, Owain left it where it lay in a crumpled wad and stepped outside. He stretched his arms wide and his spine cracked. The bones of an aging man, he thought.

He had not gone one step when he saw Nesta. Whether she had been there waiting for him or merely happened by did not matter. She was there and he wanted her, had since he first saw her. Wanted her so much his chest ached. Without saying a word, she came to him, joined him inside, and stayed with him until the first birds heralded the dawn.

Arranging to be with her had not been easy in a city of tents, where doors did not exist and walls were no thicker than a sheet of oiled canvas. He might have been less secretive of his trysts with her, if not for Gruffydd. Not since Elise had his eldest son taken interest in a woman. Until now.

Owain stumbled into his room at Carmarthen bleary-eyed and angst-ridden. He found Nesta there, although it was not her usual habit to come without being called. If not for the incident with Gruffydd earlier in the day, he would have taken delight in her presence.

She sat upon the window ledge, one knee pulled up to her chest, the other leg dangling bare with her toes just touching the floor. She yawned and stretched one arm high above her, showing off the silhouette of her deep curves framed in the pale glow of moonlight.

"He came to me," Owain began, his tongue thick with . . . guilt, perhaps? "Gruffydd told me, told me he wanted to make you his wife. Asked if it would be fitting, given your —"

"Lack of lineage?" She tilted her head at him.

Owain lowered his eyes. "Not those exact words, but yes, that is what he inferred."

"And you told him —?"

"Nothing. I told him I couldn't answer him. Told him . . ."—he looked up at her—"told him he must speak with you first."

A long minute passed before she said, "But you don't want him to have me, do you? You want me for yourself?"

God help me, I do. More than I need to breathe. He nodded. *And yet*

I know I should let you go.

"What if I consented to be his wife? Gruffydd is a good man. Very much like you."

"Then I would not stand in your way . . . though my heart would shatter."

She pushed herself up from the window ledge and stood. "I shall tell him 'no', then."

"He'll want to know why."

"Perhaps. I'll simply tell him I love another. Don't worry—I won't tell him it's you. He'll figure that out on his own, eventually, if he hasn't already."

She was more right than he cared to admit. And when it happened, Gruffydd would be angry—for stealing Nesta from him, for betraying his mother. But he could not give Nesta up. Not now. Not ever. So much of what lay ahead was unclear to him. Having Nesta beside him at night eased his worries. Her words imbued him with confidence and courage. Yet why this knot of anxiety twisting at his insides?

It would have numbed him to his troubles to simply pull her close and lose himself in her. But instead he just stood there in the doorway, his feet firmly rooted, his eyes lacking focus, his shoulders stooped. The weight he bore was tenfold that of his armor. He was beginning to wonder if the plans he had suggested to Hotspur were beyond their means.

She pressed a goblet of wine into his fingers. When he was done with it, she took his hand and led him to stand in front of a chair. Kneeling at his feet, she began to unfasten the straps that secured his leg armor.

"My squire will be along shortly to attend to me," he told her wearily.

"There is no need for your squire when I can put you in a comfortable state." Her fingers flew from one strap to the next. She laid each piece aside with practiced precision. "I have been in the company of a knight or two before you, my lord."

"I would never have flattered myself by assuming I was your first, but I am scarcely in the mood for pleasures tonight, my love."

"I can plainly see that. You'll need your rest. You have much to consider on the morrow."

Suddenly, he clamped a hand on her fingers. "Did they find him?"

She answered with a glance and a nod.

"And did he agree to come?"

"He's in the kitchen."

Owain squeezed her hand tighter. "How will I know if what he says is true?"

There was a piercing sincerity in her dark eyes. "Hopkyn ap Thomas is no charlatan, Owain. He is a Master of Brut. For many, many years he has studied the divinations of Myrddin Emrys."

"Merlin? King Arthur's Merlin? The wizard?"

"Or prophet, some say. Yes, Merlin, Merlinus Ambrosius, Myrddin Emrys—they're all the same man."

"I still don't understand why I should listen to this Master Hopkyn."

"Do you believe Arthur existed?"

He scoffed. "Of course. What Welshman does not?"

"Many believe he will come again and that the time of his return was foretold by Myrddin Emrys. As for his prophecies, there is no man alive who knows them better than Master Hopkyn. If you seek to know what is in the stars, he will tell you their meaning."

"But I have heard soothsayers before, and they speak of bears and wolves, of boars and foxes, swans and ravens, not men. Things that make no sense."

She pressed a pair of fingers to his lips. "Owain, to the rest of us it seems they all speak in riddles. You were born with a vision that only of late you have allowed yourself to follow. Do not let doubt cloud that. Go, listen to Master Hopkyn. Heed him."

"Mind you, I'm curious, nothing more." Freeing himself from the last of his body armor, he laid it thoughtfully aside, and then wriggled out of his chain mail with her help. Finally, he removed his shirt and leggings. There was no modesty between them anymore. "Nesta, I lived a quiet life until a few years ago. When Grey stole my father's lands I could have lain at his feet like a beaten dog, but when he began his selfish plotting to turn me into a rebel, I vowed to become a more troublesome one than he could ever have counted on. I was put in that position. God knows I did not seek it. My only 'visions' are of freedom for my countrymen and to have my own peaceful life back." He was painfully aware, as the last words left his tongue, that the life he had been fighting to return to was the one he had before her, one without her.

"My love,"—she wrapped her arms about his neck, her fingers teasing at the tangles in his hair—"you will not fail. There is too much greatness in you. Your brow was made for a crown. Take what is meant to be yours. Let no one and nothing stand in your way."

He buried his cheek against the wild crown of her curls and held her tight. "I need you, Nesta. I need your faith. And I will need it in days to come more than ever."

THE FACE OF HOPKYN ap Thomas of Gower was obscured behind a veil of steam. A pair of peppered, feathery eyebrows flicked upward as Owain entered the kitchen.

"A bit warm for stew, is it not?" Owain said. The cooks, upon seeing him duck his head to enter through the doorway, scurried to clear the table of bowls and plates. He waved them away.

In slow motion, Hopkyn lowered his bowl. He stared at Owain as if struck by awe. Finally, he shoved his stool back, toppling it, and dropped to his knees. The bald top of his head shone in the firelight.

"Please, get up." Owain had never become accustomed to these reverent displays. They gave him a sense of feeling unattached. Back at Sycharth, the hasty bows and respectful greetings were but formalities that were quickly dispensed with. But frequently now he found people kneeling at his feet, drinking in his image as if he were Jesus Christ walking upon water and he found it all ridiculous. "I'm pleased to see that you agreed to come. I wasn't sure if you would."

Hopkyn's chin rose slowly. "But I have been waiting so long."

Nesta was right. He was already speaking in riddles. Too anxious to sit still, Owain paced before the cooking hearth. A pot of beans boiled slowly on a hook above the flames. "Tell me, if you will, how the future will fall out for Wales."

"For Wales? Or for you?"

His hands clasped tightly behind his back, Owain turned to him. "Tell me what you will. Tell me what course I should follow tomorrow and in the days to come."

Straightening his spine, Hopkyn stood. "The prophecies are not always so clear."

"Then what good are they, if not to guide us?"

"You misunderstand." Hopkyn fumbled for the stool, righted it, and sat again. He wove his fingers together. "Many were foretold centuries ago by those who knew not the names or places of which they spoke. And time is a relative matter. The time for the prophecies to unfold comes not when we beckon it, but when it is right."

With a sweep of his arm, Owain sent every bowl, knife and spoon clattering to the floor. One of the cooks peeked worriedly through a crack in the door, and then disappeared quickly. Owain slammed his fists on the table. "I have no time for guessing games, Master Hopkyn. There is too much at stake. Hotspur is headed for Chester, where we will join together to march on London. I must know—and save your riddles—how it will fall out, if this is the right course to follow. Tell me . . . or be gone from here."

Hopkyn closed his eyes and breathed deeply, drawing from within. "You will be captured under a black banner between Gower and Carmarthen,"—he raised his eyes to meet Owain's—"if you go."

"That leaves only one route, to the west. A narrow strip between Carmarthen and the sea via Laugharne." It would delay them greatly. He could only pray that any diversion Hotspur had created for Henry would buy enough time for that not to matter. "Are you certain? Is there no other way?"

"None," Hopkyn replied.

"And what of the future? Some have said that Arthur would return one day to free his people. Do the prophecies foretell this? And is it possible that I . . . that I am *him*?"

Hopkyn drew a finger through a puddle of spilled stew and shrugged. "Do *you* believe you are?"

"No."

"If that's true, if you don't believe you are him, why ask me? Would it matter what I said?" He fell silent then, pulling his folded hands in close to him and letting his chin sink as if he had nothing more to say . . . or nothing more he cared to say.

Owain dug beneath his shirt for the pouch he carried, opened it and pushed a few coins across the table. "For your troubles."

Hopkyn slid the glittering coins back at Owain. "I did not come for that. I came to fight the English."

"Very well." Owain nodded. The soothsayer was an old man, but he would keep him safe behind the lines with other duties. "I may have need of you . . . from time to time."

Hopkyn was shown to a pallet in a back room by a servant. Owain returned to his own room, where Nesta lay waiting. He did not need her in the sense that a man needs to prove that his appetite for women had not waned with the years, but he needed her in subtler ways. Although Owain would not readily confess to it to her, he believed that this Hopkyn had a gift beyond the scope of ordinary man. He would do as he said.

Owain was up well before dawn, the skin beneath his eyes drooping heavily. He sent a detachment into the hills beyond Carmarthen to see if the routes north toward Gower were safe. Two days later he received the news: his party had been slaughtered by a column under the English Lord Carew. Had he gone that way himself, he would not have lived. Owain's deference to Hopkyn's premonitions became even firmer.

Chester, England — Summer, 1403

HARRY HOTSPUR GALLOPED THROUGH Chester's gates in all his flamboyance. His horse was caparisoned in a festival of color. The feathery crest of his helmet flowed behind him as he shouted, "Long live King Richard!"

Townspeople poured out of their shops and homes. They raised their fists in the air and echoed him: "Long live King Richard!"

Chester had been the very breeding ground for Richard's famed Cheshire archers, who sported their white hart badges and brandished their bows like lightning rods before all who defied them. Those archers had not come from noble houses, but from the fields and towns.

In his innately contagious and charismatic manner, Hotspur rallied the people to him. The ten thousand seasoned fighters he had brought from Northumberland were augmented by the thousands there who pledged themselves in Richard's name, waving rusty billhooks and broadaxes above their heads. Hotspur truly doubted that Richard still lived; he knew Henry too well to think for a moment that the man would have allowed his cousin to survive and complicate his reign, but it was in Hotspur's interest at the moment not to crush the hopes of those who now clamored before him.

A message from Glyndwr stated that he had been delayed in the south and if Hotspur could secure Chester, then he and Mortimer would join him shortly for the march on London. His father had not yet sent word and while that was a matter of some concern to Hotspur, it was also to be expected, given the complications of their plan. In his possession, Hotspur had letters from various nobles throughout the land swearing to bring Henry to his knees and make him relinquish what he had so wrongly and vilely stolen.

In Shrewsbury, Prince Harry was biding his time. It was a temptation too fantastic to resist. If Hotspur waited for the others, it would be too late. He had enough numbers to take the city now.

King Henry's days were numbered. England would be restored to its proper order in due course. Shrewsbury—and if fortune smiled on him, Prince Harry—would be Hotspur's, as well.

35

Shrewsbury, England — July, 1403

HARRY HOTSPUR HAD NO words for what he heard. His heart clogged his throat. They had halted just five miles northwest of Shrewsbury when a scout arrived with the fires of hell burning at his heels and the terrible news on his tongue: the leopard banner of King Henry IV of England was fluttering above the town walls of Shrewsbury, its statement bold and clear.

Hotspur had lost the race. Worse than that, his betrayal had been discovered. There was no turning back now.

His uncle, the Earl of Worcester, grabbed Hotspur's shoulder and inclined his head toward the hand-wringing, slight-framed man behind him in cleric's robes. "The abbot brings terms from King Henry."

Clutching his helmet tightly under his arm, Hotspur stared at the horizon. The sharp scent of spearmint and thyme filled the air in William Bretton's garden, where they had been directed to receive Henry's envoy. "Send him back."

"But you must at least hear what the king has to say."

"No," Hotspur said, "I will hear nothing from that liar. He swore to my father and me at Doncaster, as he kissed the Holy

Gospel, that he had come to claim only what had been taken from him. And what did he do? Stole the crown from his own cousin—who, most conveniently, died soon afterward. What measure of a man is that, to knowingly perjure himself in the name of Almighty God? He means *nothing* of what he says."

Worcester reeled his nephew closer, pinching Hotspur's neck with the force of his grip. "We've heard nothing from your father. I fear he is not coming."

Hotspur jerked away. "He gave his word! He *will* come. He said he would. I'll not renounce him, nor should you."

"He swore allegiance to Henry, yet he is swayed by you. The man is riven in two. The fact is that we are without him. The others who swore they would come . . . I see none of them. And where—where is Glyndwr?"

"Where is your spine, Thomas?" Hotspur snarled.

"Attached to my head." Worcester glanced over his shoulder at the abbot, who was straining to hear their words. A green sea of herbs stood between them. "Listen to me, Harry. I am with you in this until the brutal end—whatever that may be. I know what will happen to us if we fail. But I believe in what has brought us here, just as you do. The cowards who did not come—they will get their due. And you are right—Henry is a liar and a thief of the lowest sort."

"Then go to him . . . Go back with the abbot and tell him so." Hotspur flexed his gauntleted hand before him. "Tell him that we will prove by our own hands that he, Henry, Duke of Lancaster, named himself king without right to that title. By his own mouth he came to this land for naught but his inheritance. Tell him he may have it, but let the throne pass to the heir of Lionel, Duke of Clarence. The Earl of March is the true king. Go. Tell him God is on our side."

"Pray I return,"—Worcester pulled a kerchief from beneath his armor and mopped away the perspiration gathering on his forehead—"given that we already know his answer. At this point, I don't think he would listen to God either."

"I suppose this means a battle, then."

Worcester grinned wryly. "Did you come here *not* expecting one?"

Motioning to the abbot to follow him, he turned and left through the garden gate. Hotspur settled on a bench, mindful of splinters, for its planks were weathered from sun and rain. Nearby, a pair of doves nestled wing to wing on the top rail of the wicket fence surrounding the garden, cooing softly to one another. Today, he would write to Elizabeth, tell her he would return home as soon as he could, but that she should go ahead with the plans to arrange the marriage of their daughter to the Clifford boy. He would also tell her that—and God forbid it should come to pass—if he were taken prisoner or died in battle, the Earl of Douglas would see to it their son was given safe haven in Scotland.

A man should always hope for victory, but it was not a bad thing to prepare for defeat. There were others to consider besides just himself.

DOUGLAS AND HOTSPUR WERE slouched over the kitchen table in Bretton's house, nursing their tankards, when Worcester returned. The candles were burnt down to stubs and the cooking hearth was stone cold.

Hotspur took a long pull of ale and dragged a sleeve across his mouth before letting out a low belch. "Henry was overjoyed to see you, I assume. Showered you with gifts and promises, did he? Pray tell, what did he have to say?"

"Very little." Worcester shook his head when his nephew offered him a drink. "As to your statements regarding whose right it is to sit upon the throne, he says England has already spoken on his behalf."

"What of it, Archibald?" Hotspur cuffed Douglas on the arm. "Are you up for a fight?"

Douglas gave his friend a drunken smile and raised his tankard with a wink of his one good eye. "English fighting English? I would no' miss it for all the whores in Babylon."

ON THE MORNING OF the 21st of July, 1403, Hotspur was awakened with the news that the king's forces were already advancing from Shrewsbury. He sped to the nearby village to join his troops as they prepared to march, Douglas and Worcester riding abreast of him. The dew was heavy on the fields and birds sang gleefully without regard to the serious nature of the men who had risen that day at their heralding.

"You're unusually silent on this fine morning, Hotspur," Douglas said.

"I have but one thought on my mind today," Hotspur said, his eyes fixed on the road ahead. "To beat my way through Henry's army, cut out his false tongue and ram my sword through his ungrateful heart."

Douglas snorted. "You'll have a rough time of it with only your dagger. Where is your long sword? Does your squire have it?"

Hotspur's hand flew to his side. Empty! At once he remembered walking past his long sword on a table beside his bed as his squires and page flew around him in a frantic swirl. A cold dread flooded his chest. "What village is this beyond the camp?"

"Berwick," Worcester said. "Why do you ask?"

Hotspur hauled back on his reins and stopped dead in the middle of the road.

Worcester waved their accompaniment on by. His wizened face was gray with concern. "What is it, Nephew? You look as though the sheet of death has just been drawn over your face. You've no cause for concern. There are extra weapons about. I'll have my man fetch you one."

But as Worcester raised his arm to call upon his squire, Hotspur shook his head. "I was once told by a wizard, when I was a roistering brat in Northumberland, that I would die in Berwick. All my life, I have avoided Berwick-upon-Tweed in the north. What a fool I was. How vain to believe I could trick fate."

Worcester studied him a moment and then motioned to a squire. "Find him a worthy sword. He has a high purpose for it."

As the squire rode off to locate a weapon, Worcester readjusted his position in his saddle and arched his back, stretching. "Prophecies are for fools who have no faith, Harry. If our fates were already written, what reason to even rise from bed in the morning? We're here. And we're damn well going to fight. God willing, we'll win."

At that moment, however, the only unwavering faith Hotspur had was that his uncle would not abandon him. Not like his father had.

They took to the road with dire haste. Hotspur's men were hard pressed to move quickly—the previous two days' march from Chester had left them with badly blistered feet and rapidly decaying loyalties. Given the inexperience of some of those who had recently joined the ranks, Hotspur knew he had to keep the pace controlled— fast enough to find good ground to stand on before Henry claimed it, yet measured enough to keep from losing anyone, for he needed every man.

The terrain was level. His choices were few. Finally, he chose to array them on the crest of a low ridge that crossed the road. There they would have an advantage, however small.

Iolo Goch:

That same day, between St. Clears and Laugharne far to the southwest, the Welsh army was already fighting its own battle with their backs to the Bay of Carmarthen. An army of Flemings, still bitter over the humiliation that my lord Owain had dealt them at Hyddgen, had their enemies in a very compromising position.

By the time Owain and his fierce fighters overwhelmed them and broke through, they were still over a hundred miles away from Shrewsbury. If only Owain had known, he would have been there to fight gloriously beside the valiant Harry Hotspur.

36

Shrewsbury, England — July, 1403

THE SOLEMN CHANTING OF Latin syllables drummed from the lips of tonsured priests as they said Mass for the king's ranks. Even Henry was down on one knee, his head bare. As one of the priests floated past with one hand tracing the sign of the cross in the air, the king dug through the dew-slicked grass with his fingernails and placed a pinch of brown earth on his tongue.

On the opposite side of the emerald field, soon to be trampled to a pulp, Hotspur leaned forward in his saddle.

"That's it," he said above his already sweat-drenched mustache. "Pray fast, Henry of Bolingbroke, and mean it well. The Almighty is about to deliver His judgment."

He ripped off his helmet and nudged his horse's flanks with the rowels of his silver spurs. Halfway between the front ranks of his Cheshire archers and his cavalry on Harlescott Ridge, he claimed a solitary spot.

The plainsong of priests droned on as he raised his voice above it: "We will retreat no more! Take up your arms against those who come against us. If we conquer, we will be promoted in our cause. If we fall, let God deliver us swiftly from our usurper. It is far better to die in battle for one's country, than afterward by the unjust judgment of your foes.

"So stand, my men, stand with strong hearts!"

With a borrowed sword thrust heavenward, he galloped along to the rowdy cheers of his men. Then, he returned to his position and nodded to his uncle. The Earl of Worcester eased his horse through the watchful ranks and onto the low slope above a green field of peas. Once out into the open, his horse broke into a canter.

Moving his mount next to Hotspur's, Douglas growled, "You were wise to no' send me. I would ha' chafed Bolingbroke's pride so sore they would riddle me full of holes. There would be nothing left of me but bloody boots."

Hotspur shooed a fly from his horse's withers. "I am not so certain Thomas will not do the same."

WORCESTER EYED THE KING with contempt. "Every year, you rob England and turn about and say you have not enough. You make no payments to those you owe. And you are no more the rightful heir to your grandfather's throne than my stable groom."

"England has chosen its king," Henry said, indignant. The fatigue of a forced march had dampened his rage considerably. How much better for all this would be if Worcester and Hotspur would just lay down their arms and slink back home. "May I remind you the taxes you eschew as robbery are what run this realm and provide for even you, my good earl." He extended his gauntleted hand palm up toward Worcester, imploring. "Trust in me, Thomas, as once you did. You were England's Constable . . . and could be again. I am trying to keep this kingdom in one piece. Do not be the one to tear it apart."

Worcester spat at Henry's outstretched hand. "The devil I should trust you." Then he jerked violently on his reins and sped back to his nephew's side.

Henry turned to his left and nodded to his son. The cry went up as Prince Harry trotted toward his waiting column.

"Sound the trumpets!"

The royal archers advanced onto the field, their arrows nocked. As they halted to form their lines and take aim, Hotspur's Cheshire archers already had them in their sights. Beneath gathering clouds, deadly rain descended.

HOTSPUR WATCHED AS A scattering of the king's archers fell with their fingers still clutching their bows. Of those that survived, many turned and fled for their lives, leaping and stumbling over corpses, ignoring the outstretched hands of the wounded. But the way was not entirely clear for the king's escaping archers, for before them stood a wall of cavalry horses a mile long and beyond that a maze of the king's men-at-arms. Desperate to save themselves, they lashed out with their bow staves and broke through wherever they could. The horses, frightened by the mayhem, threw riders into the panicked jumble.

Douglas nudged his mount forward a step. "Now?"

Before Hotspur could even reply, his bowmen advanced further, putting them within range of the king's army. Once more, their requiem sang out.

The wave of victory was turning in Hotspur's favor. His fingers fluttered over the binding on his borrowed sword, but he did not yet draw it from its scabbard.

Perhaps his uncle had been right? It was foolish to put stake in a charlatan's prophecies. Only God knew what the outcome of any given day would be—and thus far, it seemed He did indeed frown upon Henry of Bolingbroke's folly.

ABOVE THE BLOODY FIELD, a bank of dove-white clouds raced eastward. The sun broke through, its rays streaming down in golden fingers.

Prince Harry, vigilant and anxious, looked on with his visor still open, helplessly observing the chaos unfolding before him. He brought his hand up to shade his eyes from the sun's brilliance. A moment later, the clouds rolled back across the sky and he lowered his hand. Just as he did so, an arrow glanced off his gauntlet and grazed his cheekbone. He pitched backward, ground and sky whirling around him.

"Mother of Christ!" Harry gripped the edge of his saddle and righted himself. Blood streamed down his chest plate. One of his knights rushed to his side and handed him a kerchief to sop up the blood. The reddening cloth pressed to his face, Harry bit back further blasphemous curses. He was wounded, but he would not go down. Ever.

Although he was burning to lead a charge, he remembered his father's orders from early that morning: to withhold from the fight until the moment he was absolutely needed.

'When' was purely a matter of conjecture. The moment would arrive as soon as he could stop the blood well enough to see.

ON THE OTHER SIDE of the field, Douglas grabbed at Hotspur's reins. His eyes flashed wildly. "There was ne'er a finer time. A king's head and the day is ours!"

Hotspur broke into a huge smile. "Ah, you tempt me too greatly. I will beat you to him."

"I would no' dare take the pleasure from you." Douglas swept his arm wide.

The pennons on the lances of Hotspur's knights flapped as they descended onto the plain. Hooves rumbled over soft earth. The battlefield glittered like a mountain lake with the reflection of the July sun off polished armor.

Henry's foot soldiers planted the ends of their spears in the ground and hugged their shafts tight, points aligned in a wall warning of death by impalement. But it was not enough. The spearmen crumpled under the onslaught. The royal standard was trampled underfoot like a rag.

Knight engaged knight. Sword striking flesh. Axe meeting bone.

Cries of "Esperaunce Percy!" saturated the air.

Henry's force was fast losing ground. What remained of Hotspur's army poured onto the field and engaged in what was quickly becoming a rout.

Then, Douglas saw the king in striking distance, the plume of his helmet fluttering arrogantly in the hot wind. The earl could not believe his fortune. The king's back to him, he raised his axe and swung with a roar of triumph. His adversary turned at the warning bellow. The blade glanced off the king's shoulder with a sharp click. The axe had been wielded with such force, that it flew from Douglas's grasp. In a tangle of man and beast, the king's horse reared, tossing him earthward.

Douglas kicked his feet free of his stirrups and dropped to the ground, laughter cascading from his throat. He unsheathed his sword and approached. The king lay there, unmoving, defeated. Only the slight rise and fall of his chest plate gave evidence that he yet breathed. But not for long.

Bending over, Douglas peered down into the frightened eyes that stared back at him from the visor slit. "What a momentous day this is, Henry. I promised you to my good friend, Sir Henry Percy, but I don't think he would begrudge me this. You have but a moment to say your prayers and then —"

Douglas flipped the king's visor up, only . . . it was not the king at all, but some imposter, wearing Bolingbroke's surcoat. Douglas cursed and spat at the ground.

He killed him anyway.

PRINCE HARRY THREW DOWN the blood-soaked rag and gave the command. He swung his wing wide behind Hotspur's column, trapping them.

They crashed into the confused rebels. Harry wielded his sword until his arm ached. The blood on his face had dried to a crust, but every time he moved his facial muscles, he felt the hot sting of the arrow wound as fresh as a new cut.

A foot soldier rushed at him with a howl. Harry flicked his spear away. Before the man could raise his shield, Harry's sword bit deep into his throat. He yanked his arm back, ready to strike another blow, but the man fell in a gurgling twitch.

"Here, Harry!"

The prince looked toward the sound of the familiar voice and saw his father, still seated on his horse, blood spattered, but very much alive and well. The king lifted his visor and smiled. For a breath, their eyes locked and Harry knew the day was not yet done.

They would win. They would!

Then his father flipped his visor back down and engaged the nearest rebel, striking blow after blow, his movements perhaps more sluggish than some, as the fight had taken its toll on his infirm body, but every strike precise and deliberate.

The rebel his father was fighting —

It was Hotspur!

The prince spurred his horse and the beast lurched forward with a snort. His grip tightened on the hilt of his sword. He yanked hard on the reins, meaning to halt, but his horse threw his head back and reared, hooves circling in the air.

Hotspur thrust his shield up to protect himself, but hooves

crashed down on his head, again and again, the final blow hard enough to unseat him. His body slammed onto the ground. He tried to roll away, but it was his own horse then that trampled him. Bones cracked beneath the creature's weight. When the horse finally bolted away, Hotspur did not move. There was no mistaking the result.

"Hotspur is dead!" Henry cried, raising his sword high. "Hotspur is dead!"

A WAVE OF GRIEF came over Douglas. His heart, at first so steadfast, faltered. Their lines had collapsed. Hotspur had fallen. All around him, soldiers were fleeing. He searched and searched, but saw no sign of the Earl of Worcester anywhere.

With his sword dragging the ground, he did what he never thought he would do—he ran to save his life. It would be a bloody long way back to Scotland, but what other chance did he have?

He ran. Ran until his muscles burned and his chest refused to draw air. When he stopped to catch his breath, he didn't look behind him. Then he forced himself onward, although he had no idea where he was going. He made it as far as the woods on a hill. He would hide there for awhile and then go on, perhaps finding others along the way.

It was long past sunset now. Had the battle truly lasted all day? In the darkness, he stumbled into a small ravine, slipping in a patch of mud. He tried to ram his sword into the ground to anchor himself, but his feet flew out from under him, yanking the sword from his grip. He fell, downward, downward, grasping at roots, stones, anything that would stop him. His foot struck a rock and he came to a jarring halt. Like a knifepoint perforating from within, bone pierced flesh. He was sure of it. Only, why didn't he feel anything yet? Something was not right. Several breaths passed before he looked. His leg, broken halfway down the shin was twisted oddly behind him.

Then it began to wash over him—pain so complete he would have been thankful to have someone run his gut through with a blade to end his life right there. It appeared he would just have to do it himself. He groped for his knife—gone.

He slammed his fist against the rock. Finger bones cracked. "Aghhh! God's balls! I'm here, I'm here, you stupid English swine."

No one came. He yelled until his throat was raw and his words a croak of broken curses.

It must have been close to dawn before an unfriendly face appeared above him. "Who are you?"

"Archibald, Earl of Douglas," he said to the young knight. "After you kill me, you can have my armor, but send my sword back to my son, will you? He'll need it to finish what I did not."

"Kill you?" The knight looked down at Douglas's mangled leg and shook his head. "You're far too valuable alive."

Douglas groaned as another tide of pain swept over him. "I was hoping you wouldn't say that."

Iolo Goch:

Ten thousand sons of England and Scotland gave up their lives that day outside Shrewsbury. Archibald, Earl of Douglas, was shown surprising mercy. Henry did not desire to flame his quarrels with Scotland and so he released him as soon as his ransom was met, saying that he greatly admired the man's courage. His leg set in a splint, Douglas was sent home in a litter. Worcester, who had also been taken prisoner, did not meet so happy an end. Two days after the battle, he was executed.

Stricken with a moment of clemency, Henry allowed Hotspur's body to be given to a kinsman of the Percys. But two days later, the king had Hotspur's body exhumed and put on exhibition in the market place of Shrewsbury. There, it festered under the hot summer sun, until he could decide how best to make a fitting example of him. Finally, Hotspur's corpse was beheaded and his body quartered; the parts were dispersed to the four corners of England.

Hotspur's head was set upon a pike on London Bridge to look upon that city that he and my lord Owain might have conquered if all had gone as planned.

37

Warkworth Castle, England — August, 1403

KING HENRY STRODE ACROSS the great hall of Warkworth Castle, a host of knights clipping at his heels. Their spurs chinked in a menacing percussion as they swallowed up the length of the room.

Head bowed, Northumberland bent his old, stiff knee to the king in utter submission. "My lord, I —"

"Could you not have done better in raising a son?" Henry said.

Northumberland braced a fist upon the floor to steady himself. "I tried to dissuade him, my lord. There is no way, I fear, to atone for his wrongs. Your mercy, I beg. Allow me to see my Harry and I will —"

"You haven't heard?" Henry bent over, touching the earl on the shoulder.

"Heard?" The earl drew his head back, his ragged white brows drawn tight in question.

So, he did not know of the fate of his brother and son? There was no sense in keeping it from him a moment longer then. "Your son perished on the battlefield at Shrewsbury. Your brother was taken prisoner and lost his life on the block. They rose against me, Lord

Henry. They brought against me vile, traitorous accusations. You knew of their plans. And yet you did nothing."

Northumberland paled. His arm, then his knees, began to tremble. A whimper rose to a sob as grief overcame him. He pressed his forehead against Henry's plated shins and wetted them with his tears.

Henry allowed him his sorrow. The ride northward had allotted him some time for reflection and an easing of his own anger. Northumberland may have known of their plans, but he had not joined with them. Even so, why had he not talked sense into them? Did he think they might win? Or did he fear from the first that they would lose?

Finally, Henry crouched down. His voice went low, almost soft. "What hand had you in this, Percy? Swear to me that you did not plot against me, too."

Northumberland bowed his head deeper, until his white hair brushed the floor. He drew in breath and slowly raised his face. "You know my son, sire. Harry is . . ." He seized up, another sob threatening to overtake him, but he gulped it down. "Harry was a man of his own mind. Fierce and proud. He could have returned from hell itself for all his determination. Did it matter what advice I gave him? Did it matter? He would not listen."

"You knew then? All along?" Henry's voice cracked. Deep inside, he wept for Hotspur as well. He had admired him greatly. Sometimes, he even liked him. Prince Harry, he knew, worshipped the very ground that Hotspur had walked on. The man had not been without merit. Yet he had failed to act with caution, failed to honor his oaths.

"I could only pray that he would come to his senses, my lord," Northumberland said, "and give up his grudges. Would you not have done the same for your own son?"

Henry swept a hand over his face to collect himself. "My son would never have been so rash—and if he had thought to, I would have convinced him otherwise."

"I failed to do so." Northumberland averted his eyes. "Then I should be condemned, as well."

Henry clasped his shoulders so hard, the earl could not but help to meet his gaze. "I want your solemn oath, in the name of your son and your brother and all that is holy, that you will never take up arms against me, that you will stand by me in all and do me honor. Swear it, Percy, here and now before these witnesses."

Northumberland swiped at his tear-streaked face. He looked at Henry with eyes that had seen much in his sixty years. "Tell me first my punishment."

"There is none as long as you swear and mean it. You have lost your son. I cannot inflict any more harm on you than what that loss has caused you."

"I swear," he said, hanging his head low again.

Henry helped him to his feet. He knew that without Hotspur at his father's side to exhort his assistance, Northumberland was an inert figure. But he also wondered what resentment might burn deep inside Northumberland over the loss of his heir. For now, he would take his word.

Iolo Goch:

When Henry returned to London in sore need of rest, he learned that his son's wound had become infected. The prince, still in Shrewsbury, was consumed with fever. Physicians were at his bedside constantly, but Henry, nursing his own secret ailment, stayed in London.

My lord Owain grieved over the loss of his friend Hotspur. But all was not lost. The English had ceased in their harassment of Wales, momentarily content in their victory.

Owain's letters to France finally elicited a response. French ships raided the English coastal towns to the south. Plymouth was burnt to the ground. It was enough distraction for the English that my lord was able to continue with what he had set out to do. Among Owain's new treasures were the grand castles of Aberystwyth and Beaumaris—two of the very symbols of English domination commissioned to Master James of St. George by Edward I.

In January of 1404, at Parliament's insistence, Henry conceded command of Wales fully to his son, now recovered from his wound. But Harry's task was so dire, the Welsh now so strong, and his own troops so completely discouraged by the lack of pay that by June he withdrew to Worcester, leaving Wales entirely to the Welsh—as he should have always done.

After a long, arduous siege, Harlech fell to Tudur. He delivered it into his brother's hands with serene contentment. It was a palace fit for princes and if Owain had been reluctant the year before to own up to any designs of sitting upon a throne, he was now, most seriously, considering what it might mean to Wales if he did so.

38

Harlech Castle, Wales — Spring, 1404

L ATE INTO THE SPRING, Owain's family was still establishing itself at Harlech. The children had been collected from their various transitory arrangements and at long last brought together under a single roof. But some of them were no longer children, Owain recognized. He had already lost two daughters, Alice and Janet, to bridegrooms. Gruffydd and Maredydd were often gone on soldiers' business and Madoc was yearning sorely to follow them.

With her children growing and several gone, Margaret consumed herself with arranging furniture and tapestries. That the soldiers who had occupied the castle the year past had decimated the gardens vexed her to no end. When she was not busy with those matters, she was stocking the cellars and storerooms with enough victuals to feed an entire army. She was concise and far-thinking and even though she was exacting of her servants, she knew the precise moment to grace them with a smile or a compliment that would keep them scurrying at her whisper for weeks. It may have appeared that Margaret was simply fashioning herself anew to fill the role now allotted to her—that of a princess. But in truth, her purpose was entirely different. If she did not occupy every waking moment with household affairs, a minute of thought could tear at her soul, as she wondered how Owain spent his nights away from her when he went to Aberystwyth.

In all of Wales, Harlech was the most perfectly situated castle. Like an eagle guarding its nest, it sprung from a rock, lofty and untouchable above Tremadoc Bay. On its western side, a great wall of jumbled stone fell to the sea. To the south and east, a deep ditch had been carved into the hard earth. Although Margaret and Owain ruled from a castle perched on ragged cliffs above the battering sea, Margaret no longer knew what or where 'home' was. If not for the ballads strummed by Iolo on his beloved harp in the vast great hall, nothing would have been the same. Certainly, there was something very different about Owain.

THE AFTERNOON SUN WAS at its zenith when Owain went for a long walk along the sandy shore alone. Far above, Harlech commanded everything within view. Over the cobalt waters, seagulls dipped their wings and plunged from the sky to land on foamy crested waves.

A smile of delight lifted Owain's mouth as Madoc galloped past on his new gray horse—a fine animal of Irish blood and the filly of the horse he had brought back from Ireland when he accompanied Richard there.

"Trust her, Madoc," he called out, his hands cupped around his mouth to carry his voice over the steady roar of the sea. "She'll give you her heart if you just let her go!"

Although he was of an age to be considered a young man, Madoc had not inherited the robust build his older brothers possessed. He looked perpetually underfed and had never gained the weight to match his gangly limbs. Awkward with words, curly-haired Madoc had found comfort in the company of the horses in his father's ever-growing stables. Honing in on that singular strength,

Owain had fostered it diligently and now watched with pride as Madoc relaxed his posture and flew along the glistening shoreline.

"Ho!"

Owain looked up to see Rhys trotting toward him. He must have just arrived from Aberystwyth. The castle was his to care for now, so it concerned Owain to see him away from there and approaching with such haste.

"Welcome, Rhys. Did you see Madoc there? His shield would weigh him to the ground, but by God the boy's a fine horseman. We'll make a soldier of him yet. I would not have thought it when he was four and fell from his first pony. He refused to ride again for more than three years. We gave the little beast to his twin sister, Isabel, but even jealousy would not inspire him to get back on then."

Rhys's mouth was set in a firm line, his bushy brows pinched together. His fists hung loosely at his side. "My Nesta's with child. Is it yours?"

Owain gazed out at the sea. His stomach churned with every wave that pummeled the shore. "It is." Then he looked squarely at his friend. "But she and the child will never want. I promise you, Rhys. I'll not put her aside because of it."

"Does throwing her a few coins make her less a mistress? I told you to keep from her and you ignored me to suit your own selfish needs."

Owain could see Rhys's fists tightening. "Rhys . . . you don't understand."

"Understand? *I* don't understand? Understand this: she is my daughter. *Mine.* Not some nameless wench plucked from a tavern to warm your bed on a drunken night. Now you've made her into a whore!"

"Do not speak of her that way."

"Why? Are you going to tell me that you love her? Should I tell your dear wife that?"

Owain spun around and began to stomp away. He was not fifty feet down the shore when he turned and went back to Rhys. He stopped an arm's length from him and thumped Rhys's chest with a heavy forefinger.

"You're going to be a grandfather now, too. Does that make you feel old, Rhys?"

"I am three years younger than you."

"You are three years older than me. And you're one to condemn me. How long has it been since you've seen your wife? Do you even know where she is? Bedding pretty girls is daily sport to you."

Rhys's eyebrows jumped into his hairline. "Was that supposed to hurt?"

"Not as much as this." Owain slammed his fist into Rhys's nose. Rhys staggered backward. "That's for calling your own daughter a whore."

Blood gushed from Rhys's nostrils. Covering his face, he sputtered through the blood-wet cracks between his fingers, "You broke . . . my nose. Holy Mother of God . . . I can't breathe."

Owain hooked him under the armpit and guided him along the beach toward the castle. The salty wind beat at their faces as they trudged through the sand.

Rhys sucked back the blood in his throat, coughing on it. "I would never have said anything to Margaret, Owain. It would break her heart. I would never do that."

"I know."

But Owain realized that he did not need Rhys to do that for him.

Iolo Goch:

Owain's dream was nestled in the palm of his hand like a newly hatched chick taken from its nest. The English were ousted from Wales. Gone! Henry's treasury was so empty his parliament would have been loath to finance another disastrous Welsh campaign. And while England's king had to beg for loans, money was flowing into Wales like an endless river. The monasteries of Wales and England alike were the collecting points for those who desired funds to be channeled toward the Welsh cause. Many an English baron, who despised Henry and the manner in which he had come to his present state, had no qualms about striking a blow to his purse, even though they would not openly defy him.

In early May of 1404, Owain dispatched his chancellor Griffith Young and his brother-in-law John Hanmer to Paris. They were entertained with tremendous ceremony and feasted upon delectable dishes the likes of which neither had ever before known. There were masked balls and tournaments conjured up to impress the visitors. In time, they had secured an alliance with King Charles VI of France.

Beyond its borders, Wales was gaining powerful allies and within them it was becoming nothing but stronger and surer of its own identity.

39

Machynlleth, Wales — May, 1404

W HEN THEY PLACED THE crown upon Owain's head it was nothing but a plain circlet of silver, without jewels or fancy embellishments, but it sat upon his golden brow with perfection. The ceremony was at daybreak just outside of Machynlleth, with the sun waiting behind the mountains to shine upon Owain, a robe of blue brocade draped from his high shoulders. Only his closest generals, councilors and oldest sons were there to witness the solemn, understated occasion. Owain would not have it any grander. It was the meaning of it that held value, he said, not the pomp.

In a half-timbered house in Machynlleth, with its narrow and twisted streets, Owain convened his first Welsh parliament.

The accommodations in Machynlleth were exceedingly modest and so Owain had selected the most suitable residence available: the Royal House on Penrallt Street. From his window, he could look out in the mornings to the sun climbing above the mountains. There was a knock at his chamber door and Rhys Ddu entered. The swelling was gone from his now crooked nose, but traces of bruising still remained in the dark circles under his eyes.

"You were never one to wait for an invitation." Owain slid a bulky ring onto his right hand.

"Is that it?" Squinting, Rhys walked closer to where Owain stood by the window.

Owain spread his fingers out against the bold backdrop of sunlight. "The seal of the Prince of Wales."

"Humph." Rhys crinkled his nose as he inspected it. He wiggled his fingers in a circle around it. "Does it shoot fire or give you the gift of soothsayers?"

"Not as magical as that, but yes, powerful. If all continues to go well in France with Master Young and brother-in-law John, England's Parliament will begin to consider us with some slight measure of respect. This day is only the beginning, Rhys. A parliament, laws, schools, a Welsh church—our task does not end with the dislodging of English troops."

Rhys helped himself to the bread and cheese that Owain, in his anxious anticipation, had ignored. "Best bring your head down from the clouds, Owain. You'll have to explain to the *uchelwyr* how you'll accomplish all that without making another Richard or Henry out of yourself. They're never fond of taxes, no matter what the purpose. They may love you and your Welshness, but if it weren't for the threat of their souls burning in hell they wouldn't even part with a penny to save a starving monk." He gobbled up the last crumb and wiped at his beard. "Ready?"

With a weighty sigh, Owain arranged his cloak, embroidered with his new coat of arms of four lions rampant, over his shoulders and fastened the gold clasp. "Ready."

Rhys escorted Owain down the railed stairway. Servants scattered before them, awaiting orders that did not come. Owain had requested total privacy and quiet upon arising, for he had much to think about and plan for. The tranquility had left the kitchen help bewildered about how to prepare the day's meals without some clanging. As Rhys and Owain approached the front door it was flung open before them. They went out into the street, where they met Maredydd and Gethin. A humble host of four guards fell in behind them.

Gethin gave a cursory bow. "You should have a horse, my prince."

Owain scanned the street ahead. Machynlleth was packed beyond its limit. Surely the conniving merchants and stealthy thieves would not miss their opportunities for profit. Such an auspicious occasion had drawn more gentry and their servants than the town was prepared to hold. Many had been forced to lodge far beyond the town's extremities and had begun their trek early in the morning. "It's a short walk . . . and there's no room for a horse in this crowd. Maredydd, where is your brother?"

"Late rising, I wager," Maredydd said apologetically. "He was drowning over his cup in a tavern last night and on the brink of starting an argument when I left him. He'll be along."

Townspeople spilled out of doorways and dangled from open second-story windows to glimpse their prince. They shouted his name and scrambled backward to clear a path for him. Small children, hanging onto their mother's skirts, giggled with delight at the sight of him—a golden-haired giant, his temples and beard streaked with silver, his red and gold robes flowing with each robust stride. The creases that fanned from the outer corners of his eyes betrayed his age even more, but none who saw him would have argued that he still did not strike a handsome figure. He was charismatic and commanding. He was regal. It was obvious in the way he held his chin aloft and the square set of his shoulders. Had he been the dirtiest, lowliest peasant in the land clad in soiled rags with no coin in his purse, his bearing alone would have convinced anyone that he was a force to be reckoned with and a man to be followed and obeyed, nothing less.

They moved along the streets toward the Parliament House.

Owain took his time. He enjoyed witnessing the hope he saw shining bright in the people's eyes and the cheers that burst from their smiling lips. Beside him, Gethin surveyed every movement with his hawkish eyes. The soldier in Gethin was more at ease on the battlefield than in public. Owain was smiling and waving and in no great hurry to get to his most important meeting where all of Wales' gentry, the *uchelwyr*, had gathered.

A small chestnut-haired girl pressed herself through a sea of legs, clutching in her delicate arms a huge bouquet of flowers. A stocky man of stunted height with a blazing bush of red hair blocked her way. As she tugged at one of his stout arms, he stared at her through a slanted eye. She shrank away and tunneled herself a new path toward Owain. Intrigued, Owain stopped and reached out to accept the flowers and grant her a kiss.

"Gruffydd?" Maredydd said quizzically.

When Owain straightened and gave him a questioning glance, Maredydd pointed ahead to where Gruffydd, in rent clothes and looking as if he had just awoken, tottered out from an alleyway, searching the crowd frantically. A deep purple bruise marked the side of his face and there was dried blood from a cut on his lip.

Rhys nudged Owain. "Must have lost his quarrel."

"Take him back to his room," Owain said to Maredydd, pulling him in close, "and make certain he is in a proper state to present himself before attending the meeting." Then he sent Maredydd off through the writhing crowd with two of the guards.

Gruffydd was leaning heavily against a wall as his brother approached. Trusting his son would be recovered within the hour, Owain returned his attention to the little girl ogling him. He touched her head of bouncy curls. "You will never love your freedom half as much as those who lived before you and only came by it after having none. But because of them, you will live in peace and know prosperity."

The din of the crowd heightened, but Owain gave it no regard. As he gazed upon the little girl with her tiny smiling mouth, he saw in her face a reminder of his little Mary when she was younger: the same wild curls and small nose, the same quiet, intense look on her brow.

"Fatherrrrr!" Gruffydd's shout sliced through the pandemonium.

Owain raised his face and saw behind the girl the red-haired man. A crooked grin tugged at the man's lips beneath a drooping eye. The countenance stirred a distant remembrance in Owain.

"You? I know you, don't I?" Owain guided the girl gently aside.

"Your kinsman, Davy Gam," the man said with a sneer. "We served Henry of Bolingbroke, both of us. At Berwick. I bring a message from him." And with that he threw himself at Owain.

A dagger flashed in Davy Gam's hand. Owain had only a fraction of a second to suck his torso backward. The blade snagged his garments just as Gethin's strong forearm deflected Gam's thrust. The dagger's edge caught Gethin across the top of his hand, but he took no notice as he loosed his sword and slammed the butt of its hilt across Gam's jaw. Gam stumbled backward. His dagger went hurtling to the ground. He lunged for it, but Gethin kicked it into the crowd and tackled him.

Gethin brought his sword up and aimed it at Gam's heart.

"No!" cried Owain. A tremor gripped him and he shook it off. "Take him! Put him in chains. Put him away. I will not have blood spilled before me today. Get him out of my sight—now."

Backing away, Gethin obeyed. The guards hoisted the flailing little madman to his feet. His face pulsed scarlet with every profane syllable as they dragged him kicking down the crowded street. Gethin followed close behind for added security, searching for accomplices in every face he passed.

Maredydd was supporting his limp brother as they shoved their way through. Owain grabbed Gruffydd and pulled him into his arms.

"Are you harmed?" Owain said with deep concern.

Wincing, Gruffydd leaned back. He was sporting a black eye. "I don't know what a broken rib feels like, but I think I may have one." He attempted a smile, but the cut on his lower lip brought a grimace. "I heard him, in the tavern last night after Maredydd left. He boasted that he would carve out your rebellious heart and bring it to his good friend Henry on a silver plate. When he left, I followed him and challenged his cowardly words. He knocked me down with the first blow. The devil is ten times stronger than he looks." He settled his forehead on his father's shoulder. "Father, there were others there who heard him and none would put him in his place. He might have killed you."

"I'm fine, Gruffydd. Very much alive, still." He hugged his son hard, not wanting to let go. "Now, let Rhys lend you a shoulder and come with us. Traitors can be taken care of in due time. We have important work this day and nothing should hinder us."

THAT NIGHT THE HOWLS of Davy Gam from the cellar of the Royal House robbed Owain and his sons of any notion of sleep. Gam was finally gagged and the following day he was transported to Dolbadarn, where Lord Grey had been shut up not so long before. The session of parliament flowed smoothly and Owain wrote many letters to rulers abroad. Attached to these letters was the Great Seal that bore his likeness and the signature that he put on them was *Owynus Dei Gratia Princeps Wallie*: 'Owain, by God's grace, Prince of Wales.'

That was how he signed the treaty with France when John Hanmer and Griffith Young returned with it that summer. Wales was no longer a wart on the cheek of England. And Owain Glyndwr was no longer a mere gnat to be swatted at.

Aberystwyth Castle, Wales — May, 1404

WHEN THE FIRST WELSH Parliament finally dispersed, Owain returned to Harlech, but not directly. He stopped with Rhys at Aberystwyth. Gruffydd, however, would not go there. Owain's oldest son feigned eagerness to greet his siblings and did not spare his father a stinging comment about how happy his mother would surely be to see them all.

That Gruffydd had fancied Nesta when she first joined their camp was an unspoken fact—just as Owain's infidelity with her was also well known. So, as Gruffydd rode off alone, passing Aberystwyth from the road without ever giving it a glance, Maredydd stayed at his father's side. Owain was beginning to discover the true character of his sons. Gruffydd was pure emotion—flaring in jealousy one minute, drowning in despondency the next. Even so, Owain could not begrudge him those feelings. Maredydd thought before he acted and he did so with a strong, unwavering silence. Thus, Maredydd found himself ever more in his father's company and privy to his thoughts and plans while Gruffydd drifted away with increasing frequency.

When they arrived at Aberystwyth, Owain and Maredydd were served a hearty meal. Famished, Owain rushed through it and excused himself before the others were halfway done. As he went from the hall, he was aware that Rhys was watching him. Maredydd, though, did not look up from his plate.

The child Nesta had given birth to was a girl: Myfanwy. She was the mirror image of her mother and secretly for that Owain was thankful. She was a robust child with a black mop of curls and dark, sparkling eyes and a set of lungs to make her mother proud. When Nesta settled the baby in his arms, his brow clouded momentarily.

"You are not pleased?" Nesta asked, tilting her head. The baby was only a month old, but already Nesta had regained her youthful figure.

He kissed Myfanwy on the forehead and placed her, sleeping, into her cradle beside Nesta's bed. "I have a granddaughter older than her. I was reminded, only for a second, of my age. I wish we were not so far apart in years, my little bird."

"I don't," Nesta said without hesitation. "Do you think that I love you only for your looks? That I will flee when your head is too gray or your steps too slow to match mine? Men my age are impetuous and selfish. If you had not lived so many years upon this earth you would not be the man you are and not half as intriguing to me."

He sat on the edge of the bed, his hands folded in his lap. "But because of who I am, there is only so much of me I can give to you." He was not sure if she understood what he meant. No doubt he had no one to blame for the complexity of his own life, but being with her was bittersweet. "Tomorrow I must be off to Harlech . . . and I will need to stay there for awhile."

"Of course." She approached him on silent, small feet. One of her shoes could almost fit in the palm of his hand, he mused. Her next sentence cut coldly. "You have your children and your wife."

When he looked up at her he could not hide the ambiguity that wrestled in his heart. "I am sorry."

"Sorry?" She forced a smile, but in the grit of her strained voice the hurt was there. "Say it not. Just come back to us as soon as you have played the dutiful husband. Be with me. When you can."

"How could I not come back to you?" He took one of her hands and kissed her fingertips. "There is talk about us."

Nesta's eyebrows flickered. "Oh, I should love to hear what they say. Do you not see the flames shooting from my ears? It is only jealousy that makes their tongues wag."

"Perhaps." He gave a little laugh and squeezed her hands. "But it is our adultery they speak of."

Settling herself onto his lap, she whispered warmly into his ear,

"Then call on your priest tomorrow, for you will have a sin to confess."

Nesta's warm breath on his neck stirred the blood in his veins and set them on fire. With anguishing slowness, he lay back on the bed, letting her needy kisses pour over him.

Owain heard Maredydd's voice in the hallway and his eyes flicked toward the chamber door as Nesta's hands wandered over his entire body, which was growing weak with desire for her.

"The door is not latched," he said, although he could not will himself to move. Tomorrow he would be with Margaret and their children. Gruffydd would be there. Could he still be father and husband, while loving another so helplessly and completely? He closed his eyes. The solid thud of a door reverberated. Maredydd's voice was gone. The child, Myfanwy, was asleep. Margaret was miles away. The soft, promising rustle of linen stirred the air and he opened his eyes to his lover's invitation. Her waist was so tiny it amazed him that she had ever carried a child inside her at all. His child. Their child.

An unlocked door mattered not at all to him anymore. He might have died in Machynlleth by Davy Gam's knife, or at Hyddgen on the tip of a Flemish spear, or on the slopes of Cadair Idris by Hotspur's keen sword. He could die any day in battle. How many times had he cheated fate, walked away from death while others around him fell to the blade?

He had only this night to share with her, to lose himself in her, to forget all his pains. Only the now in which to live.

LATE THE NEXT DAY Owain left for Harlech, both sated in his passions for a young, fulfilling beauty and gnawed with shame over his persistent weakness toward her, but during the months following, whenever he rode out on a raid or to tend to business throughout his realm, he always tarried at Aberystwyth on his way home. With each lingering visit, the guilt that weighted his conscience became less and less and the days and nights he spent at Aberystwyth became more and more. Before the first snowflake of winter descended, Nesta's belly was already growing with another child.

40

Bangor, Wales — February, 1405

A GALE HAMMERED DOWN upon the waters of Conwy Bay. Waves that would have swallowed a ship whole slammed against the shore. It was at the home of Dafydd Daron, the Dean of Bangor, that Owain and his son-in-law, Sir Edmund Mortimer, waited in the main hall with Gruffydd and Master Hopkyn. Sixteen year-old Madoc leaned crookedly against a doorframe, watching his father vigilantly. He readjusted the short sword tucked at his belt and swallowed a yawn.

A solid day of rain had changed over to stinging, wet snow as the bleak light of a February day faded to blackness. Tiny daggers of ice scratched at the windows and the draft swooping down the chimney challenged the hearth fire.

Gruffydd stared at the logs, poking at them and adding more kindling whenever there was danger the flames were being defeated. "She keeps a lover twenty years her junior . . ." he said, "and openly. Who knows what secrets pass above her pillows?"

"Kingdoms have been toppled from between silk sheets," Edmund said. He paced back and forth across the room in obsessive rhythm. The room was not large enough to accommodate his furious stride and every four lengths he pivoted back toward the opposite wall. "We may prove ourselves fools to think that she has the means or the will to free my nephews. For years she has served Henry as their jailor. We have cast our fate into the hands of a wanton."

Inwardly, Owain cringed at Gruffydd and Edmund's pious condemnations of Lady Constance Despenser. She had been selected by Henry to watch over Edmund, the Earl of March, and his younger brother Roger, who were now being kept under lock and key at Windsor. The plan was for her to get the boys out of Windsor and off to Glamorgan where Gethin was waiting for them. As he scooted his chair back from the long table, it scraped across the floor, causing Gruffydd to cease his tending and look at his father.

"Lord Despenser's skull was caved in at the hands of a mob in Bristol six years ago after he plotted Henry's death," said Owain. "I do indeed wonder at Bolinbgroke's reasoning behind placing the Earl of March and his brother in her care, but she is, after all, the sister of the Duke of York. I suppose he must conjure up some means with which to keep his slighted kinsman in good graces. Like it or not, she is the key—and our only hope of freeing them." Lady Despenser's role in this meant everything to him, to Edmund, to Wales and England alike. "Northumberland says she loathes Bolingbroke—curses him with every breath."

"Northumberland?" Edmund said. "I tell you, he plays the tepid partner in all this. Too afraid of being found out to show his face."

"Henry's spies keep a close eye on him. If not him, who would we have then, half as powerful, to serve our cause, Edmund? Henry Percy is happy to scheme and manipulate. I will accept that of him. When the time is right, he'll reveal himself."

Edmund resumed his pacing, every once in awhile glancing out through the rain-streaked window.

"Master Hopkyn?" Owain said.

Hopkyn had sat silently at the distant end of the table the entire evening, his liver-spotted hands folded neatly in his lap and his pale, sunken eyes barely moving from one face to another as he absorbed their banter.

"Master Hopkyn, have you any encouragement for Edmund here?"

Hopkyn's gaze dropped. With spindly arms he pushed himself up from his bench and shuffled over to the fire. He stretched his hands out, the glow of the flames outlining his gnarled fingers in shifting shades of pink and yellow. "Knowing what is possible is not always enough."

"And of what possibilities do you speak?" Edmund said cynically. "Prophecies, perhaps? Whose?"

"Myrddin Emrys's," Hopkyn uttered.

Edmund darted toward Owain and spoke lowly into his ear. "It smacks of witchcraft, Owain. If Bishops Trefor and Byfort, who you wooed from England's saintly breast, caught wind of you trusting in a prophet of Myrddin Emrys's they might abandon you."

Byfort and Trefor had become some of Owain's closest advisors. They had clandestinely withdrawn at first from Henry's choking hold, preferring Owain's plan for an independent Welsh church. He knew them well enough to know which side of the Severn their God-fearing hearts lay in. "They will abandon no one. I assure you they are as political, if not more so, as they are pious."

Madoc edged closer, as if he feared he might miss something.

The clang of an iron poker shattered the air. Gruffydd shook his fist at them. "Enough of your insane visions and perilous schemes. Enough of all of you! We must beat Henry by the sword. There is no other way. Hang your hopes on the ramblings of an old man or the vengefulness of a wayward widow if you will. May as well cast your fate to the wind. I am going to bed and there I will dream of which vein, when cut, will make the King of England bleed the most."

His stormy departure was a relief to Owain. After a door

slammed shut upstairs, Owain rose and walked around the table to stand before Hopkyn. "Tell us what Myrddin Emrys foretold."

"Lord Bardolf," Edmund muttered, alerting them to the arrival of riders. His breath steamed the pane of glass to which he pressed his forehead. "And he comes on a black horse. I pray that is not an ill omen."

Owain gripped Hopkyn tightly by the shoulder.

"The mole, the dragon, the wolf, the lion," Hopkyn chanted. "The dragon and the wolf, whose tails are intertwined, will unite with the lion and divide among them the kingdom of the mole."

Northumberland was sometimes referred to as the wolf of the north. Owain, of course, was the dragon. But the lion? Could that be Mortimer, or perhaps his nephew?

Owain pinched Hopkyn's shoulders with such force that the old man whimpered. "How do you know this? I have told you nothing about the purpose of this meeting."

"It was spoken. It was spoken," Hopkyn said, his eyes pinched shut, his entire body shrinking from the force of Owain's grip. "Long ago."

Dafydd Daron, who had been woken and alerted to the overdue arrival of visitors, flew into the hall. His shirt, hastily donned, hung crookedly from his shoulders. He dispatched two of his servants out into the frozen deluge to greet them. They returned with Lord Bardolf and two of his attendants.

Bardolf, who was the same height as Owain but older by twenty years, swept back the hood of his dark cloak. Ice frosted his snowy beard. Gracefully, he bent his knee and spoke. "My Lord Prince, I come on behalf of Henry Percy, Earl of Northumberland, and am assigned to do his bidding."

"Rise, Lord Bardolf," Owain said, touching his shoulder. "We have the maps. Let us divide what will be conquered."

By lantern light, the three men—Owain Glyndwr, Sir Edmund

Mortimer and Lord Bardolf—negotiated through the night. When all was done they had divided the whole Isle of Britain, but for Scotland, amongst themselves in an agreement they termed the Tripartite Indenture. Owain's new Wales would extend far into the Midlands and give him Shrewsbury, Worcester and Chester. Northumberland was to rule over the whole north of England and the Earl of March, who would be placed upon the throne in proper course, was to have the remaining south of England.

"The mole, the dragon, the wolf, the lion," Hopkyn had chanted. *"The dragon and the wolf, whose tails are intertwined, will unite with the lion and divide among them the kingdom of the mole."*

OWAIN HAD BEEN SOUND asleep in his bed when Edmund came into his room and shook him hard.

"What is it?" Owain rubbed at his eyelids and forced himself to sit up. Judging by the weariness in his bones, he couldn't have had but a few hours of sleep.

"Gruffydd is leaving. To join Gethin." Edmund opened the shutters and scratched away the frost on the window. "They're saddling a horse for him now."

Owain sank back into his pillows. "And you want me to stop him? Let him go. Let him test whether he can brandish his sword as deftly as he does his tongue."

Quietly, Edmund watched through the window. Owain did not rise to look. He could not. Gruffydd would come back—wiser and more forgiving—when the time was right. His callow passion was simply misdirected. He would have a broad, rich land to look after one day. Gruffydd, his oldest, his heir, he would come back . . . He would. He must. Owain had done everything as much for his son as for himself.

"Owain? Madoc is with him," Edmund said.

In an instant, Owain was up on his feet and staring helplessly out the window. Young Madoc, so eager, so worshipful of his older brothers, had deigned to join Gruffydd. By then they were vanishing riders tearing along the shore northward, sprays of sand flying from their horses' hooves, the wind fierce in their tangled hair. It was too late to catch them. They were excellent horsemen, just as their father had taught them to be. Bracing himself with a hand on either side of the frosty window, Owain hung his head.

"Margaret will not forgive me for this. She cannot bear to see her sons go off to battle."

Edmund touched him reassuringly on the shoulder. "She cannot bear it when you go, Owain."

Simple words, and yet they cut so deeply into Owain's already bleeding heart.

Harlech Castle, Wales — February, 1405

OWAIN HAD BARELY RETURNED to Harlech with Edmund and Hopkyn when a letter arrived from Glamorgan. For an hour, Owain was alone in the first floor room of the Prison Tower, the letter clenched tightly in his right hand. He lingered above the trap door to the dungeon, presently empty of captives. Whenever there were any, he would not keep them there long—not with the children about. Prisoners were quickly sent off to Dolbadarn or Aberystwyth.

Finally, he sent for Edmund.

"From Gethin," Owain said, handing the letter to him. "Our Lady Despenser and your nephews were captured at Cheltenham. They were so close, Edmund. So damn close."

As Edmund looked heavenward in question, the letter slipped from his shaking fingers and floated to the floor.

41

Near Pwll Melyn, Wales — March, 1405

OWAIN GLANCED UP TO admire the red kite sailing above the foothills of the limestone-rich Black Mountains. Beside him rode Rhys, humming a tavern song. They had ridden like that for days, mostly silent, down from Harlech on their way to Monmouthshire where Gethin and Gruffydd were struggling to hold ground against Sir John Greyndour. A hundred and fifty lightly armed Welsh fighters trotted at a steady pace behind their prince.

As they slipped past Abergavenny Castle, there was still no hint of Gethin's forces to be found. They forged on, winding their way through the broad, rocky mountainsides that embraced the Usk Valley. The woodlands that crisscrossed the land both concealed them and hindered their view. Purple-gray clouds swept low through the sky, carried on a vigorous wind that whipped Owain's hair across his eyes.

When they topped a small rise, Rhys groaned at the sight of the darkening sky to the west. The wind roared more mightily. "Damn wind. Only thing I hate more than that cursed eternal Welsh wind is lightning."

"I like the wind," Owain said.

"You're insane. What is there to like about it?"

A light shrug lifted Owain's shoulders beneath his surcoat and chain mail. "I suppose because it reassures me I'm alive—the brushing of the wind on my cheeks . . . just like the rush of water through a riverbed, the smell of decaying leaves on the forest floor, the cold purity of snow, the brightness of sunlight, the cleansing of the rain. Reminds you you're alive and not dust beneath the ground."

"You've been listening to Iolo's poetry for far too long. Your brains have rotted." That Rhys did not agree with his friend in the least was obvious in his scowl. "I've never doubted for a moment I was alive. I don't need to be reminded. Whenever I hear the rumble of thunder it's all I can do to keep from shitting myself."

"Why would a grizzled, old warrior like you be frightened of storms? I've never seen you so much as flinch in the throes of battle while arrows flew around your ears."

"I was standing next to a man once who was struck by lightning. Bolt ripped from the sky quicker than you could blink. He flew up in the air and landed twenty feet away. The soles of my shoes were burnt—I was that close to him. It charred the poor bastard from the inside out. Smoke poured out of every hole in his body as he lay dead as a lump of peat."

Owain closed his eyes and inhaled deeply. "It's going to rain," he said, smelling the moisture on the air. But there was another barely detectable scent, slightly metallic like rusted iron, mingled with it. Perhaps it was time to give his chainmail a good scrub?

When he opened his eyes to take measure of the approaching clouds, his heart thudded. A puddle of carmine lay in concealment beneath a tussock of grass just beyond the roadway. He plunged from his mount and raced toward it, frantically scanning amongst the shadows of the undergrowth. Nothing but a small pool of blood and no evidence of a wounded person or unfortunate corpse. Following a crooked path marked by bent grass stems, he dove into the fringe of the woods.

Rhys was quickly at Owain's side when they spied the first Welsh body. An axe was buried deeply in the fallen man's back. He had been trying to flee.

They would find more bodies. They knew. It was no longer the scent of impending rain that permeated the air, but blood. Bloody air. The blood of battle. The blood of death. They had arrived too late.

Rhys pointed at yet another twisted body at the base of a tree fifty feet away. "Do you think the English are still about?"

Kneeling, Owain probed the wound of the nearest dead Welsh-man. The bloodstain on his shirt was dark and dry. "He has lain here a day." Then he turned the body over to study the face. It was a practice he had done without thought for years now. Thankfully, the face was no one he knew, but still, the dead man had been someone's son or father. "The English have been long gone from here. Perhaps they are busy burying their own dead."

Before Owain had lifted his eyes from the unknown face, spat-tered with dirt and blood, Rhys grabbed at Owain's shoulder with a trembling hand.

"Gethin," Rhys muttered.

Through the lacework of forest shadows, Gethin stumbled. Across his arms was draped a limp form.

Owain's guts contorted into a knot. He knew the head of hair, the long, thin limbs, the youthful, alabaster face. He sprang to his feet and even though there were already soldiers scurrying to relieve Gethin of his burden, Owain reached him first.

He scooped Madoc into his arms as Gethin crumpled. Owain settled his son to the ground. Madoc was barely breathing. Fresh streams of crimson seeped from a hole in Madoc's ribs, just below his heart.

"Madoc, Madoc, Madoc? Do you hear me?" Owain brushed the hair from Madoc's forehead. The day was warm, but Madoc's skin was dry and cold. Owain clutched him to his breast and rocked gently. He had seen Madoc ill innumerable times when he was a small boy, but never had he lain as lifeless as this. Owain felt the wet chill of Madoc's blood against his own skin.

Someone brought a blanket and they lifted Madoc onto it and propped up his head on a wadded cloak. Owain held his son's hand. "Madoc, we're going to take you home to Harlech. Look at me, Madoc. I'm here. One word. Just utter one word so I know there is fight left in you." The tears welled up in Owain's eyes, so he could hardly see. Then he felt a tiny squeeze from Madoc's icy fingers. "Madoc? Son?"

Madoc's eyelids fluttered and with all the effort he could muster he looked up at his father. "Isabel? I . . ."

"What? What of Isabel?"

His voice was so thin and frail that Owain had to put his ear to Madoc's pale lips to hear him.

"I wanted to give her my horse, but it ran."

He cupped Madoc's face in his hands. "We'll find it. And in a few days we'll be back in Harlech and you can give it to her yourself. She'll love you for that even more." But even as Owain made that desperate promise and saw the weak smile on Madoc's lips, his son's eyes went distant, looking out over other realms. Owain pressed his face against Madoc's unbreathing chest and sobbed.

A cool rain fell softly through budding trees upon the grieving father and his fallen son.

AN HOUR LATER THEY pried Madoc from Owain's arms. Madoc's body was wrapped in a sheet of gentle folds and laid at Owain's feet. But shrouded with the raiment of death, the face Owain gazed upon was no longer his son's. Madoc was gone. There was no bringing him back. Owain would carry home a corpse and lay it before his wife. He never expected to witness any of his children being tossed into a grave. To bring a life into the world and then see it fade before him . . . it was more than even he could bear.

Gethin had been given water and offered food, which he had not the stomach for and turned his face from. Rhys supported him as they approached Owain.

There was a fresh scar slanting across Gethin's right cheekbone to match an older scar on the other side. "When I saw that Madoc was in trouble, I fought through four men to get to him," Gethin said wearily. "I cut off the arm of the Englishman who was after him, but not before he had shoved his sword into Madoc. I have failed you, my prince. It is I who should be dead and gone."

Owain merely shook his head. "You did what you could. You have failed no one."

"But I have," Gethin confessed, hanging his head low. Never before had he lowered his pride to admit to such failing. "More than you yet know."

In the pause between Owain's heartbeats, grief turned to anger. If there was any reason this should not have happened, he would see that the guilty paid for it. "What do you mean? What happened? Where are all my soldiers? My sons? My brother?" Owain closed the gap between them and grabbed Gethin's surcoat, twisting it into a wad. "Where are they?!"

Gethin would not meet his eyes. He swallowed and began with the terrible news. "We took Caerleon and Usk and then fell upon Grosmont. As we gathered what loot we could, Prince Harry himself rode out from the castle and took us by surprise." Gethin glanced fleetingly at Owain and continued. "We lost eight hundred. And John Hanmer was taken prisoner."

Was it not enough for Margaret to lose a son? Now, her own brother would wither in an English prison.

"And since Grosmont?" Owain said.

"I gathered my men and we came to Usk. On the hill of Pwll

Melyn we met the forces of Greyndour. We were outnumbered, but Gruffydd wanted vainly to prove his worth to you. He led the attack and fought in a manner that would have made you greatly proud. We could not hold the hill. Our men scattered and twice as many fell as at Grosmont.”

“Gruffydd?”

“A prisoner.”

Owain let go of him. “Then he lives?”

“He does, but . . . Tudur was struck and killed. And Master Hopkyn, who came to tell us you were on your way, died as well.”

Owain did not fully hear Gethin’s last sentence. A chasm of sorrow had opened up at his feet and swallowed him whole.

Harlech Castle, Wales — March, 1405

OWAIN’S HEART WAS MORE than heavy. To fall from the pinnacle of enduring victory into an abyss of bereavement, the bottom of which he had yet to find, was completely devastating. Every time he had faced battle, it was not his own death he feared, but the loss of those close to him. And now it had come to pass. God had finally called upon him to make payment for all that he had brought unto this land.

As he neared Harlech, its lofty walls purple in the sunset of a stormy sky, all he wanted, all he longed for, was to pull Margaret into his arms and hold her. If he didn’t, he might keep falling into that endless, sucking void and never return.

With a small party on horseback, Owain rode into the courtyard of the castle. Hooves clattered on the cobbles. The customary rush of excitement on their return was absent. It was almost as if no one at all wished to see them. The black tidings of Madoc’s and Tudur’s deaths had apparently preceded his arrival.

It was Maredydd who came out first, accepted Madoc’s body

into his arms and carried his brother to the chapel. Edmund took Tudur's body to lie beside his nephew's.

Numbly, Owain dismounted. When Margaret trudged somberly down the hall steps, she gave Owain a lingering, vacuous glance, then turned and went to the chapel. He followed her. As Owain entered the chapel, he shared a look with Emund and Maredydd that said more than any words could convey—they assigned no blame to him. Margaret, however, was another matter. She was kneeling at Madoc's feet, candles flickering all about the chapel as the darkness of night came on.

Owain lowered himself to his knees beside his wife and took her hands in his. He had not gone a day without tears since Usk and now kneeling beside Margaret with the unbreathing bodies of two dear souls . . . it only brought a new rush of helplessness to his faltering spirit.

"I don't know what to say." Salty tears streaked down his face and collected in his beard. He glanced at her to see eyes that were red and sore and had already wept long and hard. "Ah, dear God, Marged, I should have ridden after Madoc when he left from Aberdaron. I want him back. I want to see him ride along the shore again. I want to sit with Tudur in the hall, stuffed to sickness with food and ale, and hear him laugh at our children's plays. My sweet Marged, it is not supposed to be this way. Mothers and fathers should not bury their children."

He squeezed her fingers hard, but it was a long minute before she at last turned her face to him.

"Was this part of your vision?" The stabbing accusation in her stare cut him deeper than any weapon ever had.

"Never," he insisted. "I am arrogant. I know. I cannot bring Madoc or Tudur back, though I would give my life in exchange if I could. I will do what I can to get John and Gruffydd back. That I swear."

She ripped her hands away. Her icy words chilled the entire room. "You think you can do that? Is there nothing beyond your power, Owain Glyndwr? Look before you at your dead son and brother. Look at them! Selfish bastard! Can you not see the price of your ambition?"

He shot to his feet and pulled her brusquely into the corridor. The chapel was no place for such brazen words. The torches rested unlit in their sconces and he could see little but the fiery whites of her eyes.

"Selfish, Marged? Is that what you think I am? If you thought of anyone but yourself, you would know that what I have done was never for the sake of ambition. I did it so that I could have back that life we shared—with our children gathered in the hall and one day their children sitting upon your knee. Love something greater than yourself and your own little world and then you will know what it is to truly live."

"Oh, Owain. I would have suffered any indignation at the whim of an English king if only to keep part of that life. Why must it be all or nothing?" Her voice trembled with each syllable as she stifled her tears. "Why must you go on? For how long? Until every child, every grandchild of yours, every Welshman is dead? Why?"

A servant, eyes averted, floated past, silently putting flame to the torches along the corridor.

Owain unbent his knuckles and studied them for a moment. So many scars—jagged ridges of pink-rimmed white flesh. The veins on the back of his hand were dark and bulging. The crevices there on his skin looked like flats of mud dried in the sun. The blackened fingernails betrayed the rugged life he had lived these past years. He dropped his hand and raised his eyes. "After so many years, you still ask why?"

She turned from him, leaning against the wall for support. "When first we met, I thought you so noble a man: proud and courageous. Your words were honey dripped into my ears. But now when I hear you speak, I hear nothing but odes of war and hatred."

"Marged . . . I know it is hard for you to understand."

"Understand what? What is it that I fail to understand, Owain?"

His chin trembled. "*I am Wales.*"

The light was dim upon her face. "Wales will live on long after you are dead, Owain."

"No, you're wrong. If Henry has his way, Wales will not live on. It will become a forgotten part of England and its people slaves to English masters. I will not have it that way. And if I must die for Wales, I will. But by the right of God, I will die in Wales and fighting for Wales. Wales belongs to the Welsh, my love."

"It does and it always will," she said. "But soon enough the only Welsh left who will be able to claim it will be those you have put in their graves."

"I regret every man who ever died. But if we do not fight to see the dream live, then we all die in the end."

"Is that how you see it? A dream? Whatever happened to dreams of peace? Dreams of our family gathered about us? Dreams of us?"

His heart clenched in anguish. "Yes, a dream. Wales for the Welsh. A country to call our own. I thought it was once your dream, too. I thought if there was at least one soul in this whole cruel world to believe in me it was you. Tudur and Madoc did not die for nothing, Marged. They died to save others. They died for that very dream you so glibly denounce. I am not the only one who believes in it."

He backed away from her, shielding his heart with words. "Damn me to hell from now until you die, if you want. It will not bring them back. I was not the one who killed them."

Iolo Goch:

Grosmont and Pwll Melyn had turned the tide of England's fortune from its lowest ebb. It was not only in the south of Wales that prospects had brightened for Henry. In the north, Gwilym and Rhys ap Tudur had been dislodged from Anglesey after a fierce fight and fled to the mountains around Snowdon, leaving the English once again in possession of vital Beaumaris.

And so Henry deigned to take on intemperate Wales once more.

By May of 1405, forty thousand Englishmen, invigorated by the evidence that my lord Owain was no longer invincible, flooded into Hereford at the summons to array.

In royal Harlech, Owain grew uneasy. He penned eloquent letters to France, day after day and on into the night, imploring for aid in his cause.

Fragmented news from Scotland was even more disheartening than France's lukewarm promises. King Robert's health was failing and his conniving brother, the Duke of Albany, was gaining control of the realm. Any chance of help from north of Hadrian's Wall had withered.

There was one hope left to save Wales. One small, fleeting hope, however unreliable: Northumberland.

My lord Owain sent John Trefor, the Bishop of St. Asaph, and Dafydd Daron, the Dean of Bangor, northward on a mission where they met Richard Scrope, who was the Archbishop of York and a kinsman of Northumberland's. He was easily won over. Leading an army of eight thousand, Scrope marched out from the city gates with the intent to join up with Northumberland, but instead he was confronted by another Percy: the Earl of Westmorland, a faithful vassal to the King of England.

For three days, Archbishop Scrope waited for Northumberland, but the earl never came. Why my lord Owain thought he could trust the man, I do not know. I daresay he would not again.

Westmorland invited Scrope to treat with him, but when the archbishop came, the earl took him prisoner.

Henry was not going to allow any rebel, no matter how heavenly an office he occupied, to go without punishment. Richard Scrope, Archbishop of York, was executed just outside the walls of York in a field of newly sprouted barley.

Within days, King Henry suffered a fit of apoplexy. It left him weak on one side. I am not alone among those who were convinced Henry's most recent affliction was the disapproving hand of God at work.

42

Doune Castle, Scotland — Summer, 1405

IT MAY HAVE BEEN summer elsewhere in the world, but Northumberland was not convinced that the season had yet visited Scotland. A miserable mist had followed him all the way from Durham. The dank chill of Doune Castle was not much improvement. For two hours, he had been kept waiting. Finally, a door to the left of the dais gave a little groan and a creak, then swung ominously open. A parade of Scottish nobles swaggered through, among them the Earl of Douglas. Archibald was the only one grinning. The others looked less than pleased, let alone impressed, to part with their time on behalf of an Englishman, even if he was one at odds with the English king.

The last one through the door was Robert Stewart, the Duke of Albany and brother to the king: an absent king on this occasion.

Albany sank into his chair and inspected his fingernails closely. "Have you at last chosen sides, good earl?"

"Where is King Robert? I was promised an audience," said Northumberland.

"My dear brother has taken ill . . . as is often the case these days."

"Then I will wait until he's better."

"That could be some time from now. I cannot promise you a meeting with him." Albany pushed down a yawn and at last gazed upon the desperate Northumberland. A smirk altered his countenance from a look of boredom to one of amusement. "So unless you plan to stay in Scotland indefinitely, which given your history might be inadvisable, I beg of you to share your business here and now."

"I can only speak with the king."

"Impossible."

Northumberland figured perhaps the king's heir would be more amenable to reason than Albany. "Then tell me where the Duke of Rothesay is."

The wry smirk evaporated from Albany's mouth. "In his grave. So young. Such a pity. He perished while a prisoner at Falkland. Put there by orders of his father, the king. The lad was rather, ah . . . free in his ways. The candle that burns the brightest is soonest spent, or so they say." He crossed his arms across a bulging chest. "It would seem, m'lord, you are stuck with me for a pair of ears. I am, again, Guardian of Scotland, and always with her best interests at heart. Now, what can we do for you? We have heard about York. That Westmorland never strayed far from opportunity. Betraying a holy man has done little to mar his conscience, no doubt."

Albany's reception was such a far cry from what Northumberland had expected that he was at a loss for words. Robert III had never been a strong king, but he had been receptive to Owain's plans, at least. In truth, it had always been Albany whom the Scottish nobles had followed. Albany who kept the country at peace. Albany who did as he damn well pleased.

"My lord," Northumberland began, bowing his head, "I only ask that you honor your brother's arrangement with Prince Owain of Wales."

Pertly, Albany flipped a hand forward. "And that so-called

arrangement was . . .?"

"An alliance. To stand against Henry of Bolingbroke until the true heir of England is restored."

Gazing out the far window, Albany scratched at an ear. "Aye, alliance. He did mention some correspondences. But I am not aware of any formal treaty with Wales . . . or yourself for that matter. So whatever it is you've come here for will have to wait until my brother's health has improved sufficiently." He slouched in his chair and stretched his legs out before him. "Stay on if you wish, but there's no telling when that will be."

Suddenly aware that the audience with Albany was a barren work, Northumberland glanced at Douglas.

"Good day, my lords." He bent at the waist, even though Albany did not acknowledge his departure.

The earl's footsteps echoed down the gray, stone corridor. Where was he to go now? Back to Northumberland? King Henry would have his head. To Wales? What use was he to Glyndwr without an army?

"Lord Henry?"

Northumberland turned to see old Archibald Douglas limping to catch up with him.

An easy smile spread over Douglas's features. He clasped Northumberland on the upper arm. "You are loyal to your son's memory. I value that in a man."

"Just biding my time, Archibald. But after all these years of waiting, now that I have chosen to act . . ."—he shook his snowy head—"after all these years, for what?"

Douglas looked both ways down the length of the corridor and pulled the earl in close. His voice was barely above a whisper. "Albany is no friend of the King of England's . . . but he does no' want war with him, either."

"I think we both know what Albany wants: his brother's crown."

Northumberland nodded to himself. He understood everything now. And yet he knew not a whit of what to do from that point onward. "Share a drink with me, Archibald, before I'm off again."

Turning his face away so that the earl could not see his good eye, Douglas shook his head. "I owe my freedom to Albany. He saw to it my ransom was paid."

"And do you blame me for putting you in English hands?"

Douglas tensed. "You should ha' been there, Henry. Things would be very different now."

"Knowing the outcome, I'm not so certain of that," Northumberland said as he walked away. It was not how he would have chosen to leave Douglas, but at that point, there were very few choices left to him.

As soon as arrangements for transport on a merchant's ship could be made, Northumberland, Trefor and Daron journeyed to Wales where long overdue news had arrived.

A French invasion force was sailing for Wales.

43

Aberystwyth Castle, Wales — June, 1405

"I THOUGHT OF NAMING her Gwenllian—after my mother." Nesta tugged her gown from her shoulder and let the baby girl, only two-days old, but bright-eyed and vigorous, nurse.

Owain had come to Aberystwyth as soon as the news arrived at Harlech. He had given Margaret no explanation for his sudden departure. None was needed. Nor had he told her where he was going. That was a given.

"Gwenllian?" Owain repeated.

"Do you not like it?" She eased back against the cushion of her chair. "Perhaps Emma or Susanna or —"

"No, Gwenllian is a fine name. It's only that, well, I have never heard Rhys talk about your mother, let alone mention her name." Owain stroked the fine golden fuzz on the top of his youngest daughter's head. It would be plain to all that this was indeed his child. "So little," he remarked. "Is it possible that Gruffydd was ever so small?" But even as his oldest son's name passed his lips he was struck with remorse. Gruffydd had disapproved of his relationship with Nesta. Ever since the day Owain had first met her that summer evening in the Tywi Valley, he and Gruffydd had drifted apart. It was as if he had traded his son's love for Nesta's. As if he could not have both. And now Gruffydd was imprisoned in London.

"I wish I could have given you a son," Nesta mused. "Perhaps I yet will."

Owain ripped himself from his thoughts. "What?"

"A son. A prince." She beamed, swaying gently from side to side as she hummed to the baby. The baby's eyelids fluttered and closed. Soon, the child's small mouth relaxed. Nesta fixed her gown and pulled a small blanket around the baby, then settled her into Owain's arms.

"She does not cry like her sister—at least not yet." A wide smile lifted Nesta's cheeks.

"Nesta, I . . ." Owain rearranged words in his mind, searching for a gentle way to phrase it. "If we had a son, I do not think he could be a prince."

"What else would he be?"

"A knight, certainly. Perhaps a lord, if he were skilled in diplomacy or soldiering."

"A knight . . . or a lord? Perhaps?" She stiffened at the insult. "Will they never be equals with your other children? In Wales, a prince's sons are all acknowledged. Many a bastard has succeeded his father."

"I am not the only one who would have a say in what title or wealth they might be granted."

"Who else would have a say? Your wife?"

"The *uchelwyr*, for one." Owain quickly directed the conversation elsewhere. "Gwenllian," he said, kissing his daughter's small forehead. "What was . . . what is she like?"

"Who?"

"Your mother. Gwenllian."

"Oh, her." Nesta crinkled her nose, as she often did. "She left him when I was very young."

"Why?"

"Oh heaven, I don't know. For some other man. Someone who wooed and flattered her more than my father could . . . or would. He has a roving eye. He likes a pretty maid. Likes them for the curl of their hair and the curve of their waist. He called her his wife, but they were never married, did you know that? Like you and me." She swished her skirts, made of the finest cloth from Flanders, and then traced a finger lightly from his neck down his arm. "At any rate, my mother, last I knew, was in Dublin. My father is a bit rough around the edges, but a good-hearted man and I felt far more love in his embrace than I ever felt at my mother's knee. When I was with her, I spent more of my youth waiting outside taverns than I care to recall. She often pretended I was her younger sister, so as not to scare away her companions. But father, he was always proud to call me his own."

Nesta looked long and hard at Owain, cradling their daughter in his arms.

That night Owain lay beside Nesta with Gwenllian sleeping soundly in a cradle an arm's reach from the bed. He did not sleep at all, for it was in the quiet hours of night that he searched for solutions to insurmountable problems. Each morning he awoke more tired than the day before. Bearing such weight upon one's soul was an exhausting vocation—even for one so determined, so brimming with conviction and so unable to turn from the path that wove on before him.

Tenby, Wales — August, 1405

NESTLED ON THE SOUTHERN coast of Pembrokeshire, the town of Tenby stirred at dawn. Owain watched as a heron stretched its wings overhead—its long, slim neck leading it out over the choppy, cobalt waters of Carmarthen Bay. The siege on Tenby had been a brief one, lasting only days. Upon hearing of the French landing at Milford Haven, twenty miles to the west, they had capitulated with little persuasion.

A string of storms had delayed the departure of the French and when they finally set sail, many of their horses had died during the Channel crossing, the result of too little drinking water to accommodate both man and beast. The parliament at Harlech had graciously voted Owain the funds to muster ten thousand Welshmen to join the French in a march on England. It had been a promise so long in coming that Owain was still in disbelief.

Owain crouched between two wind-scoured dunes. A hundred troublesome thoughts had once more robbed him of sleep and so he had risen and dressed early, long before any of his soldiers were up. Salt air and sand stung his eyes. For a minute, he closed them tightly and listened to the steady roar of the wind and the furious lapping of the water.

"Nothing awakens the senses more," came an unfamiliar, yet gentle voice, "than the wind coming in from the sea."

Startled, Owain looked over his shoulder to see a priest weaving his way through clumps of marram grass. Every step the tonsured holy man took was thoughtfully chosen. In one hand he clutched a walking stick and over the other arm swung a willow basket half full of rattling cockles.

"You're up early, Father," Owain said.

"Me? Ah, no. I rise every day at this hour. It is you who are up too early, my lord. A hundred years too early." The priest smiled innocently at Owain, before continuing down the shoreline on his way to a favored spot to dig for more treasures.

Owain blinked. He rose and started toward the priest, hungry for a snatch of conversation which had nothing to do with sappers or siege engines. But before he could interrogate the priest further,

Maredydd was sliding down the hillside of a small dune, calling after him.

"Gethin was ready to send a search party out for you." Maredydd slipped as he reached his father and landed on his buttocks. He jumped to his feet and brushed away the sand. "You might have told someone you were coming out here."

"That would have destroyed my purpose altogether. Can I not have a moment's peace? The Lord knows I could use it."

"Your forgiveness, Father, but I have a message for you."

"Will the French grace us with their presence soon?"

"By noon, if not before."

Owain raked the hair off his forehead and attacked the hillside as Maredydd followed him back toward camp. "Pay close attention, Maredydd. When Marshal de Rieux gets here, if you see me fall silent, I am collecting my patience. Pray that I find it."

44

Near Worcester, England — September, 1405

WHEN THE FIRST PENNONS of the English army could be seen fluttering above the horizon, the September sun was sinking into the western hills. The king's standard drooped in the viscous air. Behind it trudged a column of soldiers—a swarm of locusts in the distance, each man indistinguishable from the next, uncountable in the purple-gray of twilight, but an entity of unfathomable proportions.

On Woodbury Hill, the French, who had until that hour been high on pillage and slaughter, were swallowed up by dread. Their own magnificent armor had impressed the ingenuous Welsh warriors to the point of near worship. The mere sight of their chest plates glinting in the sun had sent the citizens of Worcester running for their lives. But even behind their gleaming shells, visions of restoring the new Arthur to the throne withered with the mirage that came to life before them.

Firmly encamped on a summit, with a clear view in every direction, the Welsh and French were a united force of thirteen thousand riding on the crest of a tide of triumphs. But they were also deep within the enemy's heart, gravely outnumbered, with no lines to fresh supplies and a limited amount remaining. It appeared they had marched victoriously on only to confront the impossible. But to Owain and the tattered Welsh who followed in his name, achieving the impossible was their strongpoint.

Jean de Rieux, Marshal of France, dismounted from his raven black courser with the stunted, feeble motions of an aged man who is aware how easily his bones may break. He approached Owain, who stood rock-like at the front edge of camp, watching the enemy pour into the valley and snake their way up Abberley Hill, one uncomfortably close mile to the north. At Owain's right shoulder stood Rhys Ddu.

Rieux sidled nearer. His thin lips twitched above his pointed beard. He whispered as if he were the god Mars delivering divine inspiration. "Send the archers. Cut them down."

"Now?" Owain questioned, still surveying the scene on Abberley Hill as the English just kept coming and coming like a river encircling the earth.

"*Matin*," Rieux said. "First light."

For a minute Owain remained silent, then he dropped his chin, glanced momentarily at the marshal and back again across the valley. "Do you see what they are doing?"

"*Oui*," Rieux said, as they observed Henry taking up an equally defensive position on the steep-sided mound on the opposite side of the valley. Between the two hills was cradled a perfect battle site: broad and sweeping and crying out for blood. He twisted the ends of his mustache between a thumb and finger.

"If we begin the battle now, we've only a couple of hours of daylight left. If we wait until morning and then send our archers, they will be even better positioned than they already are. Don't you agree?"

The French commander's hand fell away from his mouth. His silver-white eyebrows rose. "Then send your men now, today, while they're still —"

"Today. Tomorrow." Owain faced him. "Who leads this army, Marshal?"

"I was, eh . . . simply advising you."

"My regrets, then," Owain said, inclining his head. "I thought you were *telling* me what to do. But then, a man of your experience has much advice to offer."

Rhys grunted. "Is it the practice of the French to begin battles at nightfall? Maybe *you* ought to send Hugueville's crossbowmen now and see for yourself how quickly the English can mince them into fodder for the crows."

At that very moment, Owain's thoughts did not dwell upon tactics and geographic advantages. Instead, he remembered the day he heard the news from Shrewsbury: that Hotspur was dead, that Henry had triumphed. How it should not have been. How it needn't have been. How his heart had hardened that very day. And Pwll Melyn—Tudur murdered on the battlefield and dear, pining Gruffydd a prisoner of the King of England. That was when Owain had stopped feeling altogether. When all his passion, his dream of a free Wales metamorphosed into the cold, hard lust for revenge. Then why now was he filled with such foreboding, such smothering doubt? The rebellion in York had not fulfilled its purpose. It had merely bought them time. And once again, Northumberland had fallen short. Another ally issuing empty promises. He turned to look at the French knights stationed along the hill and those clustered behind him, their armor capturing the last rays of daylight.

Robert de la Heuse, the French commander they called Le Borgue, meaning one-eyed and aptly so, swaggered forward. His tightly tied black patch cut an angular line across his upper cheek and forehead. A deep violet crevice had been carved into his face from nose to temple. But rather than a disfigurement, he wore the evidence of his injury more like a badge of honor, strutting about with his chin thrust out and peering haughtily at others with his one stark eye. It was the insatiable Le Borgue that the French soldiers had followed into Haverfordwest to take whatever lay within their reach. When the English Lord Berkeley surprised the remainder of the French fleet in Milford Haven and sank it, it was Le Borgue who called on them to march inland and meet up with the Welsh. Worcester, among other places, had been sacked. He scanned the distant lines of English and laid an open hand against his chest plate.

"*Certainement*," Le Borgue began, squinting his good eye, "*les Anglais* . . . they have a weakness, *non?*"

Abberley Hill blackened with English soldiers. Their customary sharp movements were absent. From the hill's base a line of stragglers trailed away. Far into the distance lurched a wobbly line of supply wagons. It was nothing short of miraculous that they had made it from Hereford to York and back in so short a time.

Rieux strained his eyes to gaze across the valley, long with shadows. "*Ils sont fatigué*," he remarked. He shifted his hips and grimaced, as though some old familiar pain had been resurrected.

"*Et nous sommes fatigué, aussi, non?*" Le Borgue said.

Rieux nodded.

Sighing, Le Borgue mopped at his brow with the back of his hand, crisscrossed with fresh scars. He shrugged. "Perhaps, the prince . . . he has a plan? He knows this Bolingbroke better than we do. He and his men, they have defeated him many times."

When Owain glanced at Le Borgue, he detected a twinkle in that one dark eye and a suppressed grin. Behind his back, Owain clutched his hands. The bulk of his armor made it nearly impossible to do so. He recalled the days when he used to turn somersaults in full plate armor. How very long ago that was. Blasted eternity. He should have been an old man sitting by his hearth now, singing to his grandchildren and teaching them how to catch trout in the Dee—just as he and Tudur used to do.

Oh, Tudur . . . you always gave voice to the doubts that I never dared to. There were times I should have been more cautious, but if I had I would have gained nothing.

"Our men are hungry, Marshal de Rieux," Owain said, echoing the leonine rumble in his belly. He paced back and forth, his thumbs circling one another behind his back. Abruptly, he halted and shoved a hand up through his tangle of sweat-soaked hair. "Rhys, have Gethin cut out the remainder of their baggage train before it reaches the hill. He is an expert at that." He smiled at Rieux and then wider at Le Borgue. "Tomorrow, we will see how willing the English are to treat with us."

Rieux grimaced. His patience was obviously being pushed to the edge. "But, my prince, why not end this, now?"

Rhys spat at the ground. "We may be a crude lot, Marshal, but we aren't idiots."

"Idiots, no. But you hesitate." Rieux stretched his neck and a stream of sweat rolled from beneath his beard and down his throat. "Opportunity is in our very hands. Seize it. Do not be blind."

"Blind?" Rhys said.

"*Oui* . . . blind."

"I'd rather be a blind Welshman than a pompous, teat-sucking Frenchman." Rhys stomped closer. His rotund chest heaved as he jabbed a finger at Rieux. "You can't even control your own bloody soldiers. You didn't have the discipline to take Haverfordwest properly. You don't need wine. The smell of blood makes you drunk. Pitiful bastards. The only reason you're still in this godforsaken country is that you didn't have the ships to take you back to Brest. Worcester was a bloody shame. A bloody fucking shame. You watched while Le Borgue and his men unpenned cattle and sent them stampeding down Smock Alley, trampling little children. Innocents dying in the name of revenge. Is that your idea of reviving the legend of Arthur? Chivalry. What do you lusty, drunken Frenchmen know of it? God damn son of a —"

"Enough!" Owain flared.

"— French whore!" Rhys roared over him, his hands flailing.

Owain grabbed Rhys by the throat, cutting his air off. "Shut up! Do you hear me?"

Rhys's cheeks blazed red, and then went purple as he struggled to breathe. His feet left the ground as Owain pushed upward. The hand on his windpipe tightened. His head bobbed backward. Owain unclenched his iron fingers. Stumbling, Rhys doubled over, grabbing his knees, great gasps for air rattling in his throat like a broken down mare with the heaves. While he gathered himself, Rieux ranted in French, his hands flying in furious gestures, slashing through the heavy air.

The soldiers on Woodbury Hill turned to gawk at the squabble unfolding in their midst. Rieux's voice pitched in indignation, drawing Hugueville, Master of the Crossbowmen, and other Frenchmen into the heated ring. Le Borgue tried to calm the marshal, but soon enough Rieux was arguing with him, too.

Raising a pair of watery eyes, Rhys looked up at Owain.

"Your sense of timing is reprehensible," Owain chastised lowly. He hoisted Rhys up by the arm and jerked him aside.

"What is he blathering about?" Rhys croaked.

"You don't want to know." Owain dragged him through the ragged lines of soldiers who were wilted from days of scorching sun. When they arrived at Owain's tent, Maredydd came rushing forward, his features slack with worry. Owain spared formality altogether. He shoved Rhys ahead and through the tent flap, then turned to his son. "Send Gethin to cut out what he can of their supplies. Now!"

Without detailing anything to Maredydd, Owain stormed into the tent. He kicked at a stool and sent it flying into a pole. The whole thing shuddered and Rhys threw his arm above his head, as if it were going to crash down and bury both of them.

"Imbecile!" Owain blared so that they must have heard him halfway down the valley. "For years I have struggled to bring them to our shores, to raise arms with us against the English! *With* us, by God. And you insult them and attempt to enlighten them to their own faults? You are more hotheaded than they are, Rhys Ddu. What the French did at Worcester was no different than what Prince Edward did at Limoges. Or you yourself at Ruthin and a dozen other places. And do I have to remind you that there were as many Welshmen, *your* men, cutting down the English in Worcester? It's true. Admit to it. War makes savages of us all. Even those of us who deem ourselves compassionate and just. You are not so different. Just turn your own eyes inward and take a good, hard look." He paused only long enough to glare at Rhys. Then he commenced his berating. His bellowing hammered against the cloth walls.

In the stuffy confines of the dark tent, Rhys looked as though he had been tied to the stake and the fire had been lit. He slipped his puffy fingers beneath the leather straps that secured his arm plates and scratched. Without warning, he swooned forward.

Owain caught him under the arms. In a moment, he drew Rhys toward the stool and righted it with one hand. Still holding on to him with the other, he gently lowered him. Owain popped outside and called for a bucket of fresh water and a cloth. Moments later he was sponging Rhys's head.

"Are you all right?" Owain asked in a softer tone.

"It's a God damn inferno in here."

"Yes, well, it was just as hot out there with Rieux." He handed the cloth to Rhys, who buried his face in it.

"I'm sorry," Rhys mumbled. They weren't words Owain could ever recall him saying before.

"You needn't be. You were every bit right." Smiling, Owain crouched down on the balls of his feet before his friend and put a hand on his knee. "Listen, I had to do that. You understand? Foolish as they are, we need them. Now," he said, rising, "come outside. We'll see what Gethin can manage."

"If you don't mind, I need to crawl out of this armor first. The unlucky Englishman who gave it up to me was a size smaller." He winked at Owain, who nodded and reached a hand to part the tent flap. Rhys stretched his legs and fumbled with one of the straps that secured his greave. "Owain?"

"Yes?"

"One thing."

"Say it."

"In the future, when you need to feign a quarrel with me, could we work out a signal? If it would keep you from crushing my windpipe again, I can fake an injury amazingly well." In an instant, his eyes rolled up inside his skull. Rhys's neck bent at an odd angle and his jaw dangled, spittle dribbling from the corner of his mouth. Owain bolted back inside, but just as quick Rhys was alert and laughing. "Hell, I'd even bleed for you. Just ask, will you?"

Owain looked at him a moment and nodded. Drawing aside the stiff canvas, he strolled out into the lavender wash of twilight to gaze at his enemy.

DAWN'S FINGERS CREPT LAMBLIKE over the Herefordshire hills and rubbed the sleep from the eyes of weary soldiers. Sunlight poured over the green valley, burning brighter minute by passing minute. On Abberley Hill, the English stood at attention. It took all their strength to do so. They were short on sleep, worn to the bone, and had been harried relentlessly by their commander. York had been a sour disappointment for Henry—the whole ordeal over before they ever arrived. Then news of the French landing came to bring them slingshotting back south again.

In his tent, Henry swirled a cup of flat ale and picked at his morning meal. Sir John Greyndour shuffled in and bowed low.

"Anything yet?" Henry asked dully.

Greyndour moved reluctantly closer. "The scoundrels absconded with over half our baggage train."

Too weary to be angry, Henry found some amusement in their misfortune. "Only half? Ah, Gethin strikes again."

"I did my best, my lord."

"You did, certainly." The king stabbed at a hunk of meat and devoured it. Plucking up a linen handkerchief, he pushed his tongue around his mouth and then probed his teeth with his thumbnail to dislodge a piece of food. "An inconvenience. Send to Worcester for more provisions."

"That cannot be done, sire. They burned it on the way."

Putting down his knife, Henry leaned back on his stool. He thought a moment, and then nodded. "A wise move on their part. The French or the Welsh?"

Greyndour shrugged. "According to reports, let's just say that Glyndwr didn't stop Rieux's men."

"Humph," Henry mumbled. "Hereford?"

"I can have supplies sent from there. It will take longer. We'll have to swing out behind the Welsh rather far."

"Whatever you can manage. We won't be here long." Henry scooped up his cup and doused his throat. "Where is Harry?"

"At the front. Shall I summon him?"

"No, no need. He is where he serves best."

"Any orders, sire?" Greyndour seemed anxious to get on with this.

To Greyndour's dismay, Henry shook his head and attacked the rest of his plate. "No orders. We will wait for Glyndwr to yield. And he will."

BY NOON, NERVES WERE fraying. French knights straddling their puissant coursers began to heckle the English. Hugueville's cross-bowmen checked their weapons repeatedly and counted their bolts. They elbowed each other and laughed. The Welsh pikemen, who had been propped against their weapons, even though they understood not a syllable, grinned and rustled with anticipation.

Woodbury Hill began to awaken. Gethin, never to be omitted when there was rabble-rousing to be had, unsheathed his sword and struck it against his shield in measured beats. He nudged his mount in the flanks and wove through the tangle of men-at-arms.

Within minutes, the entire hill throbbed in rhythm. The heart-beat of Wales pulsed over the English countryside, declaring its existence, daring to be defied.

AT THE BASE OF Abberley Hill, Harry took to his own horse. With upraised blade, he sailed back and forth, rallying his troops. Infinitely pleased by his son's capacity to resurrect his dispirited army, Henry emerged but briefly from his tent.

"So it begins," Henry muttered. Then he disappeared back into his oasis of shade.

THE CLAMOR INTENSIFIED AND so did Marshal de Rieux's temper. Owain, surrounded in his tent at a table by his generals—Rhys Ddu, Edmund and Maredydd—glanced up from a long roll of parchment as Rieux blustered in. Several tight-faced Frenchmen clipped at his heels.

"Welcome. Please sit," Owain said, indicating a single stool op-posite him.

Rieux snorted and stabbed a finger northward. "You waste time. Strike now!"

Edmund, who held a white plumed quill in his hand, finished his last stroke. "Done," he proclaimed, studying the document before him. The Welsh stared intently at the lines of black, as if willing them to march from the page and achieve their purpose. Their trance was not broken until Rieux ripped the document away and the inkwell went toppling into Edmund's lap. He shot back from the table, ink seeping between the links of his mail.

Clutching the parchment in his hand, Rieux shook it at Owain. "Explain! What is this?"

Silence swallowed everyone inside the tent. The din from the troops had quelled, strangely punctuating the very moment. A long, gaping second later a single shout of '*Cymru!*' arose from ten thousand throats and the clamor went on as it had for hours. Owain rose. He circled the table, brushing past Hugueville and Le Borgue. When he halted before the marshal, their difference in build was apparent: he was a head and a half taller and twice the muscle.

"I did not come here seeking blood," Owain said. "And don't fear that I have betrayed you. Far from it."

A blank stare met Owain's revelation. Then Rieux laughed. "You are a fool! Bolingbroke's men . . . they have been marched to death. You stole provisions. Who has the advantage here? I say it is not him."

"Advantage? What advantage? This is English territory we're in. All Henry has to do is wag his finger and the next village will dump their grain and kegs onto the back of a wagon for him. Those supplies were meant to sustain us, if need be." Deeply fatigued, Owain sighed and glanced around him—at Edmund, dabbing at his armor with a kerchief, at Maredydd, studying his father with great care, and at Rhys, dampening his anger toward Rieux in deference to Owain. "We have no advantage. None. This is a stalemate. At best, we're equally matched. But only as we stand now. If we leave the hill to sally forth and attack, it is the English staring down on us, spears poised and aimed at our very hearts, arrows snug against their strings. Henry is a cautious commander. And no more or less a fool than me. So deem me the fool if you will. 'Tis that other fool watching us I have great respect for."

"Respect? For your enemy?" His chest plate heaving, Rieux clenched his teeth. The words slid out from his pinched mouth. "They have just marched thirty leagues! Their tongues—they drag the ground. Their horses are soaked with sweat. They are weak and they have come to you, mighty prince. Is this not what you have waited for? You begged my king for an army—on hands and knees! And now we come and you will not move from this hill?"

Owain's eyes met with Rhys's. For a moment, he faltered in his will. It was true what Rieux said. Any leader with a sliver of ambition would have seized at it. The English were drained. Victory on the field today—would mean an end. A final, irrevocable answer to years of passionate prayer. A deliverance from centuries of unjust oppression. From slavery and thievery. Freedom called out to him, but its price was heavy. There were too many doubts in his head chasing each other, chanting. On the opposing hand, a defeat—and all would be for nothing. If they were vanquished at the point of English swords here and now, the cause was gone forever. Sucked into some great void. And then, the misery of Wales would fall upon Owain's head.

A hundred years too early? Had Hopkyn interpreted the prophecies wrongly? Perhaps he was not *Y Mab Darogan* after all.

Owain's tongue slid over parched lips. "King Charles has played this game shrewdly all along. How sincere was his commitment I have more than often wondered, but never spoke of until now. He has sent me enough of an army to make a show, but far from enough to do the job resoundingly. In the meantime, while we have dashed about from cave to hilltop to forests thick, we have learned a thing or two about those bloody Englishmen whose ankles you have come to bite at." Hands locked behind his back, for it was the safer place for them to be, he looked at the marshal squarely. "Fatigue has *never* hindered an English army. Hotspur assumed it would and Shrewsbury was —"

"My prince!" Gethin shot into the tent and plunged at Owain's feet. Excitement gleamed in his eyes. "He will hear your terms."

In slow motion, Marshal de Rieux laid the parchment out on the table. Le Borgue and Hugueville swarmed to peer over his low shoulders. He scanned through the demands, and then stepped back. "You think that Bolingbroke will agree to any of this?" He beckoned to his men. "Fool . . . and coward," he admonished as he strode from the tent.

45

Near Worcester, England — September, 1405

WHEN THE TERMS WERE read to King Henry by Greyndour, his left eyebrow arched upward. He might not have believed Glyndwr's outlandish arrogance, except that he had dealt with the man for too many years already. The Welshman was cunning, if not a bit insane. "My silver wash basin and a candle—lit, please."

Beneath the treasured shade of a tree, Prince Harry and the English commanders watched as a soldier held the tarnished silver bowl before the king. Henry curled a finger at Greyndour, who still cradled the document in his hands.

Holding the lit candle at an angle so the hot wax would not drip on his hand, the king passed it beneath the parchment. The edge blackened. In moments, a hungry orange flame began to devour the page. Sir Gilbert Talbot received the candle and blew it out. The ashes gathered in the bowl. As the fire licked closer to Greyndour's fingers, he relinquished the document.

Sweat poured into Henry's eyes and he blinked away its sting. With a soaked palm, he pushed his hair off his forehead. Then he took the bowl and held it aloft with its smoking contents. "Deliver my answer."

Talbot took the bowl from the king's steady hands and draped a kerchief of red silk over it, smothering the fading fire into a pile of cinders. Once Greyndour was mounted and helmeted, Talbot gave the bowl to him.

As Greyndour and a small party of knights rode down into the valley, the king turned to his son and touched him on the shoulder. "We shall see if it's a fight he wants."

"Is that what *you* want?" Harry asked, glancing at his father's mottled fingers.

The king pulled his hand away. "When the time is right, I shall welcome it."

"Sooner would be better." Harry's eyes flicked skyward. "No storms today. Unless our Welsh wizard is brewing up a pot of snakes' bellies and newts' eyes as we speak. Today, at least, would seem to be in our favor."

Harry cast a long accusing look at his father. The boy liked to challenge him. Had he been so impetuous in his youth?

On the whole of his left side, Henry suddenly felt a numbness spreading rapidly. He grabbed his left shoulder and pressed with his bare fingers against the unyielding armor. The fingers of his dangling hand prickled with heat. He gasped and quickly glanced down, but there was no fire consuming his skin, only a white burning from within that flared at his fingertips and shot up his arm, to his shoulder and into his heart. He battled for a breath, eyes clenched, until the flood of pain ebbed away. In a voice so strained and dampened only his son could hear, Henry said, "*When* you are king . . . you may decide . . . when to call the charge. Until . . . such time . . ."

His voice trailed away, leaving the thought unfinished.

Harry had not budged when he saw the discomfort flare in his father's face. Always, there stood the unspoken battle between father and son. A friction that rubbed away at already fine threads. Henry knew his son had never forgiven him for his godfather's deposition.

Even worse had been the questionable manner of Richard's death. During those final months, Harry had begged his father for an audience with Richard, but any and all encounter was severely denied. In the confines of the Tower, Richard had wasted, his thin skin clinging to his bones, death's pallor upon him, his mind feebly slipping away. How could he have ever explained to his son that it was Richard's choice to forego sustenance that had killed him, not that he, Henry, had ordered food withheld? Harry would never have believed him anyway.

BEYOND EARSHOT OF HIS father, Harry pulled Gilbert away. "Bring my horse at once. I will ride out with Greyndour to meet the man who so vexes my father."

It would be fitting justice to witness the Welsh calling upon their old gods to conjure up a tempest to send Henry of Bolingbroke back to London. He wouldn't miss it for anything. Not even for a cellar full of wine and free rein in a brothel.

When Harry caught up with Greyndour, he was handing over the king's answers to the one they called Gethin the Fierce.

"Fetch your master," Harry said to Gethin. "I'll have a word with him."

Instead of a flat denial, Gethin gave a fleeting grin and sped back to the lines of the Welsh camp with the bowl of ashes in the crook of his arm.

AS GLYNDWR RODE HIS silver-maned courser across the open field, Harry was charged with excitement. He knew his father was watching this all unfold from afar—undoubtedly fuming.

Oh but let him watch. Let him see how it is done.

Glyndwr halted a hundred feet from Harry's party and dismounted alone. He stayed his men with his palm and looked toward Harry. Withdrawing his sword and handing it to Gethin, he pulled his helmet off and sat it on the ground at his feet. Then he waited.

Taking his cue, Harry leapt from his saddle and also abandoned his weapons and headgear.

"My prince," Greyndour said, a note of caution in his voice, "I do not think this wise."

Harry laughed. "It's not wise of him either." And he went forward.

Owain Glyndwr was extremely tall and his hair fell in sun-gold waves about his shoulders. His hungry strides betrayed a purpose, yet the smooth glide of his steps displayed a grace uncommon for a man of such proportions. His gaze was cool and gentle and his bearing regal in a manner that Harry had not expected. They met halfway between Abberley and Woodbury Hills—two great armies at their backs and the sun strong above them.

"I applaud your bravery," Harry said, smiling.

"I have been called a fool of late," Glyndwr said, "and this would prove me so."

"But the curiosity was killing you."

"Indeed it was," Glyndwr said. "I beg your pardon, but I am not sure how to address you."

"Henry, Prince of Wales."

"And by what descent of lineage would you make that claim?"

Harry's amusement melted. He curled the fingers of his right hand into a fist at his side. "Let us not quibble over ancestral titles, *Sir* Owain."

Glyndwr's gaze never wavered. "Is that not how this all began?"

Harry chuckled and shook his head. "Really, now. How do you think this will end?" He glanced behind him at the hill, black with English soldiers. "I must admit, I don't think my father ever expected this of you. He is a stubborn man, you see. One might think that by now he would cease to underestimate you. You have surprised us all. And with French soldiers at your bidding, no less. We are evenly matched, wouldn't you say?"

It was oddly silent. The taunting chants from both sides were absent. A long while passed before Glyndwr spoke.

"Evenly, yes. Either could win."

"And either could lose."

Glyndwr tilted his head back. "What do you want?"

"I only wanted to know whether or not we agreed . . . and I think we do."

Then Harry turned, his head bare and his back to his enemies, and went to his horse, leaving Greyndour to collect his things. He was sure the rebel now realized he was quite a different sort from his father, which had been his whole purpose in meeting with Glyndwr.

When he returned to camp his father berated him and then pressed him for information—of which Harry had none to give. Even as the king flared with indignation at his son, the soldiers glowed with admiration for Harry. They may have cowered at Henry's command, but it was Harry they followed in heart.

Iolo Goch:

My lord Owain got exactly the answer he expected. And with a very clever twist on Henry's part, he thought. But Harry, so arrogant in his bold youthfulness and yet so astute, had planted the nagging seed of doubt in Owain's mind. Years of planning hinged on this event—and how easily it could all come undone. Just as it had for Hotspur.

The following day, Edmund penned the demands again precisely as they had read before: that Henry relinquish his false claim to the throne; that the young Earl of March be rightly crowned, that the north of England be given over to Northumberland and Wales to Owain; that due compensation be paid to Wales for the destruction inflicted by the army of England, that Wales be permitted to establish its own universities and church; and that England once and forever forfeit all claim to Welsh lands.

This time, my lord Owain struck one demand from the document. One single term. He would graciously allow Henry of Bolingbroke to live out his life in exile and avoid trial.

Again, the document came back. This time in illegible shreds. For four more days, Rhys Gethin rode down into the valley and met Sir John Greyndour.

Each time, Gethin returned with the same riposte from Abberley Hill. Furious, the French would send a small party of knights onto the field. The English replied likewise. From both hills, cheers rattled the sky. Lances were lowered as French and English targeted one another. But always, the skirmishes ended the same: some wounded, others run through at the point of a sword, their bleeding corpses dragged back to camp. Nearly two hundred men from both sides died.

A terrible waste of good fighting men.

The French were not above picking fights with their own allies, leaving the Welsh a grumbling lot who despised the very men who had come to aid them.

46

Near Worcester, England — September, 1405

ON THE EIGHTH NIGHT of their standoff on the wooded hill, Owain walked among his men. Faces void of expression glanced at him in mere recognition. A bout of bloody flux had left many of them struggling to regain their strength. Half-eaten bowls of barley and beans lay scattered around. Here and there, a soldier lay curled on his side, clutching at his stomach, moaning with discomfort.

Morale was at its nethermost. Owain saw it on their faces and in their words. There was a time when all he had to do was walk amongst them and voices would raise and hearts beat anew. A time when the hope for freedom and the thirst for justice were tonics potent enough to bring the dead to life. He saw none of that now.

The conviction within him wavering, Owain returned to his tent. He parted the flap to find Nesta sitting at the very table over which he had struggled that week. A single candle flickered before her as she drew breath to speak.

"My lord, you look distraught."

"How did —"

"They know who shares your pillow," she said with contentment, rising to her feet. "A soldier's life is lonely. They understand that."

"Why did you come here?" Owain eyed her from head to foot. She was a far cry from the barefooted girl who once earned her coin by trilling ballads. Instead of a kirtle tattered at the hem, she now wore a houppelande of plush scarlet velvet, the neckline low, the belt high. Her hair, never hidden, was woven with sparkling jewels. The attire did not seem quite practical for traveling into the midst of such a predicament, but then there was never anything subtle about Nesta. Long ago she had kindled his ambitions, urged him to think far beyond yesterday or tomorrow, but well into the past and centuries ahead. Yet something about her had changed in a way that did not appeal to him.

She traced a circle on the ground with the toe of her slipper. Her hand skimmed a gilded belt and then drifted lower over her belly. "I will bear another child. This time, it will be a son . . . and I want to know that you will acknowledge him and bequeath him with proper station and means. Title. Lands."

"I have neither the luxury of time nor the inclination to discuss this with you now."

"This is exactly the time to speak of such things, Owain. My children may be bastards, but they have a prince's blood. And Welsh custom pays heed to all of a man's natural children. Do not succumb to the English ways. Their king stands paralyzed before you. A mighty army awaits your command. Destroy Henry. Right every wrong that has been dealt to you. Answer to the prophecies that Hopkyn spoke of and seize the glory that is your destiny."

Owain, however, was not so certain of that destiny any longer.

She stepped closer, but Owain shook his head to halt her. "I only ever wanted him gone from Wales. That is all."

For over a week, he had toiled in anguish—ready to strike at Henry, weighing every possible outcome, retaliation fading to reluctance. But as he said those words to Nesta, a sense of merciful deliverance swept through him. It was as if he had been Atlas, holding up the heavens, and had not known it until then. He claimed the stool on which she had sat waiting for him and buried his face in his hands.

"Our son?" Nesta said.

"It could be a girl."

"Is that what you wish?"

"I wish," he said, raising his eyes and spreading his hands on the table, "for the health of you and the child and a safe journey home."

Owain stood, went to the opening of the tent and paused. "I will arrange for an escort for you in the morning to take you back to Aberystwyth. This is not the place for you. Not in your state."

"My place is with you." She held her chin firm. Her dark eyes blazed with defiance in the dim light. "I will not abandon you, not even when there is danger."

He hung his head. "Nesta, take my word to heart—there's no reason for you to fear for my safety. Please, you will understand. Now . . . I have matters to set right. I'll return to you the very moment I can." As he reached to part the tent flap, he could see the heavy disappointment etched in the lines around her small mouth and knew she had not received what she had come for. "I would never deny our children, Nesta. Of all things, that is one fear you need not carry within your soul."

AT OWAIN'S ORDERS, FIREWOOD was gathered and heaped into a pile. When it was done, the topmost piece of kindling was at the height of a man and a half. As the flames grew, both French and Welsh commanders gathered in a wide circle about it.

"Where are the storms?" Rieux asked, moving away from the heat.

"What?" Owain said.

Rieux grinned. "The storms. You have called on them before, have you not? A drop or two of rain and Bolingbroke might run home."

An emptied cup in his hand, Rhys brushed past Owain and strode forward. "He's no wizard . . . and you're no genius."

"No." Owain pulled back on Rhys's shoulder. "Enough. No more quarrels. No more. Or the English won't have to battle us to win. We'll have beaten ourselves."

They all stood in silence for a long while—some eyes on the fire before them, others casting glances at the distant flickers on Abberley Hill.

"Gethin," Owain began, his voice low and solid, "when you won at Bryn Glas, did your army look like this? When we clutched victory at Hyddgen against insurmountable odds, we were strong and full of fire in our bellies. It takes more than numbers and weapons to win a battle." He clutched a hand over his heart. "It takes this."

Opening his arms, he walked to the other side of the circle. "All of you—look around and tell me if it is here."

Their chins sank. No answer came.

Owain stormed away and a minute later returned. In his hands was the last treaty Edmund had penned. It flew from his fingers into the fire.

"Prepare the soldiers to leave. We march out tonight."

The words fell on the commanders' ears like stones dropped into an empty well.

Only Edmund dared to speak. "But what of the Indenture? My nephew?"

Owain looked at him blankly. "I don't know, Edmund. I don't know everything. Just that today . . . and tomorrow . . . are not the days to see it through."

THE SIGHT OF WOODBURY Hill at dawn, barren and trampled, was a bitter disappointment to King Henry. For six years, he had been harassed and taunted by Owain Glyndwr, always waiting for the chance to meet him face to face and put an end to it all. Six long years. The night before, when the towering bonfire had blazed in the Welsh camp, he had resolved that the waiting would go on no longer. He was going to bring those Welsh bastards and their French hounds to their knees and drown them in their own blood.

It was a decision that came a day too late. Soon the Welsh would be safe within their own borders.

47

Westminster Palace, England — March, 1406

T HE SLEEVES OF HIS shirt were so over-sized that Henry could easily keep his hands well hidden inside them. His left shoulder still sloped from the weakness on that side, but he had learned to prop his arm and lean to one side so that no one would ever know the difference. The discoloration of his skin, if bared, could not go unnoticed however, and so he had become a master at concealing his outbreaks.

He wiggled his fingers beneath the plush velvet of his sleeve and gripped the clawed arms of his throne as the young James, heir to Scotland's crown, was marched down the long carpet of the Westminster throne room. The boy was willowy and fair, not unlike Richard as a youth, but as James's clear, blue eyes darted about the room, drinking in every detail, Henry sensed something distinctly different about him. Something very keen. Something very . . . kingly.

"On your way to France?" Henry said. "'Tis a pity the storm interrupted your journey, but perhaps not so unfortunate you came to us, my dear James."

"I was to be tutored at King Charles' court," James said plainly, with merely a trace of a Scottish accent.

Henry leaned forward, his lip curving upward on one side. "I have been to Charles' court. You might find their jewels and feasts dazzling for the short term, but it is no place to learn anything besides madness and adultery. Consider yourself a guest here . . . for now."

He fully expected the boy to bargain for his release, but James simply bowed his head and said, "I thank you, my lord."

"You are quite welcome."

Perhaps the boy would prove pliable after all.

Iolo Goch:

Not two weeks had passed between the time that young James of Scotland was captured off the coast of Yorkshire and the terrible news was delivered to his ailing father. With the name of his son on his lips, Robert drew his last breath. Scotland's king was dead. His heir was a prisoner in the Tower of London. Albany would become governor.

And Henry of Bolingbroke became a little more secure in the fit of his crown. For the time being, there was one less foe to fret over.

48

Harlech Castle, Wales — Summer, 1406

IN ONE OF THE guard rooms of the gatehouse of Harlech Castle, Owain was conversing with his chancellor, Griffith Young. Afternoon sun streamed through the tall, narrow windows and threw patches of golden light on the tiled floor. A single ray fell across Owain's palm, in which lay a pair of spurs.

"Madoc's spurs," Owain said, his words heavy with sadness. He touched a fingertip to the fine point of one of the silver rowels and pressed until he felt a prick of pain. "I gave them to him the day we left for Aberdaron. A soldier's spurs. My father was a soldier. I became one. And so did my sons. As a boy, I used to rue every time that my father would abandon us to fight for England's king. I thought wars were senseless occasions to bring one man's ego on par with God himself. I thought, through law, that I could make a difference. How naïve of me. And now, ah dear heaven, I understand all too well. I am as guilty as Henry. I have caused a great deal of suffering . . . and yet I can end none of it. But not for lack of trying.

"There are two ways I can return peace to Wales. One is to give Bolingbroke everything he wants, including my head, and subject the people of Wales to servility. The other is to stand and be strong. As strong as England. And where do we find that strength, Chancellor Young? We find it in allying ourselves with England's many enemies." Owain flicked the rowel, watching it spin, then placed both spurs on the table. He began to pace, hands folded behind his back. "Ireland has not had a fitting king since Brian Boru. Such a beautiful land. Have you seen it, Griffith?"

Chancellor Young nodded.

"They would love to have England off their backs, but they can't stop hating each other long enough to get the job done. Blood feuds. Their pride runs deep." He poured a goblet of wine and offered it to Young. Before pouring himself a drink, Owain paused with his hands fingering the stem of the jewel-encrusted goblet. "And Scotland. In another time, perhaps, we could have hoped for more from them. But with King Robert dead and Albany at the helm, that is a wasteland of hope. Albany rules so long as James is Henry's captive. He'd be a fool to give that up. So what does that leave us with?"

"France?" Young answered.

Tipping the bottle until the wine, French wine, Owain filled his cup to the brim. "You say that as a question, as if you're uncertain."

"I have been there, my lord. And I have seen . . . what goes on."

"What does go on there? Is it as we have all heard?"

Young sighed and nodded. "With the years, Charles falls further and further from sanity. His queen does little to hide her affection for Orleans. I myself saw them kiss, open-mouthed, in his very presence. She is with child again."

Owain arched an eyebrow. Young didn't need to speak the implication. The child's parentage was questionable, no doubt. The French king was both mad and a cuckold. "Charles sends us gifts—opulent, useless frivolities—and more dribbled promises of military support, but at this stage I would be even madder than he is if I believed one whit of it. So we must look to the future. Are we secure in relying on Orleans' support?"

"We are."

"And what of the Church in France?"

"So long as you stand by Pope Benedict of Avignon and against Rome —"

"I was never *against* Rome. I was against the notion that Rome would deny Wales the right to a separate church, apart from the control of English bishops. I know how reluctant Byfort and Trefor were for me to sign the letter at Pennal in support of Benedict. It puts their privileged station in jeopardy."

"Trefor has always been your man, Prince Owain."

"But Byfort?"

"His heart may yet lie with Rome, although I do not think he'll betray you."

"Think? In that case, all I can be sure of, given his piety, is that he'll not stab me in my sleep. Bishops, monks, churches, popes . . . it is its own entire world, the workings of which I would not dare pretend to understand."

In one long swallow, Owain emptied his cup. "Do you know something, Griffith? I never knew God while sitting at Mass, listening to Latin verse. But I saw God in the height of the clouds and the color of the sunset while sitting in the Berwyns in my youth. I have heard the voice of God in the waves lapping at the shore below Harlech. And when I saw my first son being born . . . I could feel God beside me . . . felt that I *knew* him. God for me is not imbued in holy relics. He is in every stone and drop of water around us. Does that make me a druid, Griffith? A heretic?"

"No. I think it makes you a truer believer than most men."

Owain grinned. "But we must learn to balance truth with impressions."

"The impressions we make upon men do not matter in the eyes of God and the after-life."

"Maybe so, Griffith, maybe so. But impressions lead to beliefs, and beliefs to actions, and actions become the course of history."

Young tilted his head in thought and then gave a small bow. "You will have your place there, my prince. Of that I have never doubted. It is an imposing task to —"

"Like bloody hell I'll wait!" Rhys burst through the door. "Jesus! Do you think I would ask to see him for —?"

"Rhys." Owain rose and met him halfway across the room. He waved off the two flustered guards scurrying after Rhys. "Is there trouble?"

"Your pardon." Rhys nodded toward Chancellor Young as Owain approached and lowered his voice. "I rode through the night to get here. You must come at once, Owain. She is ill at heart."

"Nesta? But why?" Owain motioned Rhys toward the door on the far side of the room. He waved the guards out into the corridor and gently closed the door.

Rhys glanced briefly at Young. "She delivered you a son."

It should have been joyful news to hear those words from his lips, but there was something terribly wrong in the way Rhys had forced his way in to see Owain. Ice flushed through Owain's veins and nearly stopped his heart cold. For the moment, he forgot all about Chancellor Young being in the room. He put a hand on Rhys's shoulder. "But the child was not due for another month. Will he . . . will he live?"

"Not long." Rhys clutched Owain's hand. "Owain, you cannot save the boy, but . . . *she* needs you."

Owain nodded. "I'll go."

How could he not?

WITHIN MINUTES, OWAIN'S HORSE was saddled and waiting. He and Rhys were slipping their boots into their stirrups to mount when Margaret exploded into the courtyard.

"Wait!" Margaret grabbed at the bridle of her husband's horse. Breathless, she searched his face. "Where are you going?"

Rhys sat silently on his horse, not daring a word.

For a tense moment, Owain met her eyes, but the tally of unspoken accusations was too many for him to confront just then. "There is no time to explain. I will return soon. Now, please, let go."

Margaret clenched the bridle tighter. "Are you going . . . to be with *her*?"

A bolt of shame ripped through Owain's chest. He jerked on the reins. The horse lurched forward and Margaret's hands dropped away. He steadied his mount. "This is important. Do not press me on this."

Crossing her arms, Margaret looked down. "I see. Then go." She raised her smoldering eyes. "And stay gone. Your bed here has long been cold."

As fast as she said the words, she flew up the stairs to the gatehouse and was gone.

Aberystwyth Castle, Wales — Summer, 1406

THE BOY CHILD WAS dead long before Owain arrived. He held Nesta's hand, tried to comfort her, but she did not even bother acknowledge him.

"I am so sorry, Nesta," he said, stroking her hand. "I know how much you wanted to give me a son."

Slowly, she turned a blanched face toward him. "Would it have mattered to you if I had?" Then she averted her face again and went silent.

After a long while, fraught by an odd helplessness that he was unaccustomed to when in her company, Owain ordered his horse saddled up for the return to Harlech. He went to the courtyard, where his mount was brought to him. Rhys stood there, his feet braced wide, his countenance glum.

As Owain pulled himself up into his saddle, he said to Rhys, "Tell her if there's anything I can do for her, I will. She has but to breathe the word and I'll come back."

"No," said Rhys.

"What?"

"I said 'no'. Leave her be. Let her get on with living. No more of these fleeting trysts and off again for months and months."

"Stay out of this, Rhys. 'Tis not your place." Owain steadied his eager mount by stroking its mane.

"Ah, not my place. I see. So what is my *place*? Five steps behind you, as you face a Welsh parliament debating on your right to wear a crown? Beside you, as French generals quibble over your every stratagem? Before you, as Flemings hurl spears at your head? Perhaps my place is beneath your feet, lying face down as you trample on my daughter's honor?"

"Rhys, this is not the time to flare in anger. You asked me to come. To be with Nesta. Do not make a poison of my name to her. Or the girls. I *will* come back, as soon as I —"

"No. Enough of this Owain. You have thought of no one but yourself through it all. You divide yourself between Margaret and Nesta and pretend that all is bliss. Have you never thought of what either of them feels or thinks when you leave them?"

"If you were not who you are . . ." Owain gathered his reins, gripping them tight. "You are like a brother to me, Rhys, but do not proclaim yourself my judge."

Owain kicked his horse in the flanks and flew through Aberystwyth's gate without a backward glance.

Iolo Goch:

Even if he had wanted to, Owain could not have visited Nesta. The English had descended on Aberystwyth. For summer's length, Rhys Ddu held the castle against the zealous attacks of Prince Harry. Then, with the arrival of cannons, the siege began in full.

During the previous year, the border of Owain's realm had begun to collapse in on itself. First Anglesey fell, then Gower ceded, and later Rhys Ddu's own Pembrokeshire threw its lot with England.

How much can change in so short a time

49

Aberystwyth Castle, Wales — September, 1407

IT SEEMED TO RHYS, as he watched Harry's gunners heft their colossal stones into the wide-mouthed cannons, that perhaps the notion that Wales was a country unto its own existed nowhere anymore but inside the walls of Aberystwyth. For months now there had been no contact with the outside world. Every day, from the breaking of dawn until the sun set over Cardigan Bay, he watched in desperation for Owain's dragon banner, snapping in the sea breeze, and a host of Welsh soldiers rending the air with the battle cry of liberation. And always the night came—a sweet, too short reprieve from the hammering of guns, the searing smell of sulfur, the barrage of firepots exploding in the bailey. Each morning brought yet another empty horizon, the far-off outline of the mountains etched naked against a broad sky.

With the substantial garrison that was kept at Aberystwyth, supplies had dwindled rapidly. Water was the most valuable thing to any man there; a soldier would not have given a cup of his water rations for a pile of gold. Money meant nothing to a man withering of thirst. Tauntingly, English soldiers beyond bowshot would dump casks of water over their heads and splash in the puddles. It was the least of their cruelties. Derisions flew from both directions, though, along with arrows.

On the wall-walk, Rhys sidled up to a scowling archer, who was twirling one of his last two arrows between his fingers. "What is the count today?"

"Twelve shots . . . so far," the soldier grumbled. He spat over the wall and leaned out to see how far it would go. Then he suddenly pulled back to safety and crouched beside a jar of oil. "No wind. And another coming."

The bellow of a gun shook the air. The stones beneath their feet trembled. Instinctively, Rhys honed in on the source. It was the middle cannon—the 'King's Gun', it was christened—a fire-belching beast dragged all the way from Nottingham. Harry had spared no expense or resource in his determination.

The great fist of rock hurtled through the air and crashed into the battlements not twenty feet from where Rhys stood. A cloud of mortar and stone fragments exploded. The deadly stone slammed through three Welsh soldiers, crushing their bones as it rumbled on its way, not slowing until it impacted itself on the inner wall. Then it rolled sluggishly through the outer bailey and finally came to a halt. Cautiously, Rhys and the archer peered out at the enemy as cheers rose up from the English ranks.

An armored figure rode out before the lines of English, the scarlet plume of his caparisoned horse bobbing as it galloped along. Prince Harry came to a halt before the big cannon, a thin trail of smoke still wafting from its black orifice. His chest plate gleamed in the low rays of a deep red evening sun. He plucked off his helmet and bowed to his gunners from his saddle. They cheered again as Harry urged his horse closer to the castle.

Harry halted a safe distance away and called out, "My gunners take pride in their work! Soon your walls will crumble and I have others eager to play their part. A parley, Rhys Ddu! A parley . . . and you walk unscathed from here, your honor intact! Cannons will cease for now! At daybreak, they will commence—unless you grant me cause to order their silence!"

With a subtle cue of his knees, Harry's warhorse reared up and then spun about. "Daybreak! I shall be waiting!" he shouted over his shoulder. "God and St. George be with you!"

Rhys flew down a narrow set of stairs and emerged in the outer bailey, pausing as he passed the litter of broken bodies arranged in grotesque fashion in the stone's trail. As cruel a thought as it was, he was happy to see them all dead. Better a quick, unforeseen death than the prolonged torture of starvation.

"Cadogan!" he bellowed.

An ogreish giant appeared before him. A thick mat of hair covered the man's bare arms, unencumbered by mail or plates of armor. Cadogan tucked his great axe into his belt and jerked in a bow.

"Have someone . . ."—Rhys flapped a hand at the bodies— "take care of these men."

Cadogan rattled off orders to a gathering of onlookers. His bushy eyebrows jumped up and down as he spoke. He turned back to Rhys. "Gawkin' like they never saw a dead man. Anything else, my lord?"

"Yes, Cadogan. Where is my daughter?"

"Storeroom of the far tower. Far from the fuckin' guns as she could get herself and the babes."

Rhys raced off, through a door into the inner bailey and into the tower. His knees, weak from being famished for so long, wobbled beneath him. When he arrived breathless at the door of the storeroom, he stumbled, catching himself with his hand upon the latch. With the heel of his calloused palm, he pounded against the door. Empty silence answered his urgent drumming. He threw his shoulder against the timber of the door. It would not yield.

Rhys pressed his whiskered cheek to the door. "Nesta! Please, let me in!"

A few moments later, the bar slid. The door swung open with a groan of its rusted hinges. He swallowed Nesta in his arms. Myfanwy and Gwenllian were wailing in fright. He let go of Nesta, then swept the girls up. Myfanwy buried her face in her grandfather's thick neck, while Gwenllian, fingers in mouth, blubbered, spittle and tears mixing on her chin. She had her father's dark blue eyes and golden ringlets—the resemblance was haunting.

"Ah, little ones, you're safe here. Safe, I promise." Rhys looked at Nesta. She was guarding the flame of her candle, which flickered against the draft from the doorway. He hugged both girls harder against his chest. His paunchy belly had diminished to a barely noticeable bulge. "They're so frightened, dear things."

"Frightened of the dark. And hungry. Although they're no longer afraid of rats. I think they've named one or two," Nesta said cynically.

Rhys lowered the girls to the floor, although Myfanwy clung fiercely to her grandfather's neck and had to be pried off. She wrapped herself around his knees, while Gwenllian tottered off and climbed up on one of the few remaining sacks of flour. Her dress was in sore need of mending, but for want of thread and needle it had gone undone.

"I came to ask your heart," Rhys began, "and whatever you say, I'll abide by."

The failing light of the candle painted weak shadows on Nesta's hollowed out cheeks. She would often make sure her children had enough to eat before allowing herself the first bite—although there was not that much of Nesta to be wasted. The lice had reduced her radiant veil of black curls to a wiry mop fit for scrubbing pots.

"Ask then," she muttered with dull interest. Starvation had so robbed her of strength that she spoke only when necessity demanded it. She had not sung, not even to her children, since the day the siege began.

Rhys breathed deeply. Only Nesta could give him the strength he needed. Reason to do what must be done.

THE STANDARD THAT MARKED Prince Harry's tent was emblazoned with the red roses of the House of Lancaster. Rhys regarded it momentarily, then held his breath as he ducked inside. Four well-armed guards blocked Cadogan from entering, which left the giant ranting outside, issuing visceral threats of ripping the soldiers' heads from their shoulders and swallowing them whole.

Harry rose from his chair, smiling with unusual civility. With an open hand, he offered Rhys a seat opposite him.

"The terms are generous. You will see," Harry said, sitting again.

Rhys had not bowed before the prince when entering. He had not even as yet addressed him. In mounting curiosity, he took the seat across from Harry. The prince was barely twenty-two, Maredydd's age, but already a seasoned and successful general. He had the finer features of his mother's ancestry—graceful limbs, a slender neck, and a face so endearing that even Rhys, who owed the misery of his last few months to him, could not with full conviction hate the man.

Harry slouched in his chair. "It should all be very clear, but read it twice if you must . . . just to be certain."

Rhys did take his time. So much so, that Harry finally prompted him.

"Well?"

"Why?" Rhys asked.

"Why what?"

"Full pardons? You were not so forgiving at Conwy."

Leaning forward with his elbows on the table, Harry scratched at the crown of his close-cropped head of hair. "Yes, you're quite right on that. Hotspur begged me to show some measure of mercy, ah, but I was a stripling then. Rash and hungering to be feared. I thought men would respect me if they feared me, but that's not nearly so, is it?" He plucked up a goose quill and dipped it in the inkwell. "We all change, Rhys Ddu. Times change. Circumstances change. I want your castle. You want your freedom. It's really not so complicated."

Harry signed his name at the bottom, royal titles included, and handed the quill to Rhys.

Rhys took the quill in his stubby fingers. He tried not to imagine what Owain's reaction might be as he lowered the pen to the parchment. Neither his shield nor his sword had ever felt so weighty, so condemning.

"Now," Harry began with relief, as Rhys angrily scratched his name, "we will take the sacrament together to seal our agreement. I understand you are not a, uh . . . a man of rigorous religious practices, so I will tell the priest to make it short."

Short? Rhys laid the quill down beside the document that shouted to the world his failure. Short, long, in between—the length of some drummed up ritual mattered not. He wasn't likely to hear a word of it anyway.

Harlech Castle, Wales — October, 1407

PRINCE HARRY KEPT HIS word. He withdrew to Hereford, leaving a force at nearby Strata Florida. The truce was to last six weeks, during which time the Welsh could come and go at will. If the castle was not relieved by the 24th of October, Aberystwyth would be surrendered to Harry. In return, Rhys and his entire garrison would be given full pardons and allowed to walk free. But if a Welsh relief force did arrive, the promise of pardons was null and void and Aberystwyth would again become a fair target for English cannons and siege engines.

Rhys did not immediately go to Harlech. He was too tormented. There were arrangements to be made for Nesta and the girls. A few days later, when he finally went, it was a long, slow journey up the coast. It was the weight of his heart that delayed him so, the dread of what Owain would say to him.

As Rhys Ddu pled his case in Llywelyn's Hall of Harlech Castle before all of Owain's generals and family, he could see the rage building deep within Owain. Though dormant, the sparks were there, just beneath the surface. Owain's eyes were fixed on the floor during the entirety of the report—his hands gripping the arms of his throne. To Owain's right, on the far side of the dais, stood Edmund Mortimer. To the left, Maredydd. Somewhere to the side were Margaret and Iolo. When Rhys finished, the prince pushed himself up with stiffened limbs.

Finally, Owain raised his chin and damned Rhys with a stare. The gray of his eyes was a chilling shade. His voice was remote. "How could you, in all the world, betray me?"

Rhys's jaw dropped. He had feared this. Owain was proud and determined, but still, he had done all he could—and waited weeks for Owain to do something. To save him. Did Owain claim no part in this? Rhys drew a deep breath. "Betray you? Do you call saving the lives of two hundred of your men betrayal? How could you even think to question my loyalty?"

But Owain gave his response no regard. He stood and opened his hands wide. "Once, we could ride the land from the Irish Sea to Offa's Dyke and say that it was ours." Then his arms fell to his sides, his fingers spread apart, grasping and empty. "Now, all that's left are Aberystwyth and Harlech. If either falls, the other will for certain. If we are ever to regain what we once had, we must begin here. We must hold these two castles until the last breath. Our time will come again. In the name of honor and freedom, how could you so thoughtlessly toss that aside?"

Rhys had done what he thought was the right thing—he had no other choice—and now that was being called into question by the very idol he lived to serve?

"Harry set upon Aberystwyth because he thought you were there," Rhys began, "because you so often are. What would *you* have done after endless months under siege, seeing your granddaughters begin to fall faint with hunger, watching the horizon, waiting for relief . . . relief that never came? Speaking of such—where the *hell* were you? I can damn near feel my spine when I suck in my gut, I waited so bloody long."

Owain drew back his shoulders. "I was gathering men to come to your aid. Two more weeks, Rhys. If you had just held out two more weeks I would have been there at Harry's back."

"Two more weeks and you would have arrived to a pile of stones and rotting corpses." Rhys clenched his fists. He felt as though he were trying to converse with a rock, not his closest friend or the just leader he had come to know and admire. "You're afraid that the moment you step down from this glittering perch the English will swoop down and seize your cozy little nest."

In a moment Owain had closed the distance between them, his breathing audible, his nose inches from Rhys's heated face. Owain slid his sword from its scabbard and tapped the edge of the blade across Rhys's chest plate. "You think me a liar? I should cut off your head here and now for your treason!"

"Then do it. If loyalty means nothing to you, then strike me down. I signed with Harry so that your soldiers might live to fight another day beside you. And I pray I will, too." He had tried his best. God knows he had tried. A single tear spilled from the outside corner of Rhys's eye. His voice, normally a booming, boisterous tenor, cracked. "I did it to save Myfanwy and Gwenllian. Have you forsaken your own blood, as well?"

Owain's jaw quavered. He lowered his voice. "Where is Nesta? Where are the girls?"

"Gone."

"Where? Where did you send them?"

Rhys leaned back to steel his spine. "I sent them nowhere. Nesta chose to leave Wales . . . and you."

A few eyes turned on Margaret, but she did not flinch or color— only stood with cool repose, her chin held firm, her shoulders pulled back.

Owain slammed the point of his sword to the floor. As it struck the flagstones, sparks flew from the tip. He spun away, one hand pressed to his temple and the other dragging his sword behind him. "Gethin, how many men can you have ready to ride out by tomorrow?"

Gethin shot a glance toward Rhys. The two men may have had very distinct approaches to life in general, and warfare in particular, but neither would ever have questioned the other's loyalty to Owain or Wales.

"Owain! Have you heard nothing? You can't enter the castle," Rhys protested. "If you do you will annihilate our chance at a pardon. You will sign the death warrants of your own soldiers. This is your chance to bargain. Hand over Harlech and Harry will —"

"Hand over Harlech?" Spinning on his heel, Owain hurled his admonishments, his weapon brandished before him. "As if it were a bauble that meant nothing? I can hardly believe what I am hearing. You took sacrament with the enemy! Your cowardice and assumptions are beyond comprehension. You do not speak for me, Rhys Ddu. And you do not act in the interest of Wales, either. What a black day this is for us all." He shoved his sword back into its scabbard and turned toward Gethin, motioning him to follow as he marched from the room with Edmund close behind.

"Can you have a thousand ready to go then?" Owain said to

Gethin.

Gethin shook his head, but Owain pressed on.

"Then find them. We have precious little time. The supplies are ready, I trust? If not, then we . . ."

Their voices echoed from the corridor, the heels of their shoes striking the stones in unison. Maredydd bowed to Rhys and then hurried off after his father. Rhys was shaking when Margaret laid her hand gently on top of his shoulder.

"He loves you," she said. "You know that?"

"He has a strange practice of showing it."

"He's desperate to hold on to what he fought so hard to gain, that's all. His anger will pass."

"I fear it will not pass, Margaret. Too much has been done to undo."

"Deep wounds leave scars, m'lady," Iolo said softly at her side. "Prince Owain has been abandoned by the very people he has lived to serve. They flock to Harry's promises of pardon for want of peace, to fill their bellies, to end their suffering. What our prince holds in esteem is beyond the comprehension of many."

Rhys grunted. "It's not beyond mine." He pulled himself up tall and cleared his throat. "But I'm not much of a soldier if I'm dead, now am I?"

"Take care, Rhys," Margaret said, hugging him.

"I'd advise you say nothing to him until spoken to," Iolo added.

"Don't worry." Rhys pounded the slight bard on the upper arm. "I may have grown soft around the middle with age, but I'm not senile . . . yet."

50

Harlech Castle, Wales — December, 1407

TWO DAYS BEFORE THE truce was set to expire, Owain arrived at Aberystwyth with a relief force, but with far fewer than the thousand men he had hoped for. The truth was he could barely afford the few hundred that he had ridden with, for it left Harlech in grave danger. Instead of admitting that to Rhys, he had blamed him for entering into the truce. His harsh words toward his friend had been fueled not by anger, but by desperation. Prospects were bleak. That should have been obvious to everyone. But if Owain admitted to that openly, then those around him would give up and all their efforts through all these years would have been for naught. No, he could not admit defeat. Not while he yet lived and breathed.

The first snow that fell in Wales that season came on the last day of October. Too late in the season to begin another protracted siege, Prince Harry did not return immediately, but Owain knew Harry would be back and eventually he would lose Aberystwyth. If a miracle did not turn fate in his favor, he would lose Harlech, too.

The whole world was wrapped in snow and overcome with a hush. Silver branches were still clinging to their golden leaves. The birds that summered even further north in the Shetlands and the

Orkneys had not dallied nearby as usual on their way to kinder climes. Gently the snowflakes drifted down, piling softly upon the still warm ground. By Christmas, the ground had frozen solid and the snow, now driving hard, was still coming. It blanketed not only the jagged mountain caps of Wales, but even England's tranquil valleys and stretching plains.

Rhys would not reveal the whereabouts of Owain's children or mistress. Owain could not deny that they did not belong there at Aberystwyth. And they certainly could not be brought to Harlech. So with swallowed pride, he did not hammer the matter. At Margaret's insistence, he relented on his threats of beheading Rhys and gave Aberystwyth back into his friend's reluctant care. The garrison there was fiercely loyal to Rhys and if the castle were to withstand another attack it would be better served with Rhys in command and Owain elsewhere to gather forces and formulate plans.

In early December, a letter arrived at Harlech.

The wind that shot up over the castle walls and swirled around the inner ward was deathly cold. In his hands, frozen at the fingertips, Owain numbly clutched the letter from Queen Isabelle of France, written on her husband's behalf with an infinite regret and a distress that must have seeped onto the parchment with every nudge of the quill.

The Duke of Orleans was dead—ambushed on the streets of Paris. His sword hand had been severed at the wrist before he could levy one blow in defense of himself. A poleaxe had sent his brains splattering into the gutter. The irony of it was that he was purportedly en route to visit the queen, who had given birth to a stillborn child. The struggle for power between the Burgundians and the Orleans factions was sure throw France into utter chaos.

It did not bode well for Wales, either. He needed time to make sense of it all. Time to pray. What else could he do?

WHEN THE MESSENGER ARRIVED in the hall, Margaret watched as Owain received the letter. She heard the messenger's French accent, saw her husband's shoulders droop with each sentence that his eyes took in. As though he had not noticed her, Owain disappeared through the door that led toward the kitchen.

When she found him an hour later, it was in his usual place—the turret of the Weathercock Tower in the southwest corner of the castle, overlooking the bay.

Owain gave her a long, empty look and held the letter out.

Pulling her woolen cloak tight as the sea wind pried between the seams of her clothing, she took the letter from him and read it. When she was done and her eyes wandered to his face, she saw there the deep shadows surrounding his features, the whites of his eyes gone gray, the bones of his shoulders protruding through his tunic where once there were solid, curving muscles.

"Orleans dead." He sighed, long and low. "France will soon be groveling at Henry's feet, pleading for protection from itself. I almost felt invincible . . . once. How does it all slip away so easily? Something so close. So true. So certain. And now . . . gone." His eyes went shut.

"Do you think it will be so?" Margaret said as her teeth chattered uncontrollably. It had gone a whole day without snowing, but the cold was the worst she could ever remember. "Would King Charles actually consider peace with England?"

A weak shrug lifted Owain's shoulders. "I'm thinking I am too old to go on with this. When Rhys treated with Harry, I knew. Knew that it was coming to an end. Now I understand the despair that King Richard suffered and how it was that he abandoned hope altogether."

Pressing the letter back into his palm, Margaret braved a hand beyond the warmth of her cloak and pushed the silver-golden hair from her husband's face. "Men have risen from lower depths than you, Owain Glyndwr, Prince of Wales."

"Ah, Marged . . . how strange those words sound to me now. What am I prince of? A wasteland. The world thinks of hell as being a cave of fires beneath the ground. Hot. Burning. Your flesh consumed by flames." His breath hung before his face in a cloud of frozen vapor. "But I see it like this . . . like Wales is now. Frozen. Steeped in ice and snow. Sheep and cattle dying by the hundreds because the grass is buried too far beneath the snow. The ice too thick over the streams for them to drink. Firewood scarce. Children and old people dying. Sickness and famine and pestilence in the land. What does 'freedom' mean to a man who wants nothing but food and warmth?"

Her only source of strength the past year had been in trying to hold him up, to keep his heart on the dream that she had once envied for taking him from her so often. How she yearned to return those golden days to him—the intoxication of victory, the easy power in his stride, the way he modestly looked down at his hands in his lap when the crown was upon his head, the earnest tilt of his chin as his generals argued strategies before him, the gleam in his eye when he shared plans with Griffith Young of places of learning and worship.

"Come inside," she begged. "There are no answers out here. Only the wind."

His chin touched his chest and his eyes drifted shut again, as though fighting sleep. "Marged, my sweet," he said, reaching toward her and taking her hand in his, slowly crumpling the letter in his other hand, "I love you with all my heart. I always have. Always will."

"And I you," she said.

Arm in arm, they retreated inside. Even in their grand suite, which dominated the whole of the third floor of the gatehouse, the air was frigid, but the cutting wind was held at bay by the thick walls of stone and the deeply set glazed windows. Beneath the down coverings, Margaret molded her body to his—his chest pressed to her back and his breath warm upon her neck.

Iolo Goch:

Rumors that King Henry lay mute and blind on his deathbed came as often as the rain that falls upon the Isle of Britain. But evidence was to the contrary. He was not so ill that he could not mastermind treaties with France, Brittany and Scotland. If Wales was to survive, it had no choice now but to do so entirely by itself.

Then, my lord Owain's last remaining ally fell. Henry Percy, Earl of Northumberland, ran up against the Sheriff of Yorkshire at Bramham Moor in the month of February in 1408. There, he was resoundingly defeated and killed.

The worst was yet to come. Harry, once more, set upon Aberystwyth. This time, Rhys held out as long again, but by summer's end, he surrendered. There was no fleeing to Harlech to plead with his prince, for Harry had already dispatched Sir Gilbert Talbot to begin the siege on Owain's royal stronghold.

51

Harlech Castle, Wales — October, 1408

A FEW HOURS MORE could have made all the difference in the world. One more barrel of water. One more sack of flour. A bottle of wine. A piece of fruit. All the difference in the world.

For a furious string of days, Harlech was victualed to the highest stone. Harvest was yet a couple of weeks away and that immutable fact would prove a hardship to the Welsh and provide a feast for the oncoming English. Even by night, supplies were hustled across the drawbridge, carried on aching shoulders up the one hundred and twenty-seven steps from the water gate, or hoisted hand over hand on ropes over the walls of the outer ward.

Harry's dogs were on their way. The ships came gliding up the coastline first. Owain and Margaret watched the assaults from a crack in one of the shuttered crenels along the battlements. The Welsh sailors did not put up much of a fight. They were faced with an entire fleet of English warships far outnumbering them: single-masted, oared cogs with banners fluttering in arrogant surety. Many of the English vessels had assayed the lopsided fray from a safe distance, as if to exclaim how absolutely the English could and would dominate. Jars of pitch were launched at the Welsh ships. Flaming arrows followed. Black smoke billowed upward into a crystal blue sky. As the Welsh dove overboard, trying to swim to the refuge of shore, English archers eyed their bobbing marks from the fighting castles perched at the bow and stern of each vessel. Arrows hissed through the air. Pools of blood spotted the harbor and diffused outward, staining the beach vermilion. When the first dead Welsh sailor, floating face up with the shaft of an arrow protruding from his forehead, washed ashore, Margaret clutched her belly and retreated behind the merlon. Her face as pale as a drift of winter snow, she went to her knees.

Owain crouched beside her. Stiff at first, she yielded to his protective arm and leaned her weight against him.

"More times than I could count I have nursed soldiers," she said. "Some back to health. Some I knew would die within the day. And all I could do was hold their hands and stroke their heads while they cried out in agony. I asked their names and said prayers for them when the priests were too busy with others." Closing her eyes, she reached an arm across her husband's strong chest. "I often wondered what it was like for you, to witness the killing and dying, day after day after day."

He pulled her against him even tighter. A loose strand of her still-flaxen hair fell from behind her ear. Thoughtlessly, he wound it around a forefinger. His own hair was almost entirely silver now. But Margaret was still undeniably beautiful. How was it that she had held on to her youthful appearance through so much strife and sorrow?

"There is too much danger in thinking about it," he said. "You learn not to."

The air was thick with the scent of smoke. Every now and then, ashes floated on the wind and wandered inside the castle walls.

"How long before the French come?" Margaret asked.

Owain laughed dryly. "The French? Civil war consumes them. They couldn't care less about Henry's little Welsh parasites."

"Rhys?"

Rhys? Rhys would not give me a drink of water if I were dying of thirst.

"Soon, my love. He will not fail us." How easily he had taught himself to lie to her. But how could he abandon hope before her?

A long silence settled between them. The screams of dying sailors were becoming less frequent. Even the smoke was diminishing as the Welsh ships took on water.

"I know that he wanted Nesta to leave long before she did," Margaret announced bravely. Owain realized it was the first time she had ever spoken the name of his mistress.

He swallowed and nodded once, thankful that Margaret had not looked at him just then. At any rate, he had shoved that knife into his heart himself many times over already. "She would have left a long time ago, but for the girls." Owain glanced along the wall-walk, lined with jars of sulfur, oil and sand to be dropped scalding on assailants at the foot of the castle walls when they came with their towers and ladders. "I am full of regrets, Marged, and desperate for your forgiveness . . . but I know there is nothing I deserve less."

"Let regrets go, Owain. We must think on the good times." She brought his hand to her lips and kissed his knuckles, cracked and dry and riddled with scars. Then she pressed his fingers to her cheek.

"But it seems they were so long ago. Another life," he said.

"They will come again."

"No, never again. I know now. Slowly, the dream is dying. I see it as if from a distance. And as I look back, I think on how different things might be for us . . . if only . . . if I had not . . ." His voice trailed off. "But after everything that has happened, it will be Prince Harry who will be my undoing. Do you know why?"

"Why?"

"Because he understands what his father never could. He is no bully, like Henry. Once, he was reckless, yes, but no more. His soldiers love him. And all of England will love him one day. He knows how to balance ruthlessness and kindness. For those things,

Wales will bend to him—softly, willingly . . . and with relief."

"Will you make me one last promise, Owain?"

"Anything."

"Promise me you will never, ever give yourself up. As long as you walk free, Wales will live on."

It was so much to ask. Too much. But she did believe in him. She always had. He had simply been too blind to see the toll it had taken on her.

"I promise," he said.

Iolo Goch:

A great host of English soldiers enveloped the land surrounding Harlech Castle in the ensuing days. An entire city sprang up, enclosed behind a flimsy, yet effective stockade, complete with everything including taverns and prostitutes. Behind the cover of the high-topped palisades, carpenters buzzed like insects, erecting the siege engines which, when completed, would stand as tall as the castle walls themselves.

The surrounding fields, pregnant with provender, were put to the torch. Cattle were rounded up and penned to serve as fare for the English camp throughout the duration of the siege. The decimation suffered by the Welsh peasants nearby drove them into the mountains, where the elderly and ill succumbed to famine. Others froze to death from lack of shelter.

The caltrops, which had been so stealthily scattered by our men-at-arms in the tall grass surrounding the castle grounds, were painstakingly plucked up by Englishmen, some of whom fell to the accuracy of our Welsh arrows. But every shaft launched from within the walls was one less at hand for when they would be truly needed, if and when an all-out assault ever came.

Meanwhile as winter settled in, all the inhabitants of Harlech could do was watch, wait and pray that the storms battering the coast would take their toll on the besiegers. And yet the attacks, in sundry forms, began. Half-rotten carcasses of cows were catapulted over the castle walls—their stench and decay augmenting the illness already festering within. Not only did livestock serve as ammunition, but human corpses, as well.

It was not Prince Harry who made the first demand to surrender, for he was still finishing his business at Aberystwyth, but Sir Gilbert Talbot. The demand was resolutely refused by Edmund Mortimer from the wall above the main gate. My lord Owain, for reasons I did not wholly understand, was reluctant to make his presence known.

Talbot then gave the orders. Under cover of a spate of arrows, pioneers surged forward, furiously mapping safe ground. The traps and trenches that the Welsh had riddled the ground to the east of the castle with were numerous, but in the end they only served to delay the inevitable. The English pioneers filled them in to make safe routes for the roofed mantlets beneath which the miners could carry out their work. Later, the siege engines, with which the engineers and soldiers would batter the fortress, would be rolled across the solid earth. The burning fagots and red-hot bundles of iron discharged from the castle were minor deterrents, like flies that buzz about the ears of a horse.

When the English drew close enough, their soldiers scurried forth with ladders. Those that were able to make it as far as the top of the outer wall without being skewered by a Welsh arrow found themselves face to face with their foes.

All in all, our prospects were abysmal. The English, wholly aware of that, began their first direct assault on Harlech two days before Christmas.

52

Harlech Castle, Wales — December, 1408

I N THE SILVER WASH of dusk, Owain crouched behind a merlon, waiting silently as the stifled grunts of an English soldier making fast progress up the ladder reached his ears. Holding his breath, Owain gripped his sword in his right hand and in his left he clutched a small taper axe. The ladder creaked as the invading soldier grappled at the stone block lying across the crenel to pull himself over.

Owain swung his sword in an arc and severed the thumb from the soldier's left hand. Muted by shock, the soldier flailed himself forward, his short sword scraping the stones as he attempted to position it for a counterblow. Owain shot up from his hiding place, pinned the soldier's sword against the stones with the flat of his blade and smiled slyly.

"I don't believe you were invited," Owain mocked. "Go back to where you came from." And with that he buried his axe in the meat of the soldier's neck.

With a gurgle, the soldier's eyes rolled back into his skull. A bubble of blood foamed from his crooked mouth. He leaned backward and then went limp.

Owain reclaimed his weapon with a forceful heave, and then

nudged the cleaved soldier away from the wall. The body toppled, taking with it the next soldier in line a dozen rungs down.

Before the incursion was ended, Owain snatched away the lives of four more Englishmen bent for glory. The act of placing himself in the forefront of the castle's defense lent heart to his beleaguered garrison, but Owain was painfully aware that no amount of courage could deflect the torment of starvation which could eat away at the most stalwart soul.

THE FOLLOWING NIGHT, ON the solemn eve of Christmas, Owain, who had as yet granted no indication to the besiegers that he was actually present at Harlech, summoned his son-in-law to the constable's chamber. A sorely depleted store of arrows lined the walls. It was nigh on midnight, but Owain meant to determine the extent of Edmund's resolve before declaring his plan to anyone else. A single candle on the table in the center of the room provided a small circle of light.

Bleary-eyed, Edmund stepped into the light. The square set of his shoulders was gone. Clearly, he could not stand unsupported for long.

Owain was sitting on the edge of the table, his feet swinging beneath him. A few rolls of tattered maps lay in a pile beside him. He had brought them out, perused each one cursorily and then pushed them aside, for their contents were branded on his memory, so countless were the times he had pored over them.

Edmund wiped the perspiration from his forehead with his sleeve. He pulled out a stool tucked beneath the table and settled himself with obvious weariness upon it.

"Are you unwell?" Owain probed with concern.

"I have been better, but it will pass. A slight fever, nothing more. A little ache in my marrow. These things seldom last more than a day . . . two at best." Edmund planted his elbow on the table and propped his head against a fist. "This must be serious business for you to forego sleep on the one night we might be granted peace."

"What I am going to ask of you, Edmund," Owain said, "I do so with both trust and reluctance. Reluctance, in that I must. Trust, in that I hold great faith in your leadership."

"Ask anything, m'lord. There's nothing I would not do for you."

Owain pulled air into his lungs and held it a moment before speaking. "Are you certain of that, Edmund?"

Pink-rimmed eyes betraying his weeks of sleeplessness, Edmund looked at Owain and nodded. "Has it not always been so?"

As the click of a sentry's boots rang out from the gate passage-way, Owain glanced toward the door. The footsteps diminished.

"Good then. I grant Harlech to your charge. Defend it as long as you can. But see that my family is not harmed. Do you understand?"

Edmund was obviously taken aback. "No, I don't."

"I mean hold out as long as you can. But if you must surrender to keep them well and safe, then do it." Owain hopped to the floor and paced just beyond the perimeter of the candle's power. "Tomorrow night, when there is no moon to betray us and the English are drunk on ale and stuffed to their collars, myself, Maredydd and a few others will steal away and once beyond —"

"Leave here? In God's name, my lord . . . Father, if no one can manage to get in, how are you to get out?"

Halting, Owain crossed his arms loosely and shrugged. "It will be treacherous. I don't deny that. Many, many times this past year, as Aberystwyth lay under siege, I roamed the beach, rowed up and down the length of the outer walls in the bay below Harlech, and studied the rocks from every angle. There is a way, just beyond the upper gate on the west front, but I regret that only the strongest may pass. The children and women . . . they shall have to stay behind."

"Nothing but sheer rock and the sea below."

"Yes."

"Suicide."

Owain went to Edmund and placed a hand on his drooping shoulder. "It is the only way . . . the only hope of salvation."

Edmund slid from his stool. On his knees at Owain's feet, his face downcast, Edmund shook his head in denial.

Owain settled upon his haunches and raised Edmund's stubbled chin with a finger. "As long as you can, Edmund. As long as you can. I'll find Rhys and Gethin, gather a relief force . . . and free Harlech."

The candlelight was waning to near darkness as Owain helped Edmund to his feet, up the dark stairs and back to his bed where Catrin slept. Beside her, their son Lionel, who had been roused by a nightmare, slumbered beneath the protection of her arm.

53

Harlech Castle, Wales — December, 1408

T HE SIGNIFICANCE OF THE day was overshadowed by the sobriety imposed from outside the castle walls. Whereas in the years before, the tables at Harlech and also at Sycharth had been steeped in abundance, this year the Christmas feast was merely a few rolls more than the day before: peasant's fare. The wine was watered. The salted meat, dry and sinewy. Song was forced. Even Iolo's strumming on his harp was brittle: the rhythm irregular, the pitch strained, his fingers foreign visitors to the strings which once had echoed his heart. There was no Yule log to light the hall, no mince pie or pudding to delight young stomachs, nor holly to garnish the rafters.

Only the children were mindless of the doom that was sure to commence at dawn. Sion and Mary, now both fourteen years old, led the games with their nephew Lionel and little nieces Angharad and Gwladys with an authority well beyond their years. Mary had endured the hardships of the previous year with her mother's dauntless courage, developing into a young woman whose countenance promised a rare beauty as yet to blossom. Sion, though he had been rarely in the company of his oldest brother Gruffydd while growing up, was in every way like him: moody, pensive and passionate to a fault. When Lionel, brimming constantly with the urge to move, would not stand precisely where Sion commanded him, Sion erupted into a tantrum and demanded of his sister Catrin to make her unruly son mind. Catrin merely cocked her head and admonished her younger sibling for expecting too much of a little boy. Then she flattered Sion by adding, "He is not a man yet, like you."

On the far end of the head table, Dewi and Tomos joked. The veteran of a handful of raids and the unavailing campaign that ended at Woodbury Hill, Dewi shared his vast knowledge with Tomos, who was more than eager to gut an English soldier.

"Ah," Dewi began, clasping Tomos by the shoulder with his left hand and brandishing an imaginary weapon aloft in his other, "you will yet have your chance, my little brother. Soon enough. The English have bellies soft as a hare's."

Tomos grinned and scooped up his tankard. He slurped down the remaining ale as an act of his manhood.

As Owain reached for his drink, Margaret grabbed his wrist.

"Sooner or later you will have to tell me," she said.

It was never any use hiding his thoughts from her. To those who knew him less, Owain was always given to deep thought, seldom lighthearted and rarely emotional, but Margaret could read him by the way he stared either into his drink or out the window. Into his drink meant hesitation over troubles. Out the window indicated that his mind was a maze of plots taking shape.

"Too soon," he regretfully replied, staring at his cup as he pulled it into the circle of his fingers. He then rose and offered a hand to his wife.

Margaret laid her fingers over his as they went from the hall. The uninterrupted song of the children followed them out into the ward until a servant scurried to close the massive door. The stars winked at them from above, but neither took notice, as once they did every night while they were young and intoxicated with each other. Now they were older, heaped with responsibilities and living life like mice in a cage. One step beyond and the cat would sink its teeth into them and then swallow them whole.

Although the chill of December was sharp in the air, Owain strolled toward the chapel, an array of sentries watching with sleepy curiosity from the battlements. He wanted to feel the warmth of her hand one more time and memorize the curve of her outline in the starlight. Once inside the chapel, where three tall candles illuminated the altar, he led her toward it. Taking up both her hands, he raised his chin.

"Tonight, I . . ." He urged the words from his mouth, but they were firmly lodged in the back of his throat. Abruptly, he pulled her into his arms, crushing her against his chest. A shudder ripped through him. "Ah, dear God, I cannot do this. I cannot leave you and the children."

"Leave?" Struggling against his desperate embrace, Margaret stepped back. "What do you mean?"

He traced the sloping curve of her neckline with great tenderness. "I had made plans to descend over the cliffs and escape along the shore. To join Gethin in the mountains, seek out Rhys and bring relief. Marged, Marged . . . only hours away and I can't. I can't leave you. Not for any reason or cause."

She caught his hand and pressed it to her heart. "You must go."

No, she spoke madness. He shook his head. "I must stay to protect you. They will starve us out, Marged. Eventually, we will have to surrender, because I cannot sacrifice my family for the sake of pride. I can only pray for mercy, for you, for Sion and Mary, for little Lionel and Angharad and —"

She covered his mouth with her hand. "You said yourself, when we were alone at the beginning of the siege, that there was a trace of kindness in Harry of Monmouth. When Rhys gave up Aberystwyth,

Harry allowed the entire garrison to walk free. He will relish the return of Harlech. And if you are not here, I do not think he will explode in retribution. If he puts us away it will only be for a little while. If you were him, the perfect trap would be to set your family free and wait for you to come. We'll be safe. Safe. Do not fear for us."

"No, I won't go from here and leave you in danger. I must stay and fight."

"If you stay and fight . . . you *will* die. Either in defense of this cold, heartless place you have tried to fashion as your home, or by the amusement of an executioner while all of London jeers. Leave, Owain. I beg of you—leave. For as long as you live, there is hope."

The truth was bitter. He swallowed with difficulty, turning away from her.

"My love," she said, her arms encircling him from behind as she pressed her cheek to his back, "do not abandon that which you gave so many reason to believe in."

He turned around and pulled her so tight that he felt her heart beating in rhythm with his.

Then he lifted her chin with his fingertips and pressed his mouth to hers. The kiss they shared was not long, but it singed them both as they ripped themselves away from one another.

A FEW HOURS LATER, Owain and the others were ready. A heavy blanket of clouds began to blot out the starlight as an insistent wind pushed in from the Irish Sea.

The five men crept low across the open ground. All they had with them were the clothes they were wearing, a sword and a dagger each and a length of rope. Maredydd had spent the last two hours scanning through the darkness for English scouts and when he deemed it safe he gave the signal. Maredydd descended the rope first.

Having scaled his share of castle walls, he carefully selected the best path down toward the sea. Iolo, trembling and white as alabaster, went after him. Dewi and Tomos were close behind.

Feeling her eyes still upon him, Owain turned and shared with his wife one last look. One look that said more than a thousand words could. Then he began his descent. Each footfall brought them closer to the furious sea, each handhold further from the walls that had housed them and kept them safe. The rope burned his hands raw. He had forgotten his gloves. Every now and then a loose stone slipped beneath his boot and tumbled down the steep rock face. It might have been an hour or the whole night, Owain would not look down or up, only as far as the next step. Then, quite suddenly, he found himself on a thin landing where the waters of the bay beat against the rock on which he stood.

He looked at Iolo, who was nursing his own bleeding hands, and his sons, who were fueled by the danger of their adventure, and nodded. One by one, they slipped into the water and began to wade and then tread southward.

The last to enter the water, Owain tried as hard as he could to focus on the place where he had parted with his beloved—the place where he had left his heart behind. But all was gray above. Beyond, the black sea. When he at last submitted to the fate of the sea, the cold sucked his breath away. The tide beckoned him toward deeper waters. In the darkness, Tomos called softly to him. Owain, his thoughts going numb, followed his son's voice.

The waves created by the vigorous wind tugged at Iolo. The bard's head slipped beneath the dark surface. Owain was imbued with a surge of strength and purpose greater than the mad sea. He swam to Iolo, draped his friend's arm over his shoulder and pulled him along through the water. Iolo coughed and fought for breath.

Far down the shoreline, well past the English camp, they crawled onto the beach. Seawater cascaded from their clothing. Defeated by his exertion, Iolo collapsed, pressing his face against the sand.

Maredydd was the only one who had not sunk to his knees. He stood with his back to a boulder. Teeth chattering, he stumbled forward and helped his father pull Iolo out of plain view. Dewi called them toward a clump of grasses amidst an undulating sweep of dunes. There they huddled together, battling for air, rubbing at their leaden muscles with frozen digits, and wordlessly suffering the cold that sliced them from skin to bone.

Owain collapsed beside Iolo. He tried to flex his fingers, but they were nearly paralyzed.

"I would trade a year of my life," Iolo uttered, "for a fire."

Raising his face and looking toward the northeast, Owain could see the faint flickers of light from the English camp's morning cooking fires.

Dewi struggled to his feet. "Tomos? Where is Tomos?" He sprinted clumsily back toward the open beach, frantically scanning the shoreline and the sea. He shot to the top of a dune, disavowing danger.

"Tomos!"

Before Dewi could emit another syllable, Maredydd tackled him. Dewi thrashed against his brother's hold. They tumbled down the dune in a twist of limbs as Dewi fought to free himself. Maredydd pinned him to the ground and clamped a hand across his mouth.

"Damn you," Maredydd whispered. "You'll have us all dead."

Finally, Dewi relented. His body heaved with muffled sobs.

For an hour, they combed the shore, ducking behind buffeted sprays of grass and crouching by low-swept dunes and scattered rocks as they moved like cats searching out unknown prey. A patrol of English ships floated on the bay at a comfortable distance, far enough for the escaped fugitives of Harlech Castle to go unnoticed. In full daylight, a keen sailor might have spotted them, but the pale light of pre-dawn concealed them.

When Owain saw a shapeless form bobbing in the sea, his heart clenched in sorrow. He waded out alone and pulled his lifeless son to shore. He laid Tomos in a small valley of dunes and folded his son's limp arms across his chest. Tomos's skin was as white as a snowcap on the mountains. His lips were bluish purple.

None but Dewi wept. There was no time for it. Gathering what stones they could, they laid them over his body and covered it with a blanket of grass they cut with their knives.

As they set off toward the southeast to circle beyond the ring of the enemy camp, their clothing frozen to their flesh, a weak winter sun was just beginning to top the mountain ridge ahead of them. The sounds of an army, stirring to life, drifted on the brittle air, reminding them that danger was by no means past.

54

Uplands of Wales — December, 1408

CRADLED WITHIN A DEPRESSION of a steep-sided mountain was a black-bottomed lake. Deep fissures, darkened by shadows, cut into the mountain like the lines in an old man's face which betray his age. In the springtime, melting snowcaps would send their chilled water down into the crevices, tumbling in white veils, until it finally came to rest in this magical, secret pool undisturbed by man or beast and known only to the highest flying of birds.

Maredydd flattened his chest against a rock and, clinging to its icy lip, lowered his mouth to the water. He drank long and deep, even though the frozen water cutting across his tongue drove a dagger of pain into his skull. Anything to fill his belly.

A short whistle caused him to raise his head. Dewi cupped his hand and brought it to his chest, motioning for his brother to follow. Further along the shore, making way toward a ravine, Iolo and Owain were forging on.

Maredydd glanced across the black lake and up at the clear, blue sky. For a winter's day, it was a rare beauty, but none of them had had anything at all to eat, not so much as a crumb, since Christmas dinner three days past. He forced himself to his feet and picked his way across the random stepping stones back toward shore.

"Yesterday I was famished," he said to Dewi, as he caught up with him, "but today I am too tired to feel anything. I am just empty—from my mouth down to my boots."

"Empty in the head, too, if you think you won't get any more tired or hungry than this." Dewi shoved his sleeve across his upper lip to dam the torrent that was spilling from his nose.

The walls of the ravine rose up to either side of the two brothers and the swiftly retreating winter sun disappeared, leaving them in shadows. A shallow stream, one stride across, cut through the ravine's center.

When Maredydd's steps ceased, Dewi cast a look over his shoulder. "What are you doing?"

"Gorse. Up there. On the slope." Maredydd raised a finger, wrapped in strips of cloth rent from his cloak. The pale light of a winter evening revealed a yellow clump of gorse clinging to the rock face where even the best of climbers could not have gotten to it. But Maredydd remembered the farmers grazing their cows on such rough fare in hard times and figured if it sustained such massive beasts, surely it could provide them some sustenance.

Dewi shrugged and continued on.

"Gorse." Maredydd took three leaps and clamped his brother on the shoulders, spinning him around. "Food!"

"You can't be that hungry."

"I'd eat grass right now if —"

Maredydd froze in mid sentence. His shoulders drew up stiffly.

"If what?" Dewi said.

Suddenly, Maredydd dug his fingers into the shoulder of Dewi's cloak, dragging him across the stream while he pressed a finger to his own lips to silence his brother. He jerked Dewi down behind a boulder. Their feet were immersed in the icy stream. The tails of their cloaks sopped up water.

His eyebrows weaving together, Dewi whispered, "Has the devil gotten into you? What are you doing?"

Maredydd plucked a smooth rock from the streambed. He drew his arm back and slung it in his father's direction. The rock smacked Owain squarely in the spine. It struck him so hard, he had his sword loosed and flashing in a circle behind him before he saw Maredydd crouched in the water.

Leaning out from the boulder, Maredydd pointed higher up toward a trail that crowned the ravine some thirty feet above. Braving a look, Dewi saw his brother was alerting them to an English soldier, who was pissing over the edge.

Urine splattered upon Iolo's narrow shoulders. Owain yanked the bard toward the base of the cliff.

The soldier moaned in utter relief. His urinating went on for so long that Dewi's teeth began to chatter. Maredydd wanted to sink to his haunches, but that would have put his buttocks right down in the frozen water. To stand straight up would have put his head above the rock. To move to join Iolo and Owain beneath the cliff would have thrust them into plain view. And where there was one soldier, there were more. So both he and Dewi had no choice but to stand half-stooped up to their ankles in the icy water, the chill gradually spreading up their legs.

Maredydd clamped a hand over his brother's mouth to shush the rattle of his teeth. "I will not die here, like this," he whispered. To which Dewi gave a small nod.

"Jesus!" the soldier exclaimed. "Swear my cock's on fire." He hoisted up his hose and rearranged his gear.

"Told you the girl was poison, Ralf," boomed another, much deeper voice from upstream. Laughter and gibes rang out. A second, then a third, fourth, fifth soldier crested the ridge above and joined the trail.

The soldier named Ralf hustled back a little along the trail and seconds later was huffing along with a cantankerous donkey on the rein. Ralf, short and in miserable shape, was obviously a man of lower rank who had chanced upon an oversized suit of mail and a barely dented breast plate at a rather compromised time for its former wearer. He battled the pack animal, which was duly burdened with the supplies needed to get five gluttonous soldiers through these mountains. Ralf's companions, upon witnessing the exchange of curses and braying, laughed riotously and went on their way. In short time, there was only Ralf on the upper trail in the gorge. The others had gone from view.

Maredydd's fingers slipped beneath the water and once again emerged with a smooth, flat stone. He flipped the stone between his thumb and forefinger, eyeing the abandoned soldier.

On the other side of the stream, fifteen feet away, Owain shook his head slowly at Maredydd. But Maredydd, starving and craving nothing but the contents of the donkey's packs, ignored his father. When Gruffydd quit Aberdaron, Maredydd had gradually taken on a dauntless outlook toward danger to fill the role his brother had once inhabited. And where there was no danger to be found, he would uncover it. This newfound nature made him a valuable player, a fact which he relished. But it also meant, as in that moment while he fingered the tiny missile, that he offered up the lives of those around him as well.

Even if Ralf's haughty companions came to his rescue it was four against five—and those were not bad odds. Maredydd stood up, drew his arm back and, closing his right eye, took aim. He gripped the stone securely, balanced it perfectly and tightened his muscles for the launch.

The keen point of a knife sought out his kidney. He winced in surprise.

"Easy prey, that one," Dewi said lowly in his ear, "but the rest had bows."

Maredydd met his father's disapproving gaze and slowly sank back down behind the boulder. He pressed his cheek to it. He was frozen to the core, could no longer feel his feet. It seemed like hours that the stupid English soldier jerked and pulled on the donkey's lead, giving as much ground as he gained. Finally, the stubborn animal relented and Ralf was sprinting along, trying to catch up with his companions.

When the soldier was well gone, Dewi and Maredydd slogged out of the stream, stumbling onto the rocky bank. Maredydd simply collapsed, while Dewi writhed in agony and slapped at his legs to get the feeling back.

Later, they went on another two hours, the sun long past set and only a faint scattering of stars to light the way.

It was perhaps some overdue blessing from above that placed the empty shepherd's hut directly in their path. They did not care how soon its owner might be back, or if the English soldiers they had nearly collided with would see the smoke rising through the hole in the center of the thatched roof from the paltry fire they built—but it was a dry place, a warm place . . . and there was food.

With barely enough strength to sling the heavy iron pot over the hook above the cooking fire, Iolo made a stew of melted snow and beans. With ravenous impatience, Maredydd watched the beans stewing and then sucked them down while they were still hot enough to scorch his tongue, had he taken long enough to bother tasting the bland fare. In a few hours, they had all consumed what would have sustained the shepherd for several days.

That night they slept as deeply as the dead, well past daybreak and long after their meager fire had exhausted itself. Some time past midmorning, they gathered up what they could in makeshift bundles of burlap stolen from the shepherd's hut and continued northward with renewed purpose.

55

Uplands of Wales — Winter, 1409

THE WILDERNESS INTO WHICH Owain and the others had fled was vast and uninhabited, with purple-gray walls of rock that rose up in challenge at every turn. Flakes of stone as sharp as knives cut into their flesh whenever they stumbled. Their muscles flamed with every stride. Their ears, noses and fingers were frozen numb. Each footfall was challenged by slick inclines, every breath snatched away by relentless winds.

They went without fire and food. Frigid days gave way too quickly to even colder nights. They slept fitfully, if at all, wherever they could find a windbreak. Iolo mirrored their misery with fits of coughing harsh enough to expel his entrails along with his sputum.

It was on the seventh day that the snow began before dawn. Softly, silently, it piled upon the rocky ground. As they dove deeper into the highest of the mountains, the force of the wind drove the snow into drifting banks, creating a swirling sea of azure and ivory where sky and earth collided.

Crystals of ice frosted Owain's eyebrows and beard. He wiped at them and turned in a tight circle. He once knew these mountains even in the dark, but now, given his gaunt, compromised state, all he could do was rest and pray that his bearings would return to him. Whether it was afternoon or evening was impossible to tell. The sky was thick with clouds and he had no perception of time. He questioned himself, tried with immense effort to recall some landmark.

Somewhere, not far from here, was one of the caves where he and Gethin had sworn to rejoin, should they ever need to go into hiding again. But where it was . . . he couldn't even think, wasn't sure. His mind was dense with fog. He leaned over with his hands upon his knees and glanced behind him. The other three were shifting shapes of gray. For a fleeting moment, he had to think, concentrate to recall who they were.

Iolo clung to Maredydd's arm as they struggled up the slope. Grunting, Maredydd grappled at a rock for a handhold. He heaved himself up, staggered forward and then collapsed on the snow-packed ground thirty feet from his father. Beside him, Iolo sank to the blanketed earth.

Although reluctant to retrace his steps, even so short a measure, Owain gave in to the ease of sliding downhill and joined Maredydd and Iolo. But before he could steal a moment's rest, he spied Dewi's prostrate form at the bottom of the hill, the snow drifting around him. He flew toward him and was lifting Dewi up in his arms before either Iolo or Maredydd knew what was happening.

Owain shook his son hard until Dewi pried his eyes open. Snowflakes dusted Dewi's chin, softly whiskered with his first beard. Dewi used to lament how he couldn't grow a beard when he would watch Maredydd daily scraping his away and cursing the practice while they were holed up in Harlech.

"I can't," Dewi croaked. "Too tired."

"We'll rest an hour," Owain urged, and then added with forced optimism, "Gethin will probably find us before we find him. Faith."

Maredydd shadowed them. He unclasped his cloak and tossed it over his brother.

Dewi smirked. "Save it for yourself, Brother. I can't feel past my knees . . . can't move my fingers."

Iolo knelt in the snow. Gently, he drew one of Dewi's hands from beneath the tattered cloak and unpeeled the strips of cloth that had been torn piecemeal from their garments. Dewi's fingers were tipped with black. The flesh of his fingers was as rigid as wood. From the swelling beneath his boots, his toes were likely far worse.

A wave of vomit tossed Owain's stomach upside down. *Oh God, not this way. Don't let him suffer this way. It was a bad enough blow that Tomos fought the sea and lost, but even that was a swifter death. God, don't take yet another son from me. Spare this one!*

Maredydd ripped the rags from his own hands and began to re-wrap his brother's. Like his father, Maredydd did not waste words or sink himself with worries if there was any action that could be taken. Helplessness was not an attribute that either of them conceded to.

"How much further?" Maredydd asked.

Shrugging, Owain guessed wildly. "A few hours. Maybe less."

Intently, Maredydd gazed at his father. "You don't know?"

"If we climb to the top of this peak, perhaps . . . perhaps I could be more certain. I have not been here in three years, Maredydd. More than that in a snowstorm."

In one great heave, Maredydd had hoisted Dewi up in his arms and was on his feet, struggling toward the pinnacle. Owain and Iolo scrambled after him. Despite the added weight dangling across his arms, Maredydd was at the top first. His youthful years spent flailing weapons had built in him an unusual strength, not unlike his father's.

"Ho there!" Maredydd cried.

As Owain reached his side, he saw half a dozen riders on stout hill ponies making way across the next valley. They were lightly armed, spears pointing skyward. Owain grabbed Maredydd's arm and fought to pull him down, but it was too late—the riders had already spotted them.

"Are you insane?" Owain said. "Those could be English."

Tearing himself away, Maredydd's eyes flashed with anger. "I don't give a damn! I will not let him die."

Snow exploded around the ponies' hooves as they bounded through the drifts. The riders gripped their spears and steadied their shields. Closer and closer they came.

Before Owain could make out their faces, Iolo was sliding down the hillside toward them.

"Help us!" Iolo yelled, waving his arms. He tried to shout again, but his cries were mangled by his coughing.

The front rider raised his spear in a salute and sailed past Iolo, who was clutching his abdomen as another cough gripped him. Ten feet from Owain, the rider dropped from his shaggy mount. Barrel-chested above a diminished waistline, the forest of a black beard, now frosted with silver at the chin, betrayed him. Rhys Ddu tossed his spear to the earth and swept off his helmet.

"Well, I would not have thought, when I awoke this morning, to see your handsome face today," Rhys said.

Owain's heart rebounded. "Nor I yours. But let us save our embraces for later. My son needs a fire and dry clothes."

"Embraces? Hah. A hefty presumption on your part. I've no wish to let you close enough to sever my head for my disloyalty. Is that Dewi?" Rhys said, stepping closer, yet maintaining a safe distance from Owain. He was indeed a sliver of the bulky man that used to slouch on his stool at Sycharth, quaffing ale by the barrel and singing miserably in a drunken but merry state. Rhys's eyes reduced to thin slits against the barrage of icy snow that was now coming down harder and faster. Then he shuffled back toward his mount. "Put him on my horse, Maredydd. We're not far."

Rhys grabbed at the halter and pulled the animal close. He climbed back in the saddle and helped Maredydd get his brother up.

Maredydd swept up Rhys's spear and steadied himself with it. A moment later, he leaned against Rhys's thigh, exhaustion and relief almost overwhelming him, and mumbled into his leggings, "Bless you, Rhys."

"Yes . . . bless the bloody traitor." Rhys glanced at Owain. He ruffled Maredydd's hair and then, as if realizing the gesture was too much like the affection one would share with a small boy, pounded him on the shoulder. "Get yourself to one of the other mounts. Hold tight. The ride's a treacherous one."

With the flaccid Dewi clamped against Rhys's chest, the others were mounted. Just as Rhys had said, a brief ride of a few minutes led them to a rudimentary shelter: a narrow cave, high up on the mountain, where the vestiges of the once formidable Welsh army huddled.

"YOU'RE QUITE THIN," OWAIN said, as he stretched his feet toward the small fire near the mouth of the cave.

"And you need to trim your beard," Rhys retorted. He tested the meat roasting on the spit with his knife, grimaced to see it was not yet done, and settled himself on a smooth stone that served as his stool. "Not like you to let yourself go. I've seen you in better clothes. Too far out of touch with the fashions in London, you are."

If it had been possible, Owain would have smiled upon hearing the familiar banter from Rhys. Instead, one glance at Dewi speared his heart. Dewi was past fighting or feeling pain. At least for now he slept. Maredydd had slit his brother's boots carefully with his knife when they arrived at the cave to reveal the worst of it. The toes were grotesque and rotting from the frostbite like a piece of fruit gone putrid. Already the fever had set in and there were red streaks tracing their way up his legs. All bad signs.

"Brother-in-law, it has been long." Phillip Hanmer touched Owain on the shoulder and offered him a bowl of food. "Here."

Phillip had always been on the fringes—a follower without the will to find his own way. It surprised Owain to see him there, for he imagined Phillip would have just as well freely accepted Harry's offer of pardon, but perhaps the opportunity had not been timely. For certain Phillip was no traitor, although he was never the valuable tool that John had proven to be before his capture. Just the same, he was a good enough fighting man to have lasted this long. Owain accepted the bowl and, tilting it, forced himself to swallow. It tasted more of ashes than anything. He wasn't even sure what it was—barely warmed beans with an occasional hunk of fat, perhaps.

Not including the recent arrivals, Rhys and his men totaled only seven. There was Phillip, who, despite his Englishness, was a well known rebel; the Tudur brothers, who would always prefer to be where they were bound to be the most trouble to King Henry; the bear-like Cadogan from the hills, who had split a hundred enemies each with one blow of his axe; Griffith ap David, who had brought Gethin to Owain years ago—now less his right hand and yet always trying to hide the obvious beneath an oversized sleeve; and sitting cross-legged and mute just outside the cave's entrance despite the cold, Gethin himself, recently blinded and justifiably bitter.

Maredydd scooted closer to Rhys. "What's he doing out there?"

"What he always does. What he can do." Rhys poked at the logs with his knife. "He listens."

Rhys ap Tudur, who stood just beyond the gathering, snorted loudly. "And he can hear the bloody English a league away. Like a fox, he is." He rustled through a small chest of his belongings, plucked out a needle and length of thread and joined the ring. He squinted in concentration as he threaded the needle and went to work on the dangling sleeve of Owain's padded tunic which he had spread across his lap.

"How did he lose them?" Iolo asked with a rasp in his throat, referring to the empty purple sockets in Gethin's skull. The effort made him erupt in uncontrollable coughing. He clutched at his stomach and rolled himself aside.

Gwilym spat into the fire. "Don't know. He doesn't say and we don't ask."

"Got too damn close to the English camp." Rhys ap Tudur leaned in close, showing his rotten teeth with a snarl. "Probably took him for an archer, took out his left eye and just to be sure they gouged out the other."

"So you were at Harlech . . . or at least close?" Owain asked. *They had come, after all.*

"All of us, yes. Well," Rhys paused and jabbed again at the undercooked meat, "there were more of us then. But it didn't take long to figure out there wasn't anything to be done."

Gwilym nudged his brother with an elbow. "Least when we stole Conwy, the odds were in our favor."

The knife dangled from Rhys's stubby fingers. "We *should* have done something. We used to be good at that—doing what they least expected. Odds against us or no. What happened to us, Owain?"

"Harry happened," Owain said. *Like the damn plague—Harry happened. Figured out what his father refused to acknowledge.* "Instead of descending upon the whole of the land like a tempest, he stung, as a bee does, one place and then another. He came and he waited and he found the soft, tender spots, the festering places and there he worked like a salve to heal them. He showered Welsh soldiers with clemency and spoke of peace to a people ripped apart and suffering from war. And then, he went to our very heart—first to Aberystwyth. And he squeezed and choked until there was no will left and —"

"We fought until we could fight no more!" Rhys said.

Owain touched him on the elbow. "And you fought well and honorably. As well as any could. But that is the brilliance of young Harry. He knew our strengths as well as our weaknesses and used that to his advantage. To Harlech, he brought his vast army and pounded and shot and mined and . . ."

Harlech. Margaret was still there. *What have I done?* His hands crept up over his face. He peered through his fingers at the burning embers. "Oh, dear God. How could I have left her? The children?"

His hands dropped away, wet with salty tears. No, he could not give up out of convenience and weakness.

Then he spoke, his voice suddenly steady and full of purpose. "We must go back . . . raise the siege. I cannot leave my family to English wolves."

Maredydd's eyes plunged to the ground. Inside his warm, dry wool blanket, Iolo shrank. Rhys ap Tudur looked at his brother and shook his head.

Then Rhys Ddu, as was his usual place, said what no one else dared. "You can't."

"I must. *We* must!" Owain was weeping freely by then. He had saved his own skin and in the process lost one of his sons to drowning, with another doomed to die slowly and horribly.

And Marged, what will happen to Marged?

He knelt close to the fire, so close he could feel the flames hungering to light his hair. His head sank until his forehead met with the hot stones that circled the fire. Then he rolled to his side and slammed his fist onto the rock littered floor. "Will none of you fight beside me? Or have you all turned coward? We'll raise an army and go —"

"It cannot be done!" Rhys shot to his feet and went to stand over Owain. "Look at us, Owain. What kind of an army are we? A handful of us—against the greatest force that ever was. We *have* fought. And we have won. But of late, we have only lost. With Scotland, France, Ireland to give us arms, ships, soldiers . . . there was a chance. But that's all past and gone. Gone. Long gone. And now, we don't care much anymore for the clang of battle and the glory of having beaten our foes. We're tired. Hungry. Right now, we just want to bloody live through tomorrow."

Rhys dropped his knife beside Owain and went outside to join Gethin in angry silence.

Owain contracted into a tight ball and for an hour wept. His heart cried out in agony. He felt a traitor to himself, to his family, to his country. Now that he was here and alive and without hope, he knew he would have rather died defending Harlech against the inevitable, with his Marged beside him, than without her.

How could he have known that in a last pitch to save everything, the world beyond would prove so utterly dismal?

FOR TWO EXCRUCIATING WEEKS, Dewi lingered, slipping in and out of consciousness. It was a blessing, Iolo once remarked, when Dewi slept and that comment inspired the men to give up every last drop of ale they possessed, until they were left with nothing to drink but melted snow, to ease Dewi into drunken numbness whenever he awoke to the horror of his own rotting flesh.

For Owain, seeing another of his sons so brutally dying was a torture that gnawed at his soul. Always a man of carefully measured words, he became during that course a man of almost none. The selfishness by which he had survived his own certain capture and death evolved into self-loathing. The very reasons he had lived and fought so hard for were now unknown to him. The inferno of a dream had reduced itself to cinders. Had an army of fifty thousand Welshmen come marching to his aid then, he would have denied his own identity.

One day, near the end of January, when a rare winter sun thawed the surface layers of snow and ice in the valley below the cave and the wind ceased its howling, Dewi died. He was no more the victim of burning fever or oozing, smelly green stumps where his hands and feet used to be. They dug as far into the frozen earth as they could with their weapons and covered his grave with heavy stones to thwart any scavenging animals that might come to feed on the remains of his flesh.

It seemed to Owain that they would all suffer the same fate. That winter would never end.

56

Harlech Castle, Wales — February, 1409

S EATED ON THE EDGE of their bed, Catrin combed Edmund's hair from his forehead with her fingers. As she did so, a loose lock fell from his head and onto his pillow. In the weeks that had gone by since Christmas, he had battled a fever that anchored itself deep within his marrow. At first he merely complained of being tired—rising late from bed, falling asleep on the battlements even as stones battered the walls. Gradually, his appetite waned and if not for Catrin's pleading he would have foregone many a meal. These last two weeks he had not left his bed. Margaret had taken over the command of the garrison, utilizing the instructions Owain had prudently entrusted her with before leaving.

Catrin grazed her fingertips over Edmund's cheek. The fire was gone. His skin was cool. He was a wisp of the valiant soldier he once was: dutifully brave and strong of limb, even though he was not of great stature. What she had truly loved him for was his devotion to books and the knowledge they contained, and his sincere appreciation for small gifts of beauty in the world around him. Yet the man that Catrin had tended to of late was not that person. He had withered to almost nothing, like some old man of eighty, not one less than half that age. His speech was ambling, sometimes nonsensical. His mind was undoubtedly a void through which occasionally flitted sparks of memories dulled by famine.

His sparse eyelashes fluttered. He opened his eyes and looked at her. "The children?" he uttered hoarsely, the cracks at the corners of his mouth splitting more deeply.

She clutched at his chilled fingers, nodding. Then she looked across the room, the dim light of early morning straining to penetrate the frosty windows, and curled a finger at her children. Lionel marched forward by himself, a general leading the way, and Margaret carried the girls in either arm to their ailing father's bedside. Only Lionel, nearing his sixth birthday, was old enough to guess that perhaps all was not well with his father.

Lionel crept across the bed and buried his face in Edmund's chest.

Catrin reached for her son. "Lionel, please."

But Edmund stayed her with his hand. With every ounce of his strength, he wrapped his arms around Lionel in a feeble embrace. "Courage, my son." His words were barely above a whisper. "I want you to be a good knight for your mother and sisters. Can you do that?"

Perplexed by the request, Lionel sat back, but nodded dutifully. "I'm very brave for my age. Grandfather says so."

Margaret and Catrin exchanged a glance. They had heard nothing from Owain nor seen any sign of him since his departure. Winter was on its way out and spring heralding itself in bold hints. Rain and snow had been scarce, so springtime had not come in its usual muddy fashion. Travel would have been ideal. And yet there was no sign of him. None whatsoever. No signature harassing of the invaders. No indication of a detachment of English riding out to quell some uprising elsewhere. That meant he had either failed to gather a relief force or . . . or that he had not survived. There was no way of knowing.

With curious determination, Gwladys hoisted herself up on the high edge of the bed. She wrinkled her nose at Lionel, for the two were ever arguing, and then smiled at her father. "Father," she said in a sweet, pleading tone, "can we look for seashells today?"

Edmund's eyes drifted shut for a moment. When he opened them again, his look was blank, as if he had no focus or recognition of the faces before him. Black shadows lay beneath his sunken cheekbones. Silver tipped whiskers grayed his face even more than the colorless cast of his skin. He drew a long, slow breath and held it as if that were his greatest battle left to fight.

Then Gwladys puckered her ivory forehead, clasped her tiny hands together and added, "Please?"

A faint smile curled Edmund's lips. He looked toward little Angharad, propped on her grandmother's hip, a constant stream pouring from her tiny nose. Then, he turned his face toward Catrin again. "You . . . will teach them French?"

"They have already begun, *cariad*."

Even as Catrin answered him, she knew that he did not hear her. The life faded from his eyes and a moment later his cheek fell softly to the pillow. The children could not see the vacancy in their father's pupils, nor were they keen enough to note that he did not draw breath. Gwladys tugged at her father's hand, still expecting an answer to her simple request, which even if he had been well, he would have been unable to fulfill because of the enemy surrounding them.

"Take them to the chapel," Catrin said to her mother. Lightly, she brushed her hand downward across Edmund's face, her finger-tips sweeping his eyelids closed. She would have collapsed in grief, but she wouldn't allow herself to do so in front of the children.

So many men had died all around them these last few months— from putrefying wounds or raging fevers—and some, like her dear Edmund, had simply languished away. The deaths were so many that even the children had been numbed to the meaning of mortality.

Catrin had tried to keep them inside behind shuttered windows when the missiles were flying at the fortress, but the barrage was so constant, it had proven impossible to continue for long. The girls had seen them toss the bodies of dead soldiers over the wall to bounce like straw dolls upon the cliffs above the sea. Lionel had been standing atop the Garden Tower next to a young soldier who had befriended him when an arrow split the man's forehead clean open and half his brain splattered onto Lionel's tunic. The emptiness in their bellies disturbed them more than the constancy of death.

Margaret hustled the children out the door and into the care of one of her handmaidens. Soon, she was at Catrin's side again, her hand kneading her daughter's shoulder.

When Sir Edmund Mortimer had come to Owain Glyndwr's house, it was as a servant of the English king and a captive. Owain had impressed Edmund with his leniency, intellect and leadership, but it was Catrin who had been the victor of his heart. It was she who had converted him to the cause of the Welsh, not by persuasive argument or extortion or threats, but by the innocent grace of her smile. He had gambled his lands and his birthright, if only to be by her side. Owain had placed in Edmund as much faith as any Welshman and in turn Wales had gained a champion.

But now, like so many others before him—Madoc, Dewi, Tomos, Tudur, Hopkyn, Llywelyn ap Gruffydd, Harry Hotspur and young Tom who once carried Owain's banner—his beliefs, his actions, his very life had all led him to this inconspicuous end. Men who had risen with passion burning in their souls to fight gloriously, to live completely for but one single thing, an idea, were all in the end reduced to this: a hollow shell of flesh and bones, without breath or heartbeat.

Silent tears slid down Catrin's pale cheeks. She rubbed Edmund's cold hands and squeezed them hard. "Oh Edmund, the years were hard, but happy. And yet, too few. My father will return. He will deliver us—save our children. One day they will live in peace. He will free Wales. You always believed so. And so it will be."

As Catrin tucked her chin against her chest and threaded her fingers through her beloved's hair, Margaret backed herself against the wall. What she was soon to do, she knew Catrin would never forgive her for. Before his escape, Owain had named a date and told Margaret that by the time that day came and went if he had not arrived to relieve Harlech and freed them all, or if he had tried and failed, that she was to use her soundest judgment to decide whether to hold out . . . or to give in.

She had lost count of the number of dead. As of that morning, only four soldiers were stalwart enough to keep watch and defend the castle. The rest were ill or injured. Little Angharad was waning by the hour. There was enough food to last them all a day by normal standards—if they fed the sick ones, that is. Three days if they fooled their bellies with vinegar water.

She must lay her pride down before her, because to her back there was only a crumbling wall.

When Harry strode into Harlech at the reluctant surrender of Margaret Glyndwr, he could not say he was surprised to discover that Owain was not to be found within its wasted walls. He now had in his possession the last great stronghold of Wales—and was that not what he had come for? Wales was his, as it should have been all along. The Glyndwr family, or what was left of it, was herded into the great hall. Without laying eyes on them, he ordered Sir Gilbert Talbot to escort them to London where they would be locked up in the Tower for as long as it would take for Owain Glyndwr to give himself up.

The rebels of Wales were vanquished, Scotland had been put to bed with the capture of its young king and France was consumed with its own squabbles. Only a few years before, England had been assaulted on every front. Now, it was never more secure.

57

Somewhere in Wales — Late Summer, 1410

I N THE YEAR AND a half since he had escaped from Harlech, Owain had aged two decades. The once great warrior prince wandered the land in over-mended clothes. His hair was thinning and silver-gold. The glorious mane was now cropped at chin length and the neatly trimmed beard replaced by coarse stubble. That he had changed in appearance echoed the man within.

After Dewi's death, Maredydd had broached the subject of trying to raise troops with his father, either in Wales or abroad, but Owain had defeated every suggestion, dug up some gaping flaw in it and pitched his son's resourcefulness aside. He had forbidden Iolo to sing any ballads that spoke of the glory of his house or his fight against the English. Ballads of romance were limited to only the older, well known ones. The restrictions left his friend nearly mute, for Iolo was always proudest of his own creations and not an imitator of others.

Sometimes, on rare days when he would accompany Rhys about the hills in search of game, Owain would talk with him about better times. Whenever the talk brought up Margaret's name, Owain's shoulders sank, his eyes went distant and he grew suddenly quiet.

"Are you going to blame yourself forever?" Rhys tethered his horse to a fallen tree branch and claimed a spot in the shade. It was one of the first warm days of summer and already at midmorning the heat was building. They hadn't spied so much as a hare and knew it would be another day of porridge for them all if their luck didn't change.

Owain plucked at his bowstring as he settled himself on a log. "Do I have any sway over the sun? Hardly. I don't blame myself for what others have done . . . or failed to do. I am a prince without a people. A people who could not, would not, call themselves as one. What am I, one man, to do about that?"

"So all that talk at Machynlleth," Rhys said, sitting beside Owain to look out over a meadow crowded with yellow-faced daisies, "about churches and universities was a pile of dung?"

"No, not that."

"The parliaments, the alliances, letters to kings and popes, the army you built that won back everything from border to seashore . . . what was that for? Why was it that I stretched out my neck on bitter cold nights, days drenched with rain, snow up to my ribs —"

"Point made." Owain pulled an arrow out of his bag and fitted it to the string. "I'm old, Rhys. We're all old. Look at us. Harry is the rising sun. We are the pack mules who can no longer carry our load."

"I see." Rhys reached beneath his shirt to scratch at a rash. "Harry is the greater man. And us? Just a couple of fusty arses sitting on a stump in the middle of bloody nowhere, gibbering about our aching bones and poor eyesight and how long it has been since we've tupped a wench and . . . What are you doing with that?"

A small, black cloud erupted from the grass fifty paces away. Owain squinted, pulled back and let the arrow fly. The arrow smacked the bird down with a twang.

"Grouse tonight?" Owain chimed as he rose from his seat and went to claim his prize.

"Oh, so it's just *my* eyes that are failing." Hobbling, Rhys followed on his heels.

Pierced cleanly through the breast, the grouse that Owain picked up was not full-grown. He swung it by its feet. "Not enough to go around."

"Pity. First sign of fur or feather we've seen all day."

"Or perhaps we will have had no luck at all today?" A small, crooked smile lifted one side of Owain's mouth. "Flint?"

"Never without," Rhys said, digging in the pouch at his hip.

They retreated back to the shady spot they had left and Rhys went to work breaking up the dead branches around them for a fire, while Owain plucked the bird. They both knew if the others found them out that this little private feast would not go over well.

After they had devoured their meal in famished silence, Rhys licked the fat from his fingers.

"Do you think," Rhys mused, "that you'll ever see Margaret again?"

Owain sighed. "I don't see how. She's in the Tower. Not in our best days could we have freed her from there. I have nothing to give up for ransom. Henry might take me in her stead, though."

"Would you do that?"

Scratching in the dirt with his knife, Owain gave his companion a sideways glance. "She would not want me to. And she was right in what she said to me before I left her. So long as I live, there is hope. Besides, if I were in Henry's hands, he might just execute me and my whole family all at once. My pride, as well, prevents me from giving myself up. Do you actually think I would give that devil the satisfaction?"

"Not likely." Rhys's gaze went distant, his thoughts obviously roaming. "Nesta is in Ireland with her mother's family."

An abrupt switch in the course of the conversation, Owain narrowed his eyes at Rhys. "Then I take it she is well. The girls?"

"Don't know. News travels not at all in these parts. But . . . I have been thinking . . . thinking of joining her. Her mother's family has some land where they mostly tend to sheep. It would be a lot like home. Owain? You and Maredydd can come with me. Iolo, too, if you want. I imagine the house is small, but —"

"And what of Gethin and Phillip? Rhys and Gwilym? No, it is too much to ask and we would just as easily be found out there, as well." Owain tossed a thighbone onto the remains of the fire. "I want to die on Welsh soil, not in some land not my own. You understand?"

Rhys stretched his legs and yawned. "I do. If I was going to die—and I haven't yet decided I'm ready to do that—then I want it to be while fighting the English."

"We don't have any army to fight the English."

"Yes, but we don't have to fight the whole damn English army. Remember when we used to raid their towns, just a handful of us, and come back with armloads of bounty? We weren't many then."

Owain scraped a small pit into the earth at his feet, tossed the bones and entrails of the bird there and then covered it over with dirt and a few rocks.

"Only a few," Owain echoed. He smiled at Rhys as he stood, suppressing the groan aroused by stiff joints, and collected his bow and bag of arrows. "The spark that started an inferno."

Rhys cocked his head in contemplation. "There's still plenty of tinder about."

"And Harry to douse us."

"He hasn't stepped foot on Welsh soil since Harlech. This is a dull life, Owain. One I was not born to. Neither were you."

Owain shrugged and turned along the path back toward their humble dwelling in the mountains. He could never forgive the English their arrogance. Least of all could he forgive them for the deaths of his children and for taking away his sweet, beautiful Marged.

Ah, Marged, all of Wales must think me dead, I have been so quiet, so timid. How do I give them hope when I cannot find it myself? Do they dare speak for themselves? For certain they would never have faith in a coward. Is that not what I have become?

Near Welshpool, Anglo-Welsh Border — October, 1410

THE FIRST GOLD OF the harvest season tinged the fields below the mountain ridge. To the east lay gluttonous England. To the west, wild Wales.

"We would get richer if we robbed Welshpool," Rhys hinted, looking down the valley at the town a mile away. "Money, wine . . . a few extra horses. We'll need those things."

"You and what army?" Owain said, glancing over his shoulder at the dozen faithful followers gathered on horseback. They were lightly armed, just like they would have been a decade ago—a weapon or two apiece and not a link of mail among them. At first Owain had resisted his own idea of a raid into the borders—an idea sown time and again by those around him. Maredydd with his gentle insistence and bright hope, Iolo with his odes of more glorious days, Rhys with his prodding to action . . . even blind Gethin, who bemoaned his lost purpose in distant snatches. They were only a few, but the dream was still there in their hearts, or else they would not have clung to this wandering existence. They could have taken their pardons and lived in peace. Instead, they were here, surveying this pastoral scene.

The ground was yet wet from a storm the night before, but the sun had come forth in triumph, not yet ready to yield to the slate-gray clouds of October. Dotting the valley was a healthy herd of cattle, grazing in unsuspecting tranquility.

Rhys raised a hand to shield his eyes. "Since our supper will not come to us . . . I suggest we go get it." He gathered up his reins and looked at Owain with hungry anticipation.

Owain signaled with a single finger and Rhys nudged his horse in the flanks. While Owain and the rest waited, Rhys Ddu, Rhys ap Tudur and Philip Scudamore, a brother-in-law to Owain's daughter Alice, followed close behind him on their horses. At an easy canter, they swung out wide around the slumbering valley in the direction of Welshpool to cut in behind the herd.

"We'll cover the south." Gwilym brought his mount up beside Owain's. "There are other pastures there and the cows will want to go that direction because they know the way."

"Take your time, Gwilym," Owain said. "If we can take them quietly we'll get much further along without alarm."

"And if the farmer discovers us?" Philip Hanmer added from behind them.

"Whatever it takes to silence him." Settling back in his saddle, Owain watched Rhys and the other two men move past a stand of woods.

Philip Hanmer and Gwilym took up their reins.

"Wait," Owain said lowly, squinting. "Something's wrong."

From out of the woods around Rhys, poured a host of mounted men.

"English," Maredydd muttered.

"How many?" Owain said, relying on his son's youthful vision.

Maredydd peered intensely. With the sun in his eyes, it took even him some time to assess the situation. By then, the rattle of weapons and the shouts of their commander carried across the valley.

Finally, Maredydd turned to his father. "Well over a hundred."

The others pulled on their reins. The bits of their horses jangled.

Twisting in his saddle, Owain glared hard at them. "What are you doing?"

"Leaving," Gwilym said.

Owain drew his sword, prepared to fight. "But what of Rhys and your brother?"

Gwilym simply threw his head around and with a shrug spurred his horse. All but Maredydd followed.

With sinking heart, Owain braved one more look into the distance. There had been no chance of retreat for Rhys. The English had already dragged him from his horse without him ever raising his sword in defense. A stream of soldiers raced across the valley toward Owain and Maredydd. At their head was a detachment of thirty riders in light armor.

"Father, please," Maredydd pled, his voice strained.

Owain heard the wild drumming in his ears. It was several moments before he realized that it was the sound of English hooves bearing down on them and not his heart.

THE REST OF THE Welsh were deep into the mountains before the English troops ever got near to them. Owain and Maredydd, separated from the others, did not stop riding hard for hours. When they reached a stream, Owain jumped from his saddle and threw his sword into the mists of a shallow pool at the base of a waterfall.

Maredydd retrieved his father's sword without a word. He did not offer it back. He knew his father would not take it just then— even if the English had fallen upon them that very moment.

Iolo Goch:

Rhys Ddu was granted a trial in London, albeit a mockery of justice, and was swiftly declared guilty of treason. In the same tower where he awaited his trial was the Lady Margaret. When she heard the roar of the crowd outside one day, she asked her guards what it was about. Gloatingly, they told her. She wished, then, that she had not asked.

As Rhys went down on his knees before the block, he glared at the priest who was there to hear his final words and said in a steady voice, "Prince Owain lives and he will never yield to the usurper, Henry. Take my cursed head off, if it gives you English bastards pleasure. But when I die another will take my place. I warn you all, it will go on until there are no Welshmen left for your kind to enslave. And for each one of us that goes down, we will take ten Englishmen with us. Then the Scots will come down and take over the whole bloody island."

Then he turned his eyes heavenward. "Now forgive me, Father, I have not been to Mass regularly . . . in years, maybe . . ."

58

Tower of London, England — 1411

OWAIN HAD KEPT PRISONERS, although how many and under what conditions, Margaret was never really sure. Mostly, they were kept at Dolbadarn or Aberystwyth, seldom at Harlech, for he regarded that as his home. But it had taken her a long time to share the opinion of Harlech being any sort of home. It was too much a fortress and ever full of diplomats and soldiers flooding through the gatehouse entrance. Only Edmund and Catrin's children had brought to it any hint of hominess with their perpetual attempts at song. They had been a growing army of bards for Iolo's tutelage. Lionel, in particular, had shown an interest in the harp and Iolo had sat with him many an evening in infinite patience, first teaching him how to care for the harp and then how to properly pluck the strings. But such trivialities were far too boring for bold little Lionel. He wanted to learn an entire song and his failure to do so at his first sitting nearly killed his ambitions altogether.

The children . . . ah, the children. What short, undeservedly cruel lives they had suffered. So much different from her own childhood, half at Wrexham, half in London. After Margaret's surrender of Harlech, Angharad had died on the way to London. The sweet child did not make it as far as Shrewsbury before her lungs filled with fluid, drowning her from the inside. Lionel—she was told soon after they had all been tossed into the Tower of London—had succumbed to 'natural causes'. But she had not been allowed to see his body and suspected the 'cause' was most likely poisoning. Being an heir to Owain and the son of the traitor Sir Edmund, Lionel was better removed than allowed to live and one day incite trouble.

For the first year of their imprisonment, Sion and Mary had shared quarters with their mother, but a fresh bout of the plague had taken Sion from them. He died in his mother's arms within a day of the fever coming on. Mary survived, but she was taken away and Margaret never heard from her again. Since then, she had asked regularly of Gwladys and Catrin. At first, she was cursed and spat at. As she grew more insistent, her guards became more abusive. But apparently they had been given strict orders not to cause any harm to her person, because the backlashes seldom went further than a brusque shove or a stinging slap. Except for the one time, when one of her guards became particularly perturbed at her request for unspoiled food. A lanky, greasy-haired man with foul breath, he slammed the door shut behind him, pinned her down upon the 'bed', yanked her skirt up in one well-practiced motion and as he fumbled to free his manhood and fight off her struggles, another guard entered and knocked the perpetrator clear across the floor by slamming the stool into his head.

"You'll not hurt the lady," her liberator said. Then he seized the other guard by the collar and tossed him out into the corridor.

"You all right?" he said in a softer tone to Margaret.

She smoothed her skirts and clamped her knees together, nodding. Then she rolled over on her side to face the wall and sobbed, not out of fear of her captors, but out of misery over her own helplessness.

That was the extent of the kindness she was to receive. The next day the guard who had saved her from harm brought her freshly roasted fowl. The aroma was beyond tantalizing and when she reached for it, he caught her wrist and pulled her tightly to him. He was quite young and if not handsome at least fair smelling and clean-shaven. But there was no doubt about what the payment for decent food was to be. The unspoken proposition brought him a tankard across the jaw and ever after that he treated her just as roughly as the other man.

How opposite her life was now from that which she had shared with Owain at Sycharth and Harlech. Sycharth had been a golden dream of blissful union, with a fountain of children springing from her yearly like a carefully cultivated crop. All in all, the years at Harlech had not been wholly unhappy times. It had been an exceedingly comfortable existence. And she had been a princess. But what was she now? A companion to rats. A home to lice. A bait with which to tempt her husband into the snare. As long as she was kept alive, Margaret knew, Owain was out there and still giving Henry trouble.

Sitting on her poorly mended stool, Margaret held her thread toward the candlelight. She had to bring the needle a mere hand's width from her face to try to put the thread through the eye. Her hands were cramped. She used to be able to work on a piece from dawn to dusk, her fingers flying over the cloth like a bee collecting nectar, but it was no longer so. After several failed attempts, she put the needlework back on the small bedside table, one of three pieces of furniture in her tiny, sunless room, permeated with unidentifiable odors. She studied the tray of food that had been left for her. The molded part of the bread could be torn off, but the meat was rancid . . . if she consumed any of it she would suffer the consequences.

She gathered up her blanket and shook it—a habit developed to rid it of earwigs and spiders. Carefully, she arranged the covering on her bed, if one could call it such, for it was only three planks rough with splinters and so short that her feet hung over the end. Her only pillow was her arm and sometimes, on those days she considered herself lucky, her keepers would throw her fresh straw to soften the surface of her bed. Although she did not relish the dark, she cupped her hand and blew her candle out so that she might save it for some later time. For now, sleep invited and it was the one thing, the *only* thing, that brought her peace of any kind.

She lay down and pulled her knees up inside her gown for added warmth. The single blanket she had was growing threadbare after three—no, it was going on four winters now that she had been here. All a fog. Days that melted into nights. Minutes like hours. Days like years. Nothing to mark one from the other. Like a constant state of being half asleep and half awake. A lifetime lived in a nightmare.

Hearing no scurry of rodents, Margaret closed her eyes and let her thoughts disappear and the dreams take over. Every day she prayed that she would dream of Owain and better times, but it was almost never so. For when she dreamed, she dreamed of death and dying: maimed soldiers pleading for an end to their suffering, little children screaming in agony, old people frozen to death in their beds, the ghost of Edmund walking Harlech's battlements.

Some might have feared to sleep at all with such an onslaught of nightmares. But the actuality of death had been her life since the rebellion began. And that she had survived it, even to this wretched existence . . . that was her victory.

MARGARET DREAMED OF HOUSES burning. She could smell the smoke. Taste the ashes on her tongue. Panic pounding in her chest, she rubbed her eyes and sat up. In the wavering orange glow, she saw a face. The face of a man just entering his prime, with a straight aquiline nose, narrow chin and sharp cheekbones. Below angled eyebrows were wedged a pair of clear, commanding eyes.

She tried to focus. Beneath her blanket she dug her fingernails into the palm of her hand to test whether this was real or a dream. The sting on her flesh confirmed that she was lucid. Her two disagreeable guards flanked the man at either shoulder. They gave up their rushes to the sconces beside the door. With a slight nod, the noble dismissed them.

He studied her in pensive silence, not at all lecherously, but carefully, as if weighing what he would say. As if his words held some importance.

Margaret was intensely aware of her disheveled state. Once a week, a mute girl would come and brush her hair and bring her a bucket of water and a cloth, but undoubtedly it did little to improve her appearance. Why that mattered to her at this moment, she didn't understand, but for once she was thankful to not have a looking glass. She raked the hair from her face and gazed down at the floor. A roach scampered from the light to disappear in a crack in the wall.

"Who are you?" Margaret asked.

He tilted his head, topped with shining locks of darkest auburn, and gestured to the stool. "May I sit, my lady?"

A simple request, yet put forth with the utmost respect. Margaret nodded and drew the blanket across her chest, as if to hide her dismal attire.

"You will be moved to a more fitting apartment. One with a window. Would you like that?"

His rings glittered so much as he laid his hands across his knees that they awed her. She had never seen such ornamentation on a man, not since King Richard.

Cautiously, Margaret raised her eyes, taking in every detail of his dress. Leather riding boots that buckled on the outside of each leg were snug against his legs up to mid calf. Above his yellow hose, he wore a long purple houppelande, sewn with stripes of velvet and satin. His shoulders were padded, to make him look larger than he was, for he was perhaps shorter than average, and his sleeves were slightly billowed and perfectly gathered at the cuff. And yet there was no chain draped around his neck to indicate his station, nor fur lined collar to further proclaim his wealth.

"I don't know." Margaret eyed him directly. "I think I would prefer a pig sty, even, to this. Wouldn't you?"

His gaze dropped. "Yes, that was perhaps one of the most stupid questions I have ever asked. I'll see that some amends are made." Then he stood and shifted on his feet, stalling, as if needing but not wanting to say something. "Your son, Gruffydd —"

Margaret shot up from her bed, abandoning the shoddy blanket. She touched him on the hand. "Gruffydd? How is he? May I see him?"

"It is impossible, he —"

"But why?"

"He . . . I'm sorry. He died, this morning. The plague."

She pulled back from him. "You're lying. You all lie."

"I assure you, my lady, he is dead and if not for the nature of the malady I would take you to see his body."

"If he *is* dead, then . . . then you have killed him."

"No."

"Then Owain still lives, otherwise you would have either killed me or set me free by now."

With that accusation, some hole opened up in the noble's purpose. It was plain in his face.

"Tell me," Margaret delved, "tell me who you are. Or else I have no reason to believe you. For all I know you are some dog sent by the king to torture my mind."

He drew his shoulders up to full height. "King's whelp, perhaps. I am Henry, Prince of Wales. Or as your people would call me plainly, Harry of Monmouth. Or should I say your husband's people, as you were born very much English?"

Margaret raised her hand to slap him, but he snagged her wrist and wrung it tight. She spat into his eye with remarkable precision.

"Is that the reason you keep me here? Because I married a Welshman?"

Prince Harry released her and wiped at his eye with a sleeve. "I see Sir Owain took as his wife a woman with a will to match his own."

He could have called for his guards then, Margaret realized, but he simply regarded her with greater caution. She felt like a wild animal kept for amusement.

"To answer the question you have not yet asked—yes, he lives. Where or how, I know not. But every once in a great while, he emerges from his secret lair to remind us we never completely succeeded in bringing down the dragon." Prince Harry walked toward the door. He knocked twice. "You will be moved to your new quarters on the morrow, given clean clothes, bathwater and decent fare. You will receive a visitor then, one named Adam of Usk."

As the door opened, Prince Harry glanced over his shoulder at Margaret. "So you know my intentions—I do not seek to destroy Sir Owain. The time for such squabbles is past. I have other plans, ambitions if you will, than continuing to war on Wales and Scotland. And I would rather have him and his men fighting beside me than against me."

"He will never agree to that."

"Sadly, I think you're right."

Harry turned away and slipped through the door. It shut with a boom behind his swirl of clothing. She melted to the floor in a puddle, mindless of the filth and stench. An all too familiar itching caused her to rake her fingernails across her scalp. Lice. A spider scampered across the floor, stopped in front of her and retreated. They had forgotten to take the torches away. There would be light, for awhile.

IT WAS NOT UNTIL three days after Prince Harry's unexpected visit, that Margaret was moved to her new room in the Tower. It had a real bed, a pillow and a down blanket—although none of them delighted her half as much as the window. She bathed in the sunlight more than she did the fresh water that was brought to her. As the hours dragged on while she combed through her hair, the man that the prince had referred to, Adam of Usk, failed to appear.

On the fourth day, she awoke, golden light spilling in through her barred window. But when she tried to lift her head to gaze with some small appreciation at her spacious quarters, her muscles were already burning with fever. She put a hand to her forehead and felt the fire there. She rolled over to watch the door and as she did so, an odd pain, a lump beneath her armpit brought a groan from her throat.

"No. No. How can it be?" she whispered. "Why does the plague now come to me?"

Margaret buried her hands in her face and wept hard. Even as a man entered her room and moved toward her, she did not hear him or the bar on the outside slide into place. When he touched her on the top of the head, she startled.

"Your pardon, my lady. I waited at the door some time, but you did not seem to notice me. I am Adam of Usk."

Simply dressed in a long overtunic of dark green and a tight black cap that hugged his skull, Adam bowed. "I have been abroad these past years, but I've followed your husband's doings whenever I could get news of them."

Sweat now pouring from her face, Margaret wiped it away with her sleeve, pretending it was only her tears she sought to banish. It was with great effort that she sat upright. She could not let on that she was ill or he would fly from here without another word. "I was told you would be here three days ago."

Adam hung his head and shrugged. "The Prince of Wales him-self—the younger Henry—questioned me. When he was done there were more men. More questions."

"About what?"

"About Owain Glyndwr, of course." He walked to the window. "You can see a good part of the city from here. Did you know? Not the better parts, unfortunately, but the guts of the town."

She felt a surge of energy, but it faded as quickly as it came. "Then he lives? You have seen him?"

Turning back toward her, Adam nodded and lowered his voice. "I have."

Margaret sank back into her pillow. "Then tell me all you can about him. Will you see him again?"

"I doubt I shall." Adam approached her. "Our meeting was purely business. King's business, although I do not boast of that. While I was in Brecon, I was given seven hundred marks by John Tiptoft the constable and was told to deliver it as payment for the ransom of a man called Davy Gam, who once tried to kill Sir Owain. I was able, with great pains, to find Sir Owain himself. He brought about the release of Davy Gam, but the money I tried to give him . . . he instructed me to carry it to Bleddfa Church in recompense for his having burned it many years ago."

Adam paused. His eyebrows twisted in a puzzled look. "He would not take a penny of the ransom. He said . . . that he wanted it to go to those who had need of it—that he had no more soldiers to feed. When I returned to London, it was no wonder they questioned me. I was even asked if I had taken the money for myself. I do be-lieve they were discussing whether or not they should put me on the rack and wring the truth from me. My scholarly bones would have snapped with the first pull. But heaven watches over me, I believe. This morning a letter arrived from the priest of Bleddfa in thanks and

I was finally permitted to come here."

His words came to Margaret in a thick fog. It took time for her to sift through their content. Most of it made no sense at all.

She knew, as sure as her bones flamed from within, that she would not see Owain again in the flesh. But as Adam's words took form in her mind, she was reminded of gentler, more hopeful times . . . and harder ones as well. She remembered Owain on that dark night above the walls at Harlech, looking at her as if he knew their parting was final. She had watched him descend the rock, watched the silvery waves racing toward the shore, wanting to call him back and yet knowing that their life together had ended. Their children being born . . . dying. A circle that could not meet its own end properly. A maze of injustice. Something begun with so much love and trust—all gone awry. So much loneliness and pain in her life.

Yet some good must surely have come of it all? Surely.

"Is he well?" she asked, trying to lick her lips, but as she did so it felt as though her mouth would split all the way from its corners to her ears.

"Well enough to ride after Davy Gam, after the scoundrel broke an oath to do no harm to him. Gam attacked Owain and a few of his followers and in turn Owain burned the ingrate's house down." Smiling, Adam touched her hand. His eyebrows plunged as he did so. "You are consumed by fever, my lady. I shall have them fetch a physician."

Margaret tried to smile in thanks. They would not send a physician for an unwelcome prisoner. Even if they did, it would be in vain. She would die soon. She knew. And oddly, she welcomed it. No more prison walls or sickening food or long days of boredom to make the mind think insane thoughts. She would let go. Let the angels take her. Wait for Owain. Find him. However far away he was.

She closed her eyes and heard Owain's voice:

"May God, who knows full well the hell we have endured while we have been apart one from another, reward us with heaven when we meet again."

She swam through a sea of cobwebs. At her fingertips was something heavy and solid. A crack of light showed through, running from floor to far above: a door, slightly ajar. She pushed against the door and it swung open freely. There was her love, sitting in his favorite chair by the hearth in the great hall in Sycharth, his boots dusty from a long ride. At his side stood Gruffydd, barely big enough to keep his father's sword from dragging the ground as he held it worshipfully in both hands before him. Owain's face was brown from the sun and his hair glittered like a river of gold. Sweetly, he smiled at her and then rose to his feet, arms wide.

Owain! Owain! I have come back! I knew you would be here. Hold me. Don't let go. It has been awful . . . awful without you. I could have endured anything with you beside me. It was like death not knowing anything about you. I cried so many nights, my love, not for myself, but for want of you.

59

Westminster Palace, England — 1411

"I CAME AS SOON as I could," Harry said. As he entered his father's bedchamber, which was lit by a hundred candles, he was struck by the solemnity of the scene before him. King Henry's features were lifeless: the nostrils almost pinched shut, the lips like wax, skin thin as paper, the lesions on his face now dry and pale. His heart pounding in his ears, Harry drifted toward the bed.

At last. Can it be that I am king at last?

"How long ago?" Harry eyed the glittering crown that rested on a pillow of satin on a bedside table.

Henry Beaufort, Bishop of Winchester and the king's half-brother through John of Gaunt's long-time mistress and second wife Catherine Swynford, bent over the king to listen for his breathing. He stood and shook his head solemnly. "Just now, I think. My condolences, my lord."

Harry hung his head to display a son's grief. "Will you grant me a few minutes alone with him?"

His uncle nodded and, with hands clasped beneath his long robes, retreated through the door.

Harry brushed at his father's cheek with his knuckles. Cold as ice. Quickly, he checked that the door was shut tight and then went to the bedside table. He stretched out his hands, took the crown and kissed one of its many jewels. Then, he lifted the crown above his head.

Ah, Harry, this was ever long in coming. But oh so deserved. How my uncle Richard would smile if he could see—as much that you are dead, dear Father, as to see me come to this. He favored me . . . and yet despised you. I wonder, how do you justify murdering a king, or any man for that matter? Does it matter whether you placed your bare hands around his throat yourself . . . or looked the other way while some nameless slave dripped the poison into his drink?

You will be forgotten sooner than you are buried. I shall go on to greater things.

He closed his eyes and settled the crown upon his head, felt its power, its majesty, its burden.

Just then a sharp rasp arose from the king. As Harry whirled around, the crown tumbled from his head. He caught it in quivering fingers and swallowed back his heart, sending it plummeting down through his bowels as the realization gripped him that his father was not at all dead.

The king breathed shallowly and glanced toward the empty pillow.

Briefly, Harry looked away. Then, with stinging regret, he returned the crown.

"M-my l-lord," Harry stuttered, collecting himself, "your brother told me you were dead, although plainly you are not."

"So eager. Tell me, was the fit good?" Yellow candlelight flickered in the king's pupils.

"One day it will belong to me."

"True." The king clutched weakly at his blanket and gazed up at the canopy above his bed, poised there like the dark cloud of mortality waiting to sink down on him. "Do as you see fit, my son. And pray that God has mercy on me . . . for I had so little for others."

Every muscle and vein in Harry's face and neck went taut.

A curse on you to keep lingering like this and delay what is best for England and for all of Christendom.

Iolo Goch:

A large host of lords convened at England's next parliament. Bishop Henry Beaufort, the king's own blood, demanded that he abdicate the throne in favor of his son. But upon hearing it, Henry flew into a rage and thereafter made a miraculous recovery. To show he was far from being dead or incapable, the king traveled throughout the land, although his public appearances were brief and his sojourns at various castles were notably lengthy.

For nigh on two more years, the king's health vacillated. Matters being quiet on the borders, Harry spent much of his time tending to the business of the realm that would have been his father's duty, had the king been in a competent state.

Then on the 20th of March, 1413, King Henry collapsed in prayer at Westminster Abbey. He was carried to the Abbot's House and laid in a room called the Jerusalem Chamber, where countless prayers were whispered above him without avail.

For fourteen battle-fraught years, Henry of Bolingbroke, son of the powerful John of Gaunt and grandson of the mighty Edward III, had reigned. Now, he was king no more.

A hasty month later in Westminster Abbey, the crown alighted on Harry of Monmouth's head.

One of Henry V's first acts was the issuance of pardons. Among those who seized the opportunity at a fresh beginning was Gwilym ap Tudur, Owain's cousin. The young Edmund Mortimer, Earl of March, was released from prison and the estates of the Percys were restored to Harry Hotspur's son.

Pardons being an issue of immense compromise, there was one yet to come.

UNEASY LIES THE CROWN

One which Harry thought long and hard over. One which he finally, humbly, conceded to offer—to Owain Glyndwr.

60

Kentchurch, Herefordshire, England — September, 1415

ALICE GLYNDWR, NEAR BURSTING with the child that was due any day now, loosed her flaxen hair from its pins and re-tidied it in a tight knot. The orchard trees of Kentchurch manor stood in neatly pruned rows, their limbs weighed down with their bounty, ready for harvest. She stretched an arm for an apple, dangling in crimson perfection above her. When her eager fingers could not grasp it, she attempted to leap, but her extra weight prevented her from claiming the prize.

"Your mother was the same," came a voice from two rows away.

As Alice turned around, she stumbled over the basket of apples she had already collected. Without looking up, she at once began to pick them up. "John, you startled me," she said, thinking it was her husband, Sir John Scudamore, returned from business.

A pair of hands, spotted with age and blue-veined, reached down to help her. She fell back on her bottom and gaped, open-mouthed, at her father.

"Is it you? Truly, is it you?" she said.

"Marged would go out into the orchard at Sycharth   do you remember Sycharth, Alice?" Owain began, as he plucked the apples from the ground and placed them neatly in his daughter's basket. "Out into the orchard and pick apples even after her labor had begun. She said there was no sense in pacing the floors for hours when there was work to be done. As if she had no help."

He extended a hand toward his daughter and smiled dreamily at her. "You look very much like her, too."

"I suppose you've heard?" Alice asked tentatively, laying her hand in her father's grasp and heaving her bulk up with an ungraceful grunt. She wasn't sure where to begin, not having seen her father in years and shocked to see him alive at all.

"I regret I was not there to hold her when the time came." Owain gazed out over the valley, bright in the crisp, dry warmth of the season, so rich in abundance, so peaceful.

He was gaunt, pale and bleary-eyed, not at all like the regal prince that Alice remembered. But when one is a child many things appear grander than they really are.

Owain reached up and easily picked the apple that Alice had strained over. "Shall we share this one?"

"I'd like that."

He pulled his knife from his belt and sliced through the apple. "Ach!"

His knife still partially embedded in the apple, he dropped it and clutched at a bleeding palm.

Alice grabbed at his hand to inspect it. "It was you who used to tell me to be careful when cutting up the apples. Must I chide you like one of my own children now?"

Fearing for his safety, being so close to Hereford as Kentchurch was, she took him around the back and into the kitchen where she washed his hand in a bowl of clean water. The cut continued to bleed until the water was bright red. She fetched another bowl, dabbed at his palm and then sent her old kitchen maid to find clean rags.

As she bound up her father's hand, they began to talk. He told her of his life in the mountains, living in caves, of traveling from place to place with Iolo and of the botched raid on Welshpool. He did not say so much, but his transient existence had taken a hard toll on him. He had aged so severely that it was not hard to believe he hadn't been discovered.

Then Alice told him of her life with her husband John. A quiet life, except for the noise of their two young children and another coming soon.

"John is good to you? Home often, I trust?" Owain questioned.

"Always. He is a deputy squire in Brecon, but spends no more time away than what duty calls for." She squeezed her father's good hand across the table.

"If he knew I was here —?"

Alice leaned close, even though the kitchen was now empty. "He would never betray you, Father. He's still loyal to you."

"Then you've both made a public admission of your vows?"

Alice pulled back in humiliation. She and John had been secretly married for years now. Only the servants had knowledge of their marriage and a healthy pay encouraged them all to secrecy. "We can't. You know that. Not now, at least."

An awkward silence drove between them. Alice stared down at her unadorned fingers, folded in the lap of her plain dress. She could have dressed better, being John's wife, she knew, but it was never her will to draw attention to herself or put John's good station at risk if they were found out. Finally, she recalled her manners and offered her father some food.

Owain's head drooped wearily. "A bed, please. That's all I need. A soft bed, in a safe, quiet place. One night . . . and then I'll be on my way."

"I wouldn't dream of putting you out so soon." She stroked his forearm. "I want you to see your grandson. He's going to be tall, like you, and with your deep, blue eyes and mother's hair. He has gone to

Hereford for the day with my John. They'll be back on the morrow."

Owain rose from his stool slowly, his joints cracking. "I've already put you at risk by coming here. No, I'll leave in the morning. I want you and your family, Alice, to go on living like this. In peace. Now please, a bed is all I ask. Can you indulge an old man that one single comfort?" He laid his hand on top of her head and kissed her where her hair parted.

She wrapped her arms tightly around him and pressed her cheek against his stomach, just like she used to do when she was small.

Alice showed him to a room far from the main activity of the house, where he at once laid down, closed his eyes and was sound asleep before she shut the door behind her.

When Alice rose early in the morning and went to his bed, she could not rouse him. He was burning with fever and she feared the worst—that he had come to Kentchurch to die.

THE SMELL OF BURNING peat curled inside Owain's nostrils. He burrowed deeper inside his cocoon of wool and opened his eyes.

"You've slept long. Three days." Nesta stooped over him. The long, dark plait of her hair fell forward. She tossed it back and then placed a hand across Owain's chest.

In the comfortable bed his daughter had granted him, Owain stretched his limbs. He ached from the marrow out and his hand was stiff and sore. He brought it out from beneath his blanket and noticed the clean bandage there.

Nesta touched his forehead. "Your fever has broken."

Blinking, Owain gazed at her. "Am I not in heaven, then?"

"Hardly." She grinned, then just as quickly her brow clouded over. "Maredydd sent word to me, some time ago, and asked me to come to you. I've searched for weeks now. It was only out of desperation that I came here to see if Alice knew where you were. Fate seems to have delivered us both here at just the right time. One week either way and we would have missed each other entirely."

Owain stared into her eyes, the color of rich earth. "Then he knew my needs even when I did not."

She wrapped her fingers around his.

"I have heard them talk in the taverns," he said, "of the ruin I brought upon Wales. They blame me for —"

Nesta shushed him with a finger to his lips. "Rest. I'll have Alice bring you a broth."

There was a comfortable silence between them, an unspoken need answered only by the presence of the other.

Nesta went to the door and lingered there, her hand upon the latch. "Myfanwy and Gwenllian are well and safe. Their company is a blessing to all who know them. You have not lived for nothing, Owain. If peace and freedom do not come in our time, perhaps they will come in theirs."

Her words were but a small comfort to a man who carried within his soul a burden too huge to bear.

"I outlived Bolingbroke," Owain said, his words soft in volume, but strong in conviction. "Some victory in that, don't you think?"

"Victory? Oh, more than that. The Welsh will speak the name of Owain Glyndwr with love and admiration a thousand years from now."

LATER, AS NIGHT CREPT over the world, Alice carried a pair of lit candles to her father's chamber. There she found Nesta holding her father's cold, lifeless hand and singing to him softly.

Owain Glyndwr, the one true Welsh Prince of Wales, was dead.

61

Herefordshire, England — 1416

I N THE MURKY LIGHT of a cramped tavern on the western fringe of Herefordshire, Maredydd ap Owain nursed a warm cup of cider. Across the table from him sat Sir Gilbert Talbot, the very man who had taken part in the slaughter at Grosmont and also begun the siege on Harlech.

From beneath his cloak, Sir Gilbert drew a roll of parchment and pushed it across the table. "Do you know where to find him?"

"At one time, I did," Maredydd answered carefully. He stared at the document for a long time and then took another drink.

Sir Gilbert glanced at his guards, flanking the door of the tavern. The other patrons, ten muttering townsmen avoiding the company of their nagging wives and a few travelers in need of rest, passed curious glances toward the back table where they sat.

"Then he is . . . dead?"

Maredydd suppressed a smile. "No more so than you or I."

Sir Gilbert tapped on the roll. "Then see that he gets this." He rose, but before leaving he hesitated beside Maredydd. "I will await his answer in Hereford."

Without meeting his gaze, Maredydd snagged the corner of his cloak. "I fear you will wait for nothing."

Sir Gilbert leaned close and whispered in his ear, "If he accepts, he walks freely . . . just as you now do. My king extends the same to you. Do not forget that."

Uplands of Wales — 1416

MAREDYDD KNELT BEFORE A mossy boulder blocking the entrance to a cave. Around him rose a ring of mountains deep in the heart of Wales. He placed his hand upon the rock and touched his forehead to its rough surface. It had taken ten men to put it there.

Behind him, Nesta held hands with blind Gethin. The wind lashed at her hair. At her shoulder, stood Iolo, weeping like a child.

"In our hearts you will live forever." Maredydd's lips brushed the hilt of his father's sword, and then he leaned it against the boulder. Fingers still on the blade, he exploded in grief, tears cascading down his face.

Above, the first stars of twilight pierced an endless silver sky. Around, the mountains lay in eternal slumber.

Nesta raised her face to heaven. Her voice mingled with the sigh of the wind like an angel's clarion.

Westminster Palace, England — 1416

KING HENRY V HAD recently returned from France when he received Maredydd alone. Harry watched while Maredydd strode across the length of the hall of Westminster Palace and bent his knee before the king—a gesture which elicited a raised eyebrow from the monarch seated upon his throne.

"You have presented the offer of pardon to your father and

discussed the matter with him?" the king said.

"Thoroughly."

"And?"

Maredydd rose to his feet. "He says he is a free man now and does not need your pardon. And to correct matters, he says it is you who ought to seek his pardon for stealing his title, his lands, his holdings, and using them all to your own purpose while you raped and murdered and plundered Wales."

"He says this?"

"He does."

"As I expected." Harry stroked his chin thoughtfully. "*'I would rather be bound to the soil as another man's serf, than be king of all those dead and destroyed.'* Do you know who said that? Homer. Over two thousand years ago. Who is to say he was right?

"Go from here a free man, Maredydd ap Owain. And tell your father . . . tell him he wears his crown well."

With a nod, Maredydd began toward the door behind him. After only a few steps, he paused, and then turned around to face the king. "He would say the same of you, my lord."

Iolo Goch:

Maredydd, I hear, took the pardon that was offered to him and later served in Harry's court, although in what manner I do not know. In truth, it matters not. He deserved to find his peace. To continue to fight would have been futile and I would like to think that Owain would have taken some small pleasure in knowing that a few of his children had lived out their natural lives, if not happily, then at least free of struggle and strife.

Gethin died the winter following Owain. He wandered off in a snowstorm and froze to death, sword in hand, as he would have wanted to.

I have been told Nesta returned to Ireland, although others claim to have seen her somewhere near Cardigan. She has her daughters and her voice . . . they will keep her well. Without her, my lord Owain might not have believed in himself half as much as the rest of us did. In the beginning, he had more than he needed. In the end, he had so little.

My own days are dwindling, but I bear no sadness in my soul, for I was richer than any king, more beloved than an angel.

In the hearts of the Welsh, Owain lives on. Some even say he lies sleeping in a cave beneath a mountain and one day . . . one day he will rise again.

Historical Notes

In the year 1415, Henry V crossed over the English Channel and stormed into France with his army. On a muddy field within sight of the castle of Agincourt, they met the French. Facing a force nine times their own numbers and weakened by exhaustion and hunger, the English stood their ground, arraying their archers to the fore. The French advanced across the quagmire. A hailstorm of arrows, many of them shot by Welsh bowmen, descended. At the end of that fateful day, over seven thousand Frenchman lay dead. It was the greatest defeat up to that time that France had ever known.

In the years following his victory at Agincourt, Henry V (Harry) returned to France and brought it begging to its knees. The French agreed to a treaty in which Harry was named the heir to the French throne. Soon afterward, he married the daughter of King Charles VI of France, Katherine de Valois. He returned to England with his bride, but while awaiting the birth of their child Harry was forced to return to France to settle a disturbance. There he received news of the birth of his son, Henry. He was at Vincennes, not far from Paris, when a bout of dysentery brought him to the verge of death.

Queen Katherine flew with all haste to France, but she did not make it to him in time. He had reigned for nine years, most of which was spent not in England, but on the battlefields of France. At the age of twenty-one, Queen Katherine was a widow. Their son, Henry VI, was a mere nine months old.

Katherine de Valois, Queen Dowager, later secretly married

Owen Tudor, whose family was of the Anglesey Tudors. Owen Tudor was Clerk of her wardrobe and had fought under Henry at Agincourt. Together they had three sons, one of which later became Edmund Tudor, Earl of Richmond. Edmund married Margaret Beaufort and their son Henry Tudor, born in Pembroke Castle in Wales, took as his wife Elizabeth of York, great granddaughter of Anne Mortimer, the sister of Sir Edmund Mortimer. A protracted civil war, called the Wars of the Roses, was fought between the Lancastrians and Yorkists, two branches of the royal family.

In 1485, the forces of Welsh-born Henry Tudor, which included a great number of Welsh followers, defeated those of Richard III at Bosworth. Henry Tudor became King Henry VII of England, thus fulfilling the ancient prophecies of Myrddin Emrys (Merlin) of which Hopkyn had spoken, that one day a Welshman would rule the island.

Except for Maredydd, Owain's sons all died before the end of the Welsh War for Independence, but today Owain's blood lives on through the present-day descendants of his daughters: Alice, Janet and Mary (Margaret). Owain also had several illegitimate children who survived him. Nesta, it should be mentioned, is a fictional character of my own invention, as is Elise.

Iolo Goch, Owain's bard, outlived him and some of Iolo's odes to his lord have survived the centuries, which is a great blessing, for after Owain's downfall much of what may have been written from the Welsh perspective was forgotten or destroyed.

For a brief time in the lengthy annals of history, Owain Glyndwr united the people of Wales under one banner and led them on to victory. He earned the admiration and respect of other countries and of another Prince of Wales, Harry.

We can only imagine how the course of history might have been altered if the alliances that Owain had so carefully woven had held up, if he had been able to join Hotspur at Shrewsbury, if he had taken the field at Woodbury Hill against Henry IV, or if he had just plain not had the misfortune of being the circumstantial adversary of the tenacious Henry V.

Acknowledgments

When this story was nothing more than a dream, a couple of very generous and tolerant friends accompanied me on two separate trips to Wales. The first was Gale Rempel, without whom I might never have journeyed overseas in the first place. After experiencing the hospitality of her extended Irish family, we took the ferry from Dublin to Holyhead and began our adventure through Wales. I'll never forget sitting in Snowdonia next to a mountain stream, drenched in sunshine, not a care in the world. It was truly one of the most peaceful moments of my life. Then there were the sheep. Lots of sheep, ambling across the road with no fear of cars whatsoever. Driving in Wales can be a very harrowing experience in unexpected ways.

A few years later, my Swedish friend Lena Stangvik-Urban was my traveling companion to Wales and Scotland. On our way to Harlech Castle, we somehow ended up driving our manual transmission car the wrong way on a single lane road through the town —and ended up having to stop uphill, unable to see in either direction. We rolled the windows down, listened and probably both said silent prayers (and a few curses) as we gunned it and pulled out. Miraculously, we survived and managed to find the castle, but later that day we barely escaped being crushed against a stone wall by a boat in tow as it swung wide around a curve. Again, two foreigners driving in the U.K. is probably not the best idea. Next time we'll take a train. Still, both trips made up some of the highlights of my life. Had I never been there—to Wales, England and Scotland—I'm not sure I could have pursued my goal of writing about them with such a clear vision. Gale and Lena, I cherish those trips and my friendship with both of you.

After that trip, when I wrote the very first draft of this book, my dear friend Joni Johnson was the first to lay eyes on it. She treated my efforts with kindness and genuine encouragement. Then she went beyond the call of duty and designed a map of medieval Wales for me, adding a much needed layer to what is now the final product.

I'd like to thank my wonderful Team ULC: my editor Derek Prior, whose enthusiasm for this story is contagiously uplifting; cover artist Lancey Ganey, who worked his special magic once again and always manages to produce a cover better than anything I can imagine; and special thanks to my readers Rebecca Lochlann and Sarah Woodbury, who always help make my writing a hundred times better and whose own talent I greatly admire.

Most importantly, thanks to all my readers out there! Without you, I'd just be another crazy person, listening to the voices in my head and hiding from the world.

About the Author

N. Gemini Sasson holds a M.S. in Biology from Wright State University where she ran cross country on athletic scholarship. She has worked as an aquatic toxicologist, an environmental engineer, a teacher and a cross country coach. A longtime breeder of Australian Shepherds, her articles on bobtail genetics have been translated into seven languages. She lives in rural Ohio with her husband, two nearly grown children and an ever-changing number of animals.

Long after writing about Robert the Bruce and Queen Isabella, Sasson learned she is a direct descendant of both historical figures.

**For more details on N. Gemini Sasson's books,
or to contact her, go to:**

www.facebook.com/NGeminiSasson

www.ngeminisasson.com

Bibliography

In Search of Owain Glyndwr, Chris Barber, Blorenge Books, Abergavenny, Gwent, 1998.

Owain Glyndwr, Terry Breverton, Amberley Publishing, Stroud, Gloucestershire, 2009.

Castles of England, Scotland and Wales, Paul Johnson, George Weidenfeld & Nicholson Ltd., London, 1989.

National Redeemer, Owain Glyndwr in Welsh Tradition, Elissa R. Henken, University of Wales Press, Cardiff, 1996.

Owain Glyn Dwr & the War of Independence in the Welsh Borders, Geoffrey Hodges, Logaston Press, Wiltshire, England, 1995.

Herefordshire Under Arms – A Military History of the County, Charles Hopkinson, The Bromyard and District Local Historical Society, Bromyard, Herefordshire, 1985.

The Fears of Henry IV, Ian Mortimer, Vintage Books, London, 2007.

Owain Glyndwr, Prince of Wales, Ian Skidmore, Christopher Davies Ltd., Swansea, Wales, 1996.

Harlech Castle, Arnold Taylor, Raithby Lawrence, Cardiff, 1997.

Medieval Wales, David Walker, Cambridge University Press, Cambridge, England, 1990.

Lightning Source UK Ltd.
Milton Keynes UK
UKOW042027070313

207323UK00002B/60/P